Praise for the award-winning novels of
SHERI S. TEPPER

"Tepper takes the traditional icons, restores their
resonance, and makes them her own."
Minneapolis Star-Tribune

"Her novels are the old-fashioned kind,
despite their futuristic settings; the kind that
wrap you in their embrace, that take over your life,
that make the world disappear."
Village Voice Literary Supplement

"One of sf's most distinctive voices."
Locus

and for
THE VISITOR

"Tepper blends science well . . . and finishes
with a startling and hopeful ending."
Booklist

"[Tepper] has created a complex and
credible future—one readers will dive into and
emerge from only reluctantly after the
adventure has run its course."
Tampa Tribune

"The book is beautifully and creatively
constructed, full of fascinating and
changeable characters and societies, all of which
interact in complex and surprising ways."
Scifi.com

SHERI S. TEPPER

The Visitor

An Imprint of HarperCollinsPublishers

This is a work of fiction. Names, characters, places, and incidents are products of the author's imagination or are used fictitiously and are not to be construed as real. Any resemblance to actual events, locales, organizations, or persons, living or dead, is entirely coincidental.

EOS
An Imprint of HarperCollins*Publishers*
10 East 53rd Street
New York, New York 10022-5299

Copyright © 2002 by Sheri S. Tepper
ISBN: 0-380-82100-1
www.eosbooks.com

First Eos paperback printing: May 2003
First Eos hardcover printing: April 2002

Eos Trademark Reg. U.S. Pat. Off. and in Other Countries, Marca Registrada, Hecho en U.S.A.
HarperCollins® is a trademark of HarperCollins Publishers Inc.

Printed in the U.S.A.

10 9 8 7 6 5 4 3 2 1

We'll turnaway, oh, we'll turnaway
from god who failed our trust
We'll turnaway, oh, we'll turnaway
and tread his name in dust.
We'll come adore, oh we'll come adore
that Rebel Angel band,
who spared us forevermore,
and gave us Bastion land.

Chorus: Praise oh praise the Rebel Angels
their story we must tell,
that none forget the Rebel Angels,
who raised the Spared from hell.

Hymn number 108
Bastion Dicta Hymnal

The Visitor

caigo faience

Picture this:

A mountain splintering the sky like a broken bone, its western precipice plummeting onto jumbled scree. Below the sheer wall, sparse grasses, growing thicker as the slope gentles through dark groves to a spread of plush pasture. Centered there, much embellished, a building white as sugar, its bizarre central tower crowned by a cupola. Like a priapic wedding cake, it poses amid a garniture of gardens, groves, mazes, all halved—west from east—by the slither of a glassy wall, while from north to south the tamed terrain is cracked by little rivers bounding from the snowy heights toward the canyons farther down.

Picture this:

Inside the towered building, galleries crammed with diagrams and devices; atria packed with idols, images, icons; libraries stacked with reference works; studios strewn with chalk-dust, marble-dust, sawdust, aromatic with incense—cedar and pine and sweet oil of lavender, yes, but more mephitic scents as well; cellar vaults hung with cobweb, strewn with parchment fragments, moldering cases stacked high in shadowed corners. All this has been culled from prior centuries, from wizards now dead, sorcerers now destroyed, mysterious places no longer recognized by name or location, people and places that once were but are no longer, or at least can no longer be found.

Even the man who built the place is no longer. He was Caigo Faience of Turnaway (ca 701–775 ATHCAW—After The Happening Came And Went), once selected by the Regime as Protector of the Spared Ones, Warden of Wizardry, but now well over a century gone. Upon his death the books were audited. When the results were known, the office of Protector was abolished and the function of Warden was transferred to the College of Sorcery under the supervision of the Department of Inexplicable Arts. DIA has taken control of the place: the building, the walls, the mazes, the warden's house (now called the Conservator's House), the whole of Faience's Folly together with all its very expensive conceits. It is now a center for preservation and restoration, a repository for the arcana of history. When The Art is recovered, Faience will become a mecca for aspiring mages under the watchful eye of the Bureau of Happiness and Enlightenment, yet another brilliant in the pavé crown of the Regime.

Picture this.

A Comador woman, her hazelnut hair drawn sleekly back into a thick, single plait, her oval face expressionless, dressed usually in a shapeless shift worn more as a lair than a garment, a shell into which she may at any moment withdraw like a turtle. She is recently come to womanhood, beautiful as only Comadors can be beautiful, but she is too diffident to let her beauty show. Possibly she could be sagacious, some Comadors are, but her green eyes betray an intellect largely unexplored. Still, she is graceful as she slips through the maze to its center, like a fish through eddies. She is agile as she climbs the tallest trees in the park in search of birds' nests. She is quiet, her green eyes ingenuous but speculative as she lurks among shadows, watching, or stands behind doors, listening, the only watcher and listener among a gaggle of egos busy with sayings and doings.

Picture her on a narrow bed in the smallest bedroom of the Conservator's House, struggling moistly out of tangle-haired, grit-eyed sleep, lost in what she calls *the mistaken moment* when her heart flutters darkly like an attic-trapped bird and she cannot remember what or where she is. This confusion comes always at the edge between sleep and waking, between being here now, at Caigo Faience, and being . . . other, another, who survives the dawn only in echoes of voices:

"Has she come? Has she brought all her children? Then let her daughter stand upon the battle drum and let war begin . . ."

"Can you smell that? The stink wafts among the very stars; the spoor of the race that moves in the direction of darkness! Look at this trail I have followed! This is the way it was, see why I have come . . ."

"Ah, see there in the shadows! This is a creature mankind has made. See how he watches you!"

"A chance yet. Still a chance you may bring them into the light . . ."

And herself whispering, "How? . . . why? . . . what is it? What can I do? . . ."

Waking, she clings to that other existence as a furry infant to an arboreal mother, dizzied but determined. She is unwilling to let go the mystery until she has unraveled it, and she tries to go back, back into dream, but it is to no purpose. With sunlight the voices vanish, along with the images and intentions she is so desperate to recover. Though they are at the brink of her consciousness, they might as well be hidden in the depths of the earth, for she is now only daylight Dismé, blinking, stretching, scratching at the insistent itch on her forehead as she wakens to the tardy sun that is just now heaving itself over the sky-blocking peak of Mt. P'Jardas to the east.

"I am Dismé," she says aloud, in a slightly quavering voice. Dismé, she thinks, who sees things that are not there. Dismé who does not believe in the Dicta. Dismé who believes this life is, perhaps, the dream and that other life the reality.

Dismé, she tries not to think, whose not-sister, Rashel Deshôll, is Conservator of the Faience Museum, tenant of the Conservator's House, and something else, far more dreadful, as well.

✴ 1

dismé the child

Deep in the night, a squall of strangled brass, a muted trumpet bray of panic: Aunt Gayla Latimer, wailing in the grip of nightmare—followed shortly by footsteps.

"Papa?" Dismé peered sleepily at her door, opened only a crack to admit her father's nose, chin, one set of bare toes.

"It's Aunt Gayla having the Terrors, Dismé. Just go back to sleep." He turned and shuffled up the attic stairs to be greeted by Roger, Dismé's older brother. Mumble, mumble.

"Val?" A petulant whine from Father's room.

Voice from upstairs. "Go back to sleep, Cora."

Corable the Horrible, said a voice in Dismé's head. Cora Call-Her-Mother.

"But she's not my mother," Dismé had said a thousand times.

"Of course not. But you call her mother anyhow. All little girls need a mother." Papa, over and over.

Fresh howls of horror from Aunt Gayla's room.

"Can't anybody shut that old bitch up?" A slightly shriller whine, from the room that had once been Dismé's and now belonged to Rashel, Call-Her-Mother's daughter, already growing into a faithful copy of her mother.

Dismé pulled the blanket around her ears and rolled an imaginary pair of dice. Odds or evens: go back to sleep or wait to see what happened. Gayla's affliction had developed into an every-third-night ordeal. Her nephew and great nephew, Val and Roger Latimer, provided solace while Call-Her-Mother and Rashel offered commentary. Dismé had no part in the ritual. If she got involved, it would only make it worse.

The clock in the hallway cleared its throat and donged, three, four, five . . . Dismé emerged from the blanket, eyes relentlessly opened by the scuffle-shuffle overhead as Roger went from Aunt Gayla's attic room to his own, and father came down the stairs, back to bed.

If everyone else was asleep, Dismé would stay up! She dressed herself in the dark, went furtively down the stairs and into the back hall, past the pre-dawn black of the gurgling, tweeping bottle room, out along the tool shed, and through the gate into a twisty adit between blank-walled tenements. Aunt Gayla wasn't the only one with night terrors, for the night was full of howls, each one bringing a suitable though impotent gesture of aversion from Dismé. She was only practicing. Everyone knew sorcerous gesticulation had no power left in it. All magic had been lost during the Happening, and no amount of arm waving or chanting would do any good until The Art was regained. Which meant no surcease for Aunt Gayla, though Dismé daren't show she cared.

"We wouldn't want the Regime to punish Gayla for your behavior, would we, Dismé?" Cora the Horrible.

"Why would the Regime do that?" Dismé, outraged.

"Those who have the night terrors are more likely to get the Disease," said Call-Her-Mother.

"Those who have the Disease affect others around them, they get un-Regimic," echoed Rashel. "Dismé, you're un-Regimic!"

"Since children do not become un-Regimic by themselves, they will search for the person who influenced you. Since Rashel is Regimic, they will not blame me," so Call-Her-Mother summed it up with a superior smile. "They will blame Aunt Gayla!"

Or Father. Or Roger. If the Regime was going to blame

people she loved just because Dismé couldn't figure things out, better keep love a secret. It was hard to do, even though True Mother used to say making the best of a bad situation was a secret way of getting even.

"Secret pleasures," True Mother had whispered, "can be compensation for a good many quotidian tribulations!" True Mother had loved words like that, long ones that rolled around in your mouth like half dissolved honey-drops, oozing flavor. It was True Mother who had introduced Dismé to the secret pleasure of early mornings as seen from the ruined tower on the western wall, where a fragment of floor and a bit of curved wall made an aerie open to the air.

On her way to the wall, Dismé made up an enchantment:

"Old wall, old wall,
defender of the Spared
lift me up into your tower,
and let me see the morning."

In the solitude of the alley no one could hear her, so she sang the words, a whisper that barely broke the hush. All the schoolchildren in Bastion were taught the elements of sorcery, and Dismé often imagined what might happen if she suddenly got The Art and said some marvelous enchantment by accident!

She began to embellish the tune, only to be stopped by a sound like a tough fingernail flicking against a wineglass. Only a ping, but pings did not stay only! Dismé turned her face away and hurried, pretending she had not heard it. No use. Before her eyes, the dark air spun into a steely vortex of whirling light with a vacancy at the center which was the ping itself. It made her head hurt to look at it, and she averted her eyes as a voice from nowhere asked, "What are you thinking?"

If she lied, it would ask again, more loudly, and then more loudly yet until she answered truthfully or someone came to fetch her. Since being out alone in the dark was forbidden, being fetched by anyone was a bad idea. She had to tell the truth. If she could decide what it was!

"I was thinking about my father . . ." she ventured. She thought she had been thinking of him, though the ping had driven all thoughts away for the moment.

"What about him?"

"About . . . about his book." It was true! She had thought of it, not long ago.

"What book is that?" asked the ping.

"One written by his ancestor."

"What does it say?"

"I don't know. I haven't read it."

A long pause while the air swirled and the ping regarded her. "Did your father say anything about it?"

Dismé dug into her memory. "He said his ancestress wrote about the time before the Happening and the voice from the sky smelled like something . . . I forget. But the prayers smelled purple, going up."

The ping said, "Thank you," in an ungrateful voice, pulled its continuing resonance into the hole after it, and vanished.

Nobody could explain pings, and Dismé didn't like them poking at her. Now all her pleasure was sullied! She tramped on, pouting, until she reached the wall where she could fulfill her own magic: arms reaching precisely, fingers gripping just so into this crack, around that protruding knob, feet finding the right niches between the stones. Up she went, clambering a stair of fractured blocks into her own high place, her only inheritance from True Mother.

The ping forgotten, she crouched quiet. The dawn was pecking away at its egg in the east and night's skirts were withdrawing westward, dark hems snagging at the roots of trees to leave draggled shreds of shadow striping the morning meadows. The air was a clear pool of expectation into which, inevitably, one bird dropped a single, seed-crystal note. Growing like frost, this note begot two, ten, a thousand, to become a dawn chorus of ice-gemmed sound, a crystalline tree thrusting upward to touch a lone high-hawk, hovering upon the forehead of the morning.

Birds were everywhere: forest birds on the hills, field birds in the furrows, water birds among the reeds around

Lake Forget—a thirsty throat that sucked the little rivers down from the heights and spewed them into a thousand wandering ditches among the fields. White skeletons of drowned trees surveyed the marshes; hunched hills approached the banks to toe the lapping wavelets. Adrift in music, Dismé watched herons unfolding from bony branches, covens of crows convening amid the stubble, bright flocks volleying from dry woods to the water's edge. In that moment, her private world was unaccountably joyous, infinitely comforting.

This morning, however, the world's wake-song was marred by a discordant and unfamiliar shriek, a protest from below her, metal against wood against stone. Dismé leaned forward, peering down the outside of the wall into a well of shadow where a barely discernable darkness gaped. A door? Yes, people emerging. No! People didn't have horns like that! They had to be demons: ten, a dozen of them, shoulders blanket-cloaked against the early chill (demons were used to hotter realms), head cloths wrapped into tall turbans halfway up their lyre-curved horns.

Some of them bore wooden yokes across their shoulders, from which bottles hung, to Dismé's bewilderment, chiming with each step. Bottling was among the most sacred rites of the Spared, and demons were forbidden, unwholesome beings whom only the diseased and deceased had any reason to encounter. Yet here they were, lugging their loads into the daylight, invisible to the guards at the nearby gate who were looking in the opposite direction, unchallenged by the sentries on the towers, their averted faces silhouetted against the sky. Why was no one paying attention?

The grassy commons between wall and forest was wide, with nothing intruding upon it but the road to the west and the low bottle wall that ran alongside it halfway to the trees, so Dismé had plenty of time to observe demonic audacity, arrogant lack of stealth, insolently workaday strides, prosaic as any ploughman's. Some of them pulled a cart heaped with straw mats, and not even they had the sensibility to skulk.

As if mere demons were not enough, an even stranger

thing rose into the morning, a roiling fog that flowed invisibly up from somewhere, coalescing at the wall's farther end. Something or somethings, faceless and ghostly, limp ashen cerements covering their forms, their hands, their feet, the thick brims of their odd headdresses thrusting out like platters around their heads—if they were heads—strange and stranger yet.

Ouphs, Dismé thought, almost at once. Her mother had spoken to her of ouphs, in a whisper, in that particular tone that meant "This is a secret. This will cause trouble if you mention it, and we do not wish to cause trouble." She watched intently as they split to flow around the demons, like water around a stone, flowing together again once the demons had moved on. Why was it Dismé could see them but the demons could not? True Mother had said those who couldn't see chose not to. Perhaps the demons just chose not to.

The ouphs coalesced into a fog which approached, gliding along the bottle wall toward the dark door from which the demons had emerged, roiling there momentarily before flowing swiftly upward, like smoke up a chimney, giving Dismé no time to escape before they were all around her. She could not apprehend them in any physical sense, and yet her mind was full of feelings, voices, smells:

Sorrow. "*. . .searching searching searching . . .*" The odor of ashes, as though dreamed.

Loss. "*. . .where where where . . .*" Cold rain on skin. Dust.

Pain. "*. . . beg, beg, beg . . .*" An ache in the bones, a scent of mold, leaf smoke, wet earth.

Regret. "*. . . no no no no never . . .*" Rose petals, drying on . . . something. Dismé almost caught the scent . . .

Imprisonment. Captivity. Enslavement. "*. . . let go . . .*"

Oh, so sad, so sad, with only this nebulous linking of words and impressions, so fragile, so frail that the moment she clutched at them they were gone. Dreams did that, when she tried to hold on to them, evaporating like mist in the wind. So, too, the ouphs were driven out into the gulf of air where they whirled, slowly at first, then more quickly, keening an immeasurable sorrow that was sucked into the vortex and away.

The demons had neither seen nor heard. They were building a new section of the wall with various snippers and twisters, hoses, connectors and gadgets. They had buckets of half-solid stuff that they troweled between the bottles to hold them fast, and they worked with deliberate speed and no wasted motions. Soon, the job was done, the bottles were embedded and labeled, the tools and empty yokes were gathered, and the demons strode off toward the crow-wing shadow of the trees as the ouph-fog slowly faded into nothingness behind them,

When the last of the fog went, a chill finger touched the back of Dismé's head, a wave of coldness crept down her neck onto her back, as though someone had reached beneath her clothing to stroke her with ice. She shivered and recoiled. The chill had been there for a while, but her concentration on the ouphs had kept her from attending to it. Now it was imminent and intent, watching her. She spun about, searching, seeing nothing, but knowing still that something was watching. She ducked under the cover of tilted slabs and stayed there, trembling, pressing her hands to her head where the thing was still present, as though looking from the inside out!

In the darkness behind her eyelids a green shadow bloomed, a voice whispered. "Gone the demons and ouphs, but not gone that other thing. You must stop thinking . . ."

The suggestion was familiar. She stopped thinking. The green shade expanded to contain her as she retreated to a central fastness she was seldom able to find. Bird song wove a crystal cage. The sun pulled itself another rung into the sky. When its rays struck her full upon her head, she looked up without thinking anything and saw before her a looped line of light.

"What is that?" she asked in a whisper.

"The Guardian's sign," the voice murmured. "Go home now."

The darkness inside her gave way to a rush of scintillant sparks, edged light, pricking fire, sticking burs of brilliance creating an instant's perfect illumination. No voice. No demons. No ouphs. No ping, no thing, only the prickling star-burn, an itch of the intellect and the memory of a familiar but unplaceable voice.

So many sharp-bright questions! So many mystery-marvels that cried out for explanation! Thousands of things she wanted to know, and among them all, not one, not a single one that she, who yesterday had celebrated her eighth birthday, was still naive enough to ask.

Among the trees, the demons met others of their fellows. From the wagon, straw mats were thrown aside to disclose a pile of bodies to be unloaded and laid on the grass. Wolf, the demon in charge, went down the line, checking off each one as they came to it.

"Malvis Jones," he read from his work sheet. "Malvis goes to Warm Point with you, Mole. Rickle Blessing? That's him, in the green overalls. He's been allocated to Benchmark along with his wife, Lula, third one down in that row."

As he spoke, demons moved forward to load the still forms into smaller wagons hitched to pairs of horses. Beside the last body, a small one, the demons gathered, their faces twisted with anger and revulsion.

"Another one," said Mole, leaning down to feel the faint pulse in the child's neck. "What hellhound did this to her?"

Wolf said between his teeth, "She goes south, all the way."

"To Chasm? You mean we call for transport?"

"You think she'd live to make it any other way? Perhaps they can salvage something . . ."

Mole cried, "Does anyone know anything about this?"

"Nothing. Except that there's more of it, all the time."

Silently, the demons wrapped what was left of the still body and laid it on a stretcher. Four of them carried it off among the trees. As the others were about to move away, every demon froze. Sections of their horns became strangely transparent, as though little windows had opened there. After a long moment, they moved, though only tentatively.

"Did you feel that?" demanded Wolf. "What was that?"

"Something watching," muttered Mole. "That's all I could get." He fished a notebook from a pocket. "How many bodies were there, all together?"

"Twenty-three. Twelve alive, eleven dead."

"No body parts removed?"

"Just that little girl," said Wolf, his lips twisting in revulsion.

"Why is it always children?"

"It isn't always, just mostly. Speaking of children, j'you notice the girl on the wall, Mole? Little thing, out there alone? How old?"

"Yeah, about that. I used to see her there with her mother. Lately I've seen her there by herself, but it's the first time she's caught us out in the open. Do we need to . . ."

"No. Let it go. There's no threat there."

Because of the watcher, Dismé was late leaving the wall, and she made it home just in time to avoid being caught. As it was, only Rashel observed her return past the bottle room.

"What were you doing out there?" she demanded imperiously, nose pinched, lips pursed, a flush of indignation on her face.

"There was a bird on the wall," said Dismé, carefully, expressionlessly. "I went to get a closer look at it."

"Mother says you're not to go out without her say so."

"What's this?" Father rumbled from the kitchen door. "Been bird watching again, Dis?"

Rashel, officiously, "Mother says she shouldn't go out, ever, without asking her."

"I scarcely think Dismé needs to ask anyone's permission to take a look at a bird, Rashel. You're living in Apocanew now, not out at the dangerous frontier."

Rashel stared at him impudently, then flounced out.

"Was it really a bird?" Father whispered. "Or were you up in that old tower again?"

"I was really watching birds," Dismé replied.

"Well, your cloak is buttoned crooked and your shoe laces are in peculiar knots, so I'd suggest getting yourself put together properly before Mother sees you."

"She isn't . . ." Dismé began.

"I know. But you're to call her Mother. You've heard Rashel call me Father."

Oh, yes. Dismé had heard Rashel say *Faahther,* like a cat growling softly, playing with the word as though it were a mouse.

Father beckoned Roger from the adjacent room. "Roger, help your sister out, or she'll be in trouble."

Roger rolled his eyes, but he took her up to her room, where she had her own little white bed with a ruffled pink pillow. The pillow was a birthday present from Father.

"Where's your pillow?" Roger asked, as he retied her shoes.

Dismé whispered, "Rashel took it."

"Rashel!" said Roger. "I can't put anything down if she's around. She's a magpie for stealing. I'll speak to Father."

"Don't Roger. Please."

"I will. I'll make her stop this!"

And Roger did. And Father spoke to Rashel. And Rashel said the kind of thing she usually said.

"I did not! I saw her throw it under her bed her own self."

And when they went to look, there the pillow was, under the bed, dusty, with a hole torn in the ruffle, though Dismé knew she hadn't put it there.

Father shook his head, his face full of disappointment. Call-Her-Mother's voice cooed: "Well, Dismé, if you're not going to take care of things, we'll give it to Rashel. She takes care of things."

"Where's your shawl, Dismé?" Father asking. "The one that was your mother's?"

"I have it put away." She had seen Rashel put it in the back of her armoire, but it would not do to say so.

"Where's your quilt that Aunty made for you, Dismé?" Aunt Gayla asking.

"In the wash." As it well might be, though Dismé hadn't put it there.

Rashel tried taking things from Roger, too, but though Roger was a year younger than Rashel, he was bigger and stronger. One day, he slapped Rashel hard, leaving a red handprint on her face, and he told her if she ever told a lie about him or Dismé again, he'd tell the Regime! Dismé saw it all from the stair landing where a pair of heavy curtains made a perfect hideaway. From the time Rashel and Call-Her-Mother had come, Dismé had watched them, desperate to figure them out. True Mother once told her, "You must always know your enemies, Dis. The more you know, the safer you are." Maybe Rashel had believed Roger's threat, for none of Dismé's few remaining belongings disappeared or turned up broken for a while.

When spring came, so did Rashel's birthday, and Call-Her-Mother planned a picnic at Riverpark for the whole family. Father and Call-Her-Mother carried the baskets, striding on ahead of the children to the Stone Bridge that curved over the River Tey, at this time of the year roaring with muddy run-off from the snows up Mt. P'Jardas way. Dismé went across and stopped in the shade to wait for Roger, who was explaining to Rashel why she should stop showing off, walking on the railing.

"It's fun," said Rashel, loftily, arms extended for balance. "You're just afraid to try it."

"I have tried it, stupid. Just not this time of year, when the river's full like this! It's dangerous!"

"That's what makes it fun. Otherwise, it's just like walking along the railroad track. You slip off, it doesn't matter. I said you were afraid of the danger, and you've just admitted it."

"I am not afraid," he said, very red in the face, as he started to climb up next to Rashel.

Dismé screamed at him. "Roger. Don't get up there!" Then, when he paid no attention, she ran as fast as she could after Father, to get him to make Roger and Rashel stop.

"They're what?" cried Father, heading back down the path. "I thought Roger had better sense than that."

Call-Her-Mother sat down on a stump and shook her head in exasperation.

Dismé halted, biting her lip, not knowing which way to go. She was still vacillating when Father's great shout came echoing up the hillside, sending her scrambling down the hill, suddenly frantic. There was Rashel, leaning over the rail, father half over the rail at her side, reaching out. There was Call-Her-Mother, suddenly white in the face, looking at Rashel with pure panic, and Roger nowhere to be seen.

"He fell," Rashel cried. "He just suddenly fell!" She wept into the hem of her skirt, wailing as though in an outburst of grief. Dismé couldn't make a sound. Her eyes were dry and hot with horror and disbelief, and she could not take them from the foam-slathered darkness of the torrent.

People searched. Men from the Department of Death Prevention went up and down the banks on both sides, during the flood and afterward. No one was allowed to die all at once in the Regime. Father searched, silently, sorrow strangled, but Roger was never found. Dismé had bad dreams about dying all at once, but Father held her and told her Roger had gone to some other place where things were lovely for him.

"Shall we go see him in the bottle wall, Father?"

"No, Dismé. Roger has escaped the bottle wall. Thank God."

"Didn't you want him in the bottle wall, Father?"

"No, love. No one I love should ever be in a bottle wall. But that must be a secret, just between us. Like our other special secret, you remember?"

"About the Latimer book the ping asked me about."

He paled and grew tense. "A ping? When? Where?"

"One morning when I was out watching birds, I forget exactly when. It was a long time ago. I saw the ping first, then demons, then ouphs, then something awful watched me, and there was a voice and a sign . . ."

"Dismé, slowly. You saw what?"

"Demons, coming through the city wall. And ouphs."

"What are ouphs?"

She remembered, just in time, that ouphs were secret. "Just a pretend, Father. Mother and I had a pretend. And the something awful was only a feeling. But the voice and the sign were real."

"What voice? What sign?"

"A voice that told me to be still . . ."

Her father smiled, "As many people have."

"And a sign, like an eight lying on its side. Glowing, sort of." She gestured, making the curve loop, out and back, crossing in the middle.

"The Guardians' sign," he said, smiling. "Tamlar's and Elnith's."

"Who are they, Father?"

"You're remembering a story your mother used to tell you when you were tiny. Tamlar was the Guardian of the fires of life who will call the other Guardians back into life, to help us, and they will all wear that sign. Your mother named you after one of the Guardians."

"What was she guardian of, Father?"

"I don't remember what she was guardian of. Maybe she was Dismé of the dust bins." He laughed. "What did you tell the ping?"

She shrugged. "I couldn't tell it much."

"You do remember where the book is? And you remember, if anything happens to me, you must hide it?"

"Nothing's going to happen to you, Father."

"I hope not, Dismé. Still, one has to think of all possibilities. Like Bahibra going away." And he shook his head slowly, tears in his eyes. Dismé knew he was wondering why mother didn't tell him she was going but did tell Dismé. Dismé couldn't explain it because it was one of the many things she didn't know.

Once Roger had gone, there was no one to threaten

Rashel into being nice. One time Father caught Dismé crying and he demanded to know why. Dismé, caught off guard, said she was lonely, and she missed having her shawl, because it was the only thing left that had belonged to Mother. Father, sounding angry, which he hardly ever did, ordered Rashel to give Dismé's shawl back to her.

Call-Her-Mother said, "The child leaves her belongings all over the house. Why don't we return everything!"

The shawl had been washed in hot water. It was shrunken to nothing, a stiff, felt-like thing the size of a kerchief. Her hat had been sat upon; her book had paint spilled over all the pretty pictures; everything was spoiled.

"There," Call-Her-Mother said. "Such a fuss over a lot of trash. I hope you're satisfied."

Father was staring at the shawl, his face very cold and still. Dismé's mother had worn it when they met. It was woven of very fine wool, printed in a design of roses, and it had been very soft, very old and an armspan each way. True Mother had given it to Dismé, particularly. Father touched it with a forefinger, his face flushing as he looked up at Cora, angry, really angry.

"Who did this?"

"Why, Val, I'm sure the child did it hers . . ."

"The child did nothing of the kind. She treasured it far too much. Who did it?"

"It probably got mixed in with the wash, accidentally."

"Accidentally. Like the hat. Like the book. Like the little pillow I gave her. There are too many accidents, Cora. Far too many *Turnaway* accidents."

Dismé had no word for the expression on his face. Anger was only part of it. Maybe disappointment? Whatever it was, it made Call-Her-Mother turn very red, then very pale, and that was enough to make Dismé lie awake at night, worrying about Father. Call-Her-Mother and Rashel were both Turnaways. It wasn't smart to fool with Turnaways. Should she stop showing she loved Father? Everything she loved disappeared, or was broken, or died . . .

* * *

Father changed after that. He became less dreamy, more solid, which puzzled Call-Her-Mother. One day he asked Dismé to help him clean the back areaway, beside the toolshed. When they were almost finished, he said softly, "Go get me the Latimer book, Dis. Hide it under your shirt. I've made a place in the shed where we can keep it safe."

Dismé went into the little room her father used as an office and listened, being sure that Call-Her-Mother and Rashel were upstairs. The Latimer book was a black book with a name in gold: Nell Latimer, Father's great great so many times great grandmother. It was on the bottom shelf, behind some other books, Dismé removed the books, first carefully, then with panic, for the space behind them was completely empty.

"It's gone," she whispered to Father, when she returned to him.

He bit his lip. "Gone?"

"Gone, Father. Really. I took every book out of the shelf. and I looked at each one."

"Rashel," he said, like a curse.

"Or her mother," whispered Dismé. "They both take things."

He didn't contradict her. He hadn't doubted her since he had seen her mother's shawl. Instead, he said bitterly, "It'll be somewhere in the house. Look for it, Dismé. Whenever you have the chance. Damn it, it's a Comador book, not a Turnaway thing. Not Cora's nor Rashel's, but ours."

"What's in it, Papa?"

"I'm ashamed to say I don't know. I started to read it once, but a lot of it was very personal and embarrassing to read. I felt as though . . . I were intruding, so I never really. . . . Well. It was written by our ancestress, a sorceress, a star-reader."

"You said there was something about purple prayer, rising from the world like smoke, and something about the monster that came in the dark to strike the world a mortal blow, and something about the part that broke away . . ."

"A voice from the sky that smelled of sandalwood and roses."

"It told her to bring her children, quickly. But she couldn't, because the Happening came right then."

"When we lost The Art," he agreed. "Try to find the book."

Which she did, often, but with no success.

✦ 2

nell latimer's book

A strange thing happened today, one I think may warrant taking some notes.

I could claim to have met Selma Ornowsky because I was so conscientious and dutiful that I stayed at the observatory after closing to finish up paperwork, but it wouldn't be true. I was still there because it's getting harder every day to go home. The Jerry I'm married to is no longer the Jerry I married. He's become a stranger, a person I don't want to spend the rest of my life with. There are two children, however, who love him dearly, so wanting takes second place to being Mom. So long as I'm busy and not within the sound of his new holier-than-thou voice, I can pretend things are the way they used to be, and that's really why I was still working at 6:30 P.M. when I heard the bell that told me someone was trying to get in a side door.

The person thumbing the bell looked seventy-ish, short, chunky, white-haired, tanned, wearing chinos, a checked shirt, and a troubled expression. When I cracked the door, she said, "Neils wouldn't be here, would he, dearie? But whether he is or not, I've got to show this to somebody!"

I protested. She shrugged me off and talked her way into the foyer where she spread the contents of her portfolio out on the only available table while she continued her monologue.

"Neils has known me for donkey's years. He's the one got me started on this fool hobby. Helped me build my first eye. Pretty good eye, too, not as good as the one I've got now. No gimmicks on it. No computer. Good for finding comets, though. I've found four, one of them named after me. Taught high school science and math for forty years; made me a masochist. Name's Selma, by the way. Selma Ornowsky. Where did you say Neils is?"

"Australia," I murmured, staring in fascination at the photographs piling up on the table before her. Each one had an area of space circled in white, seemingly the same area of space on each of them. "He's helping to design some kind of wide array they're putting up in the outback."

"Well, if they finish it in a hurry, maybe he can tell me what this is. There!" One stumpy finger pointed at the center of the marked circle. "That's the first one. Then these, on subsequent nights."

"I don't see anything," I said flatly, hoping discouragement might work where excuses hadn't.

"Of course you don't. You ought to see a cluster of five faint stars." She tossed down another photograph with five stars in the marked circle, then went back to the other ones. "You do see the three that border the cluster." She flipped down another photo. "And in this subsequent one, you see only one of the three. Then . . ." She flipped rapidly. "You don't see that one, and you don't see the two very faint little ones to the left, and as we come up to the present date, you don't see even more."

I scrunched up my face, trying to convey what was still a lukewarm interest at best. "Something occluding them?"

"That would be my supposition, yes. And since it's getting bigger and bigger, I would assume it's moving in this direction."

That got my attention, and I bent over the photographs, flipping them as she had done. It could be either something huge far out or something not so huge closer in. Of course, the area of sky included in the circle was tiny.

"What do you want me to do?" I asked her.

"Do what you're supposed to," she commanded. "I presume you're more than a mere receptionist? Yes? Got some experience in the field? There's a protocol to cover discoveries, isn't there? Get some confirmation! Get something bigger looking at it! I brought you everything I have . . ."

"How did you find it?" I asked, regarding the tiny patch of blackness in amazement.

"As I said. Masochism. I enjoy sitting there flipping sheets while I have my coffee, seeing what flickers at me. Usually it's some speck of light. This time it was some speck of dark. Thought for a minute I had something wrong with my eyes, but it's there, all right."

"I can get a message to Neils," I told her. "Since he knows you personally, he probably would want to know."

"Fine. You do that. My phone number's right there. When you get it figured out, call me. I'm not going to tell anybody about it. Tell Neils that. Tell him the news junkies won't find out from me . . ."

And she was out the door. Gone. A few moments later, I saw an aged red pickup truck headed down the mountain as I stood there puzzling over Selma's last words. Why would it matter if she told anyone? Then the implication kicked in, and I shook my head, trying to dislodge the idea. The thing is headed in our direction. At this point, the only interesting thing about this darkness is that it's headed toward us.

general gregor gowl turnaway

Of the three tribes which had settled Bastion—Comadors, Praisers, and Turnaways—the strongest leaders were found among the Turnaways. General Gregor Gowl, Perpetual Chair of the Regimic Council, was a Turnaway. He'd been a leader since his youth, born to dominance and to mischief, a stocky, strong boy well able to intimidate others. He often remarked that nobody could tell him what to do, which was true. Not a day went by without Gowl doing something he'd been told not to.

A crucial point in Gowl's development came at age ten, when he heard of a parade to be held at the nearby garrison, a dress rehearsal for the annual Muster of Bastion. He told his lackeys that no boy of spirit could hold his head up unless he witnessed this event and if they weren't weak baaing ewe sheep, they could see it if they skipped school and came with him.

No Bastion boy could bear to be called a ewe sheep, for reasons to do with ovine anatomy of which they were largely ignorant, so four of them, Banner, Skiffle, Brant, and little lopsided Fortrees—whom Gowl called *the sand bur* because he never gave up sticking to them, no matter how they pounded him—went on their bellies under the school back fence and cross country to the parade ground.

Gowl had already reconnoitered the garrison fence, finding a convenient hole behind a set of bleachers where someone had haphazardly stacked a pile of straw bales for the archery butts, which Gowl, who always had an eye toward his own safety, had already identified as usable cover. He did not, however, mention the possibility of being caught to the others. Instead, Gowl led them through the hole and lined them up under the bleachers with little Fortrees nearest the parade ground and himself nearest the stray bales, lying at his ease as the event began.

Prancing from the barracks ground at the far end of the field came a white horse bearing a white-clad officer with enough gold braid on him to sink a dinghy. His aides to either side bore his battle flags, unfaded and unmarred, for the previous general had made a non-aggression pact with the demons, and there'd been no forays or wars since.

The leader was followed by gray-clad officers on black horses, then by brown-clad, brown-horsed subordinate officers, then bowmen in black leather, bows across their shoulders, quivers at their backs, then lancemen with red sleeves and spear tips glittering; then blade fighters laden with swords and daggers. Last of all came the blue-clad engineers, sappers and builders, creators of bridges and siege engines, with their support wagons behind. The buglers let loose with a great blat of brass that made all the horses go on tiptoe until the drummers came in with a steady blam, blam, blam that settled the marchers into a clockwork pace and sent echoes caroming off the nearest mountains.

Staring at the commander on the white horse, Gowl said to nobody in particular, "I'm going to be like him!"

"Yeah, right," said Skiffle. "Not with your record at school you're not."

Gowl turned to aim a punch at his detractor, catching a glimpse as he did so of some functionary or other bearing down on them from the far side. "Look there," he whispered, pointing. The moment their heads were turned away from him, he moved between two large bales of straw and then sideways between two more that supported several overhead, becoming invisible in the instant.

The functionary was swift, and he had help arriving from another direction. Within moments they had four boys by whatever part was uppermost, and were marching them away toward the command post, where the four captives found that Gowl wasn't with them. Boyish honor, admirable, certainly, though quite often misguided, required they keep quiet about this. None of them bothered to consider what Gowl would have done if he were in their place. Gowl, as was his habit, was not in their place, which he considered only right. By the time the school director was notified of the charges against the captives, trespass being the least among them, Gowl had sneaked back to school and was sitting innocently in class.

A good deal of nefarious nonsense had taken place at the school recently (the largest part of it Gowl's doing), and the school director thought it time to make an example of malefactors. Skiffle, Banner, and Brant were given twenty stripes each in the school forecourt with the student body counting the lashes aloud, and little sand bur Fortrees (who had no mother, and whose father didn't consider him worth saving) was sent away for bottling. His words to the demon who came to bottle him were, "Tell Gowl I didn't cry." The demon, though he chose not to deliver the message, took it upon himself to inquire into the matter, with results which surprised Gowl, though not until many years later.

This particular event gave Gowl his lifetime ambition. From that time on, his schoolwork improved because he kept one or two good students doing his work under threats of extreme injury. He also became increasingly adept at keeping layers of people between himself and any possible blame. He was going to be that man on the white horse, and he kept that purpose before him for three decades of his life as he rose to the rank of Over Colonel in charge of the Division of Defense. He postponed marriage until he could do so advantageously, at thirty-five, to Scilla, the twenty-year-old daughter of the Comador Clan Chief, on whom he thereafter begat a seemingly endless stream of daughters.

The general cultivated influential supporters, and it was one of these, the then-Warden of the College of Sorcery in Apocanew, who told Gowl of Hetman Gohdan Gone. An invaluable resource, the warden said, in helping others achieve their ambitions.

"Hetman Gone?" Gowl queried, brow furrowed, slightly annoyed at hearing a name he knew nothing of. "I've never heard of him!"

"Well, no reason you should, he's a lone, strange fellow," said the warden. "I wouldn't know of him except he invited me to his place. Not a well man, I'd say. Seldom goes out. Gout, maybe. Keeps his place hot as a furnace. I met him when he had some sorcerous materials that he wanted to donate to the college. It's the most extraordinary material, spells that really work, old grimoires, biographies of mages. Let me tell you, General, he had more of The Art in his hands than in all of Faience Museum! Eh!

"He told me to let him know if he could ever be of help to the Regime, eh? Now, putting you in charge of affairs would be of help to the Regime, wouldn't it?"

"Now how would he do that?" snarled Over Colonel Gowl. "The current general, my kinsman Thulger Turnaway, is still in good health and strong as an ox."

"Can't say," and the warden shrugged, laying a finger aside his nose and winking, reminding Gowl of Uncle Thulger's stinginess with funding for the College of Sorcery.

Gowl, via the warden, sent a letter of introduction to Hetman Gone, and later met with the gentleman in the subbasement of some half derelict building not far from the Fortress. It was, as the warden had said, a strange place and the Hetman was a strange man, confined to an easy-chair in his overheated room, surrounded by artifacts of the most unusual and expensive kind, and served by a group of deformed and dwarfish men who should have been bottled at birth in the ordinary course of events.

Gowl was offered some savory tidbits of food and a glass of delicious drink. He and the Hetman talked about things in Bastion, and about Gowl's ambitions, though Gowl was not thereafter able to remember just how the subject had come up. He did remember, however, the lividity of the Hetman's skin, the intensity of his eyes reflecting the red glow of the fire, the peculiar liquidity with which Gone moved his arms coupled with the odd stiffness of his legs. Most of all, however, he remembered the charm of the man's voice and the silken offers that were made.

The Hetman offered magic. Magic that worked. If Gowl wished to take his uncle's place, he had only to accomplish a certain rite, the directions for which were written out for him on an ancient sheet of parchment, and the Hetman could guarantee that Gowl would rise to the position of preeminence. Gowl took the parchment with eager fingers, glanced at it, then read it, trembling slightly. For a time he put it on his knees for his fingers seemed to have gone dead. In a moment more, however, he picked it up again, and when he left the Hetman's place, the parchment went with him.

Obtaining the necessary materials for the rite took some time. One does not walk out of one's house and find the left leg of a blind knife sharpener on any given corner. That item came via traders, from far off Mungria. When Gowl confessed this particular difficulty to the warden, that gentleman had some trouble keeping his face straight.

"You're laughing," Gowl had objected. "At what?"

"Well, you did it the hard way," the warden remarked. "It would have been easier to have the doctors blind a man here in Bastion, wouldn't it? Either a man who is now a knife sharpener, or one you would have assigned to be a knife sharpener before or after he was blinded."

Gowl hadn't thought of that. There were several other items on the list which he saw immediately could be expedited through similarly pro- or retroactive measures. Though a few surgeons declined to be helpful (unwisely, in terms of life expectancy), others were less difficult, and within two spans Gowl had the rest of the material needed, including the one item which should have been the most difficult but was actually closest at hand.

The rite was properly accomplished, and Gowl found its

accomplishment strangely satisfying. There was a moment during it when he had felt a surge of power in his veins, an ecstacy of vigor that made him feel omnipotent. A few days later the feeling returned when General Thulger Turnaway fell dead in the marketplace. The feeling continued through all the subsequent machinations through which General Gregor Gowl Turnaway ascended to the post of General of the Regime.

Gowl's association with Hetman Gohdan Gone, begun with such felicity, continued. Many impediments to Gowl's ambitions were removed through spells provided by Gohdan Gone. Since the warden of the college, who had introduced Gowl to Gone, had been bottled immediately after Gowl had assumed power, the general believed no one else knew about the Hetman. In this belief Gowl was mistaken.

✦ 4

the cooper

Far north of Bastion, across mountain and desert and over the Yellowstone Sea, lay the pleasant land of Everday. Its capital city, Ginkerle-Pale, had been named for Henery Ginkerle and Nylan Pale, twenty-first century west-coast ship-builders who had been on a ship when the Happening occurred, a ship that had been washed up, along with many others, on what had previously been a landlocked highland, perhaps in Idaho or Montana. Though the world lay mostly in darkness at this time, a hole in the cloud blanket hung above this particular spit of ocean and its adjacent coast. The opening allowed the daylight to penetrate and at night admitted reflected light from an orbiting ring of ejecta, which led the refugees to name it Everday.

Though the climate had chilled considerably, the area was largely untouched by flood, fire, ashes, plague, or monsters, and the resident population, which was tiny, scattered, and very confused, found comfort and strength in the arrival of new people. Both residents and the accidental arrivals eagerly joined in doing whatever needed doing to guarantee their survival over the terrible years that followed when the hole in the cloud cover closed.

The country around had been agricultural. As the silos had been full of grain when the Happening occurred, as an enormous food repository from the former age lay nearby, and as a seemingly bottomless abyss had opened between this repository and any neighboring population to the east, the people of Everday were able to preserve themselves and their breeding stock throughout the dark years. Rarely totally covered, the skies in Everday were among the earliest to clear, and when the sun reemerged, the people began building their stocks of fertile seed and tilling their fallow fields. Throughout this time, almost all the new arrivals had continued to live on their ships.

When the skies had cleared more generally, the shipwrights set to sea with their sons and grandsons to explore the ruins of the great cities they had known before the Happening. Though the boats returned laden with salvage, those who manned them said the original monsters had grown great and were everywhere among the ruins. No culvert was empty of them, no pipe but contained a foully crusted rootiness that emerged squirming and oozing to grasp at whatever person might be near. Those who returned from the expedition recommended that their voyage be the last. To make sure that no future generation ignored this advice, all the ships not suitable for coastal fishing were sailed up-river as far as was possible and there dragged ashore to be converted into housing for the new hamlet of Shiplea.

The people early adopted a township council system of governance for most matters, but they added the frippery of a king simply because they liked the idea of having one. There was little entertainment in Everday, and some of the settlers felt that a prolific royal family would guarantee a fountain of continuous merriment. Thereafter, the Everdayans concentrated on building, farming, and enjoying the luxury of slow time and long sagacity spent in joyful celebration of living.

It was to this mellowed land that the sign of the Guardians came to Camwar Vestavrees, an unlikely recipient for any such distinction. If one named any forceful attribute, there were a myriad others who had more of it than Camwar. He was a simple, slender, brownish man with an easy walk and plain clothes. His eyes were his most noticeable feature, for when he felt wonder or delight, they glowed with an astonishing luminosity. Camwar earned his livelihood as a cooper. He loved wood: the slip of the plane along its surface, the mute curl of the shavings, the pure arc of a stave that knew itself to be perfect and needed no puffery. He had from time to time, under unique circumstances, loved one woman or another for similar attributes of quiet perfection, begetting upon several of them children of remarkable beauty. He was unaware of this, as his partners had in each case been married to men who quite properly considered that such beautiful children had to be their own.

Camwar had been born to a couple who managed a goat dairy and nut orchard some miles north of Ginkerle-Pale. During his second year of life, a sudden storm brought down a large nut tree directly upon the Vestavrees couple who had been working beneath it. Camwar's father's body was found beneath the trunk, and it was assumed his mother's body had been washed into the river and away by the storm. After the crematory fires had died down, Camwar was adopted by his father's brother, a cooper well known for his fine kegs, barrels, watering troughs, and bathtubs.

Camwar's uncle was generous, thoughtful, and remarkably understanding for an old bachelor. He raised the child Camwar on stories of wonder, on jobs of work, and on music—the cooper's hobby was creating stringed instruments. Tales, tasks, and songs were suited to Camwar's age and became more complex with passing years.

Occasionally a ship would come by; even less frequently a traveler would come down from the mountains. These infrequent visitors always confirmed Everday's decision to keep to itself. There were still monsters and wars out there, along with a people who called themselves The Spared who were actually slavers. Still, not all that came from outside was rejected merely on that account. A Mungrian ship, for example, brought with it some remarkable maps, new and shiny, with tiny letters and immaculate labeling of places in the style of pre-Happening things.

"They come to us from the Guardian Council," said the

bearded Mungrian. "Take them. There's no cost. We are paid to distribute them for the benefit of the people."

"The Guardian Council? That's an old legend, isn't it. Are they real? Where are they?"

The Mungrian stroked his beard and pontificated upon the subject: "It is thought The Council may dwell far to the north, for in that land great mountains have risen to hide the pole from the low sun that creeps impotent upon the horizon, and in that darkness something huge has lived since the Happening and now moves southward like a great flow of ebon shadow, into the peopled lands."

The people of Everday knew that the world no longer tilted so far on its axis as in ancient times, that the year was now 400 days long, and that summer never came to the far north, but this account of flowing shadow was new to them, as was the idea that the Guardian Council, long a favorite tale of Camwar's, was a reality. Everday was to hear of The Council yet again. This time the informant came from the northern mountains.

"You will be visited," said the Messenger, "by people who will bring you a device. When the device is brought to you, put it somewhere safe, for you will need it when the sign comes."

"What sign?" asked the King, who was always sent for when there was something ceremonial to be done, such as opening the horse fair, or awarding the annual prize for preserves, or welcoming visitors.

"The sign of the Guardian Council. The sign may come anywhere, wherever Appointed Ones are to be found. The sign will appear suddenly, and you will bring that person to the device. That's all."

"Where did you learn all this?" asked the King.

"Difficult to say," said the Messenger, rubbing his brow. "The message got passed on to me from someone else, though it originated with the Guardian Council."

"What do you know of this Council?" the Everdayans asked.

"Ah, well, little enough, though it is said that Tamlar of the Flames will know the time it is to be convened. Among the first to be called will be Bertral of the Book, for it is he who calls the role of the Appointed Ones."

"Have you seen any of these Guardians?"

"No." The Messenger shook his head. "I have seen one of the devices, however, and it is quite real."

The Mungrian visit wasn't repeated, nor was there another Messenger, though as promised, the device was subsequently delivered, and when Camwar's uncle told the story, he always told how the device had arrived.

"Later on, another ship came to Everday, the first and only ship of its kind that had ever been seen. It was a black ship, flecked with gold, and on its deck was a device, wavy and glassy and strangely shaped, like a frozen flame of space, with stars in it, accompanied by some silent and dark-robed persons.

"The King directed his people to go out in a boat and get the device off the ship, and put it upon a wagon and haul it into the city, to the Temple, and there it is, in the apse behind the altar, and there it has been kept safe for generations, but no one has come bearing the sign."

Camwar learned this story along with a hundred others. By the time he graduated from the limited schooling all Everdaylings were given whether they wanted it or not, he was much sought after as a teller of tales, a singer of songs accompanied by a lute or guitar he had fashioned himself. Story tellers and song singers were much valued in Everday, where even the antics of the royal family tended to be repetitive, generation to generation. Indeed, Camwar had recited the "strange device" story so often that whenever he went about his business, buying wood or strap iron, charring vats or making a stringed instrument for a special client, he always searched for the sign, thinking to see it almost anywhere except in his own mirror.

Nonetheless, nine years after Camwar's uncle had died and left him the business, on the morning of the Festival of Lights, Camwar woke, bathed, went to his shaving mirror and stared at himself in bewilderment, for above his eyebrows, inexplicably, unexpectedly, astonishingly, there burned a twisted loop of fire that glowed like an iron white-hot from the forge.

Because it was festival, he had planned to walk among merry makers, drink a few glasses of beer, eat some hot sausages, listen to the marching bands—which cost nothing—and then come home again in the early evening to his narrow bed and the quiet of his room. The man in the mirror, however, was not the man who had planned such a day. The man in the mirror blazed with purpose, and the blazon could not be ignored, for it glowed; nor could it be covered with a cap, for it sang like the reverberation of a great peal of bells, a mighty and harmonic throbbing that spanned the range of audibility.

Trembling, he dressed himself in the best he had, garments that were clean and neatly repaired though by no means festive. He drank a glass of water to calm the queasiness he felt, an unsettling quake somewhere in his gut that was not pain but was nonetheless disturbing. He went out into the street and, keeping to the back ways as much as possible, made his way toward the palace. Unobtrusive as he tried to be, several people came trailing after him, nudging one another and whispering among themselves when he arrived at the palace gate. Though the sign had never been seen before, everyone had heard the story, and the sign could only be what had been foretold to come, so when Camwar presented himself to the guard, that man took one look at the glowing sign and asked him to wait—courteously, as it happened, which was sensible of him.

The Regent was being shaved. When the messenger arrived, in some haste, the barber dropped the razor, cutting the Regent very slightly on the chin, a fact that the Regent did not even notice. He leapt from the chair, struggled into his coat without waiting for his valet, and went bloody, belathered, and disheveled down the stairs, where he found Camwar waiting in a small reception room. He peered at him first, then he went near to him and touched the sign, drawing his hand away with an exclamation. The sign burned. The sensation was not exactly one of heat, but one could feel a force of fire when one touched it. One could, as a matter of fact, hear and taste and smell something fiery and forceful as well.

"Does it hurt?" the Regent asked in wonder.

"No, sire," Camwar replied. He had felt something when the Regent touched him, but it was not a sensation he could describe easily. It was rather as though he had answered a question without knowing what it had been.

"When?" the Regent asked.

"I've had a little itchiness there, in the forehead, for . . . oh, some years now. But this morning the itchiness was gone and *it* was there."

"Well," said the Regent, sitting down and staring at the floor. "Well. I suppose . . . I suppose we must get in touch with . . . who is it?"

"We're to go to the Temple, perhaps?"

The Regent stared for a moment more, chewing his lip, then asked Camwar to be seated, sent one footman off to bring breakfast on a tray and another one off to summon the Royal Historian and several of the younger historians as well since the Royal Historian had become somewhat forgetful and vague with advanced age. These worthies assembled quickly, in various stages of bewildered disarray, and the Regent—who had completed his shave and been properly dressed in the interim—told them in a hushed voice that the sign had come.

"You must go to the Temple," said the Royal Historian, firmly and without a moment's pause. "That is, if you're sure it's the sign."

The Regent suggested the Historian check for himself, which that man did, returning to say yes, it was the sign. "We must go to the High Priest," he repeated, with no wavering or doubt whatsoever in his voice.

"We have not thought about the device in hundreds of years," said one of the younger historians. "Is it even still here?"

"The device is in the Temple," said the Royal Historian. "You are correct that it has been there for a very long time."

"Is it really? Well, but . . . if no one has . . . oiled it or greased it or powered it up or whatever one does in all that time . . ." the Regent muttered unhappily.

The Royal Historian forgot himself so far as to pat the Regent comfortingly on the shoulder. "We need not be concerned. We were told, as everyone, everywhere was told, that when the sign came, the device would be in operating condition. We have only to bring the sign to the device. The device will function."

The Regent looked uncertainly at the mouse-quiet younger historians who would normally have been spouting contradictions to everything the old man said.

"Now?" he asked.

"Now," assented the Royal Historian, amid the others' continued silence.

They went in procession to the small audience chamber, where Camwar was enjoying a freshly baked muffin spread with something delicious he had never tasted before. Nonetheless, when the Regent appeared, he rose hurriedly and bowed.

"Finish your breakfast," said the Regent. "It will take us a few moments to have the carriages brought round and the Temple staff notified."

The Regent went off to expedite matters, but the Royal Historian stayed behind and helped himself to one of the muffins. "Tell me about yourself," he said gently, when Camwar had swallowed and wiped his lips.

"There's very little to tell, sir. I was reared by my uncle, who was a cooper. I inherited his business nine years ago. I have remained a bachelor; my shop is in Vrain Street by the bridge. I'm thirty-four years old. I had intended to spend the day at the Festival, so I allowed myself a bit more sleep than usual this morning. When I got up . . ." he shrugged. "Well, you see it."

"Yes," mused the Historian. "Yes, I certainly do. I'd wondered about that, you know. It came without warning, did it?"

"Unless the itchiness was a warning, sir. I've had that for donkey's years. Not so bad it was annoying, just enough to make me scratch at it now and then."

"Itchiness. Well. I also wondered whether the person who received the sign might not hide it . . ."

His voice trailed away as he regarded the twisted loop of shining fire, and heard the harmonic singing that changed from time to time without ever approaching melody.

Camwar said, "I don't think it would allow me to hide it away, sir."

"No, now that I see and hear it, it's clear it wouldn't."

"Do you know what the sign means, sir?" Camwar asked.

"Its shape is an ancient sign for infinity," the Historian answered. "The never ending but twisted loop of time, going out and returning. It is also the symbol for change of condition."

"Change of condition, sir?"

"The change from child to adult, from adult to age. From winter to spring. From living to dying. You go as far as you can go one way, then you go the other way, and finally, you return to the starting point."

"Ah," said Camwar politely, to show he had heard. He had heard, but he had not apprehended. He felt as though he were suspended between the sky and the city, unable to make sense of what he saw from that height. "Ah," he said again, taking a very small bite of muffin.

In mere moments he was escorted to a royal carriage that rolled silently on inflated tires behind felt-booted horses, for in Everday, people were attentive to noise as to any other form of pollution. The populace lined the streets, all the way from the palace to the Temple.

"How did they know where we were going?" the Regent asked.

"They saw him this morning, sire. As he came through the streets. I'm sure the people figured it out. They often do."

Even the temple steps were lined with quiet people. For the first time since he had risen that morning, Camwar felt a touch of panic. He started to shake, only to feel the Historian's hand comfortingly on his own. "Don't worry, young man. It's nothing you need fear. Nothing evil is said of the device or those brought to it."

"Quite right," the Regent murmured, as he alit, then offered Camwar his hand. "You need have no apprehension on that score."

They went up the steps together, the Royal Historian panting a little for the stairs, though shallow, were long. The huge iron-bound doors were open, and they walked through, down the center aisle of the lengthy nave, up more steps past the huge altar, around the reredos behind it, and into the small hidden chapel in the apse where hundreds of scented candles bloomed like flowers before images of the kindly goddesses favored in Everday. The device stood on a low dais beneath a pillared baldachin, a shadowy flame of glass, or that particular stone that comes from volcanoes, glowing with golden sparks inside it, like the ebb and flow of lights of distant cities seen through shimmering air from a mountain top. It stood above the height of a tall man, and it looked unlike anything made by hands, human or any other. The High Priest, in full vestments, including his best diadem, stood beside it.

He greeted the Regent with a low bow, murmuring as the Regent stepped near, "There's a kind of blurry place here, like a pair of handprints, and they're at the right level for a man to reach, so I suppose that's what he's to do."

The Regent beckoned to Camwar, who approached the thing and laid his hands on the indicated places in the stone. A light shot from between his thumbs to touch the sign on his forehead. The lights in the device began to spin over and under or perhaps through one another, diverse sets of them converging beneath his hands in varying combinations and colors, as a deep, pulsing hum came from the device. Camwar felt nothing except an inner vacancy, as though his self had been removed and taken elsewhere, leaving his body poised where it was, half leaning on his hands.

Those watching saw a transformation. The man leaning on the device grew taller, much taller, and larger. His face altered. His garments transformed strangely, so that he appeared alien in his dress as in his features. What stood there, only briefly, was a giant clad in skin-tight leather and fur, a bow saw across one shoulder, a great axe sheathed on his back, in one hand a drawknife and in the other an adze.

A great voice shouted:

"Behold Camwar of the Cask, in whose charge are all containments, holdings, bindings and restrainings, whether of torrents or plagues or winds. The soul of thunder is his to hold or loose . . .

"His is the discipline of the craftsman, the habit of care and attention to detail, his the accomplishment of perfection when upon the head of thunder he shall stand to account for the workmanship of his people."

In the depths of the stone, life moved and hummed. The lights glittered and faded. No one moved. The light that bathed the sign went out, the stone was still, and Camwar was only Camwar once more. Self returned, but only into the space not occupied by that larger self that had come from, or perhaps through, the machine.

"Is that all we were supposed to do?" queried the Regent.

"Yes, sire, that was all," Camwar said softly. "You are thanked for your commendable promptness."

As they turned to leave, they were stopped by a flicker of light at the top of the device, a sparkling fire which was shooting bits of it off into nothingness, the sparkle gradually lowering, eating the device as it went, within moments reducing it to a pile of dust on the floor of the apse. There seemed to be nothing anyone could say about this, as it served only to verify what Camwar had said. Indeed that had been all they were supposed to do, and the device would not be needed again.

All of them, including the High Priest, returned to the palace. Many men of importance were gathered there to be seen talking with other men of importance, resulting in an abundance of conspicuous but immaterial discourse. Some persons had already sent minions to question the neighbors and customers of Camwar Vestavrees, in case the information might be valuable, or at the very least, interesting. Meantime they discussed What It All Meant, some considering the sign a threat and others a blessing, each according to his nature.

Since Camwar was secluded in the small audience chamber with the Royal Historian and the High Priest, the talkers had nothing but opinion to work on, and even that little gave out when it was announced that Camwar would be leaving very soon, on a ship.

"What ship?" they clamored. "A fishing boat? That's all we have."

"No," said the messenger. "He says a ship will come for him."

Thus dismissed, the gathering removed itself from the palace to more comfortable surroundings where it continued to discuss What It All Meant for several days without changing in any respect the ratio of reality to opinion.

In the small audience chamber, meantime, the High Priest had asked whether Camwar had any words of wisdom to share, and Camwar had fixed him with an innocently speculative eye.

"Yes," he said at last. "A time of great danger is coming."

"For us?"

"For the world. Long ago, the people of the world cried out for help. In the reaches of heaven their cry was heard, and a Visitor came in answer to it. That Visitor began helping immediately, but secretly. Now the Visitor intends to be known to the people of the world and the people of the world must deal with that knowledge."

"What did we cry out for?" asked the Regent.

"For God to take notice of us. To correct our errors. To govern us. The first answer that came was the Happening. The second answer is about to come, and we do not yet know how terrible the governance may be."

"Why should we fear a just god?" the High Priest asked, with a little smile.

Camwar turned his full gaze upon the old man, saying in a puzzled voice, "I do not know that they prayed for a just God."

The High Priest thought upon this, his face troubled.

The Historian asked: "And what is the role of the Guardians in this?"

Camwar shook his head. "We are to be needed, but I'm not sure for what."

"You say 'we.' How many of you will there be?"

Camwar frowned, as though in deep thought. "A book exists, the Book of Bertral. All of us are in it. Fire came first. Then the two who shape the world. Then the three keepers of souls, and the four fosterers of life, and after them, the five, of whom I am one. Of the five, I was called first, for my labors will be great. The six who vary and distinguish life come last in the book, but some of them may already be at work." His voice trailed away into silence for a moment before he turned to the High Priest, saying, "You asked for wisdom? Hear these words. Nothing limits intelligence more than ignorance; nothing fosters ignorance more than one's own opinions; nothing strengthens opinions more than refusing to look at reality."

In the middle of that night, Camwar woke in his luxurious palace room, knowing a ship had sailed up the river as far as it could and was anchored there, awaiting him. He rose and dressed himself, taking with him the tools and musical instruments that had been fetched from his shop. Though they made a heavy load, they seemed unburdensome.

At the river, he was guided dowstream to the shadow-wrapped ship by whispers and nudges, as though he had a good friend at his ear. A small boat put out from the ship and came to the riverbank to pick him up. The hooded ones bowed very low before the sign, and gestured him aboard.

"Are there others?" he asked.

The master of the ship replied, saying, "You are first of the five. Of the six, who will not be involved in the great battle, Befum, Pierees, Falasti, and Ushel have long been awake and at their labors; Geshlin will soon arise; Tchandbur has been identified. The rest, like you, live in lands far from the place of battle. They, like you, will be fetched to the battle-ground, Shining One."

"I would prefer it if you called me Camwar," he said, rubbing the sign on his forehead, which by now was very pale. "I am myself, though from moment to moment something else seems to be looking on. Whatever will be required of me, however, can be best done if I remember who I am."

The ship sailed away, leaving the town behind it, and in that town the High Priest went to bed in a mood halfway between humiliation and sorrow. He was grieving over his own ignorance and the fact that his people had no way of finding out what was happening. They had come to this land in ships! Once they had had ships! Their city was named after people who built ships! How could they know the world, without ships?

He woke in the morning remembering Camwar's words of wisdom and determined upon a crusade. He began with that day's exhortation in the Temple. "We must be able to find out what really is," he said. "It is not enough merely to tell stories about what exists. We must go out into the world again. The sign has come. Therefore, build ships!"

By the time the people had been organized and begun work, building the things they would need to build the things they would need to build ships, they wondered why they had not done this centuries ago. It was exciting! It was remarkable! It was fun! And so the sign came and went and yet remained, while its coming set the people of Everday stoking the furnaces of the future.

✦ 5

the latimer book

The year after Roger died, Dismé's father fell ill. Call-Her-Mother was worried about him. She had little lines on her forehead when she looked at him, and she got cross at Rashel, which she almost never did.

"Don't forget the book," Father whispered to Dismé the night after he got back from seeing the doctor. He was lying on the couch in the living room.

"I won't," she promised him, worriedly. "But you're all right, Father. The medicine will fix whatever it is!"

He thought about this gravely for quite some time, moving his head restlessly on his pillow. "Yes," he said at last. "But remember the book anyhow."

She wanted to talk about the book, but some friends arrived just then, to visit her father.

"You ought to go to Hold, Val," one of his friends told him. "There's a doctor there, fellow named Jens Ladislav. Seems to know more about doctoring than the rest of them put together."

"I'll be all right," Father said, squeezing Dismé's hand.

When the friends left, Gayla said, "You *should* go to Hold, Val. The doctor here in Apocanew isn't helping you."

"I'm better," he said, testily. "I'm much better. I think my stomach rebelled against the seasoning Cora uses when she cooks. Turnaway food is more highly spiced than our family is used to, that's all. I'm sure this was just a passing thing."

And it seemed that it was, for Father did feel better. In a few days, he got up and went back to his work at the Office of Textual Approval, Department of Materials, Division of Education. He seemed so well recovered that it shocked them all when not long after, in the middle of the night, he became very ill indeed. His cries woke everyone. The doctor was called, and Father was taken away to the Medical Center. Dismé wanted to go visit him, but Call-Her-Mother said to wait until he was better, even though she and Rashel went to the Center the next day.

When they told her she couldn't go, Dismé felt the beast that lived inside her raise its head and sniff the air. The beast's name was Roarer. He was a strange unaccountable animal, and he was a secret, but sometimes when she was very angry he came out of his den. Father was hers, not Rashel's! They had no right to keep her from visiting him! She would get even with them by, by . . .

Roarer growled softly, cautioning her, reminding her of True Mother's words. Don't break out in anger. Get even some other way. Well then, what would be a secret pleasure she could have they wouldn't know about? Finding Father's book, of course. Finding it and hiding it in a place they'd never think to look, and doing it before they got back.

She began in the attics and searched frantically throughout the entire house, looking in all the old places plus other places she'd never dared get into before. Nothing. She sat fuming in the living room, her nails making small ragged moons in the palms of her hands. Where else was there? She'd been through the whole house except for the bottle room.

The thought resonated. She had never looked in the bottle room! She never went into the bottle room; she only passed it as quickly as possible. She hated the bottle room, which meant the bottle room would be the perfect place to hide something she wasn't supposed to find!

Half weeping over her own stupidity, she took a bit of her cheek between her teeth and bit down on it to keep her from yelping or making some other untoward noise while she lighted a candle and carried it inside the dark space, full of whispering and gurgling sounds like voices she couldn't quite hear. To drown them out, she hummed to herself, as she crawled about the room and thrust her broomstick into every corner under the bottle racks. Wonder of wonders, she found it! They—or she—hadn't even bothered to hide it very well. They—or she—had wrapped it in an old towel and stuffed it down behind one of the older bottle racks, one that dated back five or six generations.

As soon as she made sure it was the right book, she went into her father's library and found another one the same size and color. Except for the worn name, it could have been the same book that she wrapped in the same old towel and re-placed precisely in the place she had found it. Then she fled to her tiny corner room where she had already prepared a hideaway by loosening the nails in one of the boards covering the back of her closet. When she pulled all the nails out but one, the board could be pivoted aside to disclose a tiny attic under the corner of the porch roof. She took her mother's shawl, the one that had been shrunken into kerchief size, wrapped it around the book and placed the bundle inside.

When the closet board was pulled back into place with the nails re-inserted in their holes, the hiding place might as well not have existed. A row of hooks along the back of the closet held her cloak and her dresses, and no one would think of there being space behind them, not in a million years. She couldn't wait for Father to come home so she could tell him!

Call-Her-Mother came home first, saying Father would be home within a day or so. The next day, people arrived who tramped heavily through the hallway downstairs, back and forth to the bottle room. Dismé, tears running unheeded down her face, heard the clinkering sounds of tools, the mutter of voices. Outside her window a wagon was parked, and on the side was painted: Department of Health, Division of Death Prevention, Office of Bottle Maintenance.

"There he is," said a deep male voice from downstairs. "Home again."

Rashel and Call-Her-Mother went downstairs to see the visitors out. Dismé washed her face and froze it into her now usual expression of nothing.

"Now you can visit your father," Call-Her-Mother said to Dismé in a kindly though far-away voice, as if she were thinking about something else.

Rashel grinned, and Dismé could read her mind. Rashel thought Dismé would run to the bottle room, expecting to find her father there. Her father wouldn't be there. There would be a bottle with his name on it, but that was all. She didn't cry. She didn't scream or yell or cry; she just turned and went up to her room.

"I guess she doesn't care about him much," said Rashel.

Dismé heard the words but refused to react to them. She would not visit Father. She knew he would hate that, and besides, she had a half-formed intention regarding the bottle room, a thing she meant to do without any notion of how to go about it yet. She needed to find out more about many things before she did anything at all. All she could do now was watch them, and wait, and hope that something would happen to break the sad monotony.

Something did a few days later when Call-Her-Mother and Rashel left the house quite early in the morning. They didn't return until late in the evening. Dismé heard the horses and ran to her usual hiding place. She peeked out to see Call-Her-Mother half carrying Rashel into the house. Rashel's face was ashen where it wasn't bloody. Her eyes were blank. There was blood on her clothes, and she dripped blood as she walked. She looked half-dead. Dismé stepped back to be completely hidden as Call-Her-Mother dragged Rashel up the stairs.

"Come on, Rashel. Another step."

A whisper full of horror and pain. "I can't. I can't. Not after what he did . . . to me."

"Yes you can, and will. You brought this on yourself, now cope with it."

"Don't tell . . . her . . ."

"Dismé? Of course not. What business is it of hers. I think you've learned where your responsibility lies regarding

Dismé. At least, I hope you've learned it. If you haven't, we won't be living here long."

A moan. ". . . didn't know we were watching all the damned Latimers . . ."

"Now, another few steps, and you can go to bed."

The staggering, stumbling went off down the hall to Rashel's room.

When they were silent behind the closed door, Dismé sneaked back to her room without making a whisper of sound. She had thought Rashel couldn't be hurt by anything, but Rashel had been hurt and her mother either couldn't or didn't protect her. Who did it? Who or what was it that Rashel feared? For the moment it was enough to know that Rashel feared something. From its lair, Roarer also rejoiced, putting out a fiery tongue to lick her heart.

Each night she peeked into the hidden cubby before she slept, to see that the book of Nell Latimer was there, where it belonged, where it was soon joined by one of the old dictionaries from Father's office, a book so fragile that one had to hold one's breath while turning the pages. When both Rashel and Cora were away, she took the book out of hiding and read it, making a list of words to look up in the old dictionary, slowly, carefully, writing each definition down, sometimes only after looking up a dozen other words. The words weren't that different, but the spelling was. Sometimes she had to guess. What was an *observatory?* What was *6:30 p.m.* What was *conscientious?* Eventually she figured out conscientious was the same as Regimic, and observatory was some kind of place to look at the stars, and 6:30 p.m. was a way to say day-endish.

The first page took her forever to read. The second one came more quickly. Then she had read five, ten, and finally, all, still without knowing whether the story they told was true.

✦ 6

nell latimer's book

I sent Neils a message about Selma's discovery, which he didn't acknowledge, and since he was due back in two or three days and I had time, I logged some eyetime to verify what Selma had shown me, mentioning it in passing to a few close associates.

No one has been able to see anything yet. The thing is a dark body in dark space, visible only as a shadow. Neils returned eventually, I dumped the whole thing in his lap, and he in turn involved some colleagues around the world, and I heard nothing more until this morning when he told us the thing is not huge and far away but smaller and inside the orbit of Uranus. It is now reflecting a little light; it will indeed cross earth's orbit; and it may do so at an inopportune time, i.e. when that point is occupied by the human race.

However, said Neils, over our incipient panic, since the thing will be influenced by the gravitational pull of Saturn, which it will almost certainly encounter closely, or by Jupiter, which is even more likely, it's difficult to say just where it's going to end up. He hemmed and hawed and we pressed the matter until he confessed that if it hit us, even glancingly, its apparent size indicated the damage would be...ah...possibly terminal. Of life, that is. He would only say apparent size, because no one knows how big the thing actually is.

We were all sworn to secrecy. Not enough was known to get the citizenry into an uproar. We all agreed to this, even those of us with families. Most people face their own deaths as inevitable. I understand that even the death of loved ones can be grieved through. But everybody? The whole human race, every thought, every passion, every achievement wiped away? Gone? That thought creates a deep shuddery feeling, like swallowing an earthquake.

These notes are turning out to be more about me than about Selma, even though I'm only writing in it when there's something astronomical to report. It's been several months since the entry above, after which I argued with myself for almost a week before deciding that if the situation is utterly terminal, nothing I do will make any difference. If we get hit not quite that hard, however, I may be able to save our family without breaking the silence we've sworn to keep. I can't tell the truth but I can tell a plausible lie, and I do have a separate savings account with enough money in it to build a shelter.

So I babbled at Jerry while I was peeling potatoes: "A meteor shower. Something extraordinary. I'm going to build us a shelter, Jer."

"Nell, I keep telling you, if you'd just put your trust in . . ."

"Shh," I said, mock angry. "I'm not going to ask God to protect us when we're able to protect ourselves. When you started getting religious, we agreed not to fight about it. You can pray away all the meteorites in the universe and I won't mind a bit, but I'm going to build us a shelter."

When the two of us met and courted and married, we were fellow scientists. We stayed fellow scientists for five or six years, but sometime along in there, back maybe four or five years, Jerry gave up on science. I honestly don't know whether he got religion first and gave up science out of religious conviction, or his career disappointment made him use religion as an excuse. Back then I was gaining a respectable reputation as a solid, workaday hack, who had made several small discoveries and who had added some to the knowledge store of the human race by slogging away at it. That was fine by me. I've never had any huge aspirations; I just like astronomy.

Jerry, however, has . . . had big ambitions. The Nobel Prize, at least. Or some cosmological theorem named after him. He didn't like slogging, preferring innovative and highly flamboyant theorizing on the basis of very little, all of which tended to raise the hackles both of his colleagues who played by the rules and of the big names in cosmology who had totally invested themselves in other points of view. I've always known Jerry was egocentric, but he kept his ego mostly under wraps at home. Also, he has . . . had a lovely dry humor and I thought we were okay. I was busy, and I liked my work. He was busy teaching and writing and doing what cosmologists do, causing an occasional flurry but becoming no more an immortal in his field than I am in mine.

Being an immortal doesn't matter to me. If one looks out into the universe and perceives what true immortality would mean in terms of time and space, it takes monstrous hubris to even conceive of personal immortality, much less desire it. However, once Jerry turned religious it became clear that Jerry really wanted to be immortal, one way or the other, and if science wouldn't do it for him, religion might.

Personal beliefs are unarguable, even if the other side has all the facts. Jerry wasn't interested in facts, so we didn't discuss his belief in a near future apocalypse. I just went ahead and had the shelter built: reinforced concrete, buried under twelve feet of dirt with an escape hatch. I ordered dehydrated food enough for a year. In a separate pit there's a fuel tank for lanterns and stove, tied in with flexible connector lines, disconnected until time of use. There's an air filtration system run by pumping a bicycle and a water tank on heavy springs that can sway any which way without breaking. Also, in a survivalist catalogue I found a sort of hollow pipe with a folding windmill inside that can be pushed up into the wind and connected to a generator. There are bunks for four: one for Michy, who's five, and one for Tony, who's three, one for Jerry, one for Nell.

During the construction, Jerry went around with his above-it-all smile firmly fixed on his face. His actions were as affectionate and sweet toward me as always, though they didn't feel right. The only actual criticism I got was a kind of teasing: "The wrath of God Almighty approaches, and she wants to build a shelter?"

Keeping the evasions to a minimum, I usually said something like, "As a parent, it makes me feel better to have it, that's all."

"Why no solar panels?" he asked, grinning at my bicycle power source.

"Meteors can set fires and kick up dust. There might not be any sunshine for a while," I murmured. "Besides, whoever's in here will need some exercise."

He just gave me his uplifted look, as though he'd spent the morning watching Archangel Gabriel unpack his Sousaphone. "Nell, if it makes you feel better, by all means, have a shelter."

The man I married was a seeker, a man of many ardors, an amateur musician of some talent, an artist with clay (though he never worked at it). Before he turned to religion, we'd lived though several of his passing enthusiasms about different *ways of life:* a brief fling at being a vegan, a few months of yoga, a bout of transcendental meditation, none of them lasting long or changing what he was.

This last exploration, however, was different. It changed what he was, and I know with absolute certainty we would not have married if he'd been like this when we met. We have, however, two children and almost ten years of honorable and faithful history, and I've been trying to respect that.

dismé the maiden

Dismé grew from child to maiden, Rashel changed from girl to woman. Rashel was totally preoccupied by the changes, though Dismé hardly noticed them, for she was concentrated on staying out of Rashel's way. She began by moving into the attic room that Roger had used, the one nearest Aunt Gayla. There, Dismé informed Cora, she would be better located to help her great aunt when Gayla had the terrors.

"An excellent idea." Call-Her-Mother sniffed, watching Dismé's face. "You are the logical person to see to her, though I'm amazed you want to do it."

"Oh, I don't want to," murmured Dismé off-handedly. "The spiritual advisor at school said I had to."

As, indeed, he had done, after being carefully led to that suggestion during Dismé's annual citizen's review. Spiritual advisors were notably contrary, and Dismé had only to voice a well-rehearsed expression of distaste at the idea to make him insist she do it. Sacrifice for family, tribe, and country were, after all, Regimic virtues.

Attics were where servants lived, and servants were a class of people Cora and Rashel found uninteresting. The attic location coupled with the vague, slightly servile manner Dismé had adopted, made her seem inconsequential and boring. Even though playing a servant's role made her responsible for much of the housekeeping, Dismé considered the demotion to be an improvement over being watched all the time. Also, since her father's death, she had noticed that Gayla's habit of irrelevant babble made her virtually inaudible to the family. Aping this habit was easy, and between age eight and eighteen she gradually disappeared into the walls of the house, her voice heard only as background noise, while Cora and Rashel almost forgot she was there.

When Gayla had the Terrors, Dismé dealt with them. Whatever the teachers required at school, Dismé provided it. She was completely ordinary and totally obedient, requiring no "conferences" with teachers or workers from the Bureau of Happiness and Enlightenment. From her new listening post in the attic, Dismé noted that Rashel returned from periodic visits to town in moods of fury, even frenzy. She guessed that whomever they saw on these trips was the same one who had sent Rashel home bloody and bruised after Father died, and this pleased her. All in all, she spent ten years like a chip in an eddy, whirling slowly, not going anywhere, not much caring, maintaining her intrinsic buoyancy through her solitary pleasures, despite Cora and Rashel's recurrent efforts to scuttle her.

She was not physically mistreated by either of them. They had a revulsion against her being hurt or doing anything that could conceivably injure her. The endless pain they caused was not physical but emotional, for they redefined her existence from day to day by surrounding her with a torturous unreality. Rashel and Call-Her-Mother sidled along pathways Dismé could not see. They climbed scaffolding of opinion toward a goal she could not even imagine. They spoke together in a language that made no sense to her, though every word of it was a word she knew.

"Don't you see, Dismé? Are you blind?"

"Look at that! You did it. Can't you do anything right, Dismé. I'm so ashamed of you."

"Look at this, Dismé! Do you want to bring the Regime down on us all? This is most offensive!"

Sometimes they were speaking of a picture she had drawn

or a verse she had written in her notebook, or some other private something they had dragged out for collusive deconstruction. Sometimes it was merely some household chore, not completed as they would have had it, or some chance remark by a third party whom they supposed had been speaking of Dismé. Years of this might have worn her into despair, made her believe she was insane or worthless had she not found enough delight in daily life to cushion the constant abrasion.

Over those same ten years, Rashel cultivated her ambition by building a corps of dear, dear friends. She had determined upon a career in the Department of Inexplicable Arts.

"That's where the power is," she said.

"Will be," agreed her mother. "If *The* Art is recovered. Which it hasn't been, not in a thousand years. Nobody's had The Art since the Happening."

"We know *someone* who does!"

"Hush, Rashel. Be silent."

Everyone knew The Art had been lost a thousand years ago, during the Happening. Of every thousand who had lived before the Happening, nine hundred had died during the impact, flood, fire, ashes, and plague. Of every hundred who survived the initial violence, ninety had died of the cold and darkness. Of every ten who survived the cold, nine had died of the monsters. Before the Happening, men had been mighty wizards, capable of miraculous feats. After the Happening, the power of The Art was lost. The Spared, however, had been saved and led to safety by a corps of Angels who had rebelled against God's tyranny and brought their chosen people to Bastion where their duty was to discover the lost Art once again.

"Definitely the Inexplicable Arts," said Rashel, admiring herself in the mirror. "Perhaps I will be the one to restore the Great Art to humanity!" She laughed. "In the meantime, I have an invitation to a BHE soirée!"

The Office of Personnel Allocation, Department of Ephemeral Arts, Division of Culture, Bureau of Happiness and Enlightenment, often held soirées where unmarried

Regimic men could meet appropriate women. If a man married a non-Regimic woman, he gave up all hope of a successful career in government. Any such liaison betrayed a serious defect of character. Rashel, who had learned to be ultra-Regimic in public no matter what she did privately, had pulled various strings among her dear, dear friends to get an invitation.

Attending such affairs alone was considered slightly improper for women, so on the day Rashel dragged eighteen-year-old Dismé along, only to park her in a corner as soon as they arrived, which Dismé much preferred in any case. She was quite content to sit there, observing the crowd, until Rashel appeared arm in arm with an elderly man whom she introduced as a long-time friend, bidding Dismé be attentive to his wishes.

"You're the lil sisser," he announced, leering at her. "Rashel's lil sisser."

Dismé forgot to fade into the wall. "No," she said definitely. "I am not her little sister. I am not related to her at all."

He waved his finger at her. "Now, now. Mussn tell stories. Rashel says she's gotta sisser, then she's gotta sisser. C'mere, sisser. Less go out onna porch."

Dismé looked around. No one seemed to notice what the man was doing, which was to put his hands on various parts of her and try to get them under her clothing. At that point, another man came up behind him, pushed the drunken man away from Dismé and sent him away in the grip of two BHE guards.

He then returned to Dismé. "I apologize for that oaf," he said. "My name is Ayward, by the way. Professor Ayward Gazane. College of Sorcery." He lowered his voice. "That ass who was attacking you needs a flogging. Public drunkenness is prohibited, as I'm sure you know, but he's a Turnaway git, which means he 'gits' innumerable second chances not available to the rest of Bastion." He smiled, making her smile, his long, bony face grave and concerned beneath its crown of curling, slightly graying hair, his slender figure inclined toward her, his voice gentle. During the rest of the afternoon, he stayed at her side, and she was grateful for his attention, the first she had received from a man since her father died.

Rashel, whose own reception at the gathering had given her food for much profitable thought, rode home beside her sister without noticing Dismé's flushed face or shining eyes.

The next day, Ayward Gazane sent a note, which Dismé intercepted before Call-Her-Mother could see or dispose of it, and thereafter, they met in the college park, drawn to each other as two fireflies in a darkness, wandering the graveled paths through long, honeyed afternoons full of interest and enjoyment of a completely proper kind.

In truth, Ayward was not strongly sexed, and the young Dismé would only have been confused by any overt approach. She had grown through loss and confusion into a girl who lived almost entirely inside her head, taking refuge in the places she created there, not so much repulsed by others' reality as unable to perceive it. Her only other male friend had been the son of one of True Mother's friends, a little boy whom she had played with in the park. Ayward threatened her composure no more than that five-year-old boy had done, and she came to believe she loved him.

That was before Rashel noticed something different about Dismé, followed her to a couple of her trysts with Ayward, found out about the courtship—if that is what it was—and told her mother all about it.

"You're too young, Dismé!" Cora was firm. Since Father died, Dismé had called her Cora, and Cora had given up trying to change this form of address.

"But Cora, all we do is talk with one another . . ."

"Enough! He's years older than you are. No, Dismé. This can't be allowed, it's most improper."

Rashel had been less tactful. "You're too plain and too stupid to interest Ayward Gazane for very long! I mean, look how you're dressed! Like a rag-woman. He's a professor, an important asset to the Regime, and I want him for myself."

Rag-woman was probably accurate, as Cora had chosen Dismé's clothes ever since Val was bottled. The next morning, Dismé was told to pack her things, as she was being sent to her Aunt Genna's home in Newland. She had barely time to get the Latimer book out of its hiding place and conceal it beneath her cloak before she was packed off in a hired wagon.

Once there, she received letters from Ayward. The first one said that he was coming to get her. The next letter said he would come carry her away, in secret, before Rashel could stop him. The third letter said he would wait for her until she was old enough to marry without her mother's permission, since "that was the major stumbling block." His fourth complained that he didn't know what to do about Rashel. He felt he was being ensorceled by her, hag-ridden, succubus-bound. She was so powerful, so determined, so set on having him . . .

A letter from Rashel arrived shortly thereafter. Cora had been bottled, very suddenly, after a brief illness. Dismé was to return to Apocanew. And by the way, Rashel and Ayward were being married on the day Dismé returned home.

Dismé preferred to stay in Newland, with Genna, but a messenger from the Regime brought an official document saying Rashel had been appointed Dismé's guardian. Dismé was to return to Apocanew. Frozen faced, she did so, giving Ayward and Rashel her hand and wishing them well. At that meeting she also met Ayward's father, Arnole, who was in a Chair.

He was the first Chaired person Dismé had ever seen close up, and she was glad to note it was a probationary Chair and that he seemed to have all his body parts. Still, the fact that he was in a Chair at all meant he was suspected of having The Disease. Families with Diseased members were tainted, and Dismé wondered mightily at Rashel taking this risk.

After the brief ceremony, while Rashel was swanning before the guests, Dismé retreated to the garden, only to be followed there by Arnole, who parked his chair next to the bench and demanded she sit down and talk with him. At that moment her will was frozen, and if he had invited her to jump into the River Tey, she might well have done so. She sat, in icy silence.

"Why did you come back here, child?" His voice was anything but fearsome. It reminded her of Father's voice, thawing
its way through her chill. Dismé tried to explain that Rashel
was her guardian, that she had no choice in the matter.

"Why does Rashel want you here?"

She gaped at him, forced by his directness to consider a
matter she had preferred not to define. Why indeed? "Because I'm in love with . . . was in love with . . . your son and
it wouldn't be any fun for her if I were somewhere . . .
away." The moment the words were uttered, she knew they
were dangerous and wished them back, but Arnole merely
squeezed her hand and said he understood.

"*I* never understood," she cried. "I never understood
Rashel. Or her mother."

"Her mother? Not yours?"

"Not mine. Never mine."

"And what was it you didn't understand?"

"They were always seeing things I can't, hearing things I
couldn't hear! I could never figure out how to do things the
way they wanted them done . . ."

"Don't worry about anything Rashel or her mother may
have said to you," he said in a firm, dismissive tone. "They
were both—Rashel still is—headed somewhere you don't
want to go."

She laughed on an indrawn breath. "They were always
telling me their way is the only way to go!"

"Oh, no, my dear. No, not at all. So long as it harms no
one else, one's own way is always preferable."

Those few words would have been enough to make her
his friend, but there were many more words and stories and
talk. It was like being suddenly adopted by a comfortably
clucking mother hen. Or perhaps more like being taken into
the nest of a father eagle. All at once there was a strong wing
extended over her head when it began to spit lightning.
Nothing required Arnole to live with the family, but he insisted upon it, a parent's right, no matter that he was Chair-
bound. Whatever his reason, Dismé blessed him for it.
Within a season, he had taken the place of the father she had

lost, the brother who had vanished, the mother who had departed. He even extended himself to Gayla, giving her a friend to hold on to as well. During events that defied understanding, he was there, eyes alert, senses weighing what was going on. And most wonderful of all, he talked with her.

"What are you thinking about, Arnole?"

"You sound like a ping," he commented.

"You've seen pings, Arnole?"

"Oh, indeed. Always wanting to know what people think."

"Well, what are you thinking about!"

"The thing that sat at the top of the world, Dismé. At the time of the Happening, something came down at the north pole, where it stayed for centuries. Now, however, I'm told that it's moved. When it came to the coast of the New Pacific, it flowed under the water. Now it's halfway down the continent, traveling along the bed of the sea."

She stared at him, mouth open. "How do you know?"

"I have friends," he murmured, with a quick glance around, to be sure they were unobserved. "Outside friends, over the mountains."

"How do you go outside . . . I mean," she gestured, flushing, at his Chair.

He shook his head. "Ah . . . well, no. I heard about the darkness before the Chair."

Emboldened, she asked, "Is that why they put you in a Chair, Arnole? Because it's wrong to have outside friends."

"Not wrong, dear girl. Un-Regimic, yes, but not wrong."

"Rashel says they're the same thing."

"Rashel is mistaken."

"What does it mean, the thing moving?"

"It means that after sitting on top of the world for a very long time, it has finally decided to do something with, for, or about this world."

"What will it do?"

"Haven't a notion," he had said, shaking his head. "Except that it's likely to be something earth-shattering."

"The Happening was earth-shattering, Arnole. Most everybody died." She shivered.

"What do you know about the Happening?" he asked, eyebrows raised. "The usual child's version?"

She flushed, casting a quick look around. "A little more than that. My Father's great, great, great something ancestor lived through the Happening. She wrote a book about it."

"And where is this book now?" he asked, avidly.

"It's a secret. I promised Father . . ."

"Well then, did your ancestress say anything about the . . . what are we to call it? The Visitor?"

"She said it told her she must come to it, with all her children, but she only had two children, so the Visitor should have said *both*, not *all*. It sounded to me as though she were dreaming it."

After that, Arnole kept her informed about the Visitor. Now that he was in a Chair, he could not visit his sources anymore, but he knew people who did, and they told him all about it.

⋆ *8*

a disappearance

Dismé and the family learned of Rashel's promotion over breakfast. She was to be, she crowed, Chief Conservator of the Office of Conservation and Restoration.

"It's a prestigious advancement," she said, between bites. "Though the museum is ruinous both as to fabric and finance. I can manage to keep up the buildings without great trouble, but maintaining the grounds!" She shook her head in dramatic distress, rolling her eyes, making jagged gestures that were definitely Turnaway, not Comador, all elbows and long fingers conveying her horror at the waste and ostentation allowed by the builder. "A monument to extravagance!"

"How will you manage?" Ayward asked in a peculiarly toneless voice that caught Dismé's attention at once. A strident alarm could not have alerted her more.

"I've hired a maintenance crew," Rashel said off-handedly. "We'll move into the Conservator's House early this spring, and the crew will arrive immediately thereafter."

"Move?" Ayward responded, this time even sharper, his voice splintering on the words. "I don't recall being hired, or even given an honorary appointment at the Caigo Faience. By all the Rebel Angels, Rashel, it's up on the mountain! My work with the college is here in Apocanew."

Rashel shook her head impatiently. "My staff will be

commuting to Faience from Apocanew; you can do the opposite."

"Do you want to go to this new place?" Dismé queried of Arnole, when they were alone.

"In Bastion, one place is pretty much like another," Arnole said, his lips smiling but his eyes watchful. "I get around."

It was true that Arnole wasn't unduly immobilized by his Chair. It was powered by demon magic, a Black Box, which no one was allowed to touch. Not even the researchers were allowed to investigate demon magic, for it was said to be closely akin to the dark arts that had brought about the Happening.

"Nobody asked me if I wanted to go to Caigo Faience," Dismé murmured softly, thinking of her treasured places in Apocanew.

Arnole patted her arm. "I know, child. Our opinions are irrelevant. Once Rashel has decided on something, I doubt she could be stopped even by a Second Happening. She is very centered on her career, and her reputation continues to grow. I'm surprised Ayward goes along with this."

"I'm not," said Dismé. "Ayward says he couldn't have married anyone with serious faults, so Rashel is simply not well-informed." Dismé had heard this as both ludicrous and infuriating, but she had seen no purpose in asserting the truth.

"Thank heaven you didn't marry him, Dismé," said Arnole. "I'm glad your mother prevented it."

Dismé's eyes filled. "Cora wasn't my mother. She married Father when Rashel was twelve. My real mother . . . she may still be alive, Arnole. When I was about five she took me to our special place on the tower and she told me she had to go away. She said what she had to do was more important than she was, or I was, or any one person was, and she told me to remember that, to tell Father."

Arnole seemed lost in thought. "What did she look like?"

"She had red-gold hair and soft brown skin, like brown wood, silky. I remember her voice better than I do her face.

She had a magic voice. If I hurt myself, she could make the hurt go away just by ordering it to. Or make me go to sleep, or stop the flies biting."

"That's very mysterious," he said, in a strange voice.

"Father thought so. His feelings were hurt when she went, because she didn't tell him herself. Then he met Corable the Horrible, and right away he began behaving as though he didn't have good sense. I think she put a spell on him."

Arnole mused, "When you speak of your mother, it makes me wish I'd had one."

"You had to have a mother, Arnole. Everybody does. You can't get born without one."

He grinned at her. "What I meant was, I never knew my mother. When I was an infant, a flood came through our town, and when it was over, she was missing."

In the evening, Dismé often sat in the oriel window of the library, half hidden behind the curtains, pretending to read.

"Ayward," Rashel said, "I wonder if we shouldn't make some other provision for your father?"

He looked up from his papers, suddenly alert, and Dismé's fingers, poised to turn a page, froze in place.

He said, "What do you mean, some other provision?"

"I don't think he'll enjoy living up at Caigo Faience. Here in Apocanew, he manages to get out, see his friends, visit the tavern. Up there, he'll have no company."

"He has his own funds, Rashel, and if I rent a faculty toe-hold here in town, he can live with me."

She did not answer, though Ayward continued to watch her for a time, his face pale and troubled. Dismé bit her lip anxiously. Rashel had opened the subject, then fallen silent. Dismé had known Rashel too long not to understand the convention. The snake rattled, then stopped, which did not mean the snake had gone away.

At breakfast, Ayward announced his intention of renting a place in the city for himself and Arnole, but he had done nothing about it two days later when the agents from the Bureau of Happiness and Enlightenment came to tell Arnole his probation was about to expire. In three day's time, they said, he was to be examined anew to determine whether The Disease was chronic. If found guilty he would be put in a more restrictive Chair.

"You're not guilty," Dismé whispered to him, reaching up from her cushion on the floor to touch his face. "You're not guilty of anything!"

He laughed, a slightly shaky laugh. "I'm a mocker, guilty of doing what I've warned you against, Dismé, and I'm afraid they won't accept you as a character witness. The only one they would listen to is your sister Rashel, and I'd take long odds she wouldn't help."

"I would help you if I could, Arnole!"

"Well then. There is something you can do for me." He reached under the carapace of his Chair and brought forth a little bag, like a dozen other such he had given her over the years since Ayward's marriage. "I want you to hold this for me."

"I'm already holding a lot of your money, Arnole."

"Not a lot, Dismé. It doesn't total a great sum. What? A few hundred Holdmarks? Twenty or thirty Dominions? Add this to the others. If anything happens to me, if I am . . . unable to be with you in future, it is yours."

"Are you sure?" she asked, troubled. "Ayward is your son. Don't you think . . . ?"

"Of course I think," he snapped. "As you are capable of doing, though you consistently behave as though it were an arcane art known only to initiates! I *do* think, and you know very well *what* I think! You know what I want you to use this money for, and it has nothing to do with Ayward!"

She flushed for she understood both his mood and his meaning. He wanted her to leave Ayward and Rashel's house and make a life for herself. Though the Regime taught self-sacrifice as a virtue, Arnole had little patience with it. He had said over and over, "Sacrifice for sacrifice's sake does no one any good!"

Now he said in a pleading tone, "Dismé, I have known you since you were eighteen. Once you turned twenty, Rashel had no legal claim on you. I know you have the intelligence and the will to recognize good advice! I keep thinking you are . . . perhaps . . ."

"Perhaps what, Arnole."

He shook his head, then smiled, more at himself than her. "I had thought . . . I still think there's more to you than meets the eye. But then, we all have hopeful dreams about our children, and I think of you very much as I would a daughter." He held out the sack of coins, gazing fixedly at her.

Silenced equally by his love and his vexation, Dismé took the little bag of coins—splits and bits of Holdmarks—and hid it under the quilting scraps at the bottom of her ragbag with what was left of the others he had given her. Whenever Dismé was sent to Apocanew on an errand, she exchanged the smaller coins for Holdmarks. Then, rarely, when she actually had time to herself in Apocanew, she went to the money-changer's with ten Holdmarks and a split, the changer's fee, to buy a little gold Dominion with a Rebel Angel on the face and the words "I Spare the Righteous" on the back. These she sewed into the hem of her petticoat, for the fewer the coins, the easier they were to hide. Her underclothing was far wealthier than she.

If Arnole had meant this additional gift to distract her from worrying over him, however, it failed. Dismé spent the night in her aerie on the ruined tower, crouching against the stones, head on her knees, body shaking as though she were having an attack of the Terrors. Arnole was her father in all ways that mattered. Whenever Rashel had been most dangerous and threatening, Arnole had been her refuge, now *he* was threatened and there was nothing she could do for him. Her rage was futile; intervention would be childish and useless. She had clung to him like a vine to a tree, determined to share his life, now he was being severed from her and she could not bear it!

Nor, seemingly, could somethings else, for they were all around her before she knew they were there.

". . . *search, search, search* . . ." the ouphs wept, their salt wetness running into her mouth.

"Pain, see, here, like, like, who?" Rocking, moaning, tormented.

"Come. Com-fort. Come-forth. Oh, see."

She was deep in a smothering fog-bank of them, their voices like sleet in storm, their smell like old cellars full of mold, the feel of them like corpses, cold and empty! She buried her face in her hands and tried not to gag as she breathed them in, drowning in them, horrified at them, at herself, for Arnole. The horror was paralyzing, and she crouched upon the wall in a state that was almost coma.

Toward dawn, she surfaced, cold and shivering, wet through with dew. The ouphs were gone leaving behind a natural cold and warranted despair. She climbed down from the tower, plodded back to the house and fell into sodden sleep on top of her bed, only to be wakened an hour or two later by a turmoil of shouting, cursing, and running feet.

Arnole's Chair had been found burbling and tweeping to itself in an alley near by. Its carapace was ripped apart, and Arnole was gone.

Aunt Gayla had hysterics; Rashel went about with a white, angry face; Ayward closed himself in his den, and shortly the agents from the Office of Chair Support showed up, accompanied by Major Mace Marchant, a thin, wiry, sharp-faced man who headed the Apocanew sub-office of the BHE Department of Inexplicable Arts. This made him Rashel's boss, responsible for oversight of the Caigo Faience as well as for investigating anything "questionable" that happened in Rashel's family.

"I recognize the Major," Gayla whispered. "He's one of Rashel's dear, dear friends."

She and Dismé were waiting to be given injections of Holy Truth Serum before they were questioned about Arnole's disappearance. Everyone said the Regime got the serum from the demons, along with the bottles and the chairs and certain other things the Regime couldn't make for itself. After the injection, Dismé heard herself babbling on and on about how much she would miss Arnole while Major Marchant nodded sympathetically, his triangular eyebrows jiggling up and down like bouncing balls and his mouth pursing in and out with every word she said.

"Your sister is very upset," he told Rashel, laying a fond hand on her shoulder.

"My sister will get over it," Rashel replied, with a silky little laugh.

Dismé, hearing and seeing this as she heard and saw everything, thought she would not get over it. All her memories of father, mother, and brother put together were less than her memories of Arnole. Getting over it this time would be impossible. If he had died all at once, as Roger had, she could have grieved openly. Unexplained vanishment, however, was shameful, and Arnole's departure had exposed the family to censure, which, in Rashel's estimation, was best excised by relentlessly inflicting it upon others, particularly those she lived with.

Gayla wept almost without ceasing and had the Terrors every night. Ayward kept a frozen countenance and a jaw clenched shut, like someone with a mouth full of untamed utterance it would be dangerous to loose. Dismé was trapped on a frantic carousel of the unalterable, incessantly circling the pain of his loss, the regret that she had not really confided in him.

Arnole had scolded her for babbling; he had advised silence. She had not taken his advice but she had never told him why! She had never said that she poured out her blatherbrook to make a moat between herself and the world. Though the habit had labeled her a fool, years of being thought foolish had concealed her stubborn persistence as a separate person, one not defined by the roles Rashel assigned her. She could not give up the protection it afforded. Until now.

Now, she felt Arnole's reproaches turn in her mind like rusty valves, shuddering open under the twist of grief. Language ran out of her like bath water, leaving a damp vacancy, a necessary vacuum that would not accept being refilled. The only monument she could offer Arnole was this empty silence. He had urged quiet, and though she had failed when he was with her, she succeeded now that he was gone.

It was all she had to give him. She could not consider leaving, though for years she had told Arnole yes, someday, tomorrow, next season, when the summer comes. Becalmed amidst her grief, barely afloat, she knew any attempt to leave would expose her to dangers too dreadful to speak of. Once thoughts were put into words, they tended to slip out. Better let her fear be unspoken, another oozy monster like those in childhood closets, under childhood beds, out of sight. She could only keep her head beneath her blankets, hoping that so long as she did not meet evil's eyes, she was safe.

Even as she averted her eyes from old evils, however, she had to recognize the new threat. Here in Apocanew, there were people around, nosy people, Regimic officialdom, inveterate intervenors. There, at Faience, she would be far from help, easy prey. Each time this thought occurred, she struggled to unthink it.

✴ 9

nell latimer's book

It seems I'm not alone in taking precautions. My colleagues from around the country, those few who are in on the discovery, are also building shelters or making plans to take their wives and children to visit high places at the time of impact, if there is an impact. The Andes, maybe, or the Himalayas. Actually, my family is already high enough and far enough inland to avoid tidal waves. There's a huge fault line running north and south through Yellowstone, so I worry more about earthquakes. And, of course, if we're in the path of a direct hit, forget it.

Also, I'm troubled by this purple smell that comes and goes. I'm one of those people whose senses are all linked together, synesthetes, people whose minds apply color to things like letters or numbers or smells. I do it in various ways; I sometimes taste things I hear; I sometimes hear things I see; and I smell in all the hues of the rainbow, and then some, and lately I've had spells of smelling a deep, bluish purple odor no matter where I happen to be. Not a bad smell exactly, just slightly stifling. I've never smelled it before.

The thing keeps coming, big and black and already near the orbit of Saturn, which just happens to be in the way. We'll know the effect in a few days.

*   *   *

Well, it seems Saturn wasn't enough in the way to swallow the thing, but it was close enough to swerve it around and away from Earth, into an orbit that will take it out of the system without ever coming any nearer than the back side of Jupiter.

This has changed everything! The various observatories that had been keeping their mouths tight shut are opening them wide and the science popularizers are already having a field day. Naturally, certain senators and congressmen, the headline grabbers, are starting a witch hunt, demanding to know why they hadn't been informed. Neils says we star watchers will no doubt be summoned to appear before congressional committees. All we'll be able to say is that everyone was informed as soon as we had anything to tell them and we still don't have much. We still can't tell what it is or even how big it is, since it seems to have some kind of smoky field around it, sort of like a black comet, throwing off matter into its tail which is no longer directly behind it and is therefore slightly visible to us.

I'm not alone in being frustrated at being unable to provide data and answer questions without saying *approximately* or *perhaps* or *it seems*. By this time, of course, everyone knows it had been headed directly at us. There isn't any widespread hysteria about that; on the whole the discussions are scholarly and rather self-congratulatory. Other things are grabbing the headlines just now, all of them totally foreseeable. Doomsday sects have decided this thing is the Second Coming. A nihilist bunch claims to have a lethal virus they'll release if their terrorist comrades aren't let out of prison before their god arrives on the comet. In the space of a few days, there have been half a dozen plane hijackings, people trying to go to Antarctica or Nepal.

And of course, as Neils points out with irritating frequency, there are still fifty-six separate wars taking place on this planet, mostly between religious or ethnic or cultural tribes who have to rub shoulders with other religions, ethnicities, or cultures they don't like, can't tolerate, and feel a traditional hatred for. There is no longer anywhere on earth for refugees to go. Earth is fully populated, but people still can't get that through their heads.

At supper last week, Michy asked what an *asseroid* was, and I explained.

Jerry said to me, "That's what you were really worried about, weren't you. Well, observe the power of prayer. It moved."

"It didn't move," I said indignantly. "Saturn moved it, as we had thought it might." I was grumpy, but then, I'd been living on nerves and black coffee for weeks. "Besides, you didn't even know it was there, so you couldn't have prayed it away."

"We didn't pray it away. We prayed for safety and peace and good will among men, and . . ."

"Jerry, who is this 'we' you keep talking about?"

He looked at me as though I'd just crawled out of a hole. "The International Prayer Crusade, of course. www.inter-pray.edu. Where've you been? We have members all over the world, millions of us by now." He looked fondly at Michy and rumpled her hair, which she hated. "Each day we're given a topic of prayer over the net, and a time on the following day that will be simultaneous for all of us, and we all pray for that thing, at that time, all joining together with one voice."

"What do you pray for?" I asked, dumbfounded.

"We ask that God intervene in man's affairs. We ask that peace be enforced, that wars cease. We ask that . . ."

"You really mean that, Jer? You want God to reach down and solve our problems?"

He frowned into his plate. "We pray for people who need to be converted, people who are willfully blind and intellectually arrogant."

He turned from Michy to give me the full blast of his admonitory gaze. He meant me! The heat of that glare was enough to raise blisters, and the idea of forest fires popped into my head. All those fires in recent decades that have started from a spark, a lightning flash, a cigarette butt, and then gone on to burn everything and everyone in their paths because the forests were too thick, too heavily populated with trees and brush because we had fought the fires that had kept the forests balanced. Now here were millions of Jerries, all praying for God to reach down and take charge of an earth that was vastly overpopulated because we had fought the diseases that had kept it balanced! Did he know what he was asking for? Good Lord!

The next morning, Saturday, he left his computer to go answer the phone, and the flashing monitor screen attracted my attention. He'd called up that day's prayer time for the IPC, in our time zone, ten A.M. The topic was another call for divine intervention.

Saturday is my day to do the laundry. I still hang things outside when the weather is nice, because I love the smell of sun-dried sheets. So, I had the first load ready, pegging them to the lines out back, and all of a sudden the purple smell filled my nose, the same hue I'd been smelling at odd times for weeks now.

It was ten oh five by the kitchen clock when I went inside, prayer time. Maybe it was the power of suggestion, but I swear I smelled it. Not like wood smoke or leaf smoke in autumn. More like incense smoke, with its own faint fragrance, something resinous and unfamiliar, with this background odor hanging in it, powerful and purple, rising from millions of people asking God to reach down and solve all the world's problems.

I told myself it's just more of the millennial fever we've been through recently. It will go on a while, and then it will fade. The purple smell won't kill me; the prayers won't hurt anything. Maybe Jerry's new enthusiasm will turn out to be, as others have been, a passing phase.

✴ *10*

at faience

When Arnole vanished, Ayward stopped protesting the move to Faience, but that didn't prevent his drinking too much on moving day and spending the afternoon arguing with Rashel. Dismé and Aunt Gayla exchanged glances and decided to explore the grounds. When discord threatened to become overt, it was better to be at a distance.

The stone-floored loggia looked westward into thick forest. Graveled garden walks led beside grass-tangled gardens star-eyed with tiny tulips and blue squill. The entrance drive to the arboretum went over carved stone bridges where chuckling waters ran icy and clear from the snowmelt of Mount P'Jardas. When the shade grew chilly, they moved south into sunlight, toward the serpentine bottle wall, which Dismé avoided, though Gayla went along the wall, reading labels aloud.

"Meggie Ovelon Voliant. I remember her. A great tall woman with red hair. Hello, Meggie. It's a beautiful day, isn't it? Jerome Clarent. There were some Clarents living down the street from Genna and me when we were in Newland. I wonder if Jerome was the son . . . Hello, here's Cynth Fragas-Turnaway. Fragas was a minor family, not one of the big Turnaways . . ."

And then, "Oh, look. All that argument between Ayward and Rashel, and the movers have already put our bottles here!"

And indeed, there was a new section of wall containing Father's and Gayla's families' bottles as well as Rashel's . . . Not Roger's, however. Not Mother's.

Gayla chirruped, "Mother Gazane, I know you'll enjoy this place! Cousin Fram Deshôll! Isn't it lovely today . . . Oh, Nephew Val, this is a beautiful place!"

Dismé heard the words like a knell, hastening to lead Gayla south to the great yew maze, every aisle of it sentried by white marble statues standing in neatly clipped niches. Fearful of becoming lost, Gayla urged that they not go far inside, so they wandered northward again, across an extent of tufted grass to the dilapidated barns, stables, and storage sheds that occupied the northwest corner of the museum land.

Everything except the museum and house was overgrown and unkempt and—so Dismé thought—quite marvelous. Arnole would have loved it. When they finally returned to the Director's House, Rashel and Ayward weren't speaking, though the house was more or less orderly and full of dinner smells. Rashel left immediately for the museum, and Ayward settled into his chair to wax sarcastic about the place and its manifold "conceits."

Conceits or not, Dismé liked them. Her walk had made her unusually happy, a worrisome pleasure, for with Arnole so recently gone, should she be happy? Since the Regime did everything it could to inculcate guilt, a task in which Rashel was an expert confederate, Dismé had more acquaintance with regret than she did with joy. Even asking "why" usually brought rue as an answer.

Arnole had said, when she had complained about never getting proper answers, "Ah, Dismé, how many interesting questions are there? An infinite number? Here inside the Regime, however, we are told that all the answers are in the Dicta, which has many words but little pith, so the permissible number of answers is quite small."

"That's exactly right," she said angrily. "No matter who I ask, they answer out of the Dicta! Even when it doesn't fit."

"Doing such is not a new thing. In the former world,

there were people who said all truth was contained in this
or that holy book, this or that holy image, these or those
holy beliefs. No matter how complicated their world became, no matter how much it changed, the only answers
permitted were those that grew ever more tortuous and
convoluted."

"Until?"

"Until, some say, God turned his back on them for their
failure to use the minds they had been given."

"Is that why the angels rebelled? Because God gave up
on us?"

"I have often thought so. What should happen, of course,
is that people should stop trying to answer with plockutta."

"Plockutta?"

"In ancient times the mages of Tabitu printed approved
spells and prayers on cloth flags. The mages believed every
time the flag fluttered in the wind, making a sound like
plockutta, plockutta, the spell or prayer was communicated
to the powers that be. Plockutta, of course, is only the sound
of a rag in the wind, as are many of the answers we are
given."

Though Rashel talked plockutta most of the time, Dismé
did not make the mistake of considering her a fool. It was
safer if Dismé went on playing the fool, the spinster aunt,
the perpetual adolescent, roles she had played convincingly
for years. This despite the fact she knew some part of her
was stronger and more savage than such roles allowed.
Sometimes she dreamed of this part, this Roarer, pacing
back and forth in its inner lair, or she heard the echoes of its
bellowing when she was frightened. At times of ultimate
frustration, she imagined herself throwing Rashel's bloodied
carcass into Roarer's den, assuming she could find its den,
for when Roarer came from hiding, it rushed through her
consciousness with a great thunder of drums or wind, leaving no way to track it to its lair.

Despite her fears, problems and disappointments were
easier to bear at Caigo Faience than they had been in Apocanew. In Faience, beauty surrounded her. She had a pleasant

room instead of the unfinished attic she'd had in Apocanew, and even on the first night the aromas from the kitchen made her salivate. The food turned out to be as good as it smelled, and except for Rashel—who remained at the museum until late—they had their supper with the staff so they could get acquainted.

The housekeeper was dignified, white-haired Mrs. Stemfall, with her pocketful of keys; the coachman was hawk-handsome dark-haired Michael Pigeon; the maid was broom-thin, sniffly Joan Uphand, and the cook, Molly, Joan's mother, was a stouter version of the same. It was Dismé's birthday, her twenty-fifth, which no one had remembered but herself, but she did not mind. She had long felt it was better not to have a birthday than to be reminded one had spent another year meeting no one's expectations. Lacking remembrances from others, she gave herself a gift. Very early next morning, before anyone else was up, she would go out into the grounds by herself and see the dawn in all its glory.

She went to bed full of anticipation and slept the night through without waking. When she emerged from the house shortly before dawn, however, she encountered a wandering, melancholy smell totally incompatible with her plan. The spring morning should smell of mist, mint, and damp soil, as it had the day before, but a smell of lonely autumn was wafting about instead, a redolence of fading gold, wet leaves, and campfire smoke. She followed her nose to the riding field, where tents had sprouted overnight like so many mushrooms, where horses stood in a roped off paddock, knee deep in tufty grass, and men gathered around breakfast fires as they hailed one another in hearty, vulgar voices.

Ayward had already left for the city when Dismé came in for breakfast. Rashel, about to leave, directed her to stay indoors, out of the way of the workmen who had arrived to clean up the grounds. Though Dismé felt Roarer raise its head and growl in its throat, she merely nodded, fully intending to return to the ferment outside. All day she delighted in the bustle of men stumping about in muttering bunches, in or on or behind barrows of brush going out, wagons of stones coming in; sledges of rotted bridge timbers out, whole bridge timbers in; broken roof tiles out, bright new roof tiles in. Her earliest impressions of Faience were of clamor and transformation: the chink of chisel on stone as one day's gap in a tumbled wall became the next day's barrier; the slither of spilling gravel as a morning's wandering, weedy path turned into a neatly edged and surfaced one by evening; the bark of axes and the sibilant, cracking rustle of falling trees as fountaining copses frilled all over with mouse-ear leaves vanished overnight, leaving not even the stumps to mark where they had been. The continuing metamorphosis seemed natural, part of the place itself, exhilarating as being in a balloon, with everything changing moment by moment, and nothing to hang onto but the sky.

Which was how she thought sorcery must have been, changeful and marvelous. Oh, how the Regime longed for the restoration of that Art! Even though magic had destroyed their former world, they wanted it.

"Oh, yes, they want it," Arnole had commented. "But since they are deathly afraid of it, and terrified that the wrong person may find it first, they insist upon controlling the search so minutely that they will never find it."

This had been a new thought. "Why, Arnole?"

"Ah, Dismé. Well." He had looked at the sky for inspiration, as he often did. "I've heard you drumming on pots and pans and boxes and what not."

"Father said I inherited twiddling from him."

"Well then, let us suppose you want to discover drumming. Sit here and twiddle me something."

Dismé sat down at the table and began to tap out a rhythm with both hands.

"Stop," said Arnole. "Have you filled out a Regime application to explore the rhythm you are using?"

Her mouth dropped open.

He cocked his head to the left. "Have you researched

through all the documents at the College of Sorcery to establish that that particular rhythm is, so far as we know, harmless?" He glared at her straight on. "Do you have an appointment to discuss this exploration with the appropriate committee of the Ephemeral Arts Department?" He cocked his head to the right. "When you have received permission from them, you will need to explain why you wish to tap out this particular rhythm rather than some other rhythm."

"Oh, for the love of Plip, Arnole! It's just drumming!"

"Exactly," he said, wide-eyed and with a dramatic shiver. "But I am afraid of drumming. Drumming may incite people's emotions. Drumming could stir people into pathological behavior or overt sexuality. Someone might be attacked. I am afraid of drumming."

She frowned. "And the Regime is afraid of magic?"

"The Regime is very, very much afraid of magic. It has reason to be afraid."

"And what reason is that?" she had asked in a whisper.

He had looked around, being sure they were alone, and his voice dropped to match her own. "They fear it first because it could be used against them. They fear it more because they believe some of their fellows have actually found it, and it has turned out to be a dreadful thing. I hear rumors to that effect." He had put a finger to his lips, giving her a look.

"Dreadful?" she asked incredulously. "How?"

"The rumor is that human sacrifice is part of any spell they cast."

This had accorded so ill with Dismé's beliefs that she had tried to unhear it. She still refused to believe it. The sorcery she felt deep in her bones could not . . . would not require anything of the kind! If the true Art were found, it would be like the change and clamor of spring! Nothing cumbersome, nothing burdensome. Weightless. Anchorless. Free flying.

The landscaping commotion went on long enough that Dismé was quite giddy with it. Then, without warning, on the morning of eightday, Spring-span five, it was done.

She arrived at the riding field to find the last few horses drawing their wagons through the rusty back gates. Only one of the younger workmen was still there, cleaning up the campground. He greeted her by name, winked at her, and gave her a little sack of well rooted but unsprouted bulbs he and his fellows had come upon while digging out weeds.

The wink acknowledged the existence of her private garden, which she could not have kept secret from the men who helped her make it. In order to clip the hedges, the men had gone in and out of the maze by means of ropes laid on the ground and chalk marks to indicate which lanes had been finished. Dismé, however, had figured out the secret code of the maze itself: the statues of angels that stood along the aisles had a code of signals. They pointed the way past every turn and dead end into the very heart of the place, and there stood Dismé's garden, planted around a particularly enigmatic and wonderful six-armed and six-winged being carved from glassy black stone with golden lights in it, as though it were sprinkled inside with stars.

The black statue was unlike any of the other statues, and if one applied the statuary code to this being, it seemed to be saying at least half a dozen things at once! Come here and go there simultaneously, quickly! Though Dismé had not given up trying to understand its message, she accepted that mystery was appropriate for the heart of the maze, including the fact that each time she saw the statue it seemed to be a different size or in a different position. That puzzle was as nothing, however, compared to the conundrum of the following wind or the disappearing gifts. Each time she went through the maze, a little wind came after her, redistributing the soft bark of the aisles to hide her footprints. Every time she made a gift to the enigmatic black figure—a flower, a spray of leaves, or a mountain bluebird feather—it had vanished by the time Dismé returned.

When she carried the bulbs into her garden, she thought the black being was larger than when she had last seen it. As she knelt on the moist earth to plant the bulbs, she spoke to the being of the marvelous turmoil that had gone on, of the eventual emergence of the beauty that was implicit in every part of Faience. Though the carving did not answer, Dismé went away feeling soothed, as she often had after a conversation with Arnole.

The only cloud over Faience was caused by Rashel's conflict with Ayward. Some years before, Ayward had founded the Inclusionist School of The Art, an academic faction that believed the ancient magic could be found even in simplest things from pre-Happening times, things that actually were what they seemed to be—a bowl, a spoon, a painting, a table. Inclusionists preferred accessibility, clarity, and utilitarianism to the arcane, mystical, and difficult study that Selectivists espoused. Rashel, shortly after marrying Ayward, became a Selectivist, as though to spite him, and though Ayward had greater scholarship among the old books, Rashel had more prestige within the Regime.

Gayla said this was because Rashel had more "friends aloft," tallying them on her fingers: Major Mace Marchant, of the Inexplicable Arts sub-office in Apocanew; Bice Dufor, Warden of the College of Sorcery; Ardis Flenstil, Chief of the Department of Inexplicable Arts—all of them, "Men of a certain age and disposition who are Rashel's dear, dear friends."

Rashel made dear, dear friends because they helped her get what she wanted. What Rashel wanted—often because someone else had it—Rashel always got. To foil Rashel, therefore, one should have nothing she could possibly want and should stay, as much as possible, out of her sight.

At Faience, Dismé's refuge was the barn-loft, a site not unlike the aerie in Apocanew, for it too was high and concealed, with a view into the air. Often she crouched there with a rusty water bucket turned upside down before her, her hands moving upon it to make one-atum, two-atum, three-atuma, four-tum, keeping time to the song she sang, any one of the many she and her father had sung together when she was a child. Dismé never sang where Rashel could hear her.

Rashel could not carry a tune, and she disliked music from those who could.

It was from the loft she first saw ouphs at Faience. The white-trunked trees along the rivulet trembled to her pam-atum/pam-atum/pam-atuma/pam-tum, shivering leaves flicking silver undersides into a momentary glitter, and through this evanescent sparkle the phantoms wafted in time with the drumming, like waterweed shifted by the currents of a pond. Left-atum/right-atum/left-atuma/right-tum.

They oozed from the serpentine bottle wall until some dozens of them were assembled, impossible to distinguish or count, like identical minnows in an eddy. The word eddy stuck in her head as she noticed that the circular brims, which she had thought to be part of their headdresses, were actually whirls of their own substance like a vortex in a draining basin, made visible only through the twirl of reflected light.

Without moving her lips, Dismé pronounced their name. "Ouphs." She marveled at them, making the word fill her mouth as Mother had done when she spoke of them. "Ow-ufs."

As though they had heard her, all the heads turned in her direction. After a moment, however, they gave it up and began their play. Four of them harnessed themselves to an old cart and drew it around the barnyard while others sat inside it. Two others stopped the cart, some got on, some got off. Those who got off turned away and galloped off, as children gallop when riding a stick horse, lumpetty, lumpetty, whipping their thighs (if they had thighs) as they ran. There was a peculiarity in their play. Though they harnessed themselves to a real cart, one that stood on broken wheels against a far fence, when they moved away, it was a ghost cart that they pulled around and around. Dismé could not, in fact, see it, but she could imagine it well enough for the ouph passengers were really being carried by something!

When the invisible wagon returned, several of the ouphs picked up old buckets and broken pots—bending to the real, taking up the shadow—and pretended to feed animals in the empty pens, leaning upon the rails and scratching imaginary pigs with shadow sticks. Dismé had no trouble deciphering what they were doing. Her mind filled in the blanks. Though it looked like play, the mood was melancholy. Even the air took on a brown, smoked-leather smell. In time, they left what they were doing and drifted off past the barn, toward the south.

Bucket in hand, Dismé slipped down the ladder to follow them at some distance. They were headed toward the western end of the bottle wall, where they flattened themselves against the bottles, drifting upward along them, separating and shifting like shreds of smoke. She pressed forward, to get a closer look, and felt them:

"Wait, oh, wait." Smell of damp chill. Taste of mildew.

"Going, coming, where?" Smell of silence, taste of dust.

"Gone, something, wasn't it?" Nothingness, cold, mold.

"Not here. Never here. Look for it, oh, look for it . . ."

Dismé stared after them, but for a time they disappeared, only to reassemble and return toward her, stopping once more near the bottle wall, where they spiralled over the shining bottles, across and back, across and back.

"It?"

"No. Where. Where."

"Lost, lost, lost, nowhere, lost . . ."

Sadness overwhelmed her and she went astray in it as the ouphs surrounded her, wrapped her briefly in a soggy blanket of woe, then departed in a skein of fog among the trees. They were mist and memory and old things falling to ruin. They were shadow and sorrow and recollections of gifts long lost.

Tears on her cheeks, Dismé took up her bucket again. If she turned it on its side, it had a sharper sound. So she drummed, pam-atum, pam-atum, PAM-atuma . . .

Something cracked. She searched around herself, finding nothing, trying it again with that sharp PAM, this time hearing the crack as coming from the bottle wall. More than one bottle! Several! Had she done that?

She ran to tell Arnole about ouphs and drumming, remembering he was gone only when she was almost at the house. She thought briefly of telling Ayward, but if she did, she would have to tell him how she knew about ouphs. The Dicta did not mention ouphs. Since they were not in the Dicta, knowledge of them would be considered evidence of heresy, or of imagination, which was almost as bad. Besides, could she trust Ayward not to tell Rashel?

It took only a moment to decide not to tell anyone at all.

✳ *11*

colonel doctor jens ladislav

In the capital of Bastion, the city of Strong Hold, or, as it was usually called, simply Hold, the central area around the Fortress and the three great Avenues leading northwest to Turnaway, southwest to Comador, and eastward to Praise were kept clean and orderly by order of the general. These were the only parts of Bastion seen by most visitors.

The farther from the Fortress one moved, however, the less attention was given to maintaining streets, buildings, or alleys. Toward the edges of the city, the numbering of buildings became erratic; one street was indistinguishable from another; the collection of trash was an irregular exercise carried out by punishment battalions; and the state of the sewers could be determined by a diagnostic sniff of the air. It was here that housing for the workers was built, and from one such building, known to its inhabitants as Old Stink Fifty-four, a man came running very late at night into Comador Boulevard, then along that thoroughfare toward a clinic run under the aegis of the Department of Medicine.

It was far too late for any official agency to be open, but since the runner would pass the clinic on his way to the nearest carriage halt he had decided he could spare ten seconds to find out if anyone was there. Remarkably, a doctor unlocked the door.

"What is it?" he asked crisply, putting his hands on the

man's shoulders to keep him from falling down. The doctor's uniform identified him as of too high a rank to work nights or to be called out on late-night emergencies, and the running man's experience with ranking officers of the Regime made him tongue-tied for the moment, unable to do anything but stare at the long, narrow face, the long elegantly shaped nose, and the upward curving lips beneath. This latter characteristic made the running man remember not only why he had come, but, with sudden hope, who this doctor was.

"Dr. Jens Ladislav," said the doctor, offering his hand.

So stimulated, the man remembered his own name. "Millus," he panted, wiping his hand, which was somewhat bloody, along his trousers. "Forgive me, Dr. Jens, sir, but I came to fetch a doctor. It's my friends. One woke with the Terrors, the other got cut, and he's bleeding bad."

"I'll get my bag," said the doctor, doing so, and taking up a heavy cloak at the same time, for the night was turning chill, as it often did at this altitude, irrespective of the season.

"You say the man woke in a frenzy?" the doctor asked, when they were in the carriage he had fortuitously been able to hail as it went by on the thoroughfare. "What was his name, again?"

"Les Tarig, sir. That's the man who did the damage. He woke like a wild man, screaming, and calling out the names of people I'd never heard of. 'Dismé, Dismé,' he called, and 'Where are you Dis, leave her alone, get off her,' and such like things. So it was Matt tried to calm him, Matt's always a one to make peace, and Tarig grabbed up the scissors from the table and went for Matt, and it was all we could do to get him tied down."

The doctor looked extremely thoughtful at this intelligence. "And where is Tarig now?"

"He's there still, sir. Tied up on the bed. Fomenting and furying like one possessed. And here we are, sir. It's because we are so near I came running past the clinic on my way to the carriages, not expecting to find your eminence there . . ."

"Nothing eminent about it. I'm a doctor. I work there."

"Oh, yes sir, but you're a Colonel Doctor, and you work there daytimes, and even that is surprising." This was said in a tone of approval. "Most of the ranking doctors, they leave it to the student sorcerers to care for people like us."

"Let's see to Matt," said the doctor, somewhat embarrassed by this encomium, as he got out of the carriage, bag in hand.

Inside the place was a warren of rooms that the doctor recognized as being typical of bachelor quarters anywhere in Bastion, rooms repeatedly split and redone and refurbished and unfurbished, while over all rose a reek that denoted carelessness in the toilets, burned pans in the kitchen, and the miasma of unwashed clothing. In the army, where the doctor had spent some years of service, men managed somewhat better, for sergeants always had a supply of miscreants for latrine duty and kitchen duty and laundry duty, plus the power to keep them at it until the job was done better than passably. Here, however, there was no assigning or doing, but only a slothful slope ever steepening into piggery.

Their destination was an airless and bloody room where a sturdy man lay bound upon the bed, still heaving, staring, and making urgent noises even through the tight gag someone had put on him. The doctor spared him only a glance, for the injured man, Matt, lay on the floor, unconscious. One of the inhabitants pressed a pad of cloth to his cheek, which, when the doctor lifted it, displayed a lengthy cut that went across the cheekbone from near the corner of the eye almost to the corner of the mouth. Luckily, it had not gone all the way through the cheek. "Ah," said the doctor in a tone of concern, "this is bad enough, but was he hit on the head, as well?"

"He was, sir. He fell back against those pipes."

The doctor examined his eyes, felt of the head, sighed and mumbled to himself in an unconscious litany, ahwell, ahwell, ahwell, then aloud: "Ahwell, is there an anchorite here?"

"Old Ben," suggested someone, without moving.

"Right enough, Old Ben," agreed another, who also lacked the power of motion. Anchorites worshipped a goddess called Elnith of the Silences. They took vows of silence and of helpfulness toward others. Though they were said to be numerous, they were rare birds in Bastion, and inoffensive ones, or they would not have been allowed to exist.

"Can he be fetched?" queried the doctor in some temper.

"Tssh, tssh, get Old Ben," said someone else. "The doctor's about doing sorcery."

The whisper of sorcery brought out those few denizens who had not yet appeared, so that Old Ben had to fight his way through a clutter of them when he arrived. The doctor gestured, and the mob vacated the room, not without curious glances. Though inquisitive, they had no wish to be exposed to sorcery. The anchorite shut the door behind them.

"Clean water," the doctor demanded. "Possible?"

"There's a kettle there on the stove," said the anchorite with one lordly gesture, his mouth tight shut.

The doctor grinned and beckoned; the steaming kettle was brought. The doctor removed clean cloths and a little basin from his kit and added something from his bag to the wash water before cleaning out the wound. He then directed the anchorite to turn away, which he did, closing his eyes to give the doctor complete privacy for his magic.

The doctor took two vials from a secret compartment in his bag, pouring the contents of one around and deeply into the wound before sucking up the contents of the other into a glass device with a needle at its end which he then stabbed into the injured man's leg, leaving scarcely a mark when he withdrew it. Such needles were used by chair attendants, and only by them. No ordinary person used this kind of needle, for doing so might be interpreted as attempting a form of magic.

During this process the doctor whispered urgently, under his breath, his usual enchantment for such occasions, a list from his herbal:

> *"Aconite, adder's tongue, agrimony, aloes,*
> *Bugloss, burdock, calamintha, pussy toes,*
> *chamomile, cherry bark, clover, common clary,*
> *chickweed, chicory, black chokecherry, . . ."*

The list could go on to the letter Z, and Jens knew medical uses for virtually all of them, though some, he suspected, depended more upon faith than fact. When he had finished, both vials and device went back in the secret pocket he used for illicit materials. Owning illicit devices was sin enough to get the doctor either chaired or bottled, no matter that he customarily achieved a cure rate six times that of any of his colleagues.

Jens Ladislav had been a colonel for three years. He was a bronzed and active man of forty-two who had spent a lengthy apprenticeship with doctors of the previous generation. He had also traveled extensively along the borders of Bastion, and while still a mere Lieutenant-Medic had "discovered" (through the help of an outsider) a huge cache of medical books and implements, a feat which had put him in good odor with the Regime.

While still in favor, Jens had slipped away for a season and returned with useful information concerning cures for the ailments that afflicted his superior officers. When proffering these cures, previously unknown to Bastion physicians, he said he had learned them from "herbalists" who lived in the mountains. He cured the OC Bishop of a persistent infection acquired by rapine among outlanders in his youth. The bishop was grateful enough that he allowed some latitude for the doctor's "studies," but neither he nor General Gowl quite trusted the doctor. He was too well liked to be trustworthy, and they spied on him from time to time.

Once the illicit materials were safely hidden, the doctor turned the anchorite around once more, telling him to press here, and here, so, to hold the lips of the wound together while he sewed it, and the two of them cooperated with neatness and dispatch, the doctor taking notice of the fact that the old man's hands were quite clean, even the nails. When the sewing was done, the doctor cleaned the surface of the wound once more, then placed a pad of cloth across it and sealed this to the face with several lengths of sticky stuff at which the anchorite widened his eyes.

"The Regime knows all about this stuff," said the doctor

with a shrug. "It's not artful and it's not demonic, it's just a kind of cloth with some rubbery cement along one side of it, to hold bandages on."

The anchorite smiled, which the doctor found pleasant, since he got few enough of those during a day's work. Pain usually preoccupied people to the exclusion of politeness, no matter how grateful they might be. He went to the door, called Millus into the room, gave him instructions as to the care of the patient and the command to bring him to the clinic in two days' time. Then he rose and approached the boar's nest of a bed where the bound man had continued heaving and snorting. Leaving him tightly bound, the doctor took off the gag and gave the fellow a drink.

"Can you talk sense?" he asked.

"Yes, sir," said the bound man in a panicky voice. "Is he all right, Matt? I didn't even know it was him . . ."

"He's all right. Here. Let me look at your eyes. Ah. Yes. Now, let me listen here, like this. Good. Let's remove the ropes. Ben, take those scissors outside, as well as anything else that looks dangerous, and thank you for your help.

"Ah. Now, suppose you tell me about it?"

"It . . . it was the Terrors, sir. That is, I guess it was. I hadn't had them before, but I've heard people tell. All I knew was, the monsters had me, and my little friend Dismé, like in the Time of Desperation, sir, horrid things, oh, with such a taste and smell to them, like choking, and they had me and they had Dismé, and I was trying to get to her, and suddenly I had a weapon in my hand and I started stabbing the thing that held me . . ." He sobbed drily. "It was Matt."

"Dismé who?" the doctor asked. "And where is she?"

"Oh, sir, the only Dismé I ever knew was a little girl I played with in Apocanew, when I was a child. Dismé Latimer, and she's all grown up by now, still in Apocanew so far as I know. In my dream she was only a tiny girl, but it seemed real . . ."

The doctor took a notebook from his pocket and perched on the bed like an angular bird. "Now, I want you to be very patient with me and answer a great many questions. Let's start with everything you ate or drank all day yesterday?"

When he left the room an hour later, the doctor was no less puzzled than he had been on other similar occasions when hanging about the clinics at night had garnered him a victim of the Terrors. Last span there had been four dead when he arrived, and two more dying, for that man had laid hands on a bludgeon and the house had been asleep. Nothing seemed to unite those who had the Terrors. Some were young, some old, some women, some men, some workers, some farmers, some do-nothings, some who had eaten little or nothing, some who had feasted and drunk enough cider to fill a bull's bath. Most of them, though not all, had been to market recently, which meant little or nothing, since almost everyone went to market every day or so.

The doctor stopped in the entry of the place and trumpeted for the inhabitants to attend upon an announcement. When they were all more or less gathered, he said:

"I have found demonic magic in Tarig's room, and if it is there, it is likely to be elsewhere in this building and you will need to exorcise it at once."

This brought forth a gabble which subsided only when Old Ben raised his arms, invoking silence.

"Every bit of cloth in the building must be washed in hot water and soap and dried in the sun," said the doctor. "That includes all clothing, bedclothes, blankets, curtains, rag rugs. Every floor and wall must be washed. Every cooking utensil. The magic has been painted invisibly by a night demon, and only by washing everything can you dispose of it. When you have washed *everything*, then each light a candle and go through every room singing all nine verses of hymn number forty-three, the one that begins, 'Oh, forfend all demons . . .' "

"The whole thing?" complained one surly young man. "I don't even know the whole thing."

"Learn it," said the doctor severely. "The demon may come back and paint the magic on things again, so it would be a good idea to wash things regularly." He then turned aside, catching, as he did so, a glimpse of laughter in Old Ben's eyes. He winked. The anchorite returned the wink.

"Thank you, Colonel-Doctor Ladislav," said Millus, with a low bow. "Thank you very much, sir."

"What place is this?" the doctor asked.

"Office of Housing, Unmarried Men's Quarters, Number Fifty-four, sir. The tenants call her Old Stink, but officially, she's Hold Housing Fifty-four."

Outside the door, the doctor was surprised to find Old Ben waiting for him. The anchorite drew him away from the windows and whispered, "Doctor, may I ask a favor, sir?"

The doctor hid his surprise at hearing speech. "Of course."

"My order . . . they need healers, and they authorized my speaking to you. Would you consider allowing me to apprentice to you? The clinic isn't far from here, and I can work hard and learn well."

The doctor stared at him for a moment, considering whether such an arrangement might involve him in any greater danger than he ran from day to day without it, deciding finally that it would not. "Be there in the morning," he said. "I am glad to have an extra pair of hands, particularly clean ones." And he shook the man by the hand and went back to the carriage, which had waited for him.

On the way back to the Fortress, the doctor took out his notebook and wrote down an account of the evening, as he did whenever he encountered anything at all strange. He concluded his account with a few words about Old Ben, who was an interesting fellow very much to the doctor's taste. He also wrote down the name Dismé Latimer, for it was the second time he had been made aware of that name recently.

✳ *12*

nell latimer's book

Over the last few weeks, the International Prayer group has been covered by every magazine, the lead item in every webcast. It's been on the cover of MILLENNIUM THREE, NEWS-OP, and FAME. It's been praised by several prominent conservative pastors and acknowledged by the President. The hundred or so Congressmen who have always made a ballyhoo about attending prayer breakfasts were pictured last week participating in a daily IPC prayer session. I am still able to sense the daily prayer time without knowing it in advance. The world can be smelling of sunshine one moment, and the next moment it is adrift in this thick purple odor that accumulates, like smoke, hiding the horizon.

Our interstellar visitor, meantime, even though it's no longer headed toward us, is still a major mystery. It does not act like a comet, or an asteroid. It's getting closer and closer to Jupiter—it will actually come closer to Jupiter than it did to Saturn—and every observatory in the world is watching, not that they'll see much since the transit will be behind the planet. General scientific opinion is that it'll be deflected slightly toward the sun, crossing the orbits of the outer planets again as it exits the system.

Whenever I see my carefully constructed shelter, I laugh at the irony. It'll take me years to save up that much money again. Oh, well, maybe I can use it for storage.

* * *

The transit of Jupiter has occurred. Everyone was wrong. The thing didn't hit the planet, it didn't get slightly deflected. It was whipped around Jupiter like a skater at the end of a line, and snapped into a new trajectory that's headed straight toward Earth, or, where Earth will be when it gets there. Incredulity and fury are the emotions of the day. Everyone's up against the wall, politicians, scientists, media people. Everyone feels betrayed. The danger was past, and now it's not, despite the fact that the math *does not check out*. This is fairly simple Newtonian physics after all, nothing arcane about it. The mass figures obtained from the speed and orbital change when the thing was nudged by Saturn are not compatible with the diversion caused by Jupiter. A thing with the mass derived from the Saturn transit could not have approached Jupiter at that speed from that angle and been changed to its current speed and its current direction. Some unknown force has been involved in changing the trajectory.

Everybody was watching, of course, so any conspiracy of silence is impossible. This time there is no chance at keeping it quiet. All the hysteria and panic we tried to prevent is happening. There is looting. There are rapes. There are riots. The National Guard has been called out. Order is being restored. This morning the President announced, totally without factual foundation, that even though Earth would be hit, the damage would be "sustainable." At the observatory, the questions keep coming, over scrambled lines and by encrypted e-mail. Should the government recommend evacuation? Should people be told to dig storm cellars? It takes forever to get the answers, because we still don't have any figures that work! All we know for sure is that it's big—if one measures the outside, smoky layers—and what's inside can't be seen. Infrared does not help. The newest gimmick for looking inside things, "lazar," yields only nonsense. Hubble shows us a featureless blob that looks faintly dumbbell shaped. A bitch. That's what we star-geeks had started calling it, the Bitch, an epithet soon picked up by the press, and the critter is living up to its name.

Day before yesterday, Neils put all the papers into his brief-case and he and I went to D.C. where the Joint Chiefs of Staff were waiting to hear the final words. How big. How fast. How much damage.

The answers were: Too big. Too fast. Total damage. I didn't do any talking; I just pulled up the proper pages as Neils needed them, but I saw the very high brass swallowing deeply before they admitted they had nothing in the arsenal that could possibly shove it away or blow it up. They might crack it, they said, but Neils brushed this off with a don't bother. Cracking it wouldn't help. The pieces will still come down. One piece or twenty, the effects will be pretty much the same. We'd worked on that equation for weeks.

The biology-geeks, who were also present, said yes, well, it looked to them as if the Bitch intends extinction on a wide scale. Fimbulwinter, so to speak. No sunshine for a very long, long time, and Ragnarök, or at least the death of us lit-tle terran Gods, though it's entirely possible that some peo-ple, some animals, some green and growing stuff could survive if it or they could find enough to eat during a very long cold spell and didn't freeze to death in the interim. We left them with this faint ray of hope. I guess it was better than nothing.

Jerry professes to being "hurt" that I hadn't told him about the Bitch, originally, even though I explained that we'd all been sworn to secrecy in order not to start a panic. His response to the situation is to join the IPC in the mass local prayer meetings they've started in addition to their si-multaneous international sessions. Jerry said I could make up for *lying* to him by going to the meeting with him. I did not lie, but it isn't worth arguing over.

I've always been a deist, in the sense of having a belief in the essential order and purpose of the universe, but my idea of an omnipotent and omniscient God has always been of a being utterly beyond our comprehension who sets creation in motion knowing that intelligence will inevitably evolve inside the system, either because He, She, or It just knows, or because He, She, or It has played this game before. God intends that intelligence (or those intelligences) will apply itself (themselves) to the development of purpose and meaning. If I prayed to my God, the only response my belief would allow would be, "I gave you a mind, now use it!" When we married, I thought Jerry had similar ideas.

Jerry now believes, however, in a God concerned almost entirely with mankind on this one planet, a deity who spends a good part of his time peeking through people's bedroom windows and who has a hell and lots of roasting spits ready for sinners. Despite this, I felt I owed it to Jerry to share his feelings and needs with him; he'd done the same for me often enough. I'm fairly good at sitting quietly while others go about their pursuits, anybody who's worked in any kind of a hierarchy can do that, so I did sit quietly in the middle of a considerable crowd, though I was almost overcome by the purple.

During the last few days the Bitch has changed course and speed several times. The first time, everyone cried and slapped someone else on the back and took a deep breath. Then it changed back again. Then it slowed down. This time the elation was muted and brief, because within hours it speeded up again. On one of the TV religion channels that Jerry has begun leaving on all day, someone finally said what a lot of people had been thinking: Earth isn't going to be an accidental collision. Earth is the target. I'd had the thought, but I'd rejected it. I glared at the screen, yelling, "That's crazy. That's crazy. Why would we be the target?"

And Jerry patted my shoulder like he'd pat a pet dog, and he smiled his lofty smile and told me since everyone had been praying for divine intervention, I shouldn't be surprised it was coming. He put his arms around me tenderly, and sort of rocked me, as though I were an infant with the colic.

I yelled at him. "How can you smile! How can you be so calm?"

"Stop tearing yourself apart, Sweetheart."

"Jer, I'm not . . . tearing myself apart any more than is justified! I'm just terrified, that's all. For all of us!"

"You have to submit to it, Nell. Nothing you can do in the next few months will change what's going to happen. The children and I have accepted it. Stop crying." Something in the satisfied, almost luxurious way he said it bothered me a great deal more than the mere content of the words.

Meantime the high level conferences went on, every day, late into the night. How much should the public be told? After interminable top secret debates it was decided there was no point in telling the world that everyone and everything was going to be almost totally destroyed. There is nothing people can do about that, so why spend the last months of life in hysteria and panic and mass rape and looting and god knows what? Let people alone. Lie to them. Tell people it's going to hit in the Arctic, there'll be some damage but nothing we can't overcome. Let people die with some dignity. The insiders issued this from on high, like the Ten Commandments, graven in stone. Let governments do what they can to provide help for survivors, if any, but don't panic the populace, because if you do, there'll be no survivors.

Neils says there have been a series of one-to-one summit meetings among the leaders of those countries who either know the truth or are likely to find out on their own, and after a lot of breast beating they've all agreed to what they called "Death with Dignity Solution." What all the governments did do, including our own, was to pick up amateur astronomers, confiscate their telescopes, and swear all the professionals to secrecy. After this happened I saw Selma Ornowsky again. She dropped by the observatory (which was guarded) and when I went down to get them to release her, she and I had a few words together.

"They're calling it the Bitch," she said, only slightly bitterly. "I guess that's all right. I don't want it called the Ornowsky Catastrophe."

I hugged her, and we parted. There was nothing I could

say. The grapevine had it that some mavericks, including friends of mine, had been locked up when they wouldn't swear not to talk. There's also a worldwide clamp on the media. The media moguls and the ACLU fought it at first, sort of a knee-jerk reaction, but they sagged once they got it through their heads that widespread disorder will reduce the chance of any survival at all, and the right to sell a few more papers in the months we have left is irrelevant.

Of course, all the top level meetings haven't gone unnoticed. Even with the media gagged, there's still the Web, and the powers that be are floating several outer space stories to cover all the astro-cum-military activity that's going on. The U.S., in cooperation with the Russians and the Chinese, announced a new international lunar settlement, "To be accomplished before our space effort is compromised by the asteroid." The best we can figure, the moon will not be hit. A sizeable agglomeration of hackers has been hired to do nothing but flood the Web with details about the new moon colony.

The publicized Lunar mission is also the basis for a secret Mars Mission. Half the hardware needed to start a settlement is already on Mars, but the Mars settlement was planned to take place in "pulses," with automatic, robotic accumulations of hydrogen and oxygen going on between arrivals, each arrival scheduled after the essentials have been stored. Since there won't be time for that to happen, we're putting everything we can on the moon or in orbit around it, including the international space station and some of the telescopes, hoping the people there can pick up on the Mars Mission. For long-term survival, it's estimated Mars gives four or five times the probable success Luna does. The selected colonists will be young and fertile, and if they don't go to Mars, they can possibly get back to Earth later on, if they survive and there's anything here to come back to.

While that's being done, the powers-that-be have also adopted a last-ditch survival plan for earth. Everyone in the field agrees it's the lengthy period of darkness that's the major threat, so warehouses full of survival goods will help.

Builders have already started on a great many huge, widely scattered, "Disaster Relief Warehouses."

In addition, the U.S. Government wants to build a redoubt, a kind of combination fortress and library, in which all mankind's knowledge and art can be preserved so the survivors won't have to discover it all over again. Geologists and engineers are doing studies of several widely separated sites for this redoubt, and they'll decide where it goes once they figure out where the Bitch is going to hit, which is a damned frustrating question because the thing continues to change speed and course for no discernable reason except, perhaps, to show us it can.

✳ *13*

the fortress at strong hold

The Fortress of Strong Hold was built originally as a simple castle with a keep and a wall. Over time, however, it grew like a cancer, bulging at first into the area between keep and wall, then breaching the wall itself from within. Masonry piled on masonry as roofs became balconies for higher rooms, as walls became foundations for higher walls, as the shadows of seasons and centuries flickered across stones heaving upward as though thrust from below.

Each addition brought new chimneys and flues, little pipes entering bigger ones that plunged into larger yet, eventually evolving into enormous smokestacks that pythoned aloft through a stony accretion that reared and ramified, heaving itself into an irregularly pinnacled mountain, stabbed through with light wells and air shafts, pierced with alleyways and wandering flights of precipitous stairs, with so many tunnels penetrating the fabric of the place as to make it spongelike, mostly dark within, terribly dark below where tenebrous tunnels lit by feeble lanterns stank of mold and tallow.

Every scraggy pinnacle was topped by a roof, some large, some small, some peaked, some flat, many of them occupied by attic itinerants, transients of the tiles, migrants among roof-mesas and airshaft-arroyos, sooty dwellers both upon and within the massive chimney whose many vents spewed filthy smoke into a reproving sky. Here lay a plank athwart a chasm, and across it scampered scrawny chimney boys, brush laden and black from brow to ankle. There a century-old tree, rooted in a soil-filled gutter amid the stones, was slanted by the wind over a vertiginous shaft to become a leafy bridge between abutments. There on a larger flat were towering treadmills occupied by teams of a dozen or more felons, walking endlessly in all weathers to pump water up into the tanks suspended in the great chimneys whose smoke warmed the baths of the officers. Another even larger set of lawbreakers walked sporadically, in accordance with a system of bells, to raise or lower the elevator that served the highest ranks on the upper floors.

Here was a chimney-side huddle of huts whose denizens performed some necessary if unspeakable function in the structure upon which they lived, like so many ticks upon a dog, invisible in their poverty, hunger, and dirt. Here was the Bat-keeper of the Shrilling Cave (once the rooftop chapel of a sub-sub-sect, now fallen into ruin) and the Pigeon-keeper with his apprentice boys and their cooing cote. Here too was the roof-dwellers' own treadmill-winch, hidden in a far recess behind an ancient parapet, cobbled together from short bits of lumber and tangles of wire, its rope woven of a hundred shorter pieces, its line dropping deep into a half forgotten airshaft so its creaking would be lost in the sound of the ever turning water-mill. This winch brought up any and everything needed for the rooftop community to survive: a few bricks, a sack of flour, a stolen bucket, an abandoned baby. All such was on the lee side of the chimney, the dirty side, ash-laden, smoke-spewing from a thousand hearths, boilers, laundries, ovens, oasts, and incinerators.

The windward side of the great chimney is a different matter indeed. There, sandwiched between the great chimney and the parapet wall that plunges sheer to the clangorous cobbles and shout-echoing walls of the street, a roof garden floats like a green islet above the fetid humors of the town below. The elaborate and elegant penthouse that gives access to this marvel is the territory of the Commander in Chief of Bastion, General Gregor Gowl. If the Fortress is the armory of Bastion, its barracks, its HQ, its market, and—in its higher reaches—the living quarters of its officers and their families, then this roof garden is their park, their promenade, their place to take the sun and air and let the babies play, all by kind permission of sorrowful Scilla, the Commander's wife.

On this afternoon the rooms of the penthouse are thronged with brightly dressed visitors. Beneath gay umbrellas, the tables beside the reflecting pool are crowded. Flowers nod in the light wind. People chat. Members of the Bishop's Holy Guard set aside their weapons to pass trays of sandwiches and cookies. Scilla pours tea and her younger girls, including five-year-old Angelica, join the children of guests to dart like hummingbirds among potted roses, toddler voices rising in shrill gaiety over the ritual feigning and fencing of their elders.

The general is at the center of all this, impeccably dressed in his white dress uniform, belted, bemedaled, roped and ribboned in gold, affably accepting the compliments of his guests on this, the sixtieth anniversary of his birth and the twentieth of his accession to the leadership of the Spared. He is hand in hand with Gregor Gowl III, penultimate child got by Gowl upon Scilla, only son, much longed-for heir, a boy who can be neither disciplined nor swayed. "A chip off the old block," cries Gowl, as he admires this six-year-old terror of the Fortress. When Angelica was born, yet another girl, Gowl declared himself weary of begetting, and Scilla spent most of a span saying fervid thanks in the tiny, hidden Lady's chapel where men did not go.

The roof garden is no less a symbol of the general's power than the uniform he wears. On the day six years ago when his wife finally presented him with a son, he decreed into existence the garden Scilla had long begged for. Within days, it was a fact: arbor, potted trees, reflecting pool, fountain and all. Some of the guests arrive at the garden easily, for they are of the Regime's elite who live only a floor or two below.

They are entitled to use the elevator, and they have servants to climb and carry for them. On today's occasion, however, they are joined by their counterparts from Apocanew and Newland and Amen-city who have been clambering toward this height all their lives, a longer ascent by far than merely a walk up the hill to the Fortress capped by a climb of fifteen or twenty stories to the top. Here are the pretenders to power, the holders of irrelevant office, the receivers of trivial titles, the elected but impotent representatives to the Congress of the Spared. As compensation for their inconsequence, they are accorded the honor of an invitation to the general's birthday gala. Some of them, aware that fortunate liaisons have been known to arise from mere childhood acquaintance, have brought their children along today, to meet the general's children and bask in their glow.

The general moves among his guests with a sham congeniality that fools no one. Even five-year-old Angelica, currently in hot pursuit of the Colonel Bishop's youngest daughter, plans her darting and fluttering to keep herself well away from her father. The general's wife occupies herself at the tea table where her handing of cups is aided by the wives of senior officers, one of whom, the Colonel Bishop's wife, leans forward to say, with some envy, "Angelica's turning out to be so very pretty!"

"Yes," agrees the general's wife, with a wary glance at her youngest daughter. "It's surprising, for she was an ugly baby. Every day she looks more like my first child, Ovelda, the daughter who died."

"I remember her, of course," says the bishop's wife. "She was a sweet, dear girl. Every time I go to the Hold bottle wall, I stop and greet her."

"Kind of you," murmurs the general's wife, tears filling her eyes.

"I notice there's a fence around the roof garden now," the bishop's wife comments approvingly. "So much safer."

"Oh, it wasn't a roof garden then," said the general's wife, staring at the fence atop the parapet that surrounds the roof on three sides, the fourth guarded by the looming mass of the great chimney. "Our quarters were down two floors from here. We never came up here. We never knew how Ovelda got up here. There was nothing here, no reason for her to come."

"But there is a fence now," persisted the bishop's wife.

"Yes. No other child will fall all that terrible way again. Crush themselves like that. Die like that."

"Now, now, my dear, she isn't dead. She's in the bottle wall, awaiting the final days. She was just Angelica's age, wasn't she?"

The general's wife looks down at the hands writhing in her lap, for a moment unable to understand they are her own. She clenches them until they will lie still, and when she looks up again, it is with guileless and tear-washed eyes. "It was twenty years ago, and she was my first child as Angelica is my last. She was just Angelica's age, yes."

The bishop's wife, who is a kindly woman, reproaches herself for being so thoughtless as to have raised the matter and to have continued it thereafter. Through sheer ineptitude, she is about to make matters worse when a tall, uniformed figure steps forward to call Scilla's attention to a grassfire that has blazed up in the commons outside the city wall, a scene full of smoke and much comic rushing about of horses and wagons, with people waving rakes, falling over their feet and getting in one another's way. The intervenor is Colonel Doctor Jens Ladislav, and with a jester's charm he gathers a clamor of nearby ladies into an appreciative chorus that laughs at the preposterous spectacle until the painful subject of Ovelda's death has obviously been forgotten.

"Thank you," murmurs the bishop's wife, as the doctor moves away. "I shouldn't have reminded her of Ovelda. You know about that?"

"I've been told that the general's wife has never recovered from her daughter's death," the doctor says softly. "Strange, with so many other daughters, that Ovelda should still preoccupy her attentions."

"It was the way she died," says the bishop's wife. "So strangely."

"Oh, very strangely," agrees the doctor, his eyes wandering from the ladies at the parapet to the general, who is standing beneath the arbor at the center of a congratulatory group. The doctor was twenty-two when Ovelda fell, and he has heard the story. A plunge from the roof and a small body lying unseen long enough that some predator—dog? cat? wild creature?—had time to eat certain organs before it was discovered, leaving the rest untouched. There had been mention of demons, of course. Whenever anything of the sort happened, there was always mention of demons.

From his vantage point among his colleagues, the general also notices the resemblance between Angelica—now dancing in jubilation at having tagged her quarry—and the long-dead Ovelda. The likeness evokes a disturbing itch-ache of both body and mind, and the general moves restlessly in discomfort and distraction.

"I'm sorry?" he says to the young man who is being introduced. "What was your name again?"

"Trublood, sir. Captain James Trublood-Turnaway."

"Ah. Part of the great Turnaway clan, eh, Captain?"

"Yes, sir. Definitely part of the clan, and proud to be under your leadership, sir."

For the moment, though only for the moment, the general forgets the feelings that have troubled him in recent days and preens himself on being a man among men.

The general had recently grown slightly dissatisfied with his life. He told himself he had been a man among men even before receiving help from Hetman Gohdan Gone, that he was entitled to flattery and honors on his own, but still, on the morning following his birthday celebration he woke discontented. He thought it odd to stumble upon disquiet now, after everything he'd achieved, but he had to admit he had mostly pretended at enjoyment during the festivities. And though he could recall rewarding moments in his past, he was not truly enjoying his life as it went on, day by day. During the past few days, in fact, he had been recalling the desires and feelings of his youth, drawing contemptuous comparisons between what was and what he had once imagined.

Long ago, he had seen himself all in white on a white horse, and he had become that figure, yes, but it was a long time between parades. Even when there were parades, horseback was not an unmixed pleasure for a man who spent most of his time at the dining table, in bed, or behind a desk.

On this particular morning, every memory and thought was complicit in convincing him something essential had been missed along the way, something of enormous importance, something that would make a lasting mark on the people of Bastion or even on the people of the world! Certainly he could not be satisfied by simply growing older, holding on by his fingernails until he could be decently bottled! He didn't want a mere place in the bottlewall, subject to the insincere blather of those making Cheerful and Supportive visits. He wanted to be remembered for more than a few years' duty to the Regime. Oh, by all the Rebel Angels, he wanted a shrine to himself, a monument to a reputation that would survive his bottling by a thousand years! Or until the world ended, whichever came first!

The idea kept him sleepless three nights in succession, and in the end he did what he had done many times before. He sent a messenger to Hetman Gone, requesting an appointment, and he comforted himself with such ritual phrases as "He's always helped me; I'm sure he'll help me now."

These incantations were purely formulaic. General Gowl had never really thought about Hetman Gone except as an adjunct to his own life, as a man may do when he says, my spouse, my children, my doctor, my man of business, or, as in this case, my sorcerer. General Gowl took at simplest face value all matters unrelated to himself. Since he had never come face to face with a relentless opponent or fought a real war, such easy presumption had served him well enough. Though there was a good deal of evidence that Gone was not merely a man (if only Gowl had paid attention) Gowl thought of him as a person, one with many talents, but still, only a man.

He had not seen the Hetman during the Hetman's nocturnal pursuits. He had not accompanied the Hetman when he moved with unnatural speed down the roads of Bastion in the late hours of moonless nights. He had not attended the revels that the Hetman directed in mist-filled chasms or on stretches of lonely shore beside rain-pocked seas. He had not seen the Hetman's servants without clothing, or the Hetman himself in like déshabillé. In fact, though he had listened to the Hetman quite closely on many occasions, he had never really looked at him with the speculative eye of an alert and skeptical nature. He had never asked himself whence the Hetman had come, and when, and why.

He did not ask those questions now. He merely went to the meeting as he always went to the meeting, with his own needs uppermost in his mind. The room in which he was received was hotter than before, the smells were more offensive than usual. The drink he was offered was, at best, noisome, as it had been during his last several visits. As the general explained his feelings, the Hetman seemed almost preoccupied—perhaps as a chess player might be who is already ten moves ahead and knows it no longer matters what his opponent does.

"You need to call upon power," said the Hetman in a peremptory tone, when the general had finished. "The great achievement you seek will require great power."

"What power?" the general asked, somewhat confused. "The Rebel Angels?"

The Hetman shrugged, a rippling gesture peculiar to himself. "If that is your preferred source of power, then that is the power you should call upon. In anticipation of your need, I have researched a spell you can use. I am afraid I must charge you for it, for it is what we call a lapsing spell. Such enchantments are rare; they are usable only a few times before becoming impotent. This one is still new and strong, but it will only work two or three times."

The general looked over the parchment, moving uncomfortably as he did so. There were things written there . . . nothing he hadn't done before, of course, but still . . . "Charge me?" he murmured at last. "What charge?"

"In addition to the item specified in the spell, only a little of your blood. For magical potions of my own that require the blood of a powerful man."

The general looked at the spell, and at the Hetman, and he thought of the spell he had used twenty years before, and of how this spell was both different from and similar to that one, and he thought what sorcerers could do to a person if they had a sample of his blood, so it was said, and he consulted his ambition and thought again. After all, he and the Hetman had a long association. He knew so little of trust that he felt sure he could trust the Hetman.

"Very well," he murmured. "Oh, very well."

It was the twisted and dwarfish servant who took the blood, nicking the vein with a dirty blade to let it flow into a glass vial. This was done in an outer room, and the Hetman did not even say good-bye. The same servant said he would be on hand when the spell was wrought, to provide assistance and take away the item that was promised as payment. His name, he said, was Gnang.

The general took some time to obtain the ingredients for the rite, making sure that the blame for the acquisitions fell on others. He picked up the final and most important ingredient the very night that the sacrifice was made. The work was done in a deep passageway that threaded through the monstrous chimney, at the end of a dogleg passage opening through a secret door to the roof garden, a door that antedated the garden by many years. On either side of the deep passage the sheer walls of the chimneys rose; above it the scant smoke of the midnight roiled and writhed like living creatures; within it stood the necessary materials and devices, including a great iron brazier with a fire that was already burning when the general arrived with his burden. Gnang stood at one side, simply waiting.

The general set his burden down and busied himself with knives and vials and bottles, contemplating immortality as he threw certain things onto the greasy fire, as he chewed and swallowed this and that, as he turned toward the north to spill other substances upon the puddled surface around him, each thing done, chewed, swallowed, spilled, burned in accordance with the formula that Gnang prompted into his ready ear.

The thin cry of the victim scraped like a fingernail against an inner door of hell. Gowl did not respond to it. He merely uttered the final words amid the reek of burning flesh and spilled blood. Gnang picked up the item he had come for and disappeared into one of the narrow channels within the chimney. Smoke began to billow from several huge flues. At first Gowl was so preoccupied by the intricacies of the spell that he wondered at this. It was too early for the bakers to have arrived to fire up their huge ovens. It was too late for the laundry, far below in the cellars of the place, to be stoking its boilers, but there was smoke, nonetheless, first from half a dozen, then a dozen, then a dozen more of the black and twisted flues.

Gradually, the smoke turned from gray to black under the light of the late moon, and as he realized this was not mere chimney smoke, he turned to put his back against the wall. Something huge and dark emerged from a chimney pot that was not by any means large enough to have held it.

"General Gowl," whispered a voice from amid the smoke where floated a pair of red, burning eyes.

The general bethought himself of an old story concerning a woman of flame who had appeared here in Bastion when it was first discovered. Perhaps this was she. The eyes had a certain familiarity. Taking a shuddering breath, he steadied himself against a parapet and whispered a response. "I am General Gowl."

"A man who should live forever in the memory of his people," whispered the voice. "A mighty man."

The general straightened, saying more loudly, "I have always tried to be strong for my people."

A sound came from the dark mass which might have been laughter. "Of course you have. However, tonight I do not speak to strength. I speak to ambition. You want to be immortal, General Gowl."

He started to demur, but then caught himself. One did not demur with angels, and who else could this be but one of the Rebel Angels? "Yes, I want to be immortal," he admitted.

"It might be arranged," said the voice, the smoke roiling around it like a garment blown by the wind. "On certain terms."

"Which would be . . . ?" the general asked, keeping his voice level with some difficulty.

"Merely to serve us."

"But I do . . . do serve you."

"Who do you think we are, General? Who does your religion tell you we are? We will give you a clue." Again that sound that might be laughter. "We have been with the Spared Ones since the Happening itself."

The general grinned fiercely, his teeth showing. "You are the Rebel Angels! Those who came to our aid! Those who rebelled against the old God who would not save our people!"

The smoke boiled from the chimney; the eyes held steady within it; the voice purred: "You may so address us. Do you know why the glory you yearn for has so far eluded you?"

The general stopped, stunned. "Has it? It has? I thought I had had a share of it, but I wanted . . . I wanted more . . ."

The figure swirled, the voice whispered. "A man cannot want too much glory. You would have had more if you had completed the great task. Your earliest heroes were devoted to that task. In the time before the Happening, and in the time before that time, men spoke of the task. Power and vengeance are better than peace. Where is your vengeance, Gowl?"

He cried out, stung, "Against whom? All who have opposed me are dead! Who do I avenge against?"

"All those, out there, who do not accept the beliefs of the Spared. All those heretics who do not worship as you do. You have avenged yourself only against your own people, Gowl, which is like cutting off your own fingers. You must take vengeance against those outside, who refuse to follow your ways." A long pause before the keening whisper insinuated itself deeply into his mind, "You must begin a holy war against those who do not follow you and thus, who do not follow *us*."

"Everyone?" the general asked, almost witlessly. "Everyone out there?"

"Are they Spared?"

"We say . . . we say if they were, they would be in here. But some say they are not here because they do not know about us." Colonel Doctor Jens Ladislav said such things, from time to time, muddying the doctrine, in the general's opinion. It was easier to have black and white, not some peculiar shade of gray.

"Then they must be given the choice, of coming in here or . . ."

"Or death," whispered the general. "Or death."

"You are our beloved follower," whispered the familiar voice, the eyes gleaming like coals. The shadowy mass constricted and poured into the chimney once more, down, and away, perhaps into the limestone caverns and caves that pierced all the lands of Bastion like holes in a cheese. The general looked around himself. The brazier still smoked greasily, and the spell required that it be left untouched. He returned to his rooms, and though other men might have been unable to sleep considering what had been done to bring about the recent vision, Gowl fell immediately into slumber.

When he arose the next day, he had a very clear memory of what had been said on the roof. He was impatient with his wife, who came to him having paroxysms over one of the children. He told her to return to her own rooms, and to stay there. Then he sat at his desk for several hours making detailed plans. Soon he would tell his colleagues of the great future that awaited them.

✦ 14

nell latimer's book

Since the Bitch's changes of course always average out to zero, the engineers have chosen the site farthest away from where the Bitch will land. It's the last site started, Omega site, and it happens to be not quite thirty miles from here. Neils has heard all about it, and he's told us about the millennium's worth of power it will hold, and the millennium's worth of irradiated food, the gametes of people and animals in deep freeze plus state-of-the-art embryonic and suspended-animation labs. Not that life really is suspended, but the techniques are pretty good. Since the "sleepwalking" disaster on the first Mars trip, the cryobiologists have made giant strides on sleep techniques.

Omega site redoubt is designed to hold a couple of hundred scientist volunteers, youngish people who will live in the redoubt up to a thousand years. Their function is to preserve knowledge and aid survivor societies. They aren't a reproductive population. There'll be far fewer women than men because there are still far fewer young women in the sciences, and reproduction is only an ancillary concern. The real purpose is to avoid another Dark Ages, so Omega site will be a repository for all kinds of information, high tech and low, everything from how to talk to the colonists on the moon to ways of smelting iron or making a plowshare without machines. When survivors need to know how to build a generator or manufacture transistors, the redoubt will have the information. Or, if the Bitch turns out not to be a total bitch after all, survivors will have access to their cultural heritage.

So, two hundred people between twenty-four and thirty-four are being picked for Omega site, engineers, scientists, technologists, information specialists. Each of the two hundred is expected to spend ninety-six years of each century asleep and four years awake with three others. That is, theoretically. The consequences of repeated cold storage are far from certain. The best guess is that the survival chances inside the redoubt are roughly equivalent to the chances outside, that is, from one in a hundred to one in a thousand. Nobody is giving odds, either way.

It turns out that some of the Omegans—those of proven fertility and without problematic DNA—are being given the privilege of providing genetic material for storage at the redoubt. They told me I'd been picked to be one of the two hundred. I told them, no. They said, think about it.

"Don't refuse them," Jerry said, when I told them about being picked as a sleeper. He knows nothing about the plan to store gametes, and I didn't mention it to him. I told him I couldn't accept because it would mean leaving the children.

"I think you ought to put your trust where your heart is." He spoke in his uplifted voice, still calm, still smiling. It made me want to hit him.

"And what's that supposed to mean?"

"You've always trusted science. You ought to be faithful to what you've always trusted."

His face glowed when he said this, as it did when he was particularly moved. For the last several years, Jerry has been much moved by "spiritual" things. Though it's a word Jerry and his friends use quite comfortably, I've never been able to define it. It means non-material things, certainly, but also, non-intellectual, non-measurable, non-factual things. For his friend Marie, it's a belief in angels, but her husband thinks it's the feeling he gets when he sits naked in a hot spring, watching the stars. Some of Jerry's more recent friends are into Bible study, with special emphasis on revelations and predictions of the last days. Jerry's own take on spirituality is to run on "positive communications." He spends an hour every evening talking with God, coming away from the conversation with all kinds of good thoughts and good intentions he can draw power from later. He sometimes quotes what he says to God but never what God replies. "It doesn't come in words," he says.

Not all Jerry's friends think alike, but every one of them shares a belief in divine—or at least supernatural—intervention in the minutia of everyday human life. They believe in miracles, in angels, in a god who watches everything every individual man does, and sometimes reaches down and stirs his own creation. Some of them are very angry people, but others have warm, kindly and nurturing Ned Flanders sort of personalities. I always feel stifled when they're around, which seems bitchy and ungrateful of me, but it's like being smothered in nice. Still, they aren't my worry; Jerry is. I can accept whatever he believes, for him, but I can't accept being shut out. When he told me to go into the redoubt, that was the ultimate shutout.

"If I go into that redoubt, I'll be separated from the children. We belong together!"

He took my hands firmly in his own. "Nell, my dear, do listen. You and I both know that this is the end of the world. My friends and I regard it as something that's been foretold for ages. I'm not even slightly frightened because I trust in the Lord to get me and the children through the last days. I have absolute faith in that. You don't have that kind of faith."

I admit to being horrified at the indulgent calm of his voice, his unrestrained acceptance of death and devastation. "Oh, Jerry, don't go off on this now, for God's sake . . ."

He patted me as he might have patted a fractious pet. "Exactly. For God's sake. I trust we'll be taken care of if we live. If we die, it will be painlessly, fearlessly, and our afterlife will be wonderful. The children will believe me when I reassure them, because I believe it. They'll be calm because I am calm. Frankly, I'd rather they'd face the last days with me than with you. Science is cold comfort compared to finding enlightenment."

That was what he called it. I had called it "acting weird."

"And that's what you teach the children?"

He looked over my head at nothing. "When the children were old enough, I would have. As it is now, I won't have to."

Would have. Won't have to. I'd halfway accepted his indifference to his own survival, but his indifference to the children's survival hadn't penetrated until then. I should have thought of it when Michy asked me one bedtime whether she was a good girl, because "Daddy says when the asseroid comes, all the bad people will get roun-ned up and go down to hell." I told her Daddy was wrong; only cruel and vicious men create hells, a merciful God does not, and besides, she was the best little girl in the world.

So then, with the invitation to be one of the sleepers in Omega site still hanging there, I didn't know whether to scream or laugh or just run for my life. He took advantage of my being speechless.

"I believe that destruction will come, yes. But, the children and I will not feel it. I'm sure of that, Nell. Positive. And since I'm positive, I think you should relieve your mind of worry and do what your own spirit tells you to do."

"What will you feel?" I demanded, still fighting against his placid certainty.

"The children and I will feel only peace, and rapture," he intoned, like a reading from scripture, an expression of satisfaction on his face that I hadn't seen for years. "I'm sure of that. It's true, the ungodly will meet their horrible fate, we'll see that, but it won't touch us."

Something in his voice, some hint of particular satisfaction struck a sudden insight from me, like a flint hitting steel. I swallowed and said, as casually as I could, "And you want me in the redoubt rather than with you because it will be easier for the children if they don't have to watch Mommy being hauled off to hell?"

He flushed and looked sheepish, and I knew I'd hit it on

the nose. First I wanted to go into hysterics, then I felt a kind of sick fury pushing me to hit him or throw up, or both. Well, well. And he had been thinking this for some time. His recent warm affection hadn't been love, it had been piety. He was among the elect, poor little Nell was damned, and she wasn't worth trying to convert so he'd pity her until the end. Strange to believe you know someone, believe someone loves you, and then find out you don't know them and their emotions toward you are . . . well, what? Vengefulness? Born from what cause? Envy? Had all this started when I'd had that fleeting moment of journal cover eminence, five years ago? Or that article published the year later? Both were nice, but neither was important, and he knew that! Or maybe he didn't.

I tried to see myself through his eyes, a woman who had had undeserved success. It was a ten-second equivalent to a bad divorce. His look of satisfaction was a vault door closing with the time lock set on forever.

The only way I can handle what I wrote about above is to repress it. Pretend it hasn't happened. There is no further argument. There is no further discussion. Jerry goes right on conversing with God, and I'm going into the redoubt.

I am doing one sort of crazy thing. I have a friend who's an expert in surveillance, and he's agreed to put a camera and mike in the shelter at my house. It will transmit data to the Omega redoubt. If Jerry and my children are visited by angels, I honest to God want to see it happen.

✳ 15

exploring high places

Though General Gowl had received his visitation late in the spring, it was several days before he called a meeting of his officers to relay the message he had received from the Rebel Angel. One of those present was the general's closest colleague, the Colonel Bishop, Lief Laron Comador Turnaway, a long time associate, who was stunned by what the general had to say.

"We have *always* said that the Spared, all of them, are here in Bastion," said the bishop, querulously. "It's an article of faith. After the Time of Desperation, all those who were Spared were miraculously joined together in the great trek, and they all came here. Either they arrived here or they were frozen en route and bottled once we arrived and discovered how bottling could be done. We have *never* believed there were Spared . . . out there."

"I know," said the general in a strong voice. "But it was revealed to me that some, perhaps many, may be out there. Out of a great cloud of darkness lit by flame, I had a vision."

"A vision," said the Colonel Bishop, doubtfully.

"I was visited by a Rebel Angel," said the general. "Who commanded the Spared to go out into the world and bring our lost brethren into Bastion while there is yet time."

"How are you going to do that?" asked Colonel Doctor

Jens Ladislav in an interested voice. "Are we to offer an invitation, or what?"

"We are to take an army," said the general, frowning so the listeners would know this was serious. "We are to go out and offer salvation to the unenlightened. Those who are Spared will accept, and those who are not Spared will reject, and if the ones who reject fight us, we'll kill them, that's all."

"We have a non-aggression agreement with the demons," Doctor Ladislav offered. "They may object to this."

"That's why we're having this meeting," grunted the general. "We need to figure out what to do about the demons . . ."

" . . . also," said the doctor, "there's the matter of how many Spared we might find out there. Bastion won't support a great many more people than are already here."

"We can bottle a lot of our people to make room," offered Over Colonel Commander Achilles Rascan, of the Bureau of Defense. "We have lots of unproductive elderly, lots of supernumerary children among the poorer classes. Or we could bottle the outsiders before we bring them in."

"Ah," said the doctor, still in a pleasant voice. "I hadn't thought of that." He turned to the general. "Do you think it matters to the Angels? I mean, whether the Spared are bottled or not before they come in?"

"No difference at all," snorted the general. "We bring them among the Spared, either way."

"But . . ." murmured the doctor, "if that is the case, why do we need to gather them into Bastion at all? It will be most inconvenient. Surely we can just bottle them out there, build a repository and put someone in charge of maintenance."

The general squirmed slightly in his chair, frowning. "They want us to gather them, that's all. They said so. They didn't say where the bottle walls had to be."

"Ah," murmured the doctor, hiding incipient hysteria with a serious nod. "Putting the bottles outside Bastion will make it much easier. I'm glad the Angel will allow that."

He subsided, taking notice of the expressions of those around the table, which were variously interested, avid, or appalled (a junior member of Rascan's staff who hid his expression behind a handkerchief).

"Over Colonel Rascan will begin by strengthening the army," said the general. "It'll take some time as we have to deal with outsiders for the purchase of weapons and supplies. And we'll be sending out many, many small missions to start bottling any Spared Ones they find out there, as well as spying out the strengths and weaknesses of the places we'll be conquering."

The doctor kept his face expressionless as the general remarked in his direction, "And we'll need medics trained as well. To take care of the wounded."

"Perhaps we should just let the bottling teams take care of the wounded," murmured Jens. "It would be more economical."

"No," said the general. "We have to keep up our numerical strength. We can't be bottling five or ten percent of the army after every battle."

"Very true," said Over Colonel Rascan. "Though of course the doctor is correct in certain cases. I think for the seriously wounded, bottling would be more sensible. A seriously wounded man with a lengthy recovery time is a drain upon resources."

The junior officer who had retreated behind his handkerchief excused himself and slipped out the door.

"Bottling out there will be rather different from bottling in here," remarked the doctor. "In here, we merely put those to be bottled through a demon portal and the demons cut out an appropriate bit of flesh before putting the bodies down the chutes into the firepits. They do the bottling, the labeling, and add the bottles to a community wall—or leave it for our Bottle Maintenance people to install in a house if it's a private installation. If we do it out there, with our own people, we'll need a lot more maintenance people trained. Or, it would require a contingent of demons to travel with us, and since our agreement with them specifically forbids our going outside in any kind of . . . aggressive way, we may find that difficult to achieve."

"I know," said the general in a surly voice. "We all know. Of course there are problems! There are always problems, and it's your job to figure out how we can get around them! Perhaps Bottle Maintenance will have to train some people to go with us. Maybe we'll have to conquer the demons first and enslave demons to do the bottling. Get them out of the way, so to speak. At any rate, this meeting was just to announce the Vision. It was a real Vision, by the way," this with a searing glance at the Colonel Bishop. "Not something I dreamed of while I was asleep."

The general did not mention the rite he had conducted before receiving the visitation. Such things as this, Hetman Gone had impressed upon him, were not to be spoken of. Leaving the rite aside, there was no reason he could not expand upon the vision part of the thing.

"The Rebel Angel came to me up on the roof, late last night, long before dawn, in smoke and fire. It said we must . . . avenge ourselves against those who refuse the faith of the Spared. I know it will take a while to get used to the idea. It took me a while, even though I heard it from the angel's own lips. So, I thought we'd meet a span from now, same day and time, to report our progress."

The general started to rise, but the doctor stopped him by asking, "Excuse me, General, but did the being you saw actually say it was one of the Rebel Angels?"

The general frowned. "I asked who he was; he asked me who I thought he was. I said I thought he was a Rebel Angel, and he didn't contradict me. I wouldn't have dragged you all in here otherwise!"

He nodded at each man, got to his feet and departed, surrounded by the Holy Guard of Bastion. Jens stayed behind, staring moodily at the table while the others rose and departed, some silently, some whispering, all troubled to one degree or another.

"So?" asked the Colonel Bishop, from behind Jens's shoulder. "What do you think?"

"I think," said the doctor, "that I would feel more secure if the Rebel Angels had appeared to all of us."

"Visions . . . well, they tend to be solitary things," said the bishop, twisting and stretching his neck as though to unkink it, a sign the doctor well knew to be one of nervousness. "All the books say so. Which doesn't mean the visions are untrue."

"Not necessarily," said the doctor.

"No, not necessarily," agreed the bishop. "What worries me is that I'm not at all sure we have the strength to take on all the rest of the world."

"From what I know about the Outside . . ."

"Which is more than the rest of us," said the bishop, a bit sarcastically. The bishop's tolerance for the doctor's derelictions was wearing a little thin as envy and irritation gradually overtook forbearance.

"I don't know a great deal more, Bishop, but from what I do know, I'd say we aren't strong enough. Unless we have some weapon or system that I don't know about."

"Where would we have obtained such a thing?" the bishop asked.

The doctor shook his head. "I don't know, Bishop Laron."

"But you go outside! You should know!" This was said as a challenge, almost reproachfully.

The doctor replied slowly, carefully. "I go along the borders seeking medical knowledge, which I use for your benefit and the general's as well as for others of the Spared. I have never seen a weapon in Bastion or along its borders that would make Bastion stronger than the people outside."

After a moment's simmering silence, the bishop remarked, "Perhaps the general needs to talk to his vision again. Perhaps it has some special weapons to lend us."

When the bishop left the room, the doctor stared after him with a long, measuring look before murmuring, under his breath, "A prospect that I, personally, would find extremely worrying." It worried him to the extent that he brooded his way to an anonymous door giving on a narrow corridor leading to narrower passageways and steeper staircases, all of them winding through the Fortress like mold in a cheese.

With the exception of several elderly maintenance supervisors, the doctor probably knew the Fortress better than anyone else. He knew that the general's quarters were connected by a short stair to the lavish penthouse that opened directly upon the roof garden. He knew that particular stair was reputed to be the only access to the roof garden, but he also knew that chimney sweeps and roofers and people who maintained the water tanks and carried water to the garden had to have access, and they most certainly did not go through the general's quarters to get there.

Therefore, there were alternate ways to get there, and he had long ago gone looking for them, finding many, among them the route he was now following. If the general had indeed received a visitation from a Rebel Angel in the smoke from the great chimney, perhaps some sign of that visitation might still be present.

The last constricted stair went between two huge flues to end at a thick stone that pivoted near its edge, creating a door so narrow that even the slender doctor had to turn sideways to sidle through. He was deep inside the great chimney's bulk, at the inner end of a crooked passage, above which the smoke was driven horizontally, hiding the place completely. He paced slowly among alcoves and intervening chimney pots, searching for footprints or hand smears that might have been left by a soot-garbed, fiery angel as it came or went.

After a time he found a broken stone in the likeness of a threatening monster, and as he went toward it he recognized the signs of a hidden door. The mechanism took him only a few moments to solve before he entered a slit between two towering flues, a deep dogleg passage with strange signs and symbols marked upon the walls, probably with a burned stick. At the corner, the passage widened, and here he discovered a huge brazier half full of dead coals standing in an area befouled with loathsome-looking spillage that gave off repugnant stinks.

While he had no desire to touch it or, indeed, even to go closer, the matter demanded investigation. He took up a lengthy stick, partially burned, perhaps the very one that had been used to make the symbols on the walls, and used it to probe the remnants of the fire. He scratched up a lump of carbon that could have been anything. He scratched more deeply to find another lump of carbon, this one only charred. He took it between thumb and forefinger to pull it clear, stepping back with a muffled exclamation as it came into view. The charred part was a wrist. The largely unburned part was a hand, the right hand of a very small child.

The doctor stood for a moment frozen, a sick violence in his belly, eyes filling with tears that were whipped into runnels by the wind. For several days, the Fortress had buzzed with rumors that one of the general's children had disappeared. Angelica. The five-year-old daughter the doctor had seen at the general's birthday reception, playing tag with the other children. Laying the object back into the brazier, the doctor swallowed deeply and bid his bowels to contain themselves. When he was calm he went past the brazier to another stone monster head, finding another door through which he explored only far enough to verify that it gave access to the general's roof garden.

He returned to the brazier, used his handkerchief to wrap the hand and the lump, as well as several other anonymous lumps that did not seem to be merely charcoal, and put them in the deep pocket of his coat. He then stood a long, long moment in thought as his coat lashed around his legs, listening to the wind. The storm was still building. It would be windier yet before it was through, and even in this sheltered place, he could feel the rising gale.

He took the brazier by its legs and deliberately upended it, spilling the ashes upon the roof tiles to be driven about in tiny whirlwinds, like tattered gray veils. He left the brazier on its side, as though it had blown over, though he carefully checked the contents once more, this time finding nothing but ashes.

Taking a last look around and being careful not to leave either footprints or a trail of ash, he found his way back to the monster-head door, and from that to the pivoting stone, the stairs, and eventually his rooms, where he pocketed several items from a hidden closet before going down to ground level and out into the streets.

He was followed, as he often was, by one of the bishop's henchmen as he wandered aimlessly, having tea in this place and a sandwich in that, looking at shoes in that shop and then another, which finally convinced the henchman, who was tired of blinking against the wind driven dust, that the doctor was up to nothing in particular. When the henchman departed, the doctor purposefully made his way along to a ragged bit of wasteland beside the railroad where a few hardy trees were bent almost double by the wind and a good many tufts of dried grass whipped the air. A drift of white wildflower bloomed under the eaves of one of the blind-walled sheds that hid the place from view on all sides. This was the closest bit of "natural" land the doctor knew of, and "natural" land was necessary to his purpose.

From one capacious pocket he took a trowel and used it to dig first a piece of tufty sod and then a narrow but deep hole into which he put the linen-wrapped packet, replacing soil and sod above it and treading it firmly into place. In another pocket, he found a tiny book with almost minuscule print, and from that he read a prayer for the repose of the soul of the child whom he had last seen at play upon the roof garden in company with other children.

Finally, the doctor took a vial of water from his other trouser pocket, uncorked it, and poured the contents onto the tiny grave. The water came from a spring that flowed beyond the ramparts of Bastion near the cavern home of a certain seeress. It was said, not by the seeress, that the water was blessed by someone called Wogalkish, and was therefore a specific against evil. As the water sank into the ground, a faint mist rose from the tiny grave, along with a smell of flowers.

At this sign, which somewhat surprised him, he returned to the book, flipped a few pages and read, "By Shadua of the Shroud, Rankivian of the Spirits, and Yun of the Shadow, to whose care I commit her, may she whose remains lie here, whether living or dead, come to peace; may her fetters be loosed; may her spirit be freed."

He waited. The mist rose before him, to the level of his eyes, then whirled into a tiny, virtually invisible vortex and vanished. Taking a deep breath, he put the odds and ends back into his pockets and returned to the Fortress, where he saw the man who had followed him among a group of stand-abouts at the door. The doctor hailed him by name and engaged him in an unnecessary conversation about shoes.

"So you didn't buy any?" said the henchman.

"No," said the doctor in a petulant tone. "I'm going to have a pair made to order. I'm tired of these bunions springing up!"

The follower subsequently reported to the Over Colonel Bishop that the doctor had looked for new shoes because he had bunions, and that was the end of the event so far as the doctor and the bishop were concerned.

It was not the end of the consequences in another quarter, however. The city of Hold, like most of Bastion, lay atop a limestone deposit riddled with caverns, tunnels, caves, crevasses, pools, and rivers. Most of these holes were black and empty; some were tenanted only by blind fish and the skeletons of small creatures who had gone too far from the light. Others, however, were occupied, as was true of a very large cavern that lay deeply and vertically below Hold. This cavern was full of a nameless slime, an abhorrent ropiness, a stench of the pit and a darkness unutterable.

The moment that Doctor Jens Ladislav, standing by the railroad, called upon Shadua, Rankivian, and Yun, the inhabitant of that cavern started awake with a horrid yowling as though stung by some creature even more venomous than itself.

"Gnang?" the being roared, raising its jointless and terrible arms in a gesture of fury.

A servitor writhed to the door of the chamber, his usual method of locomotion when not dressed to confuse the Spared.

"The girl child," screamed the vast inhabitant. "Go look at her."

The servitor turned wordlessly and went up, once out of earshot engaging in a litany of annoyances.

"Gnash'm. Gnash and smash'm. Gnang go here. Gnang go there. Check this. See that. Serve that one the good wine, serve that one the shit from the pit. Keep this one waiting, let that one in. Cut her here. Penetrate her there. Let the Fell out of the book and step aside. Lick her blood, but don't get in the way of the Fell! All the time, do this, do that. And when's time for Gnang to have any? Ah?"

The servitor went almost to the surface, to an area of cut stone and straight corridors, down one of which it slithered until it came to a locked room in which a trio of candles gave a pallid light. There on a narrow bed lay the body of a child, one arm ending in a bandaged stump. The servitor stayed at the barred door for some moments, listening for breath, then opened the door and went to the bed, where it set its teeth into the little body and shook it, as a terrier might shake a rat. When there was no response, the creature turned back the way it had come.

When it arrived in the dark chamber, the ropiness seethed. "So?"

"Dead," said the servitor in its natural voice, which held neither concern nor pity.

"How?" came the scream, as though from a thousand throats.

The servitor had its tentacles over its sound receptors, and stayed so crouched until the echoes faded.

The servitor cringed. "There's a dreadful wind on the surface today. Maybe it blew away the ashes."

"No wind should have blown the ashes! No one should have touched the brazier in which the spell was set! The parchments have always instructed him to put it in a protected place and leave it where it was! You were there? Was it in the wind?"

"Not then," said the servitor. "Maybe now."

"He was told not to disturb it! So long as it sat there, untouched, we would have owned the child! Amused ourselves with the child! Turned the child into bait to catch others!"

Gnang shrugged, bending swiftly sideways to avoid a blow that came from a remote part of the inhabitant. "Maybe someone came upon it and decided to neaten up," Gnang offered.

"I'll neaten someone," said the being, rearing long extrusions of foul flesh up from the ooze in which it delighted. "Oh, I'll neaten someone."

✴ *16*

faience: the whipping boy

It was a rule of the Division of Education, that every citizen must be taught the essentials of Sparedness by a licensed teacher, assisted by a classroom monitor. A classroom had been set up in the Faience for the children of the workers, and a span before class was to begin, Rashel told Dismé that since she was not doing anything useful, she would take the job of monitor.

"Of course," said Dismé, as though it didn't matter. She was not displeased by the idea. The morning and evening journeys to and from the classroom would prove enjoyable: the smell of the kitchen herb garden; the hustle and jostle of squirrels in the firs; the banter of magpies; the sarcastic converse of crows; the slithery crunch of wheels on the gravel drive; the jingle of harness in the porte cochère of the Faience . . .

And at the end, the sound of Michael Pigeon's voice raised in song as he led the horses to the paddock for the day, a sound that Dismé savored. He had a high, tenor voice that soared and dipped, like the flight of a hawk, or an eagle. Looking at him, listening to him sing, and thinking about him—rather as she might think about the squirrels—was one of her daily enjoyments, so well savored that she often returned to the house smiling.

"Are you happy here?" lonely Gayla asked in wonderment.

"As happy as one can be . . ." said Dismé.

". . . who has to live with Rashel," laughed Gayla.

"There is that," Dismé acknowledged, flushing.

"Don't you long for a sweetheart?"

"I try not to think about things like that, Aunt Gayla."

"I can't understand why you stayed once you were grown!"

Dismé shook her head. "You were here, Gayla. And I had met Arnole, and having Arnole's friendship was like having Father back again. With him in the house, I felt safe. I thought of him and you as my only real family."

"Well then, the three of us should have left. Ayward and Rashel should have been a family on their own."

Should have been, perhaps, but family was not what Rashel had in mind when she had wanted Ayward for herself. She had enjoyed getting him, but even that was only preliminary to uglier pleasures that followed.

"Take Ayward his tea, won't you Dismé? He's all alone in the study." This in Apocanew, the year of the marriage.

"Of course, Rashel."

The voice without emotion. The tea carried into the study, the door pushed widely open. The cup and pot placed on the desk without comment, followed by an immediate departure, the door closed as she left. Dismé had not forgotten what had happened to her childhood treasures. From the moment of her return from Aunt Genna's, she gave no sign that she treasured Ayward. Gradually, the intention-not-to-show became an inclination-not-to-feel, until one morning, some months after the wedding, she wakened to the fact that the behavior was the reality. The real Ayward she had come to know in the household was not the dream Ayward she had lost and grieved over, and the dissonance between the two had become too obvious for her to ignore.

That morning she hummed as she brushed her hair. The next days she sang to herself. One night at the dinner table, however, Dismé noticed Rashel's eyes fixed speculatively first on Ayward, then on herself, back and forth, like a spider weaving a web, and on Rashel's face an unconscious expression of frustration.

"Arnole," she whispered to him later. "Did you notice Rashel watching me at dinner tonight?"

"Of course I noticed," he said mockingly. "What can you be thinking of? You've recently shown signs of happiness. Whipping boys are not supposed to be joyous, or even tranquil. They're supposed to cringe."

"Ah," she murmured, after a moment's thought. "Of course."

For a while, she had forgotten to behave in accordance with Rashel's script. Indifference toward Ayward was a strategic error. If Rashel could no longer gloat over the spoils of her victory, why keep the spoils lying about?

Thereafter, Dismé fashioned a fraudulent affection and rebuilt its façade, making sure that Rashel both heard and saw each act of sham solicitude. Arnole took note that Ayward had not detected either the alienation or the falsely affectionate return. The fakery was good enough. Rashel went back to gloating, and Dismé comforted herself with the hope that Rashel might somehow find some other whipping boy. When that happened, Dismé would think about having a life of her own.

✴ *17*

the advent of tamlar

On a particularly sunny day, four students took their lunches onto the lawn near the Faience where, as classroom monitor, Dismé accompanied them, enjoying the warmth of the autumn sun and the feel of the grass as much as did the four: Jem and Sanly, one pretty but rather dim, the other plainer but brighter; Horcus and Gustaf, one stout, pubescent, and jeering, the other curly-haired and gentle, Dismé's favorite.

As they finished their food, Gustaf looked at the shadows of the nearest trees, judged it to be still very noonish, and, hoping to forestall immediate return to the classroom, said, "Tell us a story, Monitor Dismé."

"What story would you like?"

"About the Trek! That's exciting," said Horcus. "When the men had to ride, and fight, and kill monsters . . ."

"And sit quiet for long years here and there growing corn," said Sanly. "Besides, we know the Trek story backwards and forwards."

Dismé offered, "I can tell you about how Hal P'Jardas discovered the woman of fire, how's that?" It was a story Arnole had been fond of, and one the children were not likely to have heard.

"When the darkness ended and the Spared had been a century in the Trek, they had become far too many to live off the country they traveled through. So, the many little tribes and families split up into three main bands named after commands in the old hymn: the Turnaways, the Come Adores, and the Praisers, but even when they had to stay in one place, to grow and harvest food, whether for a season or for years, the leaders and the scouts went on looking for a better place.

"They wanted a land that was impregnable, a place where they could rediscover The Art without the world knowing it, for the un-Spared laughed at the Spared for trying to recover what had been lost.

"One day, a scout named Hal P'Jardas was traveling deep among the canyons outside our mountains, and he came over a narrow, hidden pass and saw three wide valleys spread out like leaves of clover. He came down from the pass and went from valley to valley, fishing the streams and testing the soil, and where the three valleys ran into one another, where Hold is now, he camped near a mound covered with strangely twisted lava pillars, like glass, he said, with lights inside them. He found a fumarole nearby that served him for a campfire, and a warm pond where he could wash himself. He roasted a snared rabbit over the fumarole, and finally settled himself to sleep.

"Deep in the night, he wakened to a cracking sound and a change in the smell of the air. His eyes slitted open in time to see a line of fire come out of the fumarole, a fiery candle that stood taller than a tall man, wavering in the light wind, then broadening to take the form of a woman. She was cloaked in black so that only her shape could be seen against the predawn sky, her body visible only when the cinereous robes parted momentarily to show a blazing hand, the fiery curve of a cheek or thigh, a set of burning lips and a tongue of white flame.

" 'Why are you here,' she asked him in a voice like hissing lava, and he trembled, for in all his years on the Trek, he had seen nothing like this.

" 'Looking for a place for my people,' he said. 'A place for them to settle.'

" 'And does this place suit you?' the fiery woman asked.

"He thought he should say no, it didn't, he was leaving in the morning, but what came from his mouth was the truth. 'Yes. It is a good place. My people will like it.'

" 'And your people are called?' she asked.

" 'We are the Praise Trek-band of the Spared Ones.'

"She laughed, then, the kind of laughter a volcano might utter while it was resting."

Horcus interrupted her. "Miss Dismé, how do you know this?"

"P'Jardas wrote it all down!"

"Including the bit about the cinereous robes and the volcanic laughter?" asked Gustaf, his eyes wide.

"I'm making it vivid for you."

"So it's not all true?"

"It *is* all true," she said, annoyed. "I'm merely giving you the feel of it. One can tell from what Hal P'Jardas wrote how the woman of fire behaved, and what Hal P'Jardas wrote is in the archives in the Fortress of Hold and the person who told me the story memorized it directly from that document."

When Arnole had told her this story, Dismé had had similar doubts. "*You've* read them, Arnole? How did you get to read them?"

He had shaken his head at her. "Dismé, I was sixteen when the Spared took me for a slave, fifty years ago. After they spent a year re-educating me, they put me to working a night shift in the Fortress. Nobody notices a man with a mop, and I spent more time reading the old files than cleaning the floors."

Dismé went on, "Then the fiery woman said: 'If they are the Spared Ones, then I will spare them yet a while, explorer. Tell them, however, that if they come here, in time they will be charged a fee for the use of these lands, for this is a place dedicated to Elnith who was, Lady of the Silences who is yet to come.' "

"That's one of the Council of Guardians!" cried Jem.

Dismé nodded. "She said, 'I am her friend, her forerunner, her prophetess, if you like. Have you heard of Tamlar of the Flames?'

"Hal shook his head, too full of fear to speak, and she said, 'Elnith sleeps in this land, and it is hers, not mine, though we cohabit it in part. In time to come, Elnith will wake and set her sign on your people. Be sure to tell your masters, so they will know all about it.'

"And she moved her hand in the air, leaving a glowing line that looped upon itself, and this sign hung there even while the ashen robes closed around the radiant body and dropped back into the fumarole. That was the last he saw of Tamlar."

"Tamlar is one of the Guardians," said Sanly. "There's Tamlar of the Flames and Bertral of the Book and Camwar of the Cask . . ."

"What do we need guardians for when we got angels?" demanded Horcus, a bit truculently.

Dismé gave a careful reply. "The Dicta tell us to believe in the Rebel Angels, Horcus, but they don't name them or describe them. For all we know, the Rebel Angels and the Guardians are the same creatures under different names."

"Go on with the story, Miss Dismé," Gustaf said.

"When Hal returned to the Trekkers and announced his find, the Spared gathered together from all over the land and spent the last year of their great trek clambering their way over the mountains into this land of Bastion. When the Spared reached the center of Bastion, they found a mound topped by a number of curiously shaped lava pillars. Nearby was a dead fumarole and a recently dried-up pond, but no one connected this place with the place P'Jardas had spoken of . . ." Perhaps, thought Dismé, because they had not believed the story to begin with. ". . . and when P'Jardas next saw the place, the curving stones had been removed, and the foundations of the Fortress were already encircling the mound . . ."

Dismé reached for her shoes.

". . . so the mound where Hal P'Jardas camped is still there, in the cellars of the Fortress itself and that's how the story ends," Dismé glanced at the sky. "Look. The sun's moved past lunchtime. We need to get back to the classroom."

In the Time of Desperation, there had been darkness for a very long time and what remained of humanity had lost track of time. When the darkness lifted, someone had figured out when midsummer was and had counted days until the next midsummer to establish the solar year as lasting four hundred days. This neatly divisible annum was divided into four seasons—though there was much less difference among them than formerly—each season made up of ten spans of ten days each, yielding such calendar nomenclature as "Spring-span ten, fourday," or "Winter-span three, nineday."

In Bastion, days one through seven were work days, days eight and half nine were marketing days, while the afternoon of nine and all of ten were span-ends, given over to rest, amusements, and a required obeisance to the Rebel Angels. Dismé usually accompanied either Rashel or the housekeeper to Apocanew on marketing days, and in the latter case, it was a much relished outing.

On a particular day during Fall-span three, Rashel told Dismé she was to do the shopping while Rashel herself kept an appointment. In Apocanew, Michael stopped at a corner, and Rashel went off down the street while the carriage proceeded to the grocers' street where Dismé went into the cheese shop and the sausage shop and the green-grocer's and the bakery and half a dozen other places, in each case paying the bill with Rashel's money and exchanging her own bits and splits for Holdmarks, which she hid in her shoe. She and Michael arrived back at the corner in time to see Rashel coming down the street, obviously in a fury.

She got into the carriage and immediately went through the string bags that held the purchases, snarling about each item. Then she took Dismé's purse and went through that, pocketing the change, and then through Dismé's pockets. Dismé said nothing for Rashel had always done this, since

Dismé was very small. There was nothing in the purse except a comb, the change, and the receipts, which Rashel took. Dismé's pockets held only a couple of honey lozenges wrapped up in a clean handkerchief.

"What, no commission?" Rashel sneered, peering at the receipts. "You're a fool, girl. You should have asked for a commission," and she settled into the cushions, her face obdurate, obviously raging about something. Dismé did nothing to set her off anew, nor, she noted, did Michael.

When they arrived back at the conservator's house, Rashel was delivered at the front door while Dismé rode around to the kitchen door, to take in the groceries.

Dismé looked up through her lashes, whispering, "Where does she go, Michael? When you drop her off there? Is she always this angry, afterward?"

Michael stared at the sky. "Angry, yes. Where, I don't know. I know a way to find out, however. Perhaps I will."

"It would be interesting to know," said Dismé. "If it makes her that furious, why does she go on doing it?"

✳ 18

hetman gone

When Rashel was dropped off at a street corner in Apoc-anew, she was either on her way to visit one of her dear, dear friends or she was keeping an appointment with her "Uncle Influence." She often rehearsed upcoming visits in her mirror, mouthing this invented title with some insouciance, even impudence, the merest gloss of insolence which vanished completely when she approached the visit itself. Pretence stopped at the grilled gate in the blank wall a block or so from the Turn-away government house in Apocanew. Even knocking on the gatepost demanded an effort of will, and it was only with great difficulty that she retained an outward aplomb.

Eventually, and only when the street was totally empty except for herself, a wizened and hairy dwarf responded to the knock by appearing out of a hole in the wall, like a mar-mot. As always, he looked her up and down as though she were spoiled produce left too long at the market. Whichever one of the dwarfish servitors opened the gate, Issel, Gnang, or Thitch, he always waited for her to pronounce the correct name before unlocking it and holding it just wide enough for her to slip through.

Once admitted, she went through the hole to the flights of stairs and lengths of ill-lit hallway that ended in another gate, this one of iron, with a peephole that opened with a peculiar and mind-wrenching shriek.

"Rashel Deshôll, Thitch," she said to the eye behind the peephole.

"Known to the Hetman?" asked a sepulchral voice.

"You know I am," she muttered.

Thitch made the slobbering gargle which passed among the Hetman's servants as a laugh. It was derision, not humor. Neither the Hetman nor his minions found anything funny, though certain very horrid things afforded them amusement, but it was amusement of a gobbling kind, more akin to voracity than to joy.

The stony anteroom was lit by several iron-bracketed torches. Rashel settled herself uncomfortably on a roughly squared stone. The wait was likely to be long, and, as always, she was too vividly reminded of the first times she had come here.

It had happened only a day or two after Roger's accident, when Cora had mentioned an "acquaintance," Hetman Gone, a person of great influence who was in a position to grant Rashel many benefits—if he took a liking to her and if he offered her a job. If he did both these things, Rashel would receive expensive schooling, the finest clothing. She would be given introductions to this one and that one. Her future would be assured.

How did her mother know this? Ah, well, Cora worked for the Hetman herself, occasionally, and she had gained many benefits from that association.

It had sounded tempting. Rashel had gone with her mother to visit him in his lair by the fire, among his dwarfish assistants: Issel. Thitch. Kravel. Gnang. He had complimented her upon her appearance, her intelligence. He had mentioned the benefits she would receive for serving him, much as her mother had.

"Do you agree?" he had asked.

Rashel, age thirteen, had shrugged. "Yes," she had said. "Why not?"

"And you, Cora?" the Hetman purred. "Do you agree as well?"

"Yes, Hetman," she had said, her voice shaking slightly.

All during that first visit, Rashel had noticed that her mother was not herself. She had sat quietly, hands clenched so tightly together that they seemed bloodless. Even her face had been ashen, and it took several days for her to recover her usual appearance and manner. At the time, Rashel had thought her reaction a stupid one, for nothing bad had happened. The place had been strange, and the man had been stranger yet, but nothing had happened.

After that, everything happened as promised: schools, clothing, introductions, and the Hetman didn't even ask for a report on how well she was doing. Not until Val, Dismé's father, was installed in the bottle room.

"We must meet with Hetman Gone," her mother said, when the installation was complete. Her face was again ashen and her hands trembled when she spoke.

"I don't want to meet with him," Rashel had said in her most arrogant tone. "I have no reason to meet with him."

Her mother swallowed, gulping at nothing and having a hard time getting it down. "If you want to go on living, you will need to meet with him. If you want to accomplish all those things you desire, then you will meet with Hetman Gone."

Rashel hadn't believed it. She had thought it ridiculous, believing the actual visit would prove how silly her mother was being. So, she had returned to that dismal, fire-lit cellar and listened while Cora explained that a second one of the Latimer family had recently died, and this failure of her duty had to be reported to the Hetman.

Rashel had looked up at this. She had never heard of any duty her mother owed the Hetman.

The Hetman reached for an iron-bound box on the table beside him, opened it and took out a journal from which he read a list of all the benefits Rashel had received through his efforts—her schooling, her clothing, certain luxuries with which she had been provided.

She thanked him nicely, assuming that was what was wanted.

He had smiled, and for the first time she had felt afraid, for it was a terrible smile.

"These gifts were not so inconsiderable as to be given for a mere thank you, Rashel. They constitute an indebtedness much larger than that."

"Then you should collect from her!" she said impassively, pointing at her mother "It was she who arranged it all. I never did."

"Oh yes, you did," said the Hetman, in a particular tone that seemed to cut her tongue and freeze her throat. "You said, 'Yes.' You said, 'Why not?' You agreed. You owe the debt."

"Now, Rashel," her white-faced mother had begged. "Listen to the Hetman."

"Children are often encumbered by their parents, with chains of one kind or another." He had smiled his terrible smile. "Even though you are the cause of your mother's breach of her duty, your chains will be relatively light. You will merely visit me here, regularly, either spontaneously or at my invitation. You will merely do, from time to time, what you are told to do. These duties will not be onerous. They will be within your capability."

"And if I won't?" she had gasped, her anger still riding atop her fear.

The Hetman made his peculiar gargling, slobbering sound. "Then, surprisingly, the school you attend will find it made a mistake in admitting you. People will not want to meet you or work with you. You will find yourself isolated, friendless, and poor, as your mother once was. Soon you will catch the Disease. You will be Chaired. Your life will end."

"Rashel?" her mother begged in a frantic whisper.

"Oh, all right," she had gasped as the Hetman had turned away from her to summon his assistants.

What happened after that, Rashel preferred not to remember. At the age of fifteen, she had been dedicated to the Fell, as, evidently, her mother had been before her. The Hetman had insisted upon it. Issel and Thitch had held her mother so she could not interfere, not that her mother tried to interfere, for she merely hung there between them, ice white, with her eyes shut tight pretending she did not hear Rashel's screams. Kravel and Gnang had held Rashel. Each time Rashel screamed, she promised herself she would not scream again, and each time a new cry was wrung from her until her throat was as raw as the parts the Fell concentrated upon as he had his horrible way with her, his excruciating and dreadful way that left her bleeding and bruised and terrified. The Fell had teeth where no other creature had teeth. The Fell had poison that did not kill but only excruciated. No one had ever . . . ever before done . . . anything like that to her. Scarcely conscious, barely able to walk, she had been taken home.

Outwardly, she had healed, without scars. Inwardly, she quivered with remembrance. Since that time she had been punctilious in meeting the Hetman's expectations. Since that time, she had come here, as he ordered, regularly.

The iron door across the anteroom screeched open on rusted hinges, and the dwarfish form of the particular creature called Gnang leaned through the opening. "Are you expected?"

"I believe he knows I'm coming," she said. He always knew when she was coming, whether or not she herself had known it before she actually approached the gate.

The dwarf stood back, allowing her to enter Hetman Gone's home, or perhaps his office, or perhaps only a place in which he transacted business from time to time. The only parts of it she had ever seen were the lengthy hallways she had just traversed and this single overheated room where he waited.

As always, he was seated in a large chair before an open fire with his back to the door. The fire gave the room's only light as well as its excessive heat, though Rashel did not remark upon this. As had been pointed out to her on a previous occasion, the fire was not there for her convenience or comfort. She circled the chair to come into his view, bowing slightly.

"So, you've come visiting." Gone's expressionless voice was belied by the intent gaze of half-lidded eyes that glowed redly in the firelight. Despite the ruddiness of the fire-glow,

Rashel believed his flesh was rather gray, a hue she detected where the sides of his face and neck curved into shadow. Dark, stiff hair rose from a point almost between his brows and ran back along the center of his head in a bushy crest. His long, thick fingers bore several heavy rings set with worn intaglios, and he habitually fondled a dagger that ticked and tinged on the rings as he juggled with it. She had always seen him seated, and each time she saw him she was surprised anew that from hip to crown he did not appear to be much taller than she.

"I am astonished," he mused in an unsurprised tone. "I hear your husband may have acquired the Disease."

She remained silent, head bowed. It was not wise to comment to this person, and a bad idea, as she had to remind herself after the fact, to argue.

"So soon after his father vanished, too? Remarkable how it runs in the family. You, of course, have nothing to do with it."

"I do not know that my husband has the Disease. No one has suggested it," she murmured. "But it takes those whom it will."

"I am sure he has it. I am certain someone will soon suggest it . . ."

She flushed.

"And how is our little golden bird?" the Hetman asked.

"Less full of song than formerly."

"I'm sure you thank the Fell for that."

She swallowed deeply but could not keep from sounding strangled. "Of course, yes, I thank the Fell."

He made the sound, one peculiar to him. More like a gulp, she thought, than anything else, but not exactly that. More like a stone falling far down into a well, with echoes.

"I can remember a time when you didn't appreciate the Fell," he said, making another of his sounds, this one a counterfeit chuckle: metallic, mechanical, the rattling of a metal door or the sound of a cage shut up, *guh-khrang, guh-khrang, guh-khrang.* "Well, most of his brides don't appreciate him immediately. His ardor can be . . . agonizing. And then too, you were upset with your mother for bringing you to the Fell, and to me."

Rashel fumbled for words. She couldn't lie. The dedication to the Fell had been a ritualized violation, repeated so often by its practitioners that they had acquired a dreadful proficiency at it. The wounds still hurt, some would never heal, and the Hetman knew it.

Still, she did not dare tell the whole truth, the depth of her revulsion, her formless, furious intention to escape the Fell at some time, in some place. She temporized. "It was just that I felt annoyed she had not asked me first."

"Well, I'm sure you worked it out in time. And what of Ayward?"

She allowed herself a lifted lip. "He teaches. He writes. He collects."

"Boring for you, no doubt. And our little bird still hops and chirps? Wouldn't she be better in a smaller cage?"

"She hops. She doesn't chirp. As you once told me, Faience is a cage, and she is in it. The place is so isolated she's no trouble, now that she's given up talking all the time."

Hetman Gone showed his teeth. This was not an expression of pleasure but a voracious gape, accompanied by the lollop of a large, gray tongue. "I can understand why you would think so."

"Because it is so," she said, unwisely.

"No," he whispered, like a hot wind, like a furnace, the word drying her skin, her mouth, her eyes. "Not because it is so but because you enjoy your career, you enjoy the power it gives you over people, those who have magic in their hearts for you to destroy. You like that destruction. You enjoy pushing your authority down the girl's throat, like corn down a goose, every chance you get. It's fun, torturing her. It amuses you, seeing her and Ayward together, both of them impotent to love or be loved. You think it a diversion, heh? Entertaining and tasty to see her grieve over the old man, and the younger one. That's why you let her have her small freedoms, as an angler does a fish. The fisherman calls it play, as you do, but we know how the fish is tortured as it tries to escape the line."

As usual, she had overstepped. As usual, he had brought her back to her boundaries. "Having her there instead of locked up somewhere just makes it simpler, that's all," she murmured.

The Hetman smiled more widely, a terrible sight, from which Rashel averted her eyes. "Where did Arnole Gazane go?" he asked, almost offhandedly.

"I don't know," she answered, genuinely surprised.

"You're sure you had nothing to do with his disappearance?"

"Nothing." She raised her head and dared give him stare for stare. "I would hardly have compromised myself in that way. It did not further my reputation. In fact, it made some trouble with the Regime that I'm just now overcoming."

"Through your dear, dear friends."

She flushed, the heat of it lost in the greater heat of the fire. "Yes. Through my friends."

"Thank the Fell for the . . . skills you have learned that make you so alluring," he said. "And your new project? The artifact under the Fortress?"

She looked up, surprised. How had he found out about that? "The artifact, if it is one, is interesting, Hetman, but as yet no one knows what it is, or even if it is anything useful."

"One hopes you will be able to find out, since one put you in a position to do so."

She flushed. He? He had done it? She had thought her own merits had been quite enough to . . .

He broke into the thought with a whisper. "In the vicinity of the artifact, it is possible a book will be found. I do not say it is certainly there, but it may be. If it is there, I want it, Rashel. I want it immediately. Ordinarily, I do not tell you what you must do, Rashel Deshôll. That is not my way. I have servants to do the things I do not wish to be bothered with, and neither do I wish to be bothered telling them how their duties should be done. If they are not intelligent enough to know, then they may feed the Fell while I find others. So, I tell you only the end I desire and leave its accomplishment to you. I tell you I want a book that may be found with the artifact. I tell you the day will come when I will need the little bird alive in my hand."

"She is caged, Hetman."

"Say 'Master.' I like it when you call me Master."

Rashel moistened dry lips. "She is caged, Master."

"Ah, good. See that no one leaves the door open, so that she flies away. See that nothing is found out about the thing beneath the Fortress that you don't tell me, at once."

Rashel was in such inner tumult she did not trust herself to reply. Instead she bowed, lower than usual, to hide her flaming face. She made these occasional voluntary visits in order to avoid being summoned. Being summoned, sometimes days beforehand, meant she would have days of impotence and rage between the summons and the actual visit. Some of the times, including this one, the voluntary visits were almost as bad as the involuntary ones, and she raged nonetheless. With all the self-control she possessed she lifted her head and nodded calmly. "Of course, Master."

She could not hide her flush or her panting breath, and the Hetman smiled, mouth slightly open to show the huge teeth at the sides of his mouth. Rashel calmed herself with the thought that he resembled most some ponderous beast that habitually dined on carrion. Fell knew he smelled like it!

"Run along," he said, waving her away.

Without daring an answer, she ran along, to vent her impotent rage upon Dismé and Michael and the shopping bags.

Picture this:

Rashel fleeing, almost running away from the grilled gate, skirts fluttering around her calves, shoes making a rapid tattoo upon the paving, face set and hard as she hurries to put space between her and her tormenter, while from the opposite direction another person sedately approaches that same gate. He is a neat, smallish man, though strong and agile, and not unattractive though a bit odd-looking, with a heavily corrugated forehead above a perfectly smooth face, as though the worries of an old man have been grafted upon the wondering tranquility of a cherub. His eyebrows are smoothly curved over thickly lashed and liquid eyes, his hair is smoothly brown, like polished wood, and his lips are as sensually curved as any courtesan's. His name is Bice Dufor, and he is both the Warden of the College of Sorcery in Apocanew and one of Rashel's dear, dear friends.

Once admitted at the gate, he finds the corridors much shorter than Rashel always finds them. Once inside the lair, he meets with more hospitable arrangements than Rashel is ever afforded. He is provided with a glass of wine, a few biscuits, a seat farther from the fire.

"I received your note asking me to drop by," says the visitor, once he has been seated and provided with refreshments.

"Yes," murmurs the Hetman, softly. "It is kind of you to come to me, Warden. Alas, my poor bones still require this excessive heat for their functioning, and it is hard for me to move about."

"Not at all," murmurs the visitor, after a careful sip of the wine. When he first met the Hetman, the wine was marvelous, but evidently the Hetman has lost either his palate or his wine merchant, for the drink has become more execrable with every visit. Contorting his cherub lips into an almost believable smile of appreciation, he nods slightly. "I am happy to be of service."

"I wanted to inquire whether you have any knowledge of the device recently discovered under the Fortress in Hold? I have heard that something strange has been discovered there, and it struck a chord with some of my own research."

The Warden ponders, masking his need for thought by pretending another sip of the abominable wine. He has been told of the thing, whatever it is, but it has been only partially excavated and he knows little or nothing about it. He dislikes admitting ignorance, however, so he hums monotonously for a moment, as he decides what to say.

"Hmmm, well, Hetman, it's a bit early to say we know anything. It is said to be a monolith of glassy stone, or stony glass, as some say. No doubt volcanic. Hmmm. Black, with golden lights in it, which would lead me to suppose obsidian, if asked, though according to persons who have seen it, it is much harder than obsidian. Hmmm. They have only partly uncovered the thing, and they have been unable to detach a sample."

"Really," murmurs the Hetman.

The warden sees a strange gleam in the Hetman's eyes, no doubt from the reflection of the fire. He continues.

"Hmmm. Their failure is quite astonishing. However. The stone is not cut or shaped, apparently."

"And what do people say it is?" asks the Hetman.

"It would be sheer guesswork at this stage, Hetman. Hmmm. They speak of this and that. An igneous extrusion. Perhaps an example of pre-Happening art. Some who have seen it believe sorcery is somehow involved, which surprises me."

"Surprises you? Why?"

The warden sets down his glass and assumes an expression of thoughtfulness. "Well, I've spoken with Rashel Deshôll, the Conservator at Faience, about it. She's a true Selectivist, much more inclined to exclude sorcery than to find evidence of it. Hmmm. She hardly ever finds any among the cases that are reported to her. She goes and examines and questions, and by the time she leaves, it's evident there is no magic there, or none left, at least. Hmmm. If there ever was."

"Ah," murmurs the Hetman. "If this is so, she is a strange person to be in charge of Faience, wouldn't you say?"

Bice Dufor, who believes he has had much to do with putting Rashel in that position, flushes very slightly. "Well, she may have swung the pendulum a bit far toward Selectivism, but then, previously, it had gone too far in the opposite direction. I know Ayford Gazane well. It was he who buried us in Inclusionism through his belief that almost everything pre-Happening is, hmmm, magical, his belief that we can utilize simple magic in simple ways, without resorting to the . . . ah . . . more arcane and difficult usages. He was plausible. He built a wind-sack once, out of tough paper and cloth, with a fire pan suspended under it, and it flew! I have heard him say that even the simplest things from pre-Happening times have to be magical because of the magical age from which they came. He has a little saying, 'Sorcelsticks require no spell . . .' " Bice heard himself chattering and ceased.

"Madam Deshôll is perhaps a little too restrictive the other way, a little too driven toward the esoteric, but hmmm . . . we feel things will even out . . ."

The Hetman nods. "Well, it's all very interesting. I do hope you'll keep me informed about the device, if it is a device. In the meantime, in my research, I came across some enchantments that are new to me, and I thought I ought to pass them along to you." The Hetman draws a folded sheet of parchment from a carved box on the table beside him and holds it out to the warden, who rises to take it from him with a peculiar combination of reluctance and avidity. He seats himself and unfolds the stained and tattered sheet.

"Where you find such marvels!" He does not intend it as a question, but the Hetman answers, nonetheless.

"I have agents, out in the world. They find things for me. Have you tried those other spells I gave you? Did they work out well?"

The warden murmurs distractedly, "Oh, yes, yes. The will-bending spell, particularly. I've used it on one of the janitors at the college. Hmmm. Man was both rebellious and insolent! Now, he does better work than any of the others, doesn't raise his eyes above his shoes, works overtime without pay, doesn't even stop to eat unless I tell him to. I'm looking for an opportunity to use it again, in a way that may be more significant."

"You had no trouble with the ingredients?"

"The heart's blood of virgins . . . hmmm . . . was a trifle difficult to obtain, but nothing we couldn't manage. There are always some dying children ready for bottling, and I took it from them just before the demons arrived." He looked up, abruptly angry. "The demon had the unmitigated arrogance to be short with me about it. Said I had no business killing them before he got to them."

The Hetman waves his fingers. "I knew you'd manage somehow. Now, this new material is fascinating stuff. I've included the list of ingredients for you. Every one of these spells works. Every single one. And they work every time."

The warden says, "This invisibility spell calls for body parts from living women."

"Nothing really crippling," comments the Hetman, dismissively. "A hand. A foot."

The warden muses for a time. "I suppose when someone is bottled, we could take a finger or an ear . . ."

The Hetman shakes his head. "Oh, tsk, no, no. You misunderstand what the formula calls for. The woman must be still living, still walking about, still actively engaged in her life. Not someone who is to be bottled. No. That negates the spell entirely. You only achieve invisibility if the woman who donated the body part is still quite alive and active."

"But we say anyone in a bottle is alive . . ."

The Hetman speaks very softly. "Believe me, Warden. I know what you *say*, but this spell doesn't work on what you *say*. It works on what's real. What's in a bottle isn't a living person—it's living tissue, and that's a different thing."

The warden recalls a dozen rebuttals to this, all provided by the Dicta, but he discards them as unworthy of mention. "This requires that we maim someone who's healthy," he muses. "It is not an unheard of thing. One can always pick someone useless to take the hand from."

"You have slaves, don't you? Girl children you've captured? Others you've taken during your expeditions outside?"

"As a matter of fact . . . Yes. Just recently we've been doing a good bit more of that."

"Ah," says the Hetman, leaning back in his chair, his voice purring. "Tell me about it?"

The warden nods. "We're sending teams across the borders to make converts and bottle people who are dying. It won't be long before the army will be ready, and we'll move out across our borders in force in order to bring the blessing of Sparedness to the whole world!"

"I wonder why now?" purrs the Hetman.

The warden frowns. "I've wondered, too. Do you suppose it has something to do with the thing in the north? It's moved."

"Moved?" The Hetman freezes in startlement.

This is the first time the warden has seen him react so. He says smoothly, as though it is unimportant, "It left the northlands some time ago to move down the coast under the ocean, and now it's come up on the shore near Henceforth."

The Hetman sits like stone. After a long pause, he smiles. "I wish I were as young as you. It would be interesting to be involved in this great work of yours. Take the spell along. Whether you can use it right away or not, it's still of interest, if only as a curiosity."

"I cannot thank you enough . . ."

"You do keep the spells in a safe place, all together, do you not?"

"As you directed, of course. In my office. All in one place."

The Hetman voices his *guh-krang guh-krang,* his unamused amusement, "That's good. Very good."

The warden rises, bows, and departs with the parchment tightly gripped in one fist while the Hetman lifts a nostril at the still full glass that had been served to his guest, who was not yet sufficiently dominated to have drunk it. Then he amuses himself for a few moments wondering who of the faculty of the College of Sorcery will next fall into his hands through the use of magic which is, though not so identified on the face of it, very selective and very dark indeed.

Then he remembers what was said about the thing that had been in the north, now coming ashore near Henceforth, and the grin vanishes from his face to be replaced by an expression of obdurate, relentless fury.

✴ 19

nell latimer's book

The time is growing short. Emergency relief supplies are being produced by factories running seven days a week around the clock. The survival warehouses are being stocked with food for both humans and animals, insulated clothing and blankets and foam igloos stacked up like eggshells— even in the warmest parts of the country. One thing the planners have been told: The future, if any, is going to be damned cold.

Television has been hammering away at the techniques of surviving blizzards, of getting clean water in case of floods or earthquakes, of disposing of waste if systems break down. Every household has received a survival manual printed by the EPA, despite harangues on government wastefulness by certain congressmen who haven't yet caught on to the fact that their current term of office is going to be their last. The big quake that killed a quarter of all Californians is recent enough that people are very high on preparedness. Instead of screaming about government waste, they're giving the administration credit for its foresight.

It's crazy. The populace knows the Bitch is coming, they know it's going to hit, but by and large they believe it will hit somewhere else. All the "preparedness" is for things that will happen to other people.

*   *   *

And time has gone by, all the time there is, and I've gone on pretending to ignore what happened between Jerry and me. The last week or so the family has slept in the shelter. I want the kids used to the shelter before the thing happens, and I made it happen by removing all the beds from the house, stacking them in the garage "to have the bedrooms painted." The contractor has the rooms full of drop cloths and buckets. It's due to hit today, Saturday, but the published date is several weeks away.

When I left the kids this morning, I knew I wouldn't be back. I tried to make the morning hugs and kisses just as quick and perfunctory as usual. Jerry will be at home with the kids for the day, and I didn't tell him I wouldn't be returning.

"See you later," I said, sort of over my shoulder. "There's a meeting late afternoon. If I'm late, don't wait for me."

"Pizza for supper," he said, with his lofty smile.

"There'll be a meteor shower tonight," I warned him. "If you and the kids go to bed before I get home, be sure to shut the outside door."

"It won't be necessary," he said, still smiling.

"It would make me feel better," I begged, giving him a pitiful look and a chance to be magnanimous. If he promised, he'd do it. That was part of his code. "Please. Jerry?"

The superior smile. "Anything to make you feel better."

"Promise?"

The smile faded, but he conceded. "I promise."

I already had a small suitcase in the trunk of my car: pictures of the children, of my folks. I'm here, where Nell is supposed to be, but where Mommy had never planned on being . . .

Here I'm switching from writing to recording. There won't be time to write things, or any quiet place to do it . . .

"Here's your ID card. Muster area is down front."

That was my fellow sleeper, Hal, checking me off the list and handing me a tag. The place isn't strange to me. We've all been here several times, for briefings, and they collected ova from the sleepers here. They fertilized the ova with sperm from a number of different donors—the only one I know is my old friend Alan Block, because he told me—and then blastulas were split to provide numerous embryos. Each one of us female donors could be Eve all over again. The embryology is a lot further advanced than the artificial wombs are. There've been some successes, not a lot, but what we have at Omega site is state of the art.

The sleepers are trickling in. I don't know many of them, but I see one woman I'd just as soon not see, because I upset her needlessly one of the last times I was here. Since there are only two hundred of us, selected from all over, none of us know many of the others, so I was surprised to recognize a woman in the clinic as Janitzia Forza, a woman I knew in college. She's a chemist, and her name tag said "Janet Gerber." She asked what I was doing there, and I told her they were storing my gametes, figuring she knew all about it. Turns out she didn't know, and she was furious, accusing me of pulling strings to become a donor. She was so irrational that I asked around. Her husband is infertile and religious. He won't permit AI, and she's bitter against anyone who has children.

I'm in the largest room at Omega site, and it holds two hundred "coffins," though no one calls them that out loud. The power comes from several little nuclear plants buried in solid rock, way off thataway. Omega site is shaped like a theater, the coffins arranged in rows up the sloping floor, the shape of the place dictated by the strata it's buried in. Up top, where the lobby would be, are the current stores, the living quarters, big enough for four to eight of us at a time, and the infirmary—several of the sleepers are medical doctors, and there's a diagnostic and treatment computer.

Down where the stage would be is the control console, the monitors, and a door that goes through to the warehouses, the biology labs and cold storage, all the habitat machinery, and the enormous fuel tanks that run generators for ordinary things like lights and computers. Omega site wasn't as far along as some of the others, and the available power units were smaller than in some of the other sites, so the fuel tanks are supplementary, to be used up first, just in case. The lighting was engineered to be as close to sunshine as possible—a lot of it over the little underground garden in the bio lab where we can plant seed crops, harvest them, see that some are planted outside—conditions permitting—and keep some to start over with. Several crops a year will keep many different kinds of food and medicine plants viable, just in case.

There's Alan. Father of some of my unborn children in the cold storage. Alan Block, my colleague and fellow snoozer, evidently just arrived.

"Nell? When are you due for waking?"

"I don't know. Should I know?"

"It's on the back of your ID card. Hal gave it to you when you checked in."

"I didn't think to look . . . where is the thing, oh, here. Oh, God, Alan! Twenty-one twenty-six through twenty-one twenty-nine."

I felt dizzy, and I guess he saw it, because he took the card, and he's over talking to Hal, at the door, trying to see if it can be changed, I guess. Twenty-one twenty-six means I'm in the last waking team. Inside I'm screaming. Now, even if I make it to my first waking, my children will be gone, gone, gone, gone . . .

He's coming back.

"No luck, Nell. I'd hoped we could work together."

"When's your shift, Alan?"

"First shift. I'm one of the guys who stay awake while it happens. My second shift'll be after yours, so wake me a little early on your shift, and we can spend some time together."

"Do something for me, will you?"

"Anything, dear heart, you know that."

"I have a letter here I was going to leave the first watch, but since it's you . . . I planted a camera and a mike in the shelter, where Jerry and the kids are. They'll transmit for a couple of days, and they're being recorded on the ping recorder at the location written down here. Put the tape away for me."

"Nell, do you really want to watch that?"

"If it's too awful, just . . . don't tell me. But if they survive, tape it for me. Leave it in my stasis locker, along with my journal, here, and the tape that's in this recorder when they shut me in."

He didn't answer. He just gripped my shoulder, we pressed our cheeks together, and then he went off to take care of something. I keep reminding myself we're no better off than those outside; inside or out, we supposedly have less than one chance in a hundred of surviving.

I want to cry. I want to be with the children, no matter what, even if Jerry's demons do come drag me away into hell. Oh, God, what am I doing here . . .

There's some confusion going on . . . Something on the TV. I'm going to look. Oh, Lord, it's a hash-up. Some amateur astronomer called the media, some guy who hadn't given up his scope or who's built a new one. They're all reporting it, no response from the observatories, huge, coming fast . . . I'm turning off for a minute.

"Good lord, the moon moved. Did you see that? The moon moved, the thing actually moved the moon, it jerked backwards in its orbit, look at this thing. It's in two pieces. It's split. There's two parts of it. One looks like it's coming faster than the rest of it . . ."

Those words were a famous news anchor, just before someone turned the TV off. So I'm outside, looking up. There's time, still . . . There it is, quite visible . . . I can smell that purple smell, dense smoke rolling up from an endless brushfire of prayer. No. It went away. That smell is gone, completely. I smell something else, cedar? No, no. Sandalwood! And roses, like my grandmother's garden. Where is that coming from. And I hear . . .

There's a damned voice in my head. It's the voice that carries the smell. That doesn't make sense. It says, "Come to me quickly, with all your children." Now what the hell? over and over. "Quickly with all your children." Who's it talking to?

I shake my head to get it out of my nose, my ears, but it just hangs there. Am I smelling a sound or hearing a smell? Or maybe both hearing and smelling something I can see! I don't know. I'm going back inside to tell Alan.

Alan's busy. I ended up not telling anyone. The last few of us are being put in the coffins . . . They just gave me a sedative, to keep me calm . . .

I'm still sitting here, recording . . .

"You want to give me that recorder, Nell?"

"Take the book. Take the recorder after they put me out. Gimme a hug, Alan, for old time's sake."

He laughed and cried, and so did I. Auld lang syne. The techs are headed in this direction to connect me up. Except for me and Alan and his three shift mates, who won't be put to sleep for four more years, the coffins have been filled in order of waking, and I am the last one. Only a few hours left before the Bitch, the event, the occurrence. The happening.

And here I go. Stretched out in the sterile pod with a needle in the arm, the recorder still at my lips. Some of us have teddy bears or pictures of our families. Mine's in my locker. Thank whoever I'll be asleep before the cold. Look at the techs, so sober. Well, hell, why wouldn't they be. The Bitch will be here in a few hours, but they won't be down here when she comes. Nobody much will be down here. Just us. The selected ones, chosen because of stuff we know, or think we know, and the fact that we're young enough to have forty years left, in ten four-year chunks.

Goodbye, Jerry. You're in as safe a place as anyone could be. Goodbye, Jerry I used to love.

Goodbye Michelle, Tony. Mommy's going bye-bye. They're coming to lower the lid. I have to put this away. My throat is full of tears. Here's Alan again.

"Nell?"

"Ummmmm?"

"Sleep well."

✳ 20

sorcery

Sometimes after class, Dismé sneaked into the research wing of the museum, hid herself, and listened to sorcerous talk.

"At the College of Sorcery, Bice Dufor said the parchment or paper a spell is written on can be dangerous in and of itself."

"Why would the one who wrote it make it dangerous?"

"The one who writes it wants power over the one who uses it, and the more the magician uses it, the more power the original sorcerer has over him."

"If that's true, you wouldn't want to use someone else's spell."

"Bice says it's all right if you know what you're doing."

Faience workers wore long white coats, white wraps covering their hair, and tight goatskin gloves and visors so none of their skin or hair could fall on magical artifacts that might be what they called *potentiated* by contact. People had been mysteriously burned or crushed or infected with terrible diseases from touching ancient things the wrong way. The search for sorcery would have been given up long ago if it weren't for the rare discoveries that proved magic really worked.

Dismé had watched from a shadowed balcony when Bice Dufor, Warden of the College of Sorcery, delivered a guest lecture on sorcel-sticks.

"This is a fire spell," he began, fussily laying out materials upon the altar. "First, the magician lays the kindling. Mine is here, in this cresset, splints of wood over shavings. The implementor must be dressed as I am, in a cotton or woolen robe unmixed, with hair combed out and feet bare. Mixed fabrics and tangled hair have a tendency to 'knot' or depotentiate enchantments, and shoes separate one from the foundation of power.

"This particular kind of sorcery is called *contagious magic*, which means it catches its impetus from the intention of the 'assembly,' the materials we assemble around it, for every material and artifact conveys at least one intention, and for things with multiple intentions, the assembly serves to identify the particular intention that is meant. Since we wish to start fire, we use fire-making implements. A fire-drill, flint and steel, and a lens of glass," and he took one of these rare items from its protective covering, "sometimes called a burning glass. We also need one or two *sorcel-sticks*." He held them in his hand while the researchers gathered closely around. "They are made of ordinary wood, with clay heads colored red to signify power and no doubt also containing some sorcerous material we have not yet identified. We get them from non-demonic peddlers, who tell us they mine them from the ruins of a great old city east of here.

"Now, we have on hand some transfer fuel for the fire, a bit of soft cloth or shavings. We take a sorcel-stick and touch it to each of the fire-making implements in order that it be infected with the intention of fire before laying it on a flat surface. The spell is as follows: 'Angel of Fire, hear me! *EEG-nis EEG-nis EEG-nis FAH-tyu-us FAH-tyu-us FAH-tyu-us.*' "

Warden Dufor then struck the sorcel-stick with the arrowhead. It blazed up, and all the students gasped in astonishment, as he transferred the blaze to the kindling, remarking, "Sometimes you have to give the fire your breath to get it going—that's contagious magic also—and with hair long and loose, you risk being burned unless you're careful."

A student asked, "Warden, wouldn't it be quicker just to use the flint and steel? Why go to all that trouble?"

The warden snorted. "Well we obviously *don't* go to all that trouble. We don't use magic for simple things like this. My showing you this enchantment is like teaching the alphabet to a toddler. He must know the individual letters before he can learn to read. When The Art is totally rediscovered, our population will be ready to use it. One step leads to another until we recover all the ancient Art . . ."

"But, sir, at the Newland Fair, last year, I saw a sorcerer start a fire with one gesture and six words: She cried out, *'Hail Tamlar, let there be fire,'* and the fire blazed up. That seems more magical."

The warden scowled. "It's more efficient, certainly, but it's an unreliable spell. Only a few people can do it, and even they can't do it unfailingly. Also, we consider it suspect that those who can do it are mostly young people who have never studied the Inexplicable Arts. That smacks of demonism."

"Sir, where do we get sorcel-sticks?"

"You don't. The College of Sorcery in Apocanew buys a few for teaching purposes. The peddlers call them *matches*, because they *match* the effect of other implements, such as flint and steel, but they're terribly expensive, and used only for educational purposes."

Rashel dismissed the class, then invited the warden to tea. Dismé watched them leave—the Warden very pink and importunate, Rashel very coy—and when they had gone, Dismé came out of hiding to pilfer one of the sorcel-sticks. She would never have stolen anything from a person or from a shop, but this seemed more like research than stealing, like taking a leaf from a tree in order to identify it with the help of old books.

She left the museum grounds by a side path that led to the dilapidated barn, and once settled in the loft, she set the sorcel stick in a crack in a board and looked at it for a while. It seemed a simple enough thing. Too simple, really. Why was a thing this simple needed at all?

Inside herself, near that place where Roarer dwelt, she sensed an opening as if a gateway swung wide into an echoing space. She heard a chime of bells, very distant, almost at the far edge of hearing. She reached her hand toward the sorcel-stick, without touching it, palm upward, and murmured, "Hail, Tamlar. I summon fire."

It was there on her palm, a standing flame, burning from what fuel she could not tell. Her hand felt no heat, the flame felt no wind, for it was rock steady while all the air about it seethed with rushing and whispers. "See, see, she has called the light and it has come . . ."

She looked through the flame to see a wall of ouphs, ouphs frozen into place, fixed upon the flame, for once not grieving or wondering but silent, as though held by a core of stillness outside and beyond themselves. When she focused her eyes on her palm once more, the flame was gone. When she looked up at the ouphs, they too had gone and there was only quiet all around.

So, she could do it herself. The Art was not lost; it was here—or some small part of it was, unless Rashel learned of it and harassed it out of her. Which wasn't going to happen. She wasn't going to tell anyone about this very small talent, this tiny magic, of no use whatsoever unless one were lost in the dark.

✦ *21*

omega site

Nell awakens.

At first there is pain: a sick horror that invades bones, crawls along nerves, and surrounds every living cell. Awareness whimpers before intransigent ice. The ice does not want to let go. Pain is the battlefield on which cold contends against consciousness.

Inevitably, cold gives way, easing gradually into deep chill, then into mere clamminess, the feeling of a springhouse, where deep water flows. The sense of suffocation is strong, the panic of smothering, the frantic horror of no air, no air—nor can there be, for nothing moves, lungs are still, diaphragm is still, nothing breathes, nothing screams. When the torture becomes merely ache, when the terrible coldness becomes merely chill, then the body—not necessarily hers, it has no owner yet—rotates to one side on cushioned robot arms, the face turns downward, the head lowers, and liquid runs freely from nose and mouth, emptying lungs.

Now that the body is capable of screaming, vomiting, gasping, the need to do so has passed. It lies limp and passive as it is turned supine once more, as nozzles enter nostrils and puff to inflate lungs, once, twice, three times. The fourth time the body manages to gasp on its own. Then comes music, a soft repetitive strain in strings and woodwinds with an occasional, almost random reverberation of a deep-toned chime. The ache fades. Blanketing arms hold the body and warm it. Nose detects a minty and resinous smell; muscles click and twitch as hair-thin electrodes are inserted, *tick-a-tick-a-tick-a-tick,* an endless zipping-up which starts at the top of the head and ends at the soles of the feet. Soft pressure rolls up and down arms—they are becoming her arms—a gentle stroking as if this body were a kitten being licked down by a conscientious mother. First arms, then legs, then shoulders and back. Finally a drop of something on the tongue. The taste varies from moment to moment, but is always delicious and seductive, like the music and the stroking, all of it provided by her coffin.

She wonders dreamily—as she has before, many times—at the necessity of being seduced back into life when one has been dead such a very long time. Is it ninety-six years again?

Warm but exhausted by this near approach to living, the body dozes once more as the needles go on pulsing, making muscles and tendons tense and relax and tense again. Though not all strength is lost while deeply frozen, still it will take some time before the body feels like normal flesh. This body is now Nell, and Nell will sleep. Real sleep. Sleep that allows the dream, the one dream that returns during every waking.

In the dream she sees the shelter. Jerry is there among the meticulous stacks of supplies that fill all the space beneath beds, on top of cupboards, wherever there is a cubic inch unused. The children are there, still dressed in swimsuits, just home from the lake where Jerry takes them to swim. Nell herself is there, an observant mote hanging in the camera's eye. She knows what is coming, but they haven't been near a television all day. They haven't heard the news . . .

"Daddy, when's the meedeors coming?" Michy flops herself on the top bunk and punches her pillow. "Are we going to stay all night?"

"Don't want to," Tony, whining his pro-forma objection to life itself.

"Don't have to," Jerry replies, He can't see Nell, he doesn't know she's there. Each time she wakes, she has to remind herself that she is not, was not actually there, that she had already gone to join the sleepers.

Jerry says, "We'll just stay until the meteors stop coming down, Tony."

"Why isn't Mommy here? Won't she get hit?"

"They have a shelter at Big Eye."

"Where she washes the stars," Tony says, with satisfaction. "Mommy's a portant washer."

"Mommy's a very important watcher," Jerry agrees, with a finality that means, yes she is, but now she's away, good riddance. The dreamer watches during a brief period of ordinary living filled with ordinary doings: yawnings, scratchings, and gapings by the children while Jerry neatens and stacks, all interrupted by . . .

"Whas that?" Michy asks. "That noise."

Each time she dreams this, Nell is surprised, for she had not actually expected to hear it, not this far from the ocean where the Bitch was expected to land. Obviously, Jerry hadn't expected to hear it either. His face shows shock first, then horrified surprise. He has been confident that nothing will happen to him and the children. He has put himself in God's hands, sure that nothing will happen, but the sound *is* happening, building like an unbraked train careening down steep tracks, a rattling roar one recognizes mostly from old movies. He darts to the air lock and slams both doors. The shrill screaming is like steam engines, too, and like wheels trying to stop and the whistle going, all at once, only this one goes on and on and on, louder and louder, and the crash, when it comes is a greater sound than human ears can tolerate.

Jerry is facedown on the cot, pillows around his head, trying to block the sound. The ping lens trembles as does the room. The water tank bounces among its heavy springs, a weighty plumb bob, signifying unimaginable forces begun five, six thousand miles away.

Jerry raises his head, looking for Michy. She's on the floor, blood trickling from her ears. Tony is where? There, under the cot, pillows around his head. He is the younger, but he is the one who always has to do what Daddy does.

Jerry pulls the children onto the cots, packs comforters and pillows around them. Michy's eyes are open and her lips move, but he cannot hear her. The world is totally filled by the groaning of monstrous powers rending the earth, forces Jerry has never believed will touch him. The camera is hidden inside a box of Nell's personal supplies; it sees through a pinhole lens.

It is only a coincidence that Jerry is now facing the camera, his mouth drawn into a rictus of fury! He is not yet as frightened as he will be in a day or so, but, oh, he is raging with anger! In the dream her insect voice admonishes him. "You should have believed me, Jerry . . ."

He doesn't hear her as she hangs there, staring at that furious face, those wide, angry eyes, those lips curled back to show bared teeth. Over the vast, underground grinding, the sound changes, very gradually, and now she can hear the sound of water, a heavy downpour, as though the house had been moved beneath a waterfall. The salty ocean that had been displaced now falls upon them. Jerry struggles to the door to the airlock, to one of the listening posts, flexible pipes, one leading up into the house, one to the outside world with a rain cap at the end of it, put there so the ones inside could hear what was happening without opening the airlock.

When he takes off the inner seal, the sound of rain is a roar, a deluge. Rain trickles out the end of the tube. Jerry stares at the water stupidly. She sees his realization that this is the tube that went up into the house. The water is coming from where a house was, a dribble of liquid dark with ashes. She reads the understanding on his face: the house is gone. His world is gone. He lies down between the children while all around them the world moans like some gargantuan animal, wounded unto death but unable to die without interminable agonies.

He lies there in the yellow light of the lantern, hands clenched, still raging at the chaos around him. Though the exterior noise drowns his words, she can read his lips as he cries, "Oh, God, I turn away from you. Damn you. I turn away from you if you treat me like this . . . !"

Nell had first seen the event ninety-six years after it had been recorded. After that, each time she wakened, she relived it before she could go on. There had been later images, as well, one of them leaving the shelter, one of the children half-grown accompanied by a bearded Jerry and a small band of refugees; still another of a gray-haired Jerry leading a much larger group as they barricaded their shelter against monsters, and last of all, a lengthy recording of Jerry as a white-bearded magus, raging upon his followers like Moses down from the mountain. They were Turnaways, he cried. They were followers of the Rebel Angels who had spared them from destruction.

In each case, pings had recorded the images. Pings were the eyes of Omega site. Thousands of them, tiny and self-contained, many of them still functioning after all this time. Through them she knew that her husband and children had survived. At the end of his life, he was patriarch of a multitude that went on wandering and growing, eventually settling in Bastion, a place not far from where Jerry had begun his trek and not far from where Nell had been sleeping. Wonderful, she had thought at the time it happened. Wonderful and strange. And now that she has had the dream once more, she can rest and become flesh yet again.

✴ *22*

officers and gentlemen

General Gowl, Over Colonel Bishop Lief Laron, Doctor
Jens Ladislav, and Major Mace Marchant–Comador, from
Apocanew, were gathered in the officers' dining room late
one afternoon, sharing drinks and talking about one thing
and another. Also present was Captain James Trublood–
Turnaway, an ambitious youngster being proposed by the
bishop as an aide to the doctor. The bishop felt there was
something twisty and un-Regimic about Colonel Doctor
Jens; a certain bull-headed dedication to saving people's
lives in the body instead of just bottling them in the interest
of efficiency; a certain smiliness that wasn't always appropriate; a lack of respect, and young Captain Trublood
seemed an ideal spy to plant on the doctor, particularly inasmuch as he might also make a good husband for one of the
bishop's older daughters.

The group was discussing the first "missionary" teams
that had already crossed the border to make converts, and
the army, which was already stronger than it had been a span
or so ago. This turned their thoughts to the existing agreement between the Spared and the demons, which was the
only obstacle preventing further action.

"Why don't we just conquer them?" Captain Trublood
asked, his face flushed with enthusiasm. "Then we can go
out of Bastion whenever we want to!"

"We used to go out whenever we wanted to," said Major Marchant, reprovingly. "On salvage trips. Then the outsiders started targeting the officers, and none of them made it back. It got to the point that no one wanted to lead salvage expeditions anymore. That's when the demons offered us a deal, and we've more or less stuck with it ever since. They give us the things we need in return for our staying peaceably within Bastion."

"But now we mean to do more than merely salvage," the captain said. "We're going to conquer the world. If we're going to do that, we have to conquer the demons first."

"There's a slight problem," murmured the doctor. "They happen to be stronger than we are."

"That's heresy!" exclaimed the captain. "The Rebel Angels are at least as strong as any demons, and they're on our side."

"While your statement is doctrinally true, young man, it is practically irrelevant," interrupted the bishop, glancing at the general. "The general has not mentioned any commitments on the part of the angels."

"What angel was it?" demanded the captain.

The doctor said, reprovingly, "The general met a being who resembled one described by Hal P'Jardas, the discoverer of Bastion. In that case, the being named herself as Tamlar of the Flames. A Lady of the Silences was also mentioned."

"Angel of the Silences," corrected the bishop.

"I've never heard about that." The young captain flushed but held his ground. "What Angel of the Silences?"

It was the doctor who answered. "It's in the Archives, Captain. Look it up under Hal P'Jardas."

The bishop murmured, "The being didn't call itself an angel. P'Jardas wasn't specific, he just thought it was."

"Or we thought he thought it was," murmured the doctor.

"How mysterious," said the captain, with a slightly sinking feeling. "A little . . . well, daunting."

"Yes, I imagine angels could be intimidating—to ordinary men," murmured the bishop, "but we Spared must remember we are set apart from ordinary men."

"But when you say we can't be specific . . . You're not implying angels are an invention?" asked the captain, in a worried voice. "A fiction?"

Major Marchant bridled, saying in a monitory tone, "Of course they're not fictional, Captain . . ."

"Except," murmured the doctor, "in the sense that all human discourse upon the supernatural must be, in a sense, fictional. Supernatural creatures are by definition unknowable, and when we start being specific about essentially unknowable beings, we risk being to some extent untruthful. So, we need to be careful in our talk, careful not to say what supernaturals are, how they are named, what they do, or why they do it, because anything we say about them is clearly an assumption. We don't even know if angels are differentiable, one from the other. They may all be aspects of the same thing."

The bishop snarled silently. Leave it to Jens Ladislav to confuse the troops! He nodded ponderously, his jowls swinging. "It's possible that all angels may be uh . . . aspects of one being whose name we don't know. But it doesn't matter. The error is . . ."

"Insubstantial?" offered the doctor, irrepressibly.

"A matter of terminology," growled the bishop. "Our Dicta teach us that The Art works by invoking angels, and we know that's true because the people who actually do magic always start out by calling on Volian or Hussara or one of the others." He turned his glare at the young captain who was somewhat losing luster in his eyes. "Does that clarify it?"

Despite being both confused and set back, Captain Trublood held his peace. The conversation returned to the question of the demons.

"I'll meet with a delegation of them," growled the general. "I'll tell them if they stay out of our way, we won't harm them. If they get in our way, we'll run over them."

The gathering broke up shortly thereafter leaving Doctor Ladislav and Captain Trublood to go down the stairs together.

"Join me for a drink?" suggested the doctor.

"I'd be honored, sir," the captain replied. They had already drunk quite enough, but the doctor had a certain look in his eye.

"Tell me, young man," he said, when they were seated and served in one of the taverns on the ground floor of the Fortress. "What do you and your fellows think about demons?"

"Think, sir? You mean, do we believe?"

"Exactly. Do you believe in demons?"

"Well," the captain turned his glass somewhat uncertainly. "We do and we don't. Some of us laugh at demons when we're here in the Fortress, but the people who are sent on missionary duty tell me they worry about demons."

"Have any of the people you've talked to ever seen a demon?"

"No, sir. We know they exist, of course, because we trade with them for chairs and bottles, and we know there are times we face away from certain places because they might be there and if we don't see them, we won't aggress because we have the non-aggression agreement with them."

The doctor attempted to look sorrowful, succeeding only from the nose up, for his lips could not evert their usual smile. "Here in Bastion a cart loses a wheel and the carter utters an aversive prayer to drive off the demon who broke it. That doesn't fix the wheel, so he calls a local carpenter who probably prays for angelic intervention. That doesn't fix the wheel, either, so he drags it off to a wheelwright, who fixes it without invoking anyone."

The captain smiled. "Oh, sir, that's just human nature. Angels won't intervene with stuff we can do ourselves. That's in the Dicta."

"Which is the point. We're getting less and less able to do things for ourselves as we get further and further away from the time when our machines were designed and built. What will happen to our population when we use up the last preserving jars, the last wheels, the last drill bits and metal cog wheels? We don't make steel, we salvage it. We don't make glass, we salvage it, that's why our windows have those tiny little panes made out of old bottles. So far we've kept going by stealing from the past. What happens when there's nothing left to steal?"

The captain said severely, "What you've just said is totally unorthodox, Colonel Doctor. If I didn't know better, I'd think you'd been touched by Scientism!"

"Ah. Scientism. One of the heresies. How would you define Scientism, Captain?"

"A heretical belief that men once did the things you've mentioned through their own efforts, without angelic assistance. The Dicta teaches us that our ancestors depended upon angels for their power, just as we will when we rediscover The Art."

"Well, I wouldn't want to be taken for a heretic, Captain, but I'm a physician, and I spend a lot of time learning how to better heal people. A few times when I've been up near the border, I've even met some people who might have been outsiders."

"Unless you're on a mission for the Regime, that's against standard rules of behavior, sir!"

"It is. Quite right. But the general has been kind enough to overlook it because there are many things we don't known about healing, and some outsiders have known about herbs and cures that really work." He sighed. "They've kept the general and the bishop alive, as they wouldn't be if I'd stuck to the standard rule of behavior."

"I'm sorry, sir, but I don't get where this conversation is going!"

"It's not necessarily going anywhere, Captain. If you're going to be my assistant, as Over Colonel Bishop Lief Laron has suggested, I need to know how you feel about things. You already know that even though standard rules of behavior say we're to have no contact with demons, we do get all our Chairs from demons."

"I know that, yes." He flushed, started to speak, thought better of it.

"So you acknowledge there are exceptions? Well, from time to time I ruminate on how our lives might be improved if we made some other slight exceptions. For instance, if we saved some of what we trade for chairs and bottles, couldn't we support a medical school? I've been told they have such schools, out there."

The captain frowned. "We wouldn't want to copy anything they have out there. Even though the general's vision told him there are Spared people out there, the general population is still mostly heretical or demonic, and they use dark arts. We can't be involved with the dark arts."

The doctor ruminated for a considerable time before asking, "Don't you think we are involved with dark arts? Some of us? Perhaps only the very trustworthy ones?"

The captain paled. "You're coming close to The Disease, sir. The Spared eschew the dark arts. I learned that in kindergarten. And we don't deal with the outside, because we won't risk the possibility of contagion."

"The Chairs come from outside."

"But the Chairs are exemplary and life-ful. We can use imports if they've been made to our order, exemplifying our purity and faith. You know that, you're a doctor!"

"I'm a doctor," agreed Jens Ladislav, "and I know we've lost a lot of ground. Our maternal death rate is high . . ."

"But not a single mother dies all at once! Every one who gets in trouble in childbirth gets bottled, doesn't she? And the baby, too."

"We're unable to do tissue transplants . . ."

"Then why do we accept organ donations," the younger man asked, his voice challenging. "Why do we go on accepting organ and limb donations from people with The Disease if we won't be able to use them? We can't use the tissue of the dead. It has to come from the living . . ." His voice trailed off and he glared at the doctor, his face very pale except for flushed bars across his cheekbones.

"Ah, you see the implications," murmured the doctor. "Well, there could be a good reason for taking the organs and not using them. Prisons are expensive and the Regime would have to pay for prisons. Cripple a man and he's less likely to be a troublemaker, and Chairs are a lot cheaper than cells, and the sinner's family pays the expenses."

"We could execute people even cheaper," the captain cried. He had had this conversation with backsliders before, but he had not thought he would encounter it in the very precincts of the Hold! "If I may say so, sir, it's startling to me that the general and the bishop will let you bend the rules just to keep themselves alive! A life is a life. Whether it has a body or a mind doesn't matter so long as it's living! The Dicta say it doesn't matter if we live one second in the womb or eighty years here in Bastion or five hundred years in a bottle wall! A life is a life!"

"A few cells," dismissed the doctor.

"One cell is a human being," said the captain, quoting Dicta furiously. "The cell is the life, and the life is the soul."

"You do believe that?" asked the doctor in an interested voice.

"We've known that since the olden days! My family traces its heritage back to a famous warrior who was martyred for shooting demon baby-killers! We Spared Ones know that every fertilized egg is a human person. We've always known that! So, if a single cell egg is a human person, then any living cell out of a person is that person. All the Angels need is the pattern to resurrect the total adult person! That's the reason pious Regimic women bottle their menstrual fluid, because it may have a single cell person in it. That's why we keep cells alive in bottles from every miscarried fetus, every stillborn child . . ."

His face was red and his voice triumphant, "On the Trek, before we had bottles, we froze everyone we could. When we got here to Bastion, we revived those frozen cells in bottles, and since we've been here, we've kept living cells from everyone so everyone will still be alive when the angels come down and un-bottle us!"

He smiled beatifically, glowing with virtue. "As a good doctor, you should know that better than me."

The doctor stared at him for a moment, then beamed at him, a sweet, radiant expression of total approval. "Of course Captain Trublood. I see now what the general meant when he recommended you to me. He said you'd stand up to testing, and he was right! You're unwavering! Good for you." He smiled again, and clapped the younger man on the shoulder.

The captain cringed as though the blow had been an angry one, his mind scurrying for what he'd said, what he'd implied. So it had all been an exercise? A test? Seemingly so, for the Colonel Doctor was paying for the drinks and bidding an acquaintance good evening. It had been a test. Nonetheless, it was remarkable how sincere the doctor had sounded.

When the doctor shook his hand and bid him good night, the captain thought fleetingly that he, James Trublood, should perhaps report the conversation they had just had. Then again . . . the doctor outranked him by a good bit. A very, very good bit. And he was being considered as the doctor's aide—well, monitor, for the bishop, either one of which was definitely a step up. No. Best not say anything about it at all. It had been a test, and he'd passed, passed with flags flying, and the best thing to do was put it out of his mind and go on with his duty.

Which, except for a noticeable glow of virtue that lasted for several days, he managed to do.

✦ 23

another exploration

Following his meeting with the captain, Doctor Ladislav went slowly up several flights of stairs to his offices, taking the time to consider what he would like to do with Captain Trublood. Since everything under that heading would be imprudent, he thought what he *could* do about Captain Trublood. The man was a perfect example of Regimic discipline, which meant he was both dangerous and useless for any medical purpose. The bishop had recommended Trublood as the doctor's aide, however, and far better the spy one knew than the spy one did not!

So. He would tell the bishop that Captain Trublood was a good man, firm as a rock on doctrinal matters. And he'd take him on as an aide, and he'd wear him down with paperwork and an endless diet of the Dicta! He let himself into the reception area of his office, and through that to his private office, the door to which he locked behind him. In his desk, under a false lining of a lower drawer, was a letter, which he took from its hiding place and put in his pocket. Finally, he unlatched and swung to one side the heavy bookcase which had been immovable until the doctor had put wheels on it to conceal the hidden tunnel he had constructed behind it, a generously cut hole through the massive Fortress wall into the adjacent and more recently built annex where the doctor's rooms were.

Prior to building his tunnel, traveling from his office to his quarters, had taken almost half an hour if done at a comfortable stroll. Jens Ladislav had searched through old plans to find living quarters that were on the other side of the wall, then he put his name on the waiting list for those particular rooms, then he made sure the current occupant was reassigned to Amen City.

His new study-cum-parlor opened onto an air shaft through a heavy grille with a sliding shutter. The doctor kept the shutter as it was, but he sawed and hinged the grille so it would open. This gave him access to an otherwise windowless pit where he could dump the broken rock from the tunnel he spent many a sweaty night in digging. When it was done, and neatly plastered, the bookcase hid the office end and a carved panel hid the opening into his bedroom. The doctor could traverse it in four paces, and the resulting convenience pleased him greatly, as it allowed an extra hour a day to be spent amusing himself.

Though convenient, the tunnel did not solve all his needs. The doctor knew that he habitually skated on the edge of what the Regime allowed. He suspected that if either the general or the bishop fell seriously ill, as well they might, considering their ages and habits, the finger of blame might well be pointed at him. If that happened, he needed an escape route.

He solved that problem by building a catwalk along the side of the air shaft. Beginning below his new "window," the doctor inserted salvaged metal rods into the mortar line below his window, allowing them to protrude far enough that a narrow plank could be wired on top. This flimsy scaffold led to the corner of the air shaft where he opened another ventilation grille into a seldom-used maintenance hall. The catwalk was invisible from everywhere but the roof, and having this bolt hole allowed him to continue in unorthodoxy without constantly fearing for his life.

He seated himself in his parlor-cum-study, took the letter from his pocket and spread it flat upon his table.

To Dr. Jens Ladislav:

> *I call to your attention one Dismé Latimer. She would
> no doubt assist you in your work.*

It was signed, "An Acquaintance of Elnith."

He had no idea who had sent the letter, which he had received over a year ago. He had heard the name for the second time from a man he had treated for the Terrors, who
said Dismé Latimer had lived in Apocanew. No one by that
name was recorded as living in Apocanew now, though the
records might be in error. Regimic records almost always
were. Orthodoxy was considered far more important than
accuracy.

Every few weeks he took the letter out and read it again,
though he had memorized it the day it arrived. It nagged at
him, with a kind of mental itch, as though something were
going to happen, and the feeling had been more intense since
the general announced his Vision. The situation with the general was becoming more and more tangled, and the tempta-
tion to pull at some loose end was becoming irresistible!

He looked at his books for inspiration. Most of them were
pre-Happening, as pre-Happening writings were not greeted
with the same suspicion as outside and therefore demonic
ones. Thus far the doctor's mind, body, and library had been
let alone, but tonight the books did not inspire him. He
needed something new, some bit of discovering or unravel-
ing to do! There had been much talk recently about the device under the Fortress, which he had not yet seen. Perhaps
that device would give him a thread to pull, and there was no
better time than the present.

He acted, as usual, on the belief that the general or the
bishop or both had someone watching his door. He wore a
wig and a pair of false eyebrows of a color not his own. Over
them he wore a hooded cloak and he put on soft slippers to
replace his boots, thus depriving himself of several inches in
height. Last, he wrapped a muffler around his lower face to
hide his chin, mouth, and nose, which were too distinctive to
change without great effort and discomfort.

Thus rendered more or less anonymous, he lighted a small lantern, opened his window, went feet first down onto his catwalk and sidled along the ledge to the air vent where he stepped through into the corridor. It was, as usual, deserted and unlit. At this hour, everyone in the Fortress was at supper in their quarters or in the refectories or in some restaurant in town. It was an excellent time for spying, and of the many routes available to him, he chose a way that was least used, zigging here, and zagging there to make the discontinuous descent without being seen. At the bottom level, he moved catlike through several storage rooms which eventually debouched upon the corridor leading to the cellar.

The cressets burning in the hallway were almost out. No door closed off the archway that confronted him. No guards barred his way. The Fortress was impregnable, so everyone said, and guards were used mostly for ceremony. The pit itself was lit only by a lantern hanging askew upon the handle of a shovel that had been thrust upright into the soil beside the ladder.

Ladislav lifted his own lantern and turned its lensed side to explore an earthen area circled by low, massive arches. He went down three or four ladder rungs to the soil level and walked all the way around it, examining the device from all sides before approaching it. The device was only partially excavated, the exposed portion resembling a frozen wave, the upper edge beginning to curl, the whole an armspan wide and tall as a man. The stone bore no carving or letters. When he laid his hand upon it, however, it hummed at him, and the hum increased suddenly so that he felt the vibration all the way to his heels.

Startled, he stepped back, caught his heel upon some protrusion, and went sprawling in a graceless tangle, madly juggling the lantern. Recovering himself, he got to his knees to examine the stumbling block, a shape too regular to be natural. Putting light and eyes closer, he made out a square corner wrapped in coarse, close-woven fabric. Muffling his excitement, he knelt down and pulled at the buried thing, heaving with all his strength, but the hard clay was too rock-like to release it. A spade was nearby, however, and he thrust it here and there around the buried thing, bearing down strongly with his foot, until the soil was broken enough that the object could be levered up. Half a dozen heaves and knocks and it came loose from the clinging soil. A box of some sort. Something rectangular, in any case. Rather heavy. Wrapped in . . . no, sewn into a fabric case, a heavy canvas, thoroughly waxed and unmistakably protective in intent.

He set it down while he fetched loose soil from among the arches to refill the hole, which he stamped upon heavily, finishing the concealment by littering the spot with loose clods of soil. When he examined the place in the lantern light he could see no difference between that spot and any other.

With a last glance over his shoulder at the enigmatic humming stone, he took the mysterious bundle, restored the spade and its pendant lantern to their previous positions, and skulked back to his rooms. Once there, he placed the bundle on his small table, fetched a sharp knife and cut the threads along one edge.

Inside was a book. The cover held no title, but the first page inside took his breath away. "The Book of Bertral concerning the Guardian Council, its members and duties. For use when the signs appear . . ."

The first page was red in color, and it carried a portrait of Tamlar of the Flames opposite a page of cryptic text. The pictured Tamlar was exactly as described by P'Jardas in the documents the doctor had read. Next came two yellow pages, Ialond of the Hammer and Aarond of the Anvil. The next three pages were gray, bearing the likenesses of three figures clad in skintight clothing over which sleeveless vestments fell from shoulder to ankle: one ashen and dull; one gleaming white; one black.

"The Three," said the heading. "Rankivian of the Spirits, Shadua of the Shroud, Yun of the Shadow."

The doctor swallowed deeply, recalling where he had last seen and used those names. The next four pages were green ones bearing pictures of Hussara, Wogalkish, Volian, and Jiralk the Joyous. The next five pages were blue. They bore pictures of Bertral of the Book, clad in brown robes, leaning on his staff, book in hand; then Camwar of the Cask in leather, carrying a great axe; then Galenor the Healer, gloved and half-veiled, eyes inscrutable; and Elnith of the Silences dressed in green veils and golden wimple.

> This is Elnith of the Silences, in whose charge are the se-crets of the heart, the longings of the soul, the quiet places of the world, the silence of great canyons, the soundless depths of the sea, the still and burning deserts, the hush of forests . . .
>
> Hers the disciplines of the anchorite, the keeper of hidden things; hers the joyous fulfillment when high on daylit peaks she shall answer for the discretion of her people. No hand of man may touch her scatheless, beware her simplicity.

The next page bore the picture of a woman with a face blue at the hairline, fading to green at the jawline, fantasti-cally clad and carrying a drum. The text across from this portrait read:

> Lady Dezmai of the Drums, in whose charge are the howls of battle, the shrieking of winds, the lumbering of great herds, the mutter and clap of storm, the tumult of waves upon stone, the cry of trumpets, the clamor of the avalanche . . .
>
> Hers the disciplines of our displeasure, hers the sorrowful severities, when upon the heart of thunder she shall answer for the intentions of her people. Take care she is not slain be-fore her time! Let him who reads take heed, for he is one destined as her Protector.

Doctor Ladislav stared at the picture for some time. Dez-mai. Which was Dismé, close enough, brought to his atten-tion here for the third time. As the doctor's father had at one time pronounced: once means nothing; twice is amusing; three times conveys intent. So here she was, intentionally, but he still had no idea who she was, or where.

Was it likely that such a person should exist? Was it likely that the Guardian Council actually existed? Why should he believe it? He turned back to the gray pages, to Rankivian, Shadua, and Yun.

"So there you are," said the doctor, stroking the page. "You're in my mother's book. I've called upon you for years, old friends, not knowing whether you were real or imagined, earthly or heavenly. And here you are." He turned his eyes to the text.

> Rankivian the Gray, of the Spirits, in whose charge are the souls of those imprisoned or held by black arts, and the souls of those who cling or delay, for his is the pattern of creation into which all patterns must go.
>
> Shadua the White, of the Shroud, in whose keeping is the realm of death to which she may go and from which she may come as she pleases, for its keys are in her hands.
>
> Yun the Black, of the Shadow, by whose hand all those locked from life may be restored or safely kept until the keys may be found.

There were other pages, each bearing a male or female figure. Angels were not mentioned. Here was Falasti of the Fishes, in silver scales, and here also was Befum the Lonely, protector of the animals.

"But I know him!" cried the doctor. "I've sat by his fire eating apples with the bears!"

He put the book down and turned away from it, eyes squeezed shut, brain whirling in furious conjecture.

"Certain things one has to take on faith," he announced to the wall. "I believe the Council is not fictional. I don't care how ridiculous the idea is. P'Jardas saw one of them, and I'd wager I know one of them personally, and I've called on The Three when healing was beyond me, and here's an account of them all."

Carefully, he rewrapped the book and hid it behind a secret panel in the back of a cupboard. He had intended to put the wrapped bundle back where he had found it, if not tonight, then the next night. Now, however, he thought it best to keep it away from . . . well, away from most everyone! Somewhat reluctantly he added the new book to his hoard.

"Let one who reads take heed," it had said.

"I shall find this Dismé," he said to the wall. "I will dig her out of her burrow, from among those who hide her. If I am to be her protector, I cannot do it unless I have her here!"

nell latimer: sleepers' business

When Nell's next waking came, current time was around her, as were sight, taste, and sound. The coffin's final effort was to speak her name, echoing it several times. Nell, Nell, knell, knell . . . Remember? You are Nell?

The robot arms propelled her gracelessly upward; a lurch left, one right, a thrust of the substance beneath back and knees, pushing her into a sitting position. Leg muscles screamed protest as she wrapped her arms around her knees and put her forehead down, eyes shut, waiting until pain and dizziness passed. Getting out of the coffin was pointless until the vertigo was over; it did no good to end up sprawled on the floor, fighting nausea and despair, wishing for the comfortable dark.

Eventually, whirling space settled until it merely tilted back and forth, like a child's rocking-horse or a rowboat on a calm lake, rock-a-by, rock-a-by. When her crusted eyelids cracked open, she focused on a littered workbench, looking just as it had been when sleep came, twenty-four teams ago. No. Not that many. She had lost count. Near the door was a work table littered with parts of a ping. That meant Raymond was already up, working. He liked fixing things.

Who else this time? Oh, Janet, damn it, still full of resentment, plus someone new to take Harry's place. Jackson. Right. Janet and Jackson would wake after her, however, not before. Nell was second waker, and she was on duty again. Four years on, ninety-six off. No, no, no! That was all wrong. There were not enough of them left for ninety-six off. Now it was—was it sixteen years this time?

A channel cleared among all these confusions. Time moved and settled, allowing her to distinguish *then* from *now*, what *had* happened from what *would* happen. Now she could "remember" that Jerry and the children were long dead. The agonized simultaneity of awakening and being put to sleep, was over. She was awake, and in a moment someone would come through the door . . .

Raymond. Bearing a tray.

"You're already sitting up!" he cried in his high, fussy voice, unchanged over the centuries, "I was going to help you up. I brought tea and cookies!"

"Cookies?" She croaked through years' dryness in her throat, years' dust in her nose, a lifetime's worth of dead skin, coating her everywhere like crumpled paper.

"Well, something like. I made them yesterday, and I heated them up, and they're not bad. Here, take a sip before you try to talk." He held the cup to her lips, two vertical wrinkles between his sleekly curved eyebrows, rosebud lips pursed, still smooth-skinned after all this time, looking half his age, concentrating fully on the task at hand.

Nell sipped. Hot. Fragrant. It burned going down, but that was momentary, as was the sudden spasm when it hit the inert gastro-pac that had kept her internal systems from collapsing during sleep. Wake-up tea had a necessary solvent in it, and the only possible course of action was to drink more, little by little. After a bit, the sensation became one of pleasure, of real stuff in her stomach, of thirst quenched, of dry throat and mouth moistened. Why they should feel so dry when they had been fluid-filled for almost a century, God only knew. One of these wakes she was going to read up on cryo-suspension.

When she could hold the cup herself, Raymond left her to it, returning to the workbench where he gathered together the parts of a ping and began fitting the carapace on it as he waited for her to get to the next stage, whatever that might be. For most wakers, there was an almost equal balance between the desire to find out what had happened during null time and a determination to go back into null time. In the latter case, intervention was needed. Chosen as first wakers were those whose curiosity outweighed their languor, as with Raymond and Nell. She sipped and nibbled and finally set the cup down, demanding, "Help me out of this thing."

He returned to lower the coffin to a height she could get out of easily. All the coffins were installed at the same level, but those who slept in them were of widely varying heights, and it rather ruined a wakening—as Nell herself had experienced during briefing sleep—to collapse in a screaming heap because the floor was six inches lower than it should be. They had lost some good people, too, people who wouldn't wake up. Some of them had wakened once or twice, or even three times, but stopped at that. The people who had stopped waking were still alive in their coffins. Perhaps, Nell thought, their waking dreams were so seductive, they could not leave them. Perhaps when a certain time came, they simply had had enough.

Whichever it might be, she sympathized with them as she teetered on wooden legs that were suddenly becoming electric flesh. Tottering was next, to the nearby chair, where she flexed and stretched. By the time she could actually feel her body, Raymond had gone away, leaving her to stagger to cubicle B of the staff quarters, where she shed her sleep suit and got into the shower. At the first touch of water, all the outer skin that was already dead when she was frozen came away in sheets, sodden wads sloshing into the drain like wet tissue paper. The disposal unit came on with a whir to break up the sludge and send it into the recycling chute. An assortment of soft, whirling brushes and a liberal application of resinous smelling foamy stuff rid her of a suddenly overwhelming, all-over itch, and clothes were ready in her stasis locker when she had dried herself: underwear, dark trousers, dark shirt, lightweight lab coat. Everything soft, not to abrade the sensitive skin. Socks, soft shoes. The back of her locker door bore pictures of Michelle and Tony before the Happening. Of Tony's great granddaughter, Texy, a hundred years later, along with her four brothers and two sisters. Of assorted great to the nth grandchildren in century three, and more in century four. She had a folder thick with them. Nell was lucky in that regard. Raymond had been, as they used to say, a GASP, that is, gay and sans progeny, though he thought he had located a nephew line, somewhere south. It had become a hobby to keep track of descendants, to get ping pictures and make notes. Nell had descendants among the Spared Ones, too, and Bastion lay just over the mountain from the redoubt.

Suddenly ravenously hungry, she made her way to the kitchen, where Raymond was already poised at the cooker.

"Better?" he asked, plopping an aromatic bowl of soup onto the table before her.

"Um," she remarked, already busy with the spoon. "I forget who we're replacing?"

"Bonheur, Markle, Stetson, and John Third Jones. Blaine Markle woke me and stayed up a couple of days to get me current."

"On what?"

"Everything. The generators were out, said Blaine, because we had no fuel . . ."

"What did he mean we had no . . ." she cried.

He held up his hand, forestalling her. ". . . and it wasn't worth trying to fix it, said Blaine in a just-shoot-me-and-get-it-over-with voice, because it was inevitable that things would run out. Supplies were low, said Blaine. The embryos had spoiled, said Blaine. Everything was finite. Cleanliness. Order. Beauty. Time. Fuel. He woke a melancholy man."

"What happened to him? He used to be cheery?"

"Something happened to him during his wakening. He called it the horrors. He told me it wasn't like a regular dream, because when he was finally completely awake, he could remember every bit of it. People dying all around him. Monsters coming out of the shrubbery, up out of the earth, infecting people he loved, and he had to stand there, watching them die horribly."

"He's dreaming about the Bitch hitting earth!"

"Oh, very definitely, and not just him, apparently. His dream was odd enough to make him curious, and he started asking the pings to look for the same kind of thing outside. On the surface they call it the Terrors. Not everybody gets it. It doesn't kill anyone, though some of those who have it wake up fighting, which may be fatal for anyone within reach."

"How long had he known about this?"

"Too long. He didn't even tell me until I dragged it out of him."

"What did you do?"

"Put sedatives in the sleep juice, hoping that would stop his nightmares. Then I cleaned out the store room so I could see what we had, found the parts for the generator, pulled the pump out of tank number nine and fixed it, switched it over to tank number ten, and got the generator going again. Blaine had let all the chickens die. I took a few dozen eggs from deep storage and put them in the incubator to start a new flock."

She smiled into the teacup he'd filled from the pot on the stove. "And it took you . . . how long?"

"Two days," he said grumpily. "Blaine could perfectly well have done it, if he hadn't been completely out of it."

She stopped sipping, remembering something Raymond had said. "What did he mean, the embryos had spoiled?"

Raymond frowned at the floor. "Somewhere along the line, some one or several of our colleagues emptied the gamete storage. It's been obvious since early on that there are plenty of survivors, so we haven't paid much attention to the storage. The last routine check I could find recorded was over ninety years ago. I'm assuming there was spoilage, and whoever noticed it just did what was necessary. Blaine himself only noticed the monitor lights were off because they were near the generator cutout."

She tried to decide how she felt. Rather as she had felt when she'd miscarried that time, between Michy and Tony.

A pang, not quite grief but almost. All those little possibilities, gone. "Have you searched the log?"

"Well of course. Nothing under gametes, wombs, embryos, ova, sperm; nothing under the storage bay number or the monitor number; nothing under any other remotely pertinent designator I could come up with. I've done everything but a line-by-line read through of the last century, because if it was logged at all, which it might not have been, whoever logged it managed to do it without using any pertinent vocabulary whatsoever!"

"So what else has happened out there?" She gestured, her fingers encompassing the world outside.

"Were the Spared Ones sending out missionaries-cum-spies-cum-bottling teams when we were awake last?"

"No! They were staying at home, minding their own business, and keeping their covenants with the demons."

"Well, they've got some new bone in their craw. They've got teams fanning out putting in time as missionary-spy-bottlers. From the conversation we've picked up, it seems that General Gowl recently received a visitation from a Rebel Angel who told the general to add as many to the Spared as possible by forcibly converting anyone convertible. They've got muggers out there, knocking passers-by on the heads, sneaking into rooms where people are sick or dying and making off with bits and pieces of them."

"That's against their religion! Their Dicta said that everyone who's Spared is already in Bastion!"

Raymond sat down opposite her, swirling tea in his half-empty cup. "That's what they used to believe. Their belief now includes conquest and ruling the world. It also includes bottling a lot of their own people for no particular reason except that they're considered supernumerary."

"Are they still searching for magic?"

"I hate to tell you, Nell, but they've probably found it, or something like it. God knows how long they've had it, but what's going on is serious stuff. Raising the dead. Making zombie workers. No more sweet little fire-starting spells, now they're casting curses on people."

She gaped at him. "You're not saying it works? How?"

"Wouldn't we love to know. Crazy part is, along with the . . . well, what would you call it? Black magic? Along with that, there's a good deal of innocent stuff. Real levitators. Real firestarters. Some pretty good clairvoyants. Plus a guy who evokes animals out of thin air."

"You're joking!"

"Why would I joke about it? It's real enough. Guy they call Befun the Lonely. He conjures up creatures that look like animals, act like animals, eat and excrete like animals. When was the last time you saw a tiger? Or an elephant? We now have tigers and elephants, small ones, because the tropical rain forest they live in is where part of Texas used to be, and it isn't all that big. Whether it's hypnotism, telekinesis, manifestation, or translocation, we don't know. And we didn't do it. Hell, we couldn't do it."

"We had animal embryos. Including wild animals."

"I know, but everything spoiled, I just told you."

"Then who . . . how . . . ?"

"For all we know, he draws them from some transdimensional world. *Quien sabe.* Oh, one more thing. The visitor on top of the world has become a traveler."

"It's what?" she cried, disbelieving. "The Bitch part moved? And that wasn't at the top of your list?"

"Well, who knows." He tipped his hand: mebbe, mebbe not. "It's moved a hell of a way from the Arctic Circle. Right now it's oozing ashore about where Arizona used to be. South of Henceforth."

"Henceforth is still there?"

"The same cities as when you went to sleep last. Four along the New West Coast, north to south, Mungria, Secours, New Salt Lake, and Henceforth. Several dozen small communities in the Sierra Madre Islands. North of the Yellowstone Sea, a kingdom called Everday, quite civilized."

"And east of us, New Kansas and New Chicago."

"Both still dictatorships, but not particularly repressive as we would understand repression from our own time. More on the Singapore model. Traffic back and forth is fairly constant. Around Bastion the farms and ranches are getting more numerous, people who've moved over the hills. And there's a survivor group we didn't know about, a technological enclave, maybe scientific as well, a good way south of Bastion. Place called Chasm. They're hidden and secretive, but during the last decade the pings have spotted a couple of gateway trading communities out in the open. Evidently they've been there all along, but we didn't have any pings in that area, never thought to send any until we overheard talk about the place."

"Anything else?"

"Travelers have spotted a kind of fortress about midway between here and Henceforth, out on the plains. We can't get a ping near it, and all we know about it is that it wasn't there ten years ago. For some reason, the wagoneers call it Goldland."

"Could it be another religious bunch, like Bastion?"

"We don't know. Goldland is just what the passing wagoneers call it. It could be called something else."

She mused for a moment. "I guess the place you call Chasm answers the question about where the demons get their trade technology."

He smiled. "Probably."

"They still wearing those crazy horns?"

"They are, and we still don't know why. And we're picking up that eerie fog in other places than Bastion, now. Last team said it's moved into the countryside, and now it's beginning to show up in the nearer towns. Nobody has a clue as to what it is. It almost acts like something living, but when a ping gets close, nothing!"

"Couldn't it be some function of the monster on top of the world? Excuse me, monster who used to be on top of the world?"

He took his cup and her bowl to the sterilizer, staring into the screen that substituted for a window. A view of trees, mountains, piled white clouds with stormy bottoms. "Anything could be some function of that. We know nothing, less than nothing about it."

She sighed and rubbed her neck. "Anything from the Mars colony?"

"Moon base is still in touch with them, and they have a very slightly increasing population. Moon base itself is still teetering. And that's it." His tone of voice spoke of finality.

"Which means the human race has at least two chances to survive, maybe three, so what are we still in here for?"

He shrugged again. "We've pretty much done what we were supposed to do. Thanks to the stuff sent back by the moon team, before they left for Mars, we've been able to make accurate maps of the current surface of the earth. Three or four teams back, we printed the maps, showing the terrain, rivers, mountains and so forth. What survived seems to be anything that was a thousand feet above sea level pre-Happening. That means scattered islands where Australia and New Zealand, Indonesia and the Philippines used to be. Anyhow, we've made thousands of map copies available to peddlers and merchants and caravan leaders."

"What cover did you use?"

"As we agreed, we've printed 'Council of Guardians' at the bottom, to explain who made them."

"Right," she said, distractedly. "I'd forgotten about the 'Council of Guardians.' "

"That's our role, Nell. Can't forget our role. We haven't had anyone willing to play Allipto Gomator for eight years! Time you got back into your seeress's garb."

"Time we got out of this tomb into the fresh air," she said.

"You still want to emerge," he said in a defeated tone. "Don't you?"

"I've argued for it the past two wakings," she snarled, angrily. "I would like to meet my many-greats grandchildren."

He sighed and patted her shoulder. "Why don't we put off talking about that until the others are awake?"

"How many others, Raymond?"

"Two in this shift."

"I didn't mean just this shift, Ray. Why not wake everyone? Why go on with this?"

He stared at her, his face pale. "If we wake everyone, there'll be twelve of us, Nell. Just twelve."

She gasped. That was half as many as there had been last time she'd been awake. "My friend? Alan Block."

"He's still alive and waking."

"We didn't last as long as they thought we would, did we?"

"Long enough," he said, patting her shoulder. "We lasted long enough.

✦ 25

the fate of an inclusionist

When Rashel first took over the Faience it had been piled high with Inclusionist artifacts, which she had immediately started weeding out, including many things that Ayward had been responsible for collecting. Whenever Ayward and Rashel were together, they argued furiously about her actions.

"The painting you're talking about shows a sorcerer with his magical staff, summoning the power of the light," Ayward cried dramatically.

Rashel retorted, "It's what they used to call art, yes, but it's not part of The Inexplicable Arts. This painting is simply a piece of Durable Art! It portrays a man leaning on a rake or hoe, staring into the sunset. It's actually included in an encyclopedia of artworks dating before the Happening. You'll find it in the C of S library."

"The College of Sorcery had already declared it part of the Canon of Arcana, Rashel. It was on my Master List."

"No one refers to your old master list anymore, and I'm certainly not going to call it to their attention."

Ayward turned white. "Once something is declared part of the Canon, your job should be to find out its meaning."

"Once something is *mistakenly* declared part of the Canon of Arcana, it is my job to exclude it. Calling this simple old painting a part of the Canon destroys the integrity of The Art. Can't you see that?"

"Better a false inclusion than a false exclusion!" he cried.

"Dicta before personality! That's what the Bureau says!"

"Frash what the Bureau says."

"Hush," she sneered. "Someone might be listening."

Someone was usually listening, at the time and afterward, when Ayward complained to her.

"Everything from the time of the great mages is magical, Dis. People moved without labor, brought forth food without toil, built great structures with The Art. Ah, Dismé, I long for that time."

His longing did not impress her as once it might have done. Whatever Ayward longed for was no longer Dismé's concern, still less his marital dispute about the painting. There was nothing unusual about Ayward quarreling with Rashel, except that this was the last quarrel they would have.

A day later, three men from the Bureau of Happiness and Enlightenment came to arrest Ayward Gazane on suspicion of having The Disease. A few days later Rashel called Dismé and Gayla into the study and told them that Ayward had been found guilty and had been sentenced to body-part donation and chairing.

"He's in a Chair?" breathed Gayla.

"He's been sent to the donor center and they've taken some parts and put him in a Chair, yes. But he's quite mobile, really." She turned hot eyes on Dismé. "Stop that crying, Dismé! Ayward is my husband, not yours. Save your tears for your own family, if you're ever lucky enough to have one!"

Dismé's tears came from her revulsion at the gloating pleasure she had heard in Rashel's voice. Revulsion was also what she felt when she first visited Ayward. He was crouched in the Chair, only visible from the waist up, his head bent over so that he peered into his lap, his left arm and hand buried inside the Chair. She spoke to him, but he did not answer, though she bent near to listen, for it was hard to be heard or to hear over the constant noises the Chair made, bubbling and wheeping and an occasional shrill keening, like wind through stiff grass. Arnole's Chair had been almost silent, and Dismé found the noise of this one irritating past endurance, as though it had been designed to drive Ayward to despair.

She went to the barn and sat looking at the trees. Ouphs came out of the forest to settle on the glass towers, but she did not even glance in their direction. Oh, if she had only gone away when Arnole said to go. Now she was trapped! Rashel despised Ayward, and Gayla only irritated him. There was no one else here who was in the least sympathetic, and she could not in good conscience abandon him!

Arrangements for Ayward had been made by Rashel. A suite of rooms in the unused north wing of the Conservator's house was opened up and furnished for Ayward and his young attendant, Owen Toadlast, assigned here to expiate some minor crime through service to the Office of Chair Support. Though Dismé steeled herself to visit Ayward often, not just at the required Cheerful and Supportive visits of the whole family, he did not speak to her or to anyone. Dismé herself had become so laconic since Arnole's disappearance that she had to make a conscious effort to talk if not with Ayward, at least at him. Each day she made a mental list of ordinary topics, but even this superficial chit-chat fell into an abyss of silence, leaving her virtually mute at all other times.

Rashel noticed, of course. "Cat got your tongue, Dismé?" she asked, in her usual badgering manner. "What's the matter with you. Not feeling well?"

"I'm fine, Rashel. Just thinking about . . ." Dismé went down the list of unexceptionable things she could be thinking about. Schoolwork. The weather. What they were having for dinner, or ". . . things I have to do for school."

Recently added to the students in Dismé's class was a preadolescent girl student whose mother worked at Faience. The girl's record was much decorated with gold stars for, among other things, "Correcting other students' false ideas." Her name was Lettyne Leek, and she seemed determined to catch Dismé dispensing "false ideas" or die trying. One day in class dear Gustaf rose to his feet with an expression of wonder, gestured broadly with one hand, cried *Hail Tamlar, let there be fire*, and set his desk ablaze. Dismé bit her lip to keep from crying out, and her eyes went at once to Lettyne. Oh, if only Gustaf had not done it in public, where people could *see* him! The teacher was already bearing down on him, and Lettyne, her face screwed into righteous hauteur, was busy making a note of the time and the place and the names of all those who had been witnesses. Oh, poor boy! Now he was in for it!

Though Gustaf had always behaved in exemplary fashion, and though the spell had been mentioned the day previously in enchantments class, nonetheless, the BHE was summoned to take him away to Apocanew, keeping him overnight for interrogation. When he returned to school the next day, he was no longer able to start a fire with a gesture.

"They didn't ask me to explain how I did it," he whispered to Dismé. "They just asked about the Dicta, over and over, and did I believe in the Dicta, and didn't I know I was supposed to have a permit. Then they asked about enchantments, didn't I know what the necessary elements of enchantments were, and then they said set fire to something, and I was thinking about needing the permit and the necessary elements and I couldn't remember how I did it."

"You didn't think about it the first time," she said.

"No," he replied in a puzzled voice. "It just chimed in my head like a bell, and I did it without thinking."

She gave him a long and measuring look and dropped her voice to a whisper. "Gustaf, if you will go into quiet places, by yourself, it may be you will hear that chime again. But if you hear it when others are around, you must ask it to wait until you are alone."

He looked at her for a moment in puzzlement, then suddenly nodded in understanding. "It doesn't come from what we learn here, does it?"

She shook her head.

He smiled a secret smile. "It comes from somewhere else. Somewhere better."

During her visit to Ayward that night, Dismé spoke of

Gustaf's fire-starting, and Lettyne's continual effrontery. "The girl is trying to catch me doing or saying something wrong," she concluded. "She's ready to pounce."

To her amazement, she heard Ayward's gravelly whisper, "Anything reflecting on you would reflect on Rashel. You might be wise to mention all this to Rashel if the opportunity presents itself."

She put her hand on his cheek and cried, "Oh, Ayward, I'm so glad you're talking! I've been so concerned about you . . ."

"Shh, Dis. Talking got me into this . . ." he pounded the arm of the Chair with his right hand, though softly. "I won't talk to anyone but you and Owen." He laughed, a painful, rasping laugh that hurt her ears. "I wish this damned rain would stop. Day after day."

The rain was becoming a trial for them all. The children were depressed and moody, each day's lessons were like all those before, the hours passed like endless plockutta. At the Caigo Faience, Rashel worked even longer hours than usual, and when she made the required Cheerful and Supportive visits to Ayward's quarters, she expounded to him in a exalted, mysterious voice about the device that had been discovered under the fortress at Strong Hold.

"A momentous discovery," she said. "Perhaps the very fountainhead of the dark canon!"

Rashel was deeply involved in the project, but Ayward was against it, or against her doing it, as he wrote to her in dozens of scribbled notes.

"What is this mysterious thing?" Dismé asked him. "Rashel seems very involved in it."

"Mysterious," he snorted. "I suppose it is. The Regime decided to add a dungeon or some fool thing under the Fortress, and they've dug up a device. Rashel has been given a look at it. She's shown me a drawing, and the thing is obviously sorcerous, I told her to check the Archives for the P'Jardas account. You wouldn't know about that . . ."

She was offended by this offhand assumption. "As a matter of fact, Arnole told me about Hal P'Jardas and his fiery woman. What has that to do with this thing they've found?"

"It has to do with a letter P'Jardas sent to the Regime not long before he was bottled. He said he'd been going through his old notes, and he believed the mound where the Fortress was built was the same one the fiery spirit emerged from."

"So anything in that mound . . ."

"Anything in or on the mound would be contaminated by sorcery even if not itself magical. They've found this pillar thing inside the mound. According to P'Jardas's account, there were pillars all over the mound. Arnole told me those were taken away when the fortress was first built; the archives have records of the move. Someone should try to find them."

"But if the thing is sorcerous, shouldn't it be examined?"

"It's dangerous," he cried. "But when I tell Rashel so, she doesn't listen. If someone else had told her about the P'Jardas account, she might have paid attention."

Rashel announced loudly over dinner that there was concern among people in the Regime that Ayward was unrepentant. If that were true, come spring he might be sentenced to a second Chair!

"No," said Gayla, giving her a horrified look. "Oh, no, Rashel. Don't. Enough is enough. He couldn't . . . he couldn't stand that!"

"Well," said Rashel in a severe tone. "It isn't my decision, Gayla. Ayward knows the consequences of behavior as well as I do!"

Dismé expressed her anger at Gayla. "She married him! Doesn't she have any sympathy for him at all?"

"She's required to be cheerful and supportive, Dismé, but not sympathetic," Gayla said in a bitter voice. "Not with Ayward's father gone the way he did. If Rashel were sympathetic and then Ayward went, eyebrows would be raised, questions asked. Had she been permissive? Had Owen not done his job well? Had the rest of us, including you, Dismé, made all their required visits during which we were optimistic, cheerful, and kindly? It's almost always the family's fault if people leave. If they are well-treated, people do not leave their loved ones."

Dismé had searched Ayward's haggard face too often to believe such sentimental blather. "He hasn't the strength to love anyone," she said in an angry whisper. "It takes all his strength just to be awake every day until the Chair puts him to sleep at night. They've taken everything from him. His work . . ."

"Whatever that amounted to."

"You believe Ayward was mistaken? About Inclusionism?"

Gayla threw up her hands with an explosion of hectic laughter. "Oh, for heaven's sake, child. You know Ayward! He can't decide between a boiled egg or a fried one for his breakfast. You've seen him dither for an hour over the choice of what color shirt to wear! Coming up with Inclusionism saved him from ever having to make up his mind, that's all!"

Dismé flushed with instant humiliation. Though she had never thought of Ayward in this way, she knew it to be true the moment it was said. Who should have known it better than she? Even so, she had to warn Ayward about what Rashel had said, though she waited until Rashel went on a trip that would keep her away for several days.

Ayward didn't reply for a long time. "Did she say when?"

"She said this spring, Ayward."

"Poor Rashel," he said. "Ah, poor Rashel. So unhappy. So embittered. So willing to destroy anyone to get her way, without even knowing what her way is. I believe that when your father did what he did, and your brother disappeared, she felt betrayed. All her life since has been taking vengeance against their leaving her . . ."

"What do you mean, betrayed? What do you mean, did what he did?"

"Well, taking his own life that way. Rashel said . . ."

Dismé said in angry astonishment, "How can you think that, Ayward? Father didn't . . ."

He interrupted her. "Hush, my dear. We won't worry about it now."

Dismé's fury drove her out of the house. The rains had given way to an interlude of mist, and she felt as though the outward mist permeated her as well. Rashel had told Ayward that Val Latimer had killed himself! Why would Rashel have said such a thing? Was it only to build yet another drama around herself? To make her life more interesting and vital? Poor child, her dear, dear friends would say. Poor child. Look at what she's had to bear!

She found herself running along the path that led to the glass towers, almost invisible in the light rain. As she approached the tallest of them, she realized she had literally walked into a great pool of ouphs who swirled and eddied all around her.

"Listen." The smell of decay. The feel of slime on her lips.

"Please." Roses, their odor, the brush of their petals.

"Make them . . . no, make them . . . no, something else." Cold, the smell of smoke.

"Wrong, all wrong." Sickness, aching, feculent reek.

"Break . . . all . . . break them . . . all . . . please." Ice. Old Ice.

She felt a wave of frustration, as though all around her, minds tried to find words and move tongues with all the linkages missing. Beings trying to speak, without anything to speak with, or of.

"Oh, let go, let go, let go on, lost here"

"Lost here"

"Lost"

The ouphs poured up the tower, covering it, and the voices washed around her, through her, for the first time creating a sensible and coordinated shout.

"You . . . must help . . . only one . . . help us . . . not leave us like . . . are . . ."

When they went away she knelt on the ground, gasping for breath through an uncontrollable weeping. That last voice. It had been so familiar. So very familiar. A long time ago, hadn't she decided to do something? Some particular thing . . .

She found herself at the bottle wall, at its end, where the

family bottles had been put when they arrived at Faience. She had the old bucket, her drum, in her hands. A shallow stream was overflowing from the river, draining away under the wall where Val Latimer's bottle had been installed. She had resolved long, long ago to do this. Why had it taken her this long? It could perfectly well be washed out by this stream, perfectly well destroyed.

She struck her drum sharply, on its side, then again, then again. She summoned Roarer with her whole heart and sang as she drummed again. Her voice and hands together struck like lightning. A bottle cracked, then another. She crouched and drummed a fury, hearing Roarer's rampage, hearing the bottles crack, the crash and tinkle of their shattering, the slosh and gurgle of what had been inside.

She came to herself sitting back on her heels.

"Thank . . . blessing . . . Good child . . ." The feeling of an entity retreating, fading, vanishing, lost in a swell of fog:

"All, all, all, all, please. Rest, rest. All, all. Now . . ."

She could not destroy them all. The Regime would know she had done it. She could only . . .

Furiously she ran to the old shed near the barn where there was a pile of rusty tools including an old shovel, the handle splintering beneath her hand. Upstream, where the river was overflowing to make the slender stream beneath the bottle wall, she dug furiously into the bank to make the flow increase, digging and digging until she could dig no more. Perhaps the flood would be a large one. Perhaps it would do a lot of damage.

She washed the shovel and put it back where she had found it. She washed the mud from her own legs and arms. It was a long time before she could get back to the house. Later she went to the center of the maze and stood before the enigmatic black statue there, believing for a moment that it had actually turned its head to listen. Then it was as before, and she was still alone. There was no one at all she could talk to about this.

Rashel returned from her trip just after the worst of the flood. The rain had gone on for so long that the rivers overflowed, the torrent flooding two sections of the arboretum, the middle of the east garden, a stretch of the yew hedge that made up the southernmost aisle of the great maze, and a great length of the pilgrims' walk along the bottle wall together with a huge section of the wall itself, which left broken bottles and exposed nutrient pipes that leaked and stank. By the time anyone could get to it, the contents were too far gone to re-bottle.

Ayward complained of the odor, though he said it came from him.

He wrote, "I am drowning in my own stink, Rashel. The stench of what remains of my body, rotting."

"Nonsense," Rashel said. "Owen keeps you beautifully clean, Ayward. It's the bottle wall you smell."

It wasn't the bottle wall. It was a sad smell peculiar to Ayward's rooms that reminded Dismé of the ouphs and the foggy evening at the beginning of the flood. This was an episode which she wished to keep out of her thoughts, just in case someone asked. The damage to the Great Maze, however, drew her full attention. The news that some of the southern edge had washed out sent her running to survey the damage from the inside.

It was true. Midway along the boundary hedge, which was even taller and thicker than those inside the maze, a several-paces-long stretch of the carefully squared yews had disappeared. As she gaped at this vacancy, she heard a workman outside the maze: "The damn thing has no bottom!" She held her breath to listen, at first thinking he was joking, but soon it was clear: they honestly couldn't find a bottom with the tools at hand.

Rashel soon joined the men outside and directed that a barrier must be placed around the hole at once. This occasioned some confusion. The men could not barricade the inside of the hole from the outside of the maze, for the hedges pressed too closely on either side of the hole, and they could not barricade it from the inside, for they did not know how to get there.

Waiting until Rashel was not among them, Dismé approached the hole from inside, calling to the workmen. "Can you toss the parts in here? I'll set them up for you."

The barricades weren't heavy. One of the husky workmen pitched them across the hole, and Dismé arranged them, quickly, murmuring to the workman that she was not supposed to be in the maze, and she would appreciate his not mentioning it to Rashel. When the workmen left, she crawled to the edge of the hole—prudently anchoring one arm around the nearest trunks that were still in place—to lie prone, peering down.

Below her was a tangle of interwoven roots from which the missing section of hedge dangled upside down. Beyond that was a general darkness, but far down was a glimmer, like sunlight reflected from water. She searched for something she could drop into the hole and found a stone-littered gap at the bottom of the hedge across from it, the customary trail of some small animal, perhaps. Dismé picked up several of the smaller stones and dropped them, one by one, counting until she heard the plop. The count was the same as from the cupola of the museum tower to the bottom of the air shaft, six flights of stairs above the museum, which was itself four stories high.

She started to rise, then froze in place. From below she heard voices: the hollow, reverberating sounds of people talking in cavernous space. No one had mentioned hearing voices! She huddled down once more, trying to make out words and phrases, thinking how much this would interest Ayward while remaining naively unaware of how intensely interesting it actually was. The return of the workmen from their lunch sent her scurrying back to the Conservator's House.

Though she could tell the effort pained Ayward, he pulled his head up and looked her in the eyes.

"I've been to see the hole in the Maze. They've set up barricades around it, but I went in from the inside to see it."

"The statues still tell you the way."

"Of course they do. That's not the important thing. There were voices, Ayward! Coming up from the hole!"

He kept his head up, his jaw tight with effort as he concentrated on hearing her over the Chair noises. "Voices?" he cried. "Saying what?"

"I don't know what they were saying. It was too echoey. I couldn't hear that clearly."

"How . . . how big is this hole?" he asked.

"Oh, big. As big as this carpet," she said, indicating the one his Chair sat upon, two meters by three, perhaps less. "But it's at the far end of the maze. You can actually look out through the hole in the hedge and see the pasture, all the way down to Fels canyon. I could see water at the bottom of the hole, so I dropped a rock into it and listened for the splash. It's about as far down as from the top of the museum tower."

His eyes were suddenly fiery, as though he had a fever, and he stared across her shoulder for what seemed to be a very long time before whispering urgently, his eyes darting to be sure they were unobserved. "Dismé, early in the morning, as early as you can, listen again."

"And come tell you if I hear anything?"

"Ah . . . Oh, yes. Come tell me immediately if you hear anything."

She looked at him worriedly.

"Please," he stroked her fingers with his one usable hand. "Promise, Dismé. It's . . . it's terribly important to me."

She discerned a peculiar inflection in his voice, a famished yearning that was abhorrently intimate, like being touched by something voracious and engulfing. She had heard a hint of something similar in Arnole's voice once in a great while, a longing to be elsewhere . . .

And Arnole had gone. She remembered everything about it. Only demons could make someone disappear like that. Demons lived underground, the Dicta said so. Now, here was Ayward, speaking in the same way Arnole had sometimes spoken, wanting to know what the underground voices were saying! My fault, Dismé accused herself. My fault. I shouldn't have told him about them.

"Dismé!" he cried.

She gulped. "If it's important to you, I'll do it, Ayward. Early tomorrow morning, I promise."

"It is important. It could be . . . terribly important."

Leaving him, she tried to think of something else that would interest him more. Appallingly, until this hole was mentioned, nothing had interested him at all. This was the first time in ages he'd asked her to do anything for him, and it was such a small thing, taking little if any effort. Probably he was just curious, she told herself. That was natural. She, herself, was curious. She was making too much of the matter. How could it possibly do any harm?

✦ 26

another disappearance

Dismé kept watch on the maze all afternoon. Men had arrived who said the maze had been planted over limestone that had been eaten away by seeping water to leave a thin, unsupported shell. The flood had cut through it. The engineers drilled all around the hole, during the afternoon, looking for thicker rock from which they could bridge the gulf. Dismé, hiding nearby, heard Rashel's voice, the anger barely suppressed.

"Please estimate the cost of your repairs, Engineer. We will decide what to do when we are sure what our options are."

The engineers did not mention hearing voices, which, Dismé thought, meant the voices were not always there. If she was to be sure of hearing them, she would need to listen at various times of the day and evening, starting tonight. She would have far more privacy when everyone else was asleep.

Once the moon had risen, she went out her window and into the maze, running swiftly, her slippered feet silent on the bark-strewn paths. When she came to the barrier she was shocked into immobility by rumbling male voices she had not expected. Men. From outside or inside, she couldn't be sure.

In a panic she turned toward the narrow stone-littered gap she had found earlier in the day, flinging herself down and wriggling backwards as the rugged yew trunks tore at her with spiny twigs and serrated bark. She was bloodied but well-hidden beneath the shadowed bulk of the hedge when the men arrived, at the outside barrier.

Covering her face with her hands and peeking between her fingers Dismé made out the furtive, amber glow of a lantern with Rashel's pale face seeming to float within it. The two men were heavy, bearded, familiar: both Turnaways, members of the Committee on Inexplicable Arts who had visited Rashel at the house in Apocanew on several occasions.

"The engineers tell me they are stretched thin," said Rashel in an ingratiating voice. "We're all aware of the manpower shortage, of course. With only a few hundred thousand of us here in Bastion, we aren't enough to do everything needing doing."

"Nonetheless, the terms of the agreement are clear, Madam," one of them muttered, shaking his head so that his loose jowls flapped from side to side. "The Office of Conservation and Restoration, of which you are Conservator, is charged with maintaining the grounds as well as the buildings. The Great Maze is part of the grounds. Additionally, some believe Caigo Faience discovered an arcane significance in the pattern of the maze."

The other murmured, "May we say, Madam, that until now you have done an exemplary job of maintaining the place, and you have done so at modest cost. We applaud your stewardship, but even though it could be done cheaply, fencing off this section of the maze would not be permissible. Until the maze is formally removed from the Canon, it must be preserved as it is. If Inexplicable Arts is to retain usage of the place, the maze has to be repaired."

Rashel said firmly, "Since doing so within my budget will require me to let essential employees go, I thought, perhaps, that my cooperation with the Regime had been such that a small, very small exception might be made . . ."

The two Turnaways shared a look over Rashel's head, and one remarked in a less agreeable voice, "Your cooperation has been no greater than we expect of every citizen."

"He is my husband," she replied slowly, with some dismay. "Some women might not have been so conscientious."

The other Turnaway laughed shortly. "He is guilty of The Disease. The fact that you denounced him does not demonstrate superior adherence to the Dicta. We expect such action."

"Besides," said the first. "We know you are not fond of him. No more than you were of his father, whom you also denounced. There was in both cases, perhaps, a certain element of self-interest? As for service to the Regime, you are being well-paid for that. Few citizens live as well as you are living. And there is the matter of the *new discovery*. You would not want to miss that opportunity . . ."

"I have earned my place," she cried.

"You have earned your place? Ha ha. Well, perhaps in a sense you have. *Someone* no doubt thinks so."

Even in the amber glow, Dismé could see the flush of fury on Rashel's face, the quivering muscles, the clenched hands brought slowly, slowly under command until at last she turned away, making a half bow and uttering a few diplomatic words of apology for her presumptuousness. She led the men back the way they had come, and Dismé remained where she was, waiting for their voices to fade as their words still filled her mind. Rashel had denounced . . . Rashel had accused . . . not because they had any disease, but because Rashel wanted them, him . . . what? Gone? Dead?

Dismé trembled, furious tears sheeting her face, and deep within her, Roarer stirred. She could smell blood. Through the thunder in her ears, she could still hear the murmur of voices, retreating . . . only to be replaced by another sound, a shrilling insect voice, a mechanical keening that cut through the shrubbery like a blade. Not loud, not threatening, almost ordinary, yet it sent her into panic, her legs frantically pulling her back, toes digging in like mattocks, knees thrusting, hands and arms pushing her away from that sound through the scratchy bulk of the monstrously thick hedge, squeezing her body into impossible angles among the multiple trunks and rasping twigs, knife-edged stubs of pruned branches jabbing into her flesh, emerging breathless on the far side, bleeding from a dozen wounds. She was prickled all over with gooseflesh, sweat standing in frigid beads on her face and chest, chilled through by a deep well of horror she had not known was there.

On the far side of the hedge, the shrilling, bubbling, creaking sound continued while she remained frozen, lying with her bleeding face buried in her arms, perfectly still, scarcely breathing. The shrill creaking was replaced by the clunk of moving wood, the scrape of one board on another. Then there was only a long whisper and a cry which might have been animal or bird or even something mechanical shrieking wordlessly to its responding echo.

Dismé rose and crept down the mossy lane, slowly, very slowly. She would not be heard, not be seen, not be perceived, no one could ever know she was here, oh no. No, no, get home, make up a story, make it watertight for no one, no one must ever know she was here.

Something was rising inside her, a pressure that closed her throat and made the hedges around her spin dizzily. She gulped at the bubble, standing quite still as she tried unsuccessfully to swallow it, eyes unfocused, uncertain of what this was, what this feeling could possibly be. And then it burst, engulfing her, overwhelming her, almost lifting her on its wave.

Relief. Solace.

She stood blindly, timelessly adrift in a comfort so profound as to approach ecstasy. The euphoria did not last long. Within moments she sagged to her knees in angry self-accusation. How despicable! How contemptible! To feel joy at such a time and for such a reason!

Or for no reason! She didn't know what had happened! She was assuming, and her assumptions might well be wrong, might well be none of her business. If she had been less inquisitive, she would not have been here at all. It had nothing to do with her. She should leave it alone! And feel, feel . . . nothing. Feel nothing at all. Later she would know what was an appropriate feeling. Sadness.

Perhaps melancholy. Even grief, but not this outpouring of warm joy . . .

She ran, as from some barely discernable monster made more terrible by her recognition of it. The maze fled behind her, the museum, the woods, she went up the trellis like a squirrel, crossed the roof, stumbled through her open window and collapsed onto the bed, pulling pillows and blankets toward her, burying herself in them, wrapping herself tightly, quoting silly poems to herself, things she and Arnole had made up to amuse themselves, over and over, a litany of desperation. She didn't know anything had happened! She had heard noises, that was all! Words jingled in her head, the little tune that carried them repeating and repeating until she was lost in a dizzy buzzing that led into an exhausted sleep.

Despite the self-hatred that had possessed her, when she woke, well before dawn, her first feeling was one of peace and joy. Somewhere in the night she had come upon a gladness. What was it? What had happened? She hunted for it, coming upon it at last like a dead rat on a dinner plate. She couldn't be joyous, because she didn't know. She didn't know anything!

But she had made a promise. No matter what had happened or not happened or might have happened, she still had to keep her promise! Staggering from bed, she confronted a scabbed and battered image still wearing the trousers and torn shirt that had failed to protect her bloodied face or arms. The trousers were old ones of Michael's. She had rescued them from the rubbish, patched the holes, wore them only in secret, for tree climbing and such. The shirt was an old one of her own, ruined. Chunks of matted hair were hanging loose, gouged out during her struggle.

Flinching, she combed out the loose hair, the twigs, the bits of bark, painfully rebraiding the unruly mop into its usual smooth cap. A washcloth dipped into the pitcher removed the dried blood from neck, forehead, ears, arms, reducing the apparent damage by half though making it appear more recent. She changed the torn shirt for a long-sleeved, high-collared one; the un-Regimic trousers for a skirt, then went out into the predawn darkness, back the way she had come the night before.

The statues guided her from their topiary niches, nodding to the left, pointing to the right, lifting eyes to denote a dead end way, their fingers signaling directions, distances, and meanings, as Caigo Faience had meant them to do. She carried no lantern for the skies were paling and the bulging moon still cast its pale rays into the east-west lanes. When she reached the far south lane, she saw what she had envisioned: the barriers tumbled, the cross pieces pulled aside. She knelt at the hole and peered down. Nothing. Nothing at all.

She wept silently, her face in her hands, then wiped her face on her shirttail and rose. Quietly and carefully, making as little noise as possible, she set the barriers up as they'd been before. This was why Ayward had told her to come early in the morning. He had wanted her to come here to this place, to act in this way, before anyone else saw the barriers had been disturbed. He'd known how she would interpret the fallen barrier. He just hadn't expected her to be here when he knocked it down.

Clenching her teeth, she knelt again, then lay flat, hanging dizzily over the edge of the hole, looking down past the same rooty mass. The moon above her shoulder shone into the hole, evoking the silver glimmer she had seen before, far down. There was also a sound, not what she'd heard before, something else, low and continuing. She listened intently, trying to make sense of the noise, wondering if water running or the rustling of bats could make that noise, those words . . .

"Help me, Dis! Oh, God, help me. Please, please, turn it off."

She shoved herself away from the edge and sat shaking, knees up, arms around them, stomach heaving, trying to disbelieve what she'd heard. Though she put her head between her knees and took deep breaths, the sick feeling would not leave her. She was not mistaken. It had been Ayward's voice.

It was a long time before she could get to her feet, and

then only shakily. Dawn lightened the eastern sky, and as she climbed the trellis, a derisive caw from a crow's nest in the park suggested an acceptable excuse for her battered appearance. She went along to Aunt Gayla's room to complain of getting up at dawn to spy on a high nest only to be attacked by the parent birds. Her face was wet with tears and smeared with blood, the tale was false, but the pain was real, as the punishment no doubt would be. Compared to what had happened in the night, punishment was nothing.

Gayla applied ointments and sympathetic words and tush-tushed at her when she broke into renewed weeping. They went down to breakfast together, where Dismé was silent, busy with self-hatred. How could her first reaction have been one of release? What kind of cold, inhuman creature was she?

"Were you hurt somewhere else?" Gayla asked. "You're crying!"

"It's nothing, Aunty. Just ashamed of myself for being so clumsy."

"As well you should be," said Rashel, furiously, as she entered from the corridor. She glared at Dismé, then leaned forward to slap her sharply across her wounded face. "You're too old for nonsensical behavior like climbing trees! When are you going to grow up? As if I didn't have enough to worry about, cutting the staff to come up with the money to repair this damage! Keep out of sight until you're healed. I don't want anyone to see you looking like that!"

Dismé swallowed deeply, not sure it was sarcasm.

"I have class today, Rashel."

"I'll tell them you won't be there. You can't be, looking like a bowl of cat-meat!" She left, slamming the door behind her.

"Now why was she that angry?" wondered Gayla. "Out of all proportion, that one."

Dismé had no idea. She had never had any idea. Since Rashel obviously hated her, one would think she would relish Dismé being injured—even killed—but Rashel did not want her hurt. Whenever Dismé was in danger of being hurt, Rashel became frightened and more than usually abusive.

Gayla moved from the breakfast table into the kitchen to discuss supper with Molly Uphand. Joan came to clear, surprised to find Dismé still at the table.

"What're you waitin' for, Miss Dismé?" asked Joan. "My, that mama bird did do you damage! Lucky your eyes weren't hurt!"

"I'm waiting to see Owen," she replied. "He has a book about frogs he said I could borrow for class."

"He's late," said Joan, amid her clattering.

"Who? Owen?" asked Aunt Gayla. "He's terribly late. I wonder if something's wrong . . ." And she was off to the other wing, to check on Owen. To Gayla, all young men were nephews.

Dismé stayed stubbornly where she was. Shortly, a flurry of shrill screams came from the far end of the house, and both Molly and Joan rushed off toward the noise, joined by Michael, who had just come in the back door. Dismé didn't move.

Michael was back in a short time, giving her a hard look and reaching for the emergency alarm flags.

"Is someone hurt?" she managed, as he pulled out the flags that meant a medical emergency.

"Owen," he said. "We think he's fallen and hit his head." He hummed through his teeth for a moment. "Ayward is gone."

"Gone!" she said, astonished at her own surprise. Well, she hadn't *known*, not really. It could have been demons, trying to trick her. "How could he go anywhere without Owen?"

"We don't know. I've got to request a medic," he said, rushing out the back door to comply with the Regime's dictates about the injured. Injured people had to be seen to right away, so if necessary, they could be bottled in time.

Gritting her teeth, Dismé went along to Ayward's rooms, where she found Aunt Gayla sitting on the floor, weeping as she cradled Owen's head, Molly and Joan wailing dirges behind her. Driven by conscience, Dismé knelt to get a good look at Owen. He had a bump on his head, though not a big one; there was no blood and he was breathing very naturally. If he had fallen where he lay, he had possibly hit his head on the shelf above him.

When the medic arrived with the horse-drawn ambulance, the configuration was more or less the same, except that Rashel was contributing a raging dissonance to the chorus of lamentations. In addition to the medic from the Department of Medicine there was an agent from the Office of Chair Support, Department of Death Prevention, Division of Health, BHE. This man took Rashel and Aunt Gayla off into another room, and they returned after a time wiping their eyes, though whether from fear or anger, Dismé couldn't tell. Now the agent wanted to see Dismé.

Though Arnole had always denied it, everyone more or less believed that interrogators from the BHE could tell if someone lied to them. She would be careful not to lie. Not really.

"You're the Director's sister?" he asked.

"Step-sister, sir." Her forehead itched abominably. She rubbed at it with her fingers.

"I understand you were out early this morning?"

"Yes, sir." It was true he understood that.

"Birdnesting, your sister said. What's that about?"

"I'm interested in the wildlife here, at the edge of the forest. Since the Happening, the distribution of wildlife in the world has changed enormously, but we have few if any recent studies. I'm writing a little journal about the various species of local birds." True. All true.

"Ah." He frowned at the form before him, tapping his pen. "Do you have a permit from the Office of Textual Approval?"

"A permit from the Office is not required unless one submits for publication, sir."

"Ah, right." He stared at her face. "Did you see anything unusual?"

"After I got all scratched up, I was mostly interested in getting home, so I really wasn't paying attention." All of which, heaven knows, was true enough.

"You know your sister's husband is gone."

"That's what Michael said. I don't understand how he could be gone without Owen. Maybe when Owen wakes up, he'll know."

"The medics say Owen has been drugged."

"Drugged?" she stared with her mouth open. The Chairs used drugs, of course, to keep occupants comfortable, but she couldn't imagine how Owen could have been drugged. He was a strong young man, and Ayward could only use one hand.

The man saw her puzzlement. "This man, Ayward. Is it true his father also went away?"

"Yes, sir. He did. I miss him a great deal."

"After so long?" His voice softened. "You must have loved him."

Dismé, rubbing at her forehead once again, allowed herself a few angry tears that would no doubt pass for grief. "My father died when I was very young. Arnole became a kind of replacement father to me."

"Well, then. Don't worry about this matter. I'm sure the mystery will be solved." He patted her on the shoulder as he turned to go out, and she heard his voice in the hall, telling Rashel how puzzled and worried she was. "It is strange, Madam, to have it happen twice."

"Not at all strange," she said slowly, in a bitter tone. "They were father and son, and consequently much alike."

"Intransigent?" he asked.

"Stubborn, certainly," she replied. "My husband's father was a salvage child, saved from among outsiders. He remembered a youth among outlanders, where things were done differently."

"So your husband would have grown up with that example," the agent said. "Yes. You're right. It's not so strange as I had at first assumed."

"He went so suddenly," she blurted angrily. "Before I had a chance to . . . well. It was all very . . . unfortunate."

Dismé was behind the door, and through the crack she could see Rashel's face set in furious frustration. Had she been looking forward to that second Chair? Savoring Dismé's possible reaction to that second Chair? Had Dismé's furious pity concerning the first Chair lost its savor?

The agent nodded once more. "You'll need to be careful. Your sister has seen it happen twice. She is extremely upset."

"I know," Rashel said, with momentary satisfaction. "But my sister will get over it."

questions concerning faience

Several senior officers were together in the officers' mess when a messenger arrived with a folder for the bishop, who buttered a bit of toast, slathered it with game paté, and chewed reflectively while perusing the first page of the document.

"Post rider brought this communiqué from the Office of Conformity Assurance in Apocanew," he said at last. "The Office was called out to examine flood damage up at the Faience center. Repairs will put them over budget."

Major Marchant, on yet another visit to Hold, looked up with a startled expression. "I thought Faience came under my jurisdiction."

The bishop raised his eyebrows. "For what goes on there, yes, Mace, but when BHE took over the place the physical fabric was defined as Ephemeral Art, full of trees and mazes, and maintenance of such stuff falls under Conformity Assurance."

"Ah," murmured the major. "Does your communiqué mention the woman running the museum . . . what's her name?"

"Rashel Deshôll."

"Deshôll, ah, right. Just last year I signed a Hold-honor commendation for her exemplary reorganization of the Faience."

The doctor had seen the major's face and heard his too casual tone being a little too uncertain of the name of the "woman running the museum." Anyone at the Inexplicable Arts sub-office in Apocanew should know that name as well as he knew his own. Now the major's cheeks were a bit flushed, his manly nostrils were slightly dilated.

The bishop remarked, "No doubt she's done a commendable job, but I've also had a report from Colonel Professor Zocrat's office suggesting that she may be a nexus for demonic activity."

"What business has the Division of Education with Faience?" asked the major, now openly annoyed.

"There's a school for workers' children at Faience," said the bishop, mildly. "It's a legitimate concern."

The doctor leaned back in his chair, gray eyes flicking from one to another of his fellow officers from beneath arched brows, wide mouth impudently and forever curved beneath his long nose as he said, "What's being suggested, Bishop? Contagion?"

Marchant looked slightly stunned.

The bishop shook his head. "Our agent reports two cases of strange vanishment in Deshôll's immediate family, father-in-law and husband; both were chaired, both disappeared."

"Disappeared? How can anyone in a Chair disappear?"

The question came from Captain Trublood, who, in the doctor's opinion, showed a great deal of presumption by constantly hanging around.

"Inexplicable, indeed, Captain!" the bishop said. "The family was scrutinized very carefully on both occasions, however, and we found absolutely nothing to involve the Deshôll woman in the disappearances or in the fact that one of the students at the Faience school sorcerously set fire to his desk. In that case, Deshôll wasn't even present, though her sister—ah, Dismé Latimer—was. We brought the boy in, but as usual, the power didn't persist throughout interrogation."

"Because the kid couldn't remember how he did it?" asked the doctor.

"He wouldn't have been asked *how* he did it," said the general, irritably. "He would have received the standard interrogation we use whenever demonism is suspected. Only the doctrinally orthodox can get a permit. Needless to say, the boy had no permit!"

"Our sub-office investigated after the disappearance of both Arnole and Ayward Gazane," said the major. "In the last incident, we found no tracks, he wasn't hidden anywhere, no one in the place knows anything and the man had seen no one but family and servants for over a year. I suspect he drove his chair down the hill and over a cliff into the lake."

"Why would he have done that?" asked the doctor, just to be irritating.

The major scowled. "Gazane founded the Inclusionist school, which had proven useless. He was given a chance to refocus himself, and couldn't. He'd been quite depressed. I'm sure no one at Faience was involved. The step-sister is a bit weird, but she's not bright enough to have had anything to do with it."

The doctor noted the major's tight lips and watchful expression. All this intimate knowledge of Ayward when he couldn't remember Rashel's name? The major had lovely eyes. Altogether an attractive package, the major. Was Rashel also an attractive package?

"What's her name again?" he asked, casually.

"Who? Deshôll?"

"No, the ah . . . step-sister."

"Ah, Dismé," said the major. "Dismé Latimer. Why?"

With an effort the doctor managed to say in an indifferent voice, "No reason. Just that it's an odd name."

The general waved the matter away. "Leif, where did this nexus allegation come from?"

The bishop poured himself more wine. "We have a Special Agent at Faience, woman named Leek. She works there, her daughter attends the school and keeps an eye on the teacher, the monitor, and the other children."

"Special Agents from the Office of Investigation?" inquired the major, suddenly pale. "Why wasn't I told?"

The bishop nodded. "I'm not stepping on your toes, Major. No one is overriding your authority at Faience, but it's necessary to keep an eye on the place. It's off to hell and gone. Anyone could be up to mischief, without anyone in authority knowing anything about it."

Indeed, thought the doctor to himself. Indeed they could be up to mischief including the hiding away of a woman named Dismé Latimer whom he had been trying to locate for a very, very long time.

✦ 28

the seeress

Some distance west and over the mountains from Bastion, a single traveler made his way along a dusty road, little more than a wagon track leading over a ridge and then down again by long, winding traverses to a wide and fertile valley. He had made this trip several times during his life, whenever he could arrange it. Except that he seemed very strong and fit for a man of his obvious age, there was nothing remarkable about him.

As he neared the summit, he searched the verges of the trail, letting his eyes come to rest on a cairn of stones that marked a turn to the right and a scarcely visible path to a sheer rock wall. In an inconspicuous cleft was a metal panel with a translucent window set into it. Behind the window, a red light glowed softly. He laid his palm upon this window and sat down on a nearby rock to wait. The way might not open at all. If it did, it would not do so immediately.

After some time, a voice spoke from the rock. "You wish to confer with Allipto Gomator?"

He rose, speaking in a firm voice. "I do."

"What do you want with her?"

"I have news of this and that."

After a lengthy silence, the voice said, "Enter."

The rock moved aside, and he went through the cleft, down a short corridor of stone, and into a domed cavern, mostly natural, though he could detect places in which the stone had been cut or perhaps melted away to provide for the transparent chamber before him. Inside it sat an old woman wearing a wimple of gold beneath a robe and hood of green. Though spotted with age, her hands were lovely, with long and graceful fingers.

"Welcome, my friend," she said. "I have not seen you for years."

"I was in Bastion for some time," he grumbled. "They have ways of hampering movement." He sat silent for a moment, then said, "You're looking well."

"I'm looking old."

"You've changed little, Ma'am, since I first saw you."

"Be seated. May I offer you something to drink?"

They decided on tea, which came out of a dispenser next to the table on which the seeress kept her crystal ball and was passed to the man through a slot in the chamber. When they had sipped and spoken of nothing much for a few moments, she said, "What do you have for me."

The man twisted himself into a more comfortable position and crossed one leg over the other. "To the west of here, a new place has built up. It is called Goodland, Gladland, or Goldland, depending on who's telling. An explorer who went there said it looks like an unassailable fortress, with only one huge gate."

"Did he talk to the people who live there?"

"He didn't see any people. Just a very forbidding wall and a closed gate. Also, I have heard that the being which used to lie far in the north has come south, toward this same place."

The seeress sat as though carved in stone for a long moment. "Do you know anything else about it?"

"Nothing. The wagoneers who come by there say the place is set on the dry plain. They are amazed at this, wondering who would build such a place in the desert."

"Anything else?"

"In Bastion, beneath the Fortress, they have discovered a device. It is only partially uncovered as yet. It seems to be made of stone, but such stone has not been seen before."

The seeress took some time to think about that, as well. "And what will they do with it?"

"They have already appointed people from Inexplicable Arts to examine it. My son's wife is one of them."

"If I recall correctly, he is not your son."

"Only you and I know that, Lady. He believes he is. Certainly he was born some spans after I married his mother."

"Don't I recall that you married her out of kindness, to save her from shame and bottling."

"Kindness, yes. Or perhaps out of lust. She was very beautiful."

The old woman laughed. "I have always respected your candor. Do you think this device is important?"

"I believe, Madam, that this device is only one of several, or even many. It is my intention to find the others. I've already found a clue to their whereabouts."

"And you base all this conjecture on what?"

"My reading, Madam, done in my youth, in the archives of the Fortress itself, beginning with an account we have discussed before, concerning the discoveries of Hal P'Jardas."

"You give credence to his flaming woman, then? What was her name? Tamlar?"

"I believe in Tamlar more now than ever. We are beginning to hear much about the Council of Guardians, Seeress. Their names and attributes are known. Prayer is uttered in their names. They are too often identified with the Rebel Angels for my taste, but if one presumes the mythical nature of such angels, the mis-identification does no harm."

She regarded him narrowly. "You think this device has something to do with the Council? You think it's magical? Or perhaps merely powerful."

He thought for a moment before replying, "From a certain point of view, the two are indistinguishable. Sufficient power would always look like magic to one who lacked knowledge of it. And, yes. I think this device will turn out to be very powerful indeed."

"Ah," she murmured. "Will that affect me, at all?"

He regarded her with a slight smile for a long moment,

sipping his tea. She did not hurry him. Eventually, he set down the cup and said, "According to P'Jardas, Tamlar said this is the land of Elnith of the Silences, who sleeps beneath these lands and will emerge in time. Think on those words, Lady. If these are the lands of Elnith, then she is here. If she will emerge, in time, then she is hidden now. P'Jardas lived some centuries ago, so she has remained hidden for a long time. You are the seeress. Perhaps you can tell me who or what has slept here all that time. Who, or what will emerge."

She answered from a throat suddenly dry and rasping. "As I have said, though only to you, I am not a believer in magic."

"But you are a believer in power," he said, smiling.

She nodded. "Yes. I am a believer in that."

"In Bastion, a great deal is heard about the Council of Guardians. It begins always with Tamlar, with fire. Next are mentioned the names of Aarond of the Anvil and Ialond of the Hammer. Is this a systematic seraphium do you think? First fire, then those who shape matter. Then, who next? Rankivian, Shadua, and Yun, who are said to be caretakers of souls, and after them the tutelary deities of earth, air, and water, Hussara, Volian, and Wogalkish, along with one called Jiralk the Joyous, bringer of life. Oh, yes, definitely it is systematic. Or metaphorical."

He finished his tea and set the cup back in the slot through which it had come. "This assembly may be, of course, both metaphorical and real. There are said to be a score or more of these Guardians." He rose and bowed to her. "I will come again when I have discovered more. Have you anything to tell me in return?"

"Very little, my friend. Things are quiet here."

She said it with some bitterness, and as though in acknowledgment, he bowed again, very low, before leaving. When he had gone, the green-robed woman bent her head onto her hands, feeling both weariness and confusion. Before her, the crystal ball came alive with fire, and she raised her eyes to confront a globe of blinding light that faded, almost at once, into a fleeting image. She thought the image was herself, but it faded too quickly to be sure.

"Elnith," she said to herself. "Elnith of the Silences. Sleeping below these lands. And what does that have to do with me?"

The cavern of Allipto Gomator had been built by several successive Omega Station awake teams when the darkness of the Happening was beginning to wane and time lay heavy on their hands. At first, Nell had considered it the height of hubris to build such a place. It would be dependent for custom upon casual wanderers at a time when there were unlikely to be enough human beings left to wander anywhere! She had, however, underestimated the antsiness of mankind. The Darkness was only half lifted before people began trickling by in ones and twos and dozens, most of them eager to trade a little information about the outside world for a trifle of food or medicine. Nell had been amazed at the number of animals the wanderers had managed to keep alive: horses, cows, llamas, sheep and goats, dogs and cats, various sorts of chickens, turkeys, ducks, geese and pigeons, as well as the occasional example of native fauna: deer, squirrel, ferret, bear.

During her last two wakes, Arnole Gazane had been one of her most faithful informants. The various wakers who played "Allipto" had seen him several times, Nell herself had seen him first as a youth, then as a middle-aged man, now as one approaching age. Rising from her chair, she divested herself of her costume and went down the winding stairs into the station itself where she found Raymond, Janet, and Jackson engaged in their continuing argument about the limitations of Omega Station.

Jackson was saying, "The nuclear plants they had time to install couldn't maintain power for the habitat plus 200 coffins, but now there aren't 200 coffins."

"Strictly speaking, there are," murmured Janet. "I mean, they're all occupied. The freeze units are still on."

"But they don't have to be," Nell said as she approached.

Janet gave her an angry look. "What would we do with . . ."

"Take the sleepers with us when we go outside," Nell remarked.

Silence.

"We always planned to go out eventually," she said firmly. "Listen. It's time, isn't it? Some of the sleepers are still alive, they just won't wake up. Why don't we take them out into the sunlight! Does it matter whether we die out there or down here?"

Raymond heaved a huge sigh. "We've always known Emergence might be necessary; let's just grit our teeth and do it."

"We've maintained a presence," said Janet. "That's what we were supposed to do. We've got the old lady up there spreading useful information."

"I'm the old lady on this shift," Nell said, "and we need to get past providing information. The population is edging up toward a million. The people in Chasm probably have all the technology we had in the 21st, and the other people are relearning it. We don't have many years left, and we can best help if we're outside. Besides, things are happening. My informant just told me the Bitch thing is oozing itself toward a new construction that's sprung up on the plains southwest of us, toward Henceforth. Doesn't that entice you at all?"

"We can send some pings," murmured Janet.

Nell cried, "Pings can't get anything out of the Bitch, we've known that for centuries! They can ping at her interminably, and she just ignores them! Let us for the love of God get out of here and *learn* something . . ."

"I'd like to know something about the Bitch *before* we go out there," said Janet in a reproving tone.

"You're not going to learn anything in here," Nell snarled at her.

Janet frowned. "You're so hasty, Nell. Far too hasty. Did any of the other crews find out if it's alive?"

"How would they know, Janet? Everything we've learned about it came from the moon base. They're the ones who mapped the world for us, including the area of the Arctic covered by that critter. What difference does it make whether it's alive or not?"

"Because it barely moved at all until recently," said Jackson, putting his hand on Janet's shoulder.

She shook him off. "Something made it move. We ought to find out what before we leave the safety of the redoubt."

Nell threw up her hands and went to the dispenser for tea.

Looking after her, Raymond said, "If something made it move, it had to be the increasing population. That's the only real change, that and the improvement in natural environment over what we had in the 21st century. Benign changes in general climate. Slight lowering in sea level since the high after the Happening. More ozone. The changes from season to season are much milder now, but you knew that. No change in . . ."

"All right!" Nell cried from across the room. "Why do we keep repeating what we all know?"

Raymond raised his voice and went on, ". . . anything else except the number of people. Which has doubled in the last century."

Janet laughed. "From a half million to a million? There were over four hundred million of us in this country alone!"

Nell said impatiently, "A number we now know to have been excessive for one continent. Presumably, something under one million was about right, or at least, not wrong, because we're reaching that figure without anything else happening. That is, if anything that's happening has anything to do with humanity at all, which it may not! Let's at least *postulate* that more than a million is, if not wrong, at least on its way to becoming wrong."

Janet snarled, "Nell, who made you the arbiter of what's right or wrong?"

Nell thumped the table. "I'm not making a moral judgement, I'm making a pragmatic one! Before the Happening, the world was full of people, and we were using up the Earth's resources at a fantastic rate. Somehow we felt we'd find some other world before we used up this one, and going to space was a spectator sport. That game's over. We're not going anywhere! Therefore, all the attitudes that led to use-up-the-world-and-leave-it-behind are *wrong for us*, and whatever attitudes keep the Earth fit for what people and animals are left is *right for us*, and I defy you to come up with any better definition."

"So what else is new?" Jackson asked, flippantly, then, seeing the expression on her face, "Sorry, Nell. It's just . . . last time I fell asleep with those words ringing in my ears. I had hoped we'd have something else to discuss by now."

Nell snorted. "You don't seem to be listening! You want something else to discuss? How about the vast being that's crawling toward the new place out there on the plains? How about Raymond's weird sensor readings on the fog that's haunting Bastion. How about the really weird artifact that's been found under the Fortress in Bastion, *or* the fact that we are beginning to hear a good deal about the Council of Guardians . . ."

"*Hear* about the Council?" cried Janet. "Hear about it?"

Nell repeated, "Hear, yes. As in sound waves generated by friction, propagated through some medium such as air or water, that causes the ear drum to vibrate."

Jackson persisted. "You mean *hear from outside?*"

Raymond said, "According to the monitors, and the journals, members of the Council have been seen. Last awake team learned of a man in Everday who showed up with a glowing sign on his forehead."

"What sign?" demanded Janet, turning red.

"The sign of the Council."

Janet cried, "Hell, Raymond, we *invented* the Council! We didn't think up a sign for it!"

Raymond snapped, "I am not deaf, Janet. I know we had no sign for it."

Janet growled. "We created the Guardian Council. We spread the word about it through Allipto."

Nell snorted, "Yes we did, Janet. We did it to lay the groundwork for our eventual emergence!"

"Maybe *you* did!"

Nell said, "The old guy that came into Allipto's cavern

just a little while ago mentioned Elnith of the Silences. He says she's been sleeping under Bastion for a long time."

"Oh, come now," said Janet. "Surely none of our people who played seeresses talked to outsiders about sleepers down here. That would have been stupid."

Nell said, "I'm sure none of them did. I certainly didn't."

"You must have misunderstood him," Janet sniffed.

"The interview was recorded. They always are! Look at it if you don't believe me."

Raymond plowed on. "Janet, stop picking! Nell is right. The pings have picked up many references to a mythology about the Council of Guardians."

"My informant mentioned Tamlar, then Ialond of the hammer and Aarond of the anvil, and then Rankivian, Shadua, and Yun." Nell rubbed her forehead. "Who was it comes after them?"

Raymond shook his head. "I think it's the four who cradle life. Hussara of Earth. Wogalkish . . . or is it Wolagshik . . . I don't remember of the waters. Somebody of the sky . . ."

"Volian!" grated Nell.

". . . and then a lifebringer named . . . ah, Jiralk, I think. Jiralk the Joyous. Those are the only names I've heard, but there are said to be a score or more of them altogether."

Jackson said, "We invented a council of a dozen members, and we didn't make up any titles! It was a mystical concept! What Alan called a faith-anchor. Something for the survivors to believe in, something to give hope . . ."

Nell growled, "Well, now our faith-anchor has grown itself a hull, a mast, a set of sails, and maybe even an engine! Our mystical concept is crewed by mystical titles: Tamlar, Ialond, Aarond, et-bloody-al-onds, and Elnith is coming."

"Elnith coming? Coming where?" demanded Janet.

"How should I know." Nell grimaced impatiently. She was burning to get something done and they were so *slow*. "If you're wondering how a specific name became associated with a fictional group that we invented some hundreds of years ago, then by all means, waste your time."

She gestured widely on the "we," meaning all of them in

the chamber including those in the ranked coffins, silent or humming. Eighty lights, including all those who wouldn't wake up, plus the four of them sitting there arguing. A hundred sixteen dead. Slept into silence.

Janet said, "They've simply embroidered the idea over the years. They took the notion of a Guardian Council and just . . . made up the members of it."

Raymond nodded. "That's possible. It doesn't explain everything, however."

"Like what?" asked Janet.

"In Everday a miraculous device identified Camwar of the Cask as a member of the Council. When they are all identified, the story goes, they'll usher in the new age."

"Whoopee?" challenged Nell. "Are we going to be part of it, or are we going to stay in this hellhole until we're all dead and already buried?"

"Let's emerge," said Raymond.

"No," said Janet.

"I'm not sure that the others . . ." said Jackson.

"For the love of heaven!" Nell cried. "Wake them and let them make up their own minds! We won't force you and Janet to do anything. You can stay down here until you rot, if that's what you want! We must wake the wakeable because they have the right of decision."

"I think you're being precipitous. But then, you always have been," sneered Janet.

"There's time," soothed Jackson.

Raymond raised his eyebrows at Nell, who felt herself smothering in fury. She could not listen to them any longer. Instead, she went into the ping room, locked the door behind her, and spent the rest of her day's waking hours reviewing all that the pings had reported concerning the lands east of Henceforth where a fortress called Goodland or Goldland or Gladland had been built.

✴ 29

the spelunker

Owen's story as told to the investigators was a simple one. "I was about to inject his evening pain medicine when Ayward dropped the books he had piled on the Chair. I laid the vial down on the Chair panel in order to gather them up, which, I admit, was foolish of me. He stuck the needle into my shoulder and I passed out. That's all I know about it."

Owen's story as told to Dismé was, "It doesn't matter what happened; they're going to blame me, so I'm going to run away." Dismé heard this with some relief, for Owen's ignorance of what had really happened freed her to take whatever action she considered proper. She had heard voices in the hole. The people who owned those voices got there somehow, through a tunnel or a cavern! She knew caverns were occupied by bats, for Arnole had often pointed out clouds of flutterers rising into the evening sky. To find caverns, therefore, she would look for bats.

When supper was over that night, Rashel returned to the museum, as she often did; Gayla went to her room; Dismé packed odds and ends into a canvas sack and waited for dusk. When it came, she left the house, counting on the grief and distraction of the day to keep Gayla from noticing she was gone.

At the museum she climbed the fire escape to the roof, went across the roof to the tower and through an open arch to the winding stairs. At the top was a small, hexagonal platform surrounded by lacy iron railings and surmounted by a domed roof and spire. It was from here the signal flags were flown to say "Holiday, open to the public," or, as they had this morning, "Send Medical Help."

The light leeched from the sky above the jagged rim of the world, and within moments she saw dim clouds swirling from the canyon's rim. Dismé dismissed these. She was looking for something closer. She turned, making a slow survey of the sky. Northwest, past the stumpy black fist of the barn roof, a triangle of protruding gable pointed like a black knuckle at a whirling swarm, and unlike the amorphous shapes at the canyon rim, this cloud was clearly made up of individual flutterers.

She went down the tower and the fire escape more quickly than she had climbed it, hurrying to get to the barn before the swarm dispersed. Once there, she climbed to the familiar refuge of the loft, where the weathered and splintery loft door made a precarious support as she leaned outward beneath the beam and rusted pulley that still carried a tail of rotted rope. Though the loft seemed empty except for dust and cobwebs, a skittering sound above her presaged a score of ragged shapes diving before her startled face to fan outward in the dark.

The flight she had seen earlier was still rising, though it was difficult to see the upward spiral between the two largest trees in the area. When Dismé reached the ground, she could still see the tree tops over the intervening growth, black puffs against the lighter sky. The moon was close to full and would be rising at any moment. She had traversed the cleared area, and come into the woods beyond, mixed pines and hardwoods, traveling in as straight a line as she could manage to the trunk of what she thought was the nearer of the two huge trees. It was too dark to see farther, so she crouched at the base of the tree and waited silently while the woods came alive with rustling and chittering. As the moon rose, her eyes adjusted to the light, and she sought the other huge tree, using moon shadows to keep her direction. In the end, it was a shrill squeaking that drew her into a small clearing just in time to see a wave of bats plunging downward into an old well with a ruptured roof and half fallen stone coping.

Dismé leaned over the stones as other bats dodged past her head and dropped into darkness. It was too dark to see anything.

"Now, the lantern," she said, taking it from her pack. The flint striker was as strikers always were, uncooperative, but she managed to get it lighted at last. She fished a length of line from the pack and lowered the lantern into the well, catching it momentarily on a rusty spike jutting into the opening. Another flight of bats skimmed down the well and into a hole in its wall.

"That hole is big enough to get into," Dismé told herself. "If it were a natural cave, I would have no idea where it led, but this isn't a natural cave. This well was built by someone; someone put those spikes into the wall. That hole was hidden by someone, which means it was probably used by someone. And I can get down there."

She dropped the lantern farther, swinging it a little, until it actually entered the hole at the end of a swing, then she measured the armspans necessary to retrieve it. "About three meters," she said, nodding to herself.

On the way back through the woods, heading for the glass tower that could be seen high above the trees, Dismé took note of landmarks. An outcropping of stone like a howling dog; a tree with a huge branch hanging by a shred of bark; at the edge of the wood an apple tree in full bloom, white against the darkness of the nearby pines. At home, she lay on her bed as she made a mental list of the things she would need before searching for Ayward. Rope ladder. Lantern. Spare fuel, water, and food, warm coat. Underground places were used as wine cellars and root cellars because they were cool, even cold. Ayward had a compass; it was probably still in his rooms.

Shortly after dawn, she rose. Though no one would have expected her to monitor the class today, she went to school at the usual hour. Doing the usual thing would keep people from thinking about her, and she didn't want their attention while she got her supplies together. Everything depended on her being completely ordinary until the moment she disappeared. Rashel would report the disappearance. The BHE would make a search. They had scent hounds, or so everyone said. She mustn't leave a trail . . .

Which she had already done! She'd left a trail when she had followed the bats!

She stopped in the washroom to think about this while she cleaned her hands, hoping Lettyne Leek would be busy when she went into the classroom. Forlorn hope. Lettyne strolled over to give her the insolent up and down look that started each day.

"What happened to you?" Lettyne asked, with a leer.

"I climbed a tree to look at a bird nest, and the birds came at me," she said, as offhandedly as she could.

"You definitely look . . . damaged," Lettyne said over her shoulder as she moved back to her desk.

"Damaged" was Regimic for a family with a missing member, someone who had presumably been chaired or died all at once. Trust the brat to find the worst possible time to stir all Dismé's feelings of guilt. The Dicta required family members to rescue one another and Ayward's only "family" was Rashel, who would do nothing to help him unless BHE was watching. Besides, if anyone but Dismé found Ayward alive, they would drag him back to Bastion. Un-Regimic or not, Dismé had to do it alone.

It took all her free time that day to prepare and to lay several false trails, one of them ending at the riverside, complete with shreds of her nightgown. She walked this one several times, to leave a good strong smell. Though it distressed her to think of Ayward waiting, in pain, she had not had much sleep since Ayward went and delayed leaving until dawn. At first light, she had only to dress and pick up the pack that was ready by the door.

With her room door locked, her final task inside the house

was to go onto the roof, cushion the window to her room with a blanket and break it from the outside, the tiny panes of salvage glass crumpling in the light wooden filigree that held them. She dropped the blanket inside and locked the window. This would suggest an abduction. Her trail this time would be covered by a kind of salve that Gayla swore by, a particularly stinky mixture that she rubbed on her shoes as she went into the forest.

It was growing light as she hung her pack on a line and swung it into the opening down the shaft, put the rope ladder she had stolen from an upper room at the museum over the spikes in the wall, and then crept over the coping and down. Only two steps down, Dismé decided that it would have been far easier and safer had the ladder hung slightly away from the wall instead of tight against it. As it was, she bruised her knuckles against the stones when she pushed her fingers around the side ropes, and each time she felt for the next step below, her foot was pushed off the rungs by the wall itself. There were fifteen rungs between the well coping and the bottom of the hole, each of them a struggle.

Once at the bottom, however, getting into the hole was easy enough, though the inside was deep in dried bat droppings. She flipped the ladder several times before dislodging it from the spikes, realizing as she did so that she would be unable to return that way. There had to be some other way out. Her continued existence rather depended on it.

She had expected the tunnel to slope downward, as it did in fact, and after the first fifty feet or so, signs of human travel became obvious. The path had been cleared, the footway was smooth, although there were still many bat-caverns leading off to either side. Light fell into this tunnel through crevices in the stones above it, and mirrors had been affixed to the walls to scatter whatever light sneaked through, though only bats and spiders had been here recently.

According to Dismé's reckoning, the Great Maze was almost directly south of the well she had entered, and by referring to Ayward's compass she reassured herself she was moving in that direction, though her elation gave way to a feeling of dismay when she passed the last of the mirrors. The lantern did well enough for emergency light at home, but it wasn't well-suited for exploration. It had been easy to follow the little puddles of mirror-reflected light, and she had gone quite swiftly from one to the next. Now, however, she stood in a small globe of visibility and could go only where she carried it. She held the light high; a flight of bats went by, startling her. The lantern fell, rolled, and was gone down a deep crevice in the stone, leaving her in darkness.

She had a moment of total panic, crouching as though fearing a blow. Inside her a voice spoke, "There there, settle down." She pulled herself inward, held out her hand and said, "Tamlar, I need light." The flame bloomed on her palm, growing as she watched it, until it lit the way before her. Her hand outstretched, she continued downward and southward, making minor detours to either side. The bats were behind her; the dust lessened and she eventually was able to make out the trail itself, stone worn so smooth that it gleamed in the light, as did rock-edges of the walls that had been slicked and glossed by passing hands. The air, which had been full of motes near the surface, was clearer here, making it easier to see. She heard running water, and soon after, a few trickles came out of the wall at her left and ran along beside the path, the rivulet gaining in size as she went.

Dismé considered the water a good sign, since there had been a pool below the hole in the maze. Though the water made her hopeful, it was the appearance of light that relieved her anxiety. She blew out her flame and hurried toward the light ahead, stumbling, almost falling, coming out into a vaulted space with rays of sun filtering through a tangle of roots and twigs onto a still pool. The Chair stood beside it, set upright, its wheels bent, the carapace jagged and torn. It was empty and covered with mud.

Dismé ran to the Chair and fell to her knees beside it, uncertain whether to laugh or cry. If he had been freed from the chair . . . *If* he had been freed. She stood up, looked around, finding a level spot beside the pool where a blanket was spread, bearing the imprint of a body.

"So he did get out of the Chair," Dismé cried.

"Which was appropriate," growled a voice from the darkness.

She spun around, searching for the voice.

"If you want to talk with us," the voice commanded, "sit down on the blanket, facing the water."

After a doubtful moment, Dismé sat.

She heard someone approach from behind her and started to turn.

"No. Keep your eyes front. I'm going to blindfold you so you can't see me. I don't want my face known. I won't hurt you, and we can talk, but only with the blindfold."

Dismé said angrily, "Do it then! Tell me about Ayward!"

Dark cloth descended over her eyes and was knotted tight.

"Now," said the voice from before them. "What do you want to know about your friend?" It was a youngish male voice, a medium baritone.

"You said he was alive when you found him. Is he still alive?" Dismé demanded.

A woman laughed, the sound coming from across the pool. "Though he was irritated about that fact, yes. He planned that the fall would kill him, which it would have if he hadn't hit the water. It's deeper than it looks. The Chair floated, of course, as it's designed to do. Still, he broke one arm and several ribs, so he's been taken away to be seen to."

"Then I needn't have come at all," cried Dismé. "It was all a waste!"

"On several counts," agreed the woman. "Why did you come?"

"I came because I heard his voice . . ."

"Then you must be Dismé," the voice said, with another unamused laugh, like a snort. "Ayward said you'd show up. His faithful friend Dismé."

"He couldn't have known . . ."

"He did know. He said if you could find a way, you'd come. After he'd fallen, he saw you up there, against the moonlight."

"You took him out of the Chair," Dismé accused.

The man's voice said, "Of course we did. And we gave him painkillers that'll keep him unconscious for several days. He's been strapped into that Chair so long that his muscles and tendons are in revolt. He hasn't been able to straighten from that cramped position for years. Also, it'll be a while before his chair-sores heal, and before he can eat solid food. There are people moving his limbs for him, turning him and massaging him. We'll let him sleep until the worst of it is over."

Dismé murmured, "I didn't know you could take someone out of a Chair. With so much of their bodies missing, the Regime says only the Chairs keep them living."

After a short silence, came another of those cheerless snorts, rather like a bull or horse. "Well, the Regime says a lot of things, nine-tenths of it lies and the other tenth wishful thinking. Ayward is entirely whole, though rather bent at the moment. He'll recover."

"But the chaired ones give their flesh to people who need it," Dismé said, desperately trying to understand. "We don't take parts from the dead, that's what brought on the Happening, but we can take parts from the living! They took Arnole's legs to give to someone else, someone who didn't have the Disease, someone who needed them . . ."

"That's what they tell you," he said.

"But he couldn't raise his head," she cried. "They took tissue from his back . . ."

The person sounded exasperated. "Listen, woman! We're the ones who build the Chairs and we're the ones who put people into them. Unlike the Spared, we're not torturers. It was *after* Ayward was installed in the Chair that the Regime put metal plates over his arm and jammed a hook into the muscles of his shoulders. Every time he tried to straighten up, it dug into his flesh!"

"Why?" She shook her head. "I don't understand."

"You needn't understand. Enlightening you isn't my job."

Dismé cried, "If you were here, why did you let him suffer? I heard him from up there. He screamed out, asking someone to turn it off. He was in pain!"

The woman said, with more calm but no less annoyance, "We were here the day before, yes, but we'd left before Ayward . . . dropped in. There's an alarm system, however, and we returned as quickly as possible. I quite agree that any time is too long for a person who's suffering, but it wasn't actually very long by other standards. He terrified himself with the idea the Regime might move on him suddenly, and instead of doing what was logical, he took the sudden appearance of that hole as a portent."

"At which point," the male voice jeered, "he did a totally uncharacteristic thing! He acted!"

"You think all this is funny?" cried Dismé.

The female voice answered soothingly. "Pain isn't funny, but it is humorous that the only decisive thing Ayward Gazane ever did was try to end it all."

"It was panic," said the male voice, dismissively. "The idea of losing brain tissue horrified him. And he may have feared his link with us would be discovered . . ."

"His link with you?" she demanded. "Ayward? What link?"

"The same one we had with Arnole. If Ayward had kept his wits and asked for help, we would have come for him before anything happened, just as we did with Arnole."

Dismé put her face into her hands, pressing the heels of her hands into her eyes. "Arnole? You came for him? Where is he?"

The woman said, "A long way from here, I'm sure."

"Alive! And he never let me know?"

"Well he couldn't very well, could he? He said you were a chatterer, always busy telling anyone and everyone everything that occurred to you."

"I never saw Ayward talk to anyone!" Dismé cried.

"You wouldn't have known. We saw what he saw, heard what he heard, not that we bothered to listen or watch after the first few days. Ayward used nine-tenths of his waking time explaining himself and Rashel to himself. We grew weary of the monologue."

Dismé shook her head in frustration. "I don't understand."

There was a muttering between the two voices. Dismé started to turn, but heavy hands on her shoulders kept her faced toward the water. "Tell her," said the woman. "Arnole said to."

"If she'll be quiet and listen!"

Dismé shut her mouth. After a moment's pause the voice went on: "As soon as Bastion was settled, people began moving over the border. So far as the Regime was concerned, that was desertion, so they sent armed teams out to wipe out the deserters, along with anyone who got in the way! They used to go thundering out of Bastion on killing sprees every spring before planting and every fall after harvest."

"They always say there's no one out there," murmured Dismé. "Just demons and devils and monsters . . ."

"People," said the voice in a disgusted tone. "Just people, like you, like me, some of them farmers, some of them runaways from Bastion, some of them people traveling in caravans from one city to another."

"Cities?" Dismé breathed. "Out there?"

"Cities, yes. Some on the New West Coast. Some to the east. As far as the people outside are concerned, Bastion is a boil on the world's rear end, and they stay well away from it. There's another city in the mountains south of here, called Chasm, and it's been there since before the Happening. We people who were being slaughtered asked Chasm for help, and Chasm provided some excellent weapons so we could target the leaders of the raiders. It doesn't do any good to kill underlings, not with a Regime like Bastion. They just pop some tissue in a bottle and pretend the person is still there. We had to get the ones at the top, and we had to be sure there was nothing left of the bodies. No bodies, no bottles. No bottles, no being re-created by the Rebel Angels.

"Well, that went on for a few years, long enough to make leading war parties very unpopular. Meantime, we'd made a deal with Chasm. There's no agricultural land where they are, and we're happy to provide food in return for manufactured things. When we'd slaughtered enough of the Spared to make them more reasonable, we offered them a deal: we'd provide things they needed and couldn't make for themselves, like machines, if they'd stop raiding us and taking our children."

"Machines?" asked Dismé. "What machines?"

"Well now, that's interesting. My grandfather was one of the negotiators. According to him, our side suggested things like medical equipment and power looms and farm equipment and glass-making machinery, but that wasn't what Bastion wanted. They said comfort and contentment and health weren't important, they weren't *life-ful* things. They wanted punishment Chairs and batteries to run them and nutrient bottles for their bottle walls. Things to gain them credit when the world ends. Which they expect rather soon."

"Life-ful," said Dismé. "Yes. That's what they call Chairs and bottles. Life-ful. And if you provide them, that must mean you're demons."

"That's a Regime label. We're people, just like you are, and this series of caverns is one of our routes to and from Apocanew. A team of us goes in every day or so, to the place they put their useless people and the dead. We put the heretics in Chairs for them, and we put tissue in bottles, and we sedate and transport the so-called useless people out of Bastion. Other teams do the same in other cities. That way we can keep an eye on all of Bastion, to be sure it's living up to the agreement."

"Heretics?" breathed Dismé. "They're not heretics. They just have The Disease."

"The only disease they have is the disease of doubt or of being in someone else's way," snarled the voice. "Which is heresy so far as the Regime is concerned. Recently they've been getting uppish again, so we're going to have to settle them down."

"Who do you mean when you say we?" demanded Dismé.

The woman chuckled. "We. Let's see, if you include everyone who detests Bastion and all its works, it's a rather large group. We're allied with the rebels inside Bastion."

"Rebels?" asked Dismé. "There are rebels?"

"There are, and I'm not going to tell you about them, and you wouldn't remember if I did."

"And Arnole was one of your people?"

"Since he first volunteered to be abducted by your salvagers fifty years ago. He kept us informed of what went on inside the Regime. We could see and hear everything he saw and heard."

The woman interrupted. "He married a Bastion woman, an unfortunate marriage from our point of view, because she was already pregnant when he met her, and she had no sense to speak of. She was beautiful, however, and she was in danger of being bottled for illicit sexual relations—another thing the Regime is good at—and Arnole felt sorry for her. She was a lovely thing, a Comador girl who died when Ayward was quite young."

"Arnole wasn't Ayward's father?"

"No. Though Ayward was never told that. When Ayward was thirty . . . I guess you were the one he was attracted to."

"How did you know?"

"You're not listening again! From Arnole, obviously. We saw everything that happened to him and around him. We know your whole life history, such as it is, better than you do."

"I doubt that," muttered Dismé, offended at his tone.

"Yes we do, including the fact that Ayward was attracted to you because you resembled his mother. And the fact that Rashel seduced Ayward and then told him she was pregnant. The Regime is fairly strict about such things, immorality being a symptom of The Disease. He chose to marry her instead. Later she told him she'd miscarried, and it was his fault, so to make it up to her he should help her get a job with the BHE."

Dismé cried, "I didn't know that!"

"Of course not," the man said. "But we did, because Arnole was a snoop and a gossip and damned clever besides. He was never actually sentenced to a Chair; he had us make it for him because being in a Chair was good cover. We made sure the Chair was comfortable. He used to sleep in the Chair a lot in the daytime, and then at night, with his door locked, he could get out of the thing and move around on his own. He used to disguise himself and wander all over Apocanew, cutting a swath through the married ladies and finding out all kinds of interesting things. He probably has a dozen sons or daughters out in Bastion somewhere."

"The Chair wasn't real? And he never told me."

"That Chair wasn't. The next one would have been."

"But, didn't the Regime know he'd never been sentenced? Wouldn't their records have told them . . ."

"Records. Ha. The Regime keeps its records like it keeps its pacts. Why would anyone suspect someone in a Chair was there voluntarily, and if they can't find the records, who cares. We could have removed him from Bastion before Ayward and Rashel were married, but he chose to stay."

"Why would he stay?" Dismé demanded.

"Because he had been very fond of Ayward's mother, sense or no sense, and he grew to be fond of Ayward, and then even fonder of you," said the male voice. "He thought you were something special, though I can't see why. You never followed his advice to get away from that damned family!"

Dismé felt her inner gates open, felt Roarer come out, didn't even try to stop it. "He didn't know Rashel!" she cried. "Not half so well as I did. If I had tried to go elsewhere in Bastion, she would have hunted me down and killed me, or worse. Even if I had left Bastion, she'd have found me or died in the attempt."

There was a shocked silence among the echoes, then the female voice asked, "Why? Why would she hate you enough to . . ."

"I don't know," Dismé snarled. "Why did she hate my brother enough to kill him! Or my father enough to kill him also! If they had known, if I had known, we might have defeated her somehow. But we didn't know why."

"Do you know this to be true?" the male voice asked.

"I know they were in her way and nothing stands in her way. Not when she was a child. Not now! I don't know how I know, but I do know!"

"But she hasn't killed you," objected the male voice. "She's had plenty of opportunity."

"I've played the role she gave me, and that kept me safe . . . relatively," said Dismé tiredly. "I don't expect you to believe me. It wasn't something I could prove to Arnole. It wasn't something you'd find out merely by seeing what he saw. She doesn't show the world what she is."

"If Arnole had told you he was leaving, would you have gone with him?"

"If it wouldn't have put him at risk, and if I'd thought it would get me cleanly away from Rashel, I probably would," she said. "He never told me. He never asked me. I don't blame him for that if he really thought I couldn't keep it to myself . . ."

After a long pause, the female voice said, "It's irrelevant now, anyhow. Arnole didn't yell for help until he was threatened with a second Chair. Nobody in a second Chair is really alive, they're just cautionary examples for the populace. We came to get him in the middle of the night, and he suggested we transfer the link to you."

"Me?" she asked, surprised. "Me?"

"You. Yes. He said it might be useful to you. But we couldn't find you, not anywhere. So then he suggested Ayward."

"I went . . . out," she murmured, remembering. "That night, I went out to the wall . . ."

"Well, you picked a bad night for it," muttered the woman.

"Ayward never worked out, and when we pulled him out of that pond, he was still going on and on about Rashel betraying him and how he loved her and hated her and had to stay with her . . ."

"He was besotted with her," said Dismé bleakly.

The female voice interjected, "Say bewitched and you'll come closer to the truth. His attachment to her wasn't natural, even Ayward thought so. We've heard rumors . . ."

"Black magic," murmured Dismé. "Arnole thought so."

The male voice said, "That's nonsense. There's no such

thing. Maybe being besotted simply runs in the family. Your showing up down here might indicate so."

"I'm not part of his family, and I came because I thought Ayward was lying down here in agony. All this other stuff is just plockutta, and I'm tired of listening to it!"

The voices murmured together. The female voice said, "We'll leave you to get a bit of rest. You'll find drinking water and a privy on the other side of the pond."

Dismé, face flaming, waited until the murmurs and footsteps stopped, then took off the blindfold and laid it on the blanket beside her. She found a rock privy on the far side of the pond, and nearby, hollowed into a pillar, was a basin beneath a spring, the overflow glossing the floor of the cavern. She splashed her face and neck, cooling her anger and embarrassment as she cleaned away the dust of the caverns. A glass pitcher stood amid a clutter of cups on a nearby shelf. When she had slaked her thirst, she went back to the blanket and dug out the bread and cheese she had provisioned herself with.

She felt overcome with weariness. The cavern swayed slightly, and she put a hand to her forehead. Exhaustion was understandable, she thought. There'd been all too little sleep lately. As though on cue, the male voice called from behind the pillars to don the blindfold.

Dismé did so, keeping her balance with some difficulty. Anonymous hands steadied her, and the woman's voice said, "Don't worry about getting home. We'll pick up Owen Toadlast and use his disappearance as an explanation for yours, Dismé."

"Pick him up . . ."

"Get him out of Bastion. Ayward asked us to. The boy left Faience this morning, and he won't object to our help."

Dismé put her hand to her head, which felt as though it were rocking. "You don't want me to stay here?"

"No. What we really want, though we have no right to ask, is for you to take Ayward's place as our contact. You picked a hell of time to go out of the house that night. What was that all about?"

"I just used to go out to a certain place on the wall. For

some peace. But there were ouphs that night, a fog of them, like being lost in clouds of sad. And they were all around, I couldn't get away from them . . ."

Silence. Then, softly, "What did you say there were?"

What had she said? She couldn't remember. "Nothings," she murmured. "Nothings."

Muttering. Growling. The male voice, "So. You'd be willing to be our eyes and ears."

"If you do something for me!" The anger had stayed with her, busying itself by making white-hot red-rimmed bore holes through the haze that wrapped her. "I'll be your eyes and ears, if you'll get me safely away from Rashel."

The words took the last of her strength, and Dismé lowered her head into her hands. The dizziness increased, and had now turned into acute nausea. Perhaps it was having gone without sleep. Or all this clambering about.

There was a murmuring again, this time among several voices, one saying, "He thought she'd do well . . ." and the male voice interrupting, ". . . don't think this fear of being killed is quite credible . . . not sure she's worth the trouble."

"Wolf!" said another female voice. "That's cruel."

"Well, look at the last ten years of her life! She's behaved like a dishrag, limp as a dead snake. If she'd told Arnole what she really felt, he could have figured something out, but all she did was mush about! I say before we go to a lot of trouble, she should do something decisive herself, just to prove she can!"

"Wolf has a point," said the first woman's voice, close at Dismé's ear. "We'll arrange getting you away from Rashel, and then we'll see. We'll open some doors for you, but you'll have to walk through them on your own."

How dared they! Roarer came out of its lair again, like a red wave, and she felt it rise furiously, trying to find a way through the haze. When it could not, it slowly ebbed away. As it retreated, she followed it, floating after it, finding the place it went, a feeling place that smelled of iron and tasted of tears. In that place she heard an endless series of echoes. Mother. Roger. Father. Arnole.

She moved away, then returned to see if it was still there. It was. A twisted cavern that belonged to her, not only the structure of it but also the beast that snuffled inside it, growling and pressing against the walls to make them creak. She could feel it in there, and now she knew where it was, she could come get it, open the gate for it anytime she needed it.

She felt herself nodding, unable to speak. Oh, let a door be opened. Even a door into a furnace where she could go through and burn away this man's words, like Rashel's words, hurtful and unkind. A dishrag. A dead snake. A limp nothing. Like Ayward. Useless. The dizziness faded into a tingling quiet. The woman's voice said, "We've given you a drug, in the drinking water. It won't hurt you. Just relax."

Later she heard the woman's voice saying: "Arnole was almost always right. He would say he was sure about something, and it always came true. Then there's the matter of the light . . ."

"She probably had a candle or something!"

"We found the lantern two-thirds of the way back, Wolf. We found no evidence of a candle. How did she get here in the dark?"

Something alive was thrust into Dismé's ear where it drilled its way into her head with hard, pincher feet. Before she could complain about the pain, it was replaced by momentary euphoria.

Another time she opened her eyes to see several figures walking away from her, silhouetted against a distant light. They had horns, bull's horns, curved like a lyre.

"Demons," she said, from a dry mouth. "Demons with horns."

"Nonsense," said the woman's voice. "They aren't horns. They're Dantisfan. We need Dantisfan down here. No matter, don't ask. Hush. Drink this. Now look at this and tell me what it is, silently. Now think these words: Courage. Determination. Help. Think louder, in color, the letters H E L P, with jagged points around them! Help! Yes. That's very good."

"What I worry about," Dismé said, in a reasonable voice,

"is those shots of Holy Truth they give us. I don't know how Arnole or Ayward kept quiet about all this, but I can't . . ."

"Hush," said the woman, again. "With a dobsi in your head, their drugs can't even touch you."

Later, someone said, "We'll arrange the opportunity, but you'll have to be resolute. Wolf's right. You'll have to prove you're worth our effort. Another like Ayward would be useless."

The words resonated, humming, like a tuning fork. *Oppoooor tuuuunity. Rezz ohhhh looot.* Dismé grasped those words and hung onto them, though all else left her mind. She was inside a bell that went on ringing without ever being struck, a deep, harmonic reverberation, endless as time. She had drunk something very pleasant, and the sound had begun, fading very gradually into a quiet and welcome darkness.

✦ 30

dismé and the doctor

Dismé awoke in her room in the house at Faience, amid a circle of variously concerned, worried, or suspicious faces.

"What happened," Rashel asked, her eyes narrowed. "What happened to you, Dismé?"

Dismé asked, "Why are you all here in my room?"

Rashel snarled, "You were missing, Dismé. For two nights! Your window was broken. We brought in dogs. They couldn't find you anywhere. Then this morning, one of the restorers found you lying beside the road, right in plain sight."

"Morning?" she turned her head, seeing darkness outside.

Gayla said, "It's night, now. The doctor says you've been . . . drugged. What happened to you?"

Dismé shook her head slowly, not wanting to agitate it in any way. Her brain felt full of . . . air.

She murmured, "I can't remember . . ."

She didn't remember! There was nothing recent in her mind! Every room in her brain had space in it, the windows were open and the breeze was coming in. How interesting! She did not remark on it, however. There was no reason to invite others into this emptiness. No matter who asked her what, she couldn't remember anything about Ayward or herself or Owen during the last few days. Instead, she complained of headache, tried to get on her feet and was promptly sick, which effectively ended the questions. She slept deeply, restfully, and they let her alone.

Four days later, the agents from BHE arrived to question her about the strange occurrence. The examination took a good part of an afternoon. Though they kept at it, the usual shot of Holy Truth elicited nothing at all. In the end, the agents reported that she had been abducted and drugged by Owen, the same drugs he used in Ayward's Chair. Loss of memory from Chair sedatives was not unknown. Dismé was judged to be an innocent victim, luckily unharmed and also untainted by demonish ideas or feelings.

The senior agent reported first to Rashel. "This is a most unusual event, Madam. Your poor sister does seem to have been at the margin of a great many unusual events recently."

"My sister will get over it," said Rashel, as she had said before, though with a tone that presaged no good for Dismé. "I am sure she will be untroubled by further events of any kind."

Dismé was listening as usual—the emptiness of her mind had done nothing to moderate her habits—and she reacted to Rashel's words as to imminent peril. On the following morning she decided to follow Arnole's longtime advice and leave, as soon as possible. That same morning, Aunt Gayla whispered to Dismé that considering Rashel's moods, she had decided to move to Newland to live with Genna, and Dismé agreed this was a very good idea. Privately, she felt it solved her problem as well, and she planned to go with Gayla.

Before any further plans could be made, however, a rider brought an official letter from Hold advising her she had a morning appointment in two days' time with Colonel Doctor Jens Ladislav, to interview for a job with the Division of Health, Bureau of Happiness and Enlightenment. It was almost the answer to a prayer, an honest reason for departing, one so official that even Rashel would be unable to subvert it! Carelessly, on purpose, Dismé left the letter where Rashel would see it.

"What have you done?" Rashel screamed at her. "How dare you apply for a job in Hold! With Gayla leaving, I need you here to help with the house!"

Dismé heard herself saying, "Rashel, I have neither applied for a job in Hold nor am I interested in housekeeping for you."

Rachel's mouth dropped open, for a long moment silent, then furious with accusation: "You're not what? Since when did you have the wits to decide what you're interested in?"

Dismé gave her a level look. "Now that Gayla is leaving and Arnole and Ayward are gone, there is nothing to keep me here. This appointment might be interesting."

Rashel laughed, mockingly. "Once the Colonel Doctor has seen you, he won't want you. I can't imagine why he wrote."

"Nor can I."

"You didn't send some kind of application?"

"I wouldn't have known who to send it to. Surely you're not suggesting I should refuse to comply with their letter? If you are, I will have to tell them that I am willing to come to Hold, as they have requested, but you won't allow me to do so."

She fell silent, wondering at herself. Where had she found the courage to say that? Rashel was actually gnawing her lip in frustration, probably trying to come up with a dear, dear friend in the Division of Health whom she might prevail upon to cancel the request. Jens Ladislav was a colonel, however. He outranked all of Rashel's dear, dear friends.

In the end, Rashel merely sneered. "No, but when you return, we'll get to the bottom of this, believe me!"

Dismé had already decided not to return, and the threat in Rashel's voice buttressed her decision. She would go, and she would stay gone, whether the interview came to anything or not. Remembering Arnole's frustration with her inaction, she told herself it was the memory of Arnole that moved her, that and the money he had given her to make it possible.

Rashel did not make it easy. She was constantly in and out of Dismé's room, giving advice on what clothes to take (the ugliest) and where to stay in Hold (the cheapest). She counted Dismé's coins to be sure the amount would not suf-

fice for more than "a day or two." Dismé complied with
every suggestion. She opened one small case on the foot of
her bed and packed it with exactly what Rashel suggested.
She left her purse lying open beside it. That night, however,
when everyone else was asleep, she obtained several small
canvas sacks from the storeroom, packed them with everything else she owned, and dropped them out her window.
She then went down the trellis and carried the bags to a
seldom-used toolshed near the front gates.

The next morning, as the time for departure approached,
she changed into her ugliest clothes, picked up her small
case, and found her door had been locked from the outside.
Gritting her teeth, she went out the window and down the
trellis, in through the back door, up the back stairs, unlocked
the door—leaving the key in it—picked up the case, then
went sedately down the front stairs when she heard the carriage drive up. The front door was open and Rashel was
nowhere in evidence, though as soon as Dismé started out
the door, Rashel came around the corner, calling:

"You can unhitch the horses, Michael. Dismé won't . . ."

Rashel saw Dismé and stopped, flushing an ugly color.

Pretending she hadn't heard, Dismé called to Michael.
"My door was stuck and I had to jiggle it forever before it
opened."

Michael got down from the seat to open the carriage door.
Rashel, her face flaming, moved swiftly forward to take
hold of the case, noting its lightness.

"Let me get that for you," she said, putting it into the carriage. "You only have money enough for a day or two, so
don't delay returning." She showed a forced smile. "If they
should offer you a job in Hold, we'll have a celebration
when you come back to get your things."

"Oh, Rashel," cried Dismé, with spurious joy. "How very
thoughtful and kind of you. May we have a cake?"

"Oh, a cake, certainly," said Rashel. "Mrs. Stemfall has a
special icing she's been dying to try."

"What was all that about?" asked Michael, when they had
rounded the first curve.

"She locked me in. Decided I should miss the appointment, I guess. Can you stop at the toolshed near the gate?"

He didn't ask why, but he followed her to the shed and helped her pick up and stow her remaining baggage.

"You planned this," he said, amazed. "You've packed everything, haven't you?"

"Yes," she conceded. "Something told me it was a good time to get away. You won't tell on me, will you Michael?"

"Why would I?" he asked, peering intently into her eyes.

"No reason. It's just, I've left nothing behind to come back for, but I don't want Rashel to know that until I'm safely situated somewhere else."

"You left nothing, Dismé?"

"Nothing," she said, shaking her head. She had a little box containing seeds from her garden. The sacks contained books, her own notebooks, and the rest of her underclothes and shoes, which didn't amount to much. She did not see the disappointment on Michael's face, or the hurt in his eyes even as she wondered what else could there have been.

"I took five canvas sacks from the storeroom. I'll send them back!" she remarked, puzzled.

"Don't trouble yourself," he said, rather distantly. "There's a hundred more in the shed. No one counts them."

The drive to Apocanew was completed in virtual silence. In the town, he took her to the station and helped her transfer her baggage to the county-train that went back and forth between Apocanew and Hold, up the hill to Hold on one day, down the hill to Apocanew the next. Similar little trains ran between Hold and the other two counties.

Michael said suddenly, "How can you be back day after tomorrow. The train comes from Hold every other day."

"Yes," she said. "I know. Rashel knows, too, but she wasn't thinking. Tomorrow, tell Rashel I thought of it just now, and mentioned it to you. Please tell her you lent me enough money for an extra day. No, no." She stopped his reaching for his money. "I have enough, she just doesn't know that. Also, it might help to say I asked you to fix my door before I got back."

"It'll give you an extra day before she knows, but she'll still have a fit."

Dismé only smiled, her eyes lighting up at the thought. Michael took her by the hand, kissed her chastely on the forehead before she could object, and watched her board the train. As it pulled slowly away, Dismé leaned from the window and called something to him. Was it, "I will miss *you*, Michael?" He wasn't absolutely sure, but his step was jauntier as he returned to the carriage.

In choosing Dismé's clothing, Rashel had specialized in ugly fabrics and excremental colors. Wearing such stuff had suited Dismé's purposes well enough at Faience, where she had played her spinster-sister role with a certain numbness. If she was to chose her own role at the end of this journey, though, it might well be time to look like someone who mattered. Since she had never spent any of Arnole's money, her petticoat had wealth enough to clothe her fifty times over.

Accordingly, unobserved by anyone in the virtually empty women's car, she surreptitiously unstitched several golden dominions from her petticoat hem, and as soon as she had obtained lodging in Hold, she left the hostelry to find a shop selling women's clothing. The stock was small, as befit a Turnaway establishment, devoted to material simplicity. Nonetheless, the garments were well cut, the fabrics were enjoyable to feel and dyed in pleasant colors. She bought ankle-length skirts and soft jackets in shades of green and blue and violet, garments that draped around her body instead of enclosing it like a tent. Trousers were forbidden to Regimic women, but the saleswoman suggested at least one split skirt, for riding, and simple shirts of woven or knitted cotton or linen, with knitted sweaters and vests of wool for the colder seasons. After getting a good look at Dismé in her new clothes, the saleswoman also suggested a hairdresser.

Dismé frowned. She had always braided her hair into a single plait, the way her mother had done it for her as a tiny child. She had never thought of making a change.

"The way it is now, you mean, it isn't . . . suitable?"

"It would be most attractive if the citizen were twelve or thirteen. It is not quite what one expects of a grown woman."

Dismé unstitched another inch of petticoat hem and went to the hairdresser, where she was shown how to do her hair in several different ways. She peered at the difference the mirror showed her and considered it money well spent, only afterward wondering how such "conceits" as attractive hairstyles fit into the Regime's system. Though, come to think of it, the hairdresser had been a Praiser, and Praisers were the only Spared who seemed to have any fun, since they were known for love of theatrics and ceremony; for music, dancing, and wit; for cookery, colorful dress, and ingenious inventions. It was said of the Praisers that any long-dead chicken was an excuse for a wake and any recently dead one an excuse for a feast.

Turnaway was different. It boasted the loudest talkers, the most vicious fighters, the heaviest drinkers and the most fanatical believers. It was said of the Turnaways that any one of them would sacrifice his wife, mother, and children if he could win a battle thereby. Comadors were known as farmers, cheese and wine makers, for the soft wool of their sheep, for calm, musical talk, for muscular, handsome men and beautiful women. Of Comador it was said that their wines and their women were foretastes of heaven, a claim which Dismé, though Comador, had no proof of whatsoever.

She spent part of the late afternoon dropping off the older garments she most hated at a recycling station where they would probably be used, the manageress said, as rags for hooking rugs.

"Only for backgrounds," she said, with her head tilted as she examined Dismé's castoffs. "Whoever wore these either hated herself or someone else hated her."

The next morning, wearing soft blue and with her hair swept into a neat roll (the achievement of which had taken some time), Dismé went to her interview. She was introduced to Dr. Ladislav by his aide, Captain Trublood, who first sniffed at her and then bowed himself out, leaving them alone. The doctor rose politely to take her hand, then sat down again, waving her to a chair, taking a moment to look her over.

She regarded him as intently as he did her, for he had an interestingly narrow face with a long and pointed chin matched by an equally long and shapely nose with high arched nostrils. Between these two features, his wide mouth curved into a thin-lipped and perpetual smile which grew more pronounced when he was amused but never sagged into anything approximating solemnity. It was, she thought, a jester's face. Decks of cards had a jester card, a fool's card, one that was frequently wild.

The doctor was not a fool, but he could possibly be wild. He had wild, clever eyes surmounted by thick eyebrows of the same steel gray as the abundant hair that curled about his large, almost lobeless ears. Though she could see only his upper body, his shoulders were broad and, since his shirt sleeves were turned back, she could see that his arms looked well muscled.

"He is attractive, clean, and respectful," she decided, filing him in her *unobjectionable male* category, along with Arnole and Michael. Poor Owen had not been attractive; the teacher at the Faience school had been quite objectionable; and this list included all her male acquaintances.

The doctor asked half a dozen questions about things she had no reason to know about but did, in fact, know quite a lot about, such as the habits of birds and frogs and the geology of Bastion. He also asked her what she thought of demons, and she said she had had no opportunity to think about them, which was more or less true. He asked for a brief history of the Spared Ones, both the received version and whatever other versions she knew.

The received version for the layman was that there were no other humans than the Spared. Outside the lands of the Spared there were only demons or others of that ilk. There seemed no point in denying that she knew of other peoples who not only existed but also traded with Bastion, particularly since Colonel Doctor had already said he knew she had been told a great many things not allowed by the Dicta. Possession of non-Dicta information seemed to enhance her desirability—in a strictly professional sense—for the job the Colonel Doctor had in mind.

"On occasion, I travel along the borders of Bastion, talking with other peoples who live near there, in an effort to learn everything I can about their healing materials and techniques. You know that the demons provide us with certain supplies?"

"Yes, Colonel Doctor."

"One or the other, Citizen Dismé, if you don't mind." He found her quietness charming. She sat simply, relaxed, without fiddling about, and the Colonel Doctor admired that in anyone, especially in a woman. Besides, she was wonderful to look at. That calm face spiked by those huge, watchful eyes. Like an old painting from before the Happening. "Call me either Colonel or Doctor. Hearing both titles gives me a split personality, the two philosophies differing so widely. It is medicine's philosophy that lives should be saved, of all sorts. It is our military's philosophy that as long as a few cells are kept alive, actual lives may be dispensed with. A few inches of gut in a bottle is not, to my mind, a life, no matter what theological contortions one puts oneself through. I would prefer the company of even a cantankerous, obstinate, and opinionated old geezer to any number of bottle walls."

She smiled widely, without thinking.

"You are amused?"

She flushed. "You were describing my friend, Arnole."

"Ah. The one who vanished. A geezer, was he?"

"Cantankerous, Colonel . . . that is Doctor Ladislav."

"I do prefer doctor, yes. As I was saying, I travel about, but a man traveling alone is somewhat suspect. He might be a scout for a raiding party, for example. A man traveling with a wife and one or more children, however, is merely a traveler. I need a traveling companion with a certain flexibility of mind."

She could not keep the surprise from her face, or the shock.

He nodded. "Your maidenly sensibilities are stirred. Have no fear. I have no designs upon your virtue. On these journeys the essence of prudence is not to be distracted. Finoodling of the sort you momentarily suspected—I am sure you are too nice-minded to have thought of it more than momentarily—would be a distraction. Besides, if we are to act like old married persons, we should be quite bored with one another. I'm sure I can bore you, given only a little time. Just a few lectures on medical oddities or the sniping among Regimic officialdom should do it."

She smiled, quite without meaning to. "Is that all I am to do? Ride along with you and be bored?" Even she heard the disappointment in her voice, and it made her blush.

"Certainly not," he said in a shocked tone. "That is only what you are to appear to do. Really, of course, you will be collecting data, just as I do, only you will be collecting it from women and children and any others who might be reluctant to confide in a male person, often for very good reason."

"Data on technology, about which I know nothing."

"Data on flora and fauna, local culture and habits. I do not expect you to learn about technology, for I have spent some years trying and still find it incomprehensible. Also . . ."

He shut his mouth abruptly. He had been about to mention that he intended to warn the people over the borders about the general's new plans. It was too early to tell her that, but he would test the waters.

"I will, Citizen Dismé, make a confession to you, one I hope you will keep completely confidential." He achieved a quasi-serious face by lowering his eyebrows and leaning his chin on a fist, the knuckle of his index finger pushing up his lower lip, thus slightly reducing his expression of cheer. "I have reason to believe there is a technological survival out there."

She frowned. "Isn't that a heresy?"

"To believe there is one?"

"To believe there *can* be one? Isn't that Scientism?"

"Do you worry about Scientism?" he asked, slightly concerned at this trend of the conversation.

"No," she confessed. "But my friend Arnole told me about Scientism, and if there's technological survival, that means some scientists were spared also, and believing scientists survived would deny the Dicta's words that only the Spared survived."

He relaxed, allowing his face to resume its usual expression. "We wouldn't know a survival was heretical until we found it. It might exist under the personal direction of the Rebel Angels. I do hope to find out."

"I know so little," she murmured.

"Better admit you are up to your neck in ignorance than stand upon a pinnacle of misinformation," he said firmly. "For the immediate future you are hired as my assistant. If asked what you do for me, you say research. If asked research on what, you say, whatever Colonel Doctor tells me. If pinned down, you say you are reading nakity-nakity, blah blah, whatever it is you are reading that day—which will always be a pre-Happening book as they are less suspect than post-Happening ones . . ."

"Why is that?"

He dropped his voice to a whisper. "Pre-Happening books are very hard to read. The words are almost the same, but the spelling is different. Few if any of the people here in Hold have either the patience or inclination to burrow through them. I, myself, struggled to acquire the skill. As a result of my struggle, I can offer you a key to spelling changes which much simplifies the task."

Dismé did not mention that she already knew about reading pre-Happening books. She merely nodded, to show she understood.

He went on, "Also, everyone knows the former world was full of heresy, but since all the heretics are dead, they and their books are historic. Anything historic is tolerable. A book written post-Happening, however, would have been written by one of the Spared—since according to the Spared, only they exist—who would not have dared be heretical. If you follow me." He cocked his head questioningly.

She nodded to show she understood him.

"Now, as I was saying, if they ask why you are reading nakity-nakity, you say you don't know, ask the Colonel Doctor."

She almost chuckled. "I see. Am I to infer that some of what you do is not approved by the . . . powers that be?"

His eyes opened wide, his eyebrows rose, he appeared extravagantly shocked. "You wouldn't want to infer that, would you? If you made any such inference, your conscience would require you to report me at once to the Office of Investigation, Department of Personnel. To make any such inference would imperil you, because you are associated with me. You must not, therefore, allow yourself to infer anything to our mutual detriment. It will be far safer to assume I am perfect in every regard, that everything I do or tell you to do is commanded directly by the Rebel Angels." He scratched one ear, thoughtfully. "Or perhaps the Regime, as the angels may have no particular interest in minutia, as why on earth should they?"

She caught her breath and forbid herself to laugh. "Yes, Doctor."

"Very good. You will begin working for me only when you have settled into your own quarters. Today, you will be allocated living space and you will fill out request forms for whatever furnishings and supplies you will need. Remember to be detailed in your requests. First requests are usually filled with only moderate obfuscation and delay. Subsequent requests are met with disbelief. If you forget to ask for a chamber pot the first time around, no amount of explanation will get you one later."

She wrinkled her nose in distaste.

"While you have that expression on your face," he said, "it is appropriate for me to emphasize once more the imprudence of inference. Don't infer from my manner and deportment that others in my office share my opinions, my vocabulary, or my intentions. *It is also unwise to seem personable.* Toward others here in Hold you must convey a presence that is both dull and demure. You have, I note, a face which can be virtually vacant. Keep it that way, but do not turn off the mind behind it."

"Yes, Doctor," she said, smoothing her brow, slightly compressing her lips and half lidding her eyes.

"Excellent. Your eyes are now remote, your lips make a formidable barrier against confidences, your demeanor conveys an unqualified indifference. See that you maintain that expression as you take this note down to the supplies office on the first floor, and fill out form eleven A five thirteen."

He shooed her as he rose to open the door and put his head out. "Who's here?" he asked the air. "Ah. Trublood. Would you take Citizen Dismé to the housing office, please? Thank you."

The young officer stood up as she came out of the Doctor's office, nodded in a peremptory manner, and started out at a fast pace down the corridor. It was all she could do to keep up as they covered three hallways and two sets of stairs.

"Down there," he said, pointing.

"Thank you," she murmured breathlessly, reminding herself not to smile at him.

"Don't mention it," he said, nostrils pinched in annoyance. "We have pages who lead people about and fetch tea and the like. Colonel Doctor Ladislav never seems to remember that." And he went angrily back the way they had come while Dismé continued to the indicated door. The room was divided by a counter, the area behind it occupied by two men at large desks and two women at small ones. Dismé vacated her face as she approached the counter. She murmured a toneless, "Good morning."

One of the women cast a glance at the nearest large desk, holding herself ready to move or not, as indicated. The large man looked up briefly. Dismé had vacated her face by the time he saw her, and he muttered incuriously, "See to her Miram."

"Yes, Captain," she said, rising and advancing on Dismé with a slightly worried expression. "What?" she asked.

"I have just been hired on as an assistant to Colonel Doctor Ladislav," Dismé said in a deadly monotone. "He told me to come here and you would assign me quarters."

Miram fetched a book from a nearby shelf and turned to

a set of plans showing floors and corridors and rooms, each room with vertical lists of names neatly printed in, some with all names crossed out, some with all but one or two. "Women's corridors," she muttered. "Let's see, vacant, vacant. I've got 306 or 415. You can have your choice; Elida Ethelday was in 306, she's gone back to Comador, and her room's nearest the stairs; 415 is in the corner tower, so it's not as warm, but it has a nice view."

Increasing the distance from the stairs would also decrease traffic in the corridor outside, Dismé thought. She didn't mind a cool room, and quiet was something she preferred.

"Four-fifteen," Dismé said. "May I look at it before I go to the supply officer?"

"Oh, of course, of course. I've got the key here, but first I have to put your name down."

Dismé wrote her name and job and watched while it was inked in minuscule letters at the bottom of the 415's list of tenants.

"Key," said Miram, handing it to her. "You go out and turn right to the main corridor, where the town flags are. Turn left there and take the first stair to your left. There's a sign that says women's corridors. Go up three flights, tell the fourth floor keeper who you are, she'll put you on the roll."

"Keeper?" murmured Dismé.

"Women's corridors have keepers," said Miram, surprised. "To protect their tranquility. Of course."

"Oh, of course." She followed directions, main corridor lit by a skylight five stories up, three flights of stairs lit by inadequate lanterns. The sad-faced keeper had a few candles and a little alcove at the head of the stair where she could see anyone who came up or went down. Dismé introduced herself, was properly enrolled, and was read the rules:

"No men visitors in your quarters, not even relatives. Women relatives who visit may stay overnight if you're not on duty. No pets except birds in cages, small ones. Inspection irregularly, at least every twenty days, with reprovals for untidiness. Five reprovals equals a beating, and I don't recommend it. Keep food put away, it attracts mice. You're lucky, there's a slop chute right next to your door on the outside wall. Chamber pots are to be emptied and rinsed out promptly. You can get reprovals for smelly quarters."

The room at the end of the hall was shaped like a fat raindrop, with the door almost at the angle of two right-angled straight walls, a third wall curving into the three-quarter circle of the tower at the corner of the building. The curved wall had a narrow window in each quarter-circle arc, each with a separate view across the city and surrounding countryside. Dismé carried pen, ink, and paper in her bag, and she sat down to make a list. The room already had a bed, a chair, and a wash stand. There was room for a desk, a bookshelf, and a commode. A stove stood between two windows on the curved wall. When she had her list complete, she asked the keeper how to find the supply office and went there.

The supply officer took forever to read the list.

"Y'say sheets and blankets and a pillow, but you don't say bed," he commented.

"There's a bed already there."

"Not your bed. Whadever you're gonna use, you godda ast for. Otherwise, somebody fines a bed there and no bed on your rekazishun, they take the bed."

"Give me a moment," asked Dismé. "I'll put down the bed and the chair and the wash stand that's already there." She did so, then resubmitted the list.

"You got down here curdens or shades but you don' say how many winnows."

She amended her list once more. Three windows, curtain rods.

"There's curden rods already there," he said.

"Not my curtain rods," she responded.

"They're fas'ened in. Stuff that's fas'ened in, you don't got to rekazition. Like a stove. Id's build in, so take it offa the lis."

"I see."

"You don' got down here no rug."

"Am I allowed a rug?"

"You don' know 'less you ast for one."

"All right," she murmured, "I'll ask for a rug."

They continued in this wise for some little time, adding an oil lamp, a fuel box (a limited supply of firewood and coal was provided), and concluding with a grudging agreement on the part of the supply officer that most of what she'd asked for could be delivered to the room by the following day.

Dismé returned to the Division of Health offices, where she was ostentatiously ignored by Captain Trublood. An officer of lesser rank gave her meal chits, an overnight chit for the hostelry where she was staying, and another one that allowed her to go on living there until her quarters had been furnished. "Do some sightseeing," this one suggested kindly. "Go over to Mill Street. It has all kinds of nice shops, and there's respectable places to eat, and a little park."

Accordingly, Dismé went to Mill Street and spent the afternoon wandering in the dull little shops and having a barely edible meal at a cafe and sitting in the little park, which had more weeds than grass and no flowers except six badly maimed marigolds around a broken sundial. Noting her own lack of appreciation, she realized she had been spoiled by Faience. Molly Uphand was a superlative cook with access to unlimited milk, cream, eggs, meat, vegetables, and fruit from the surrounding farms; the grounds were visually exciting; and the contents of the Museum, at least the artistic ones, put any shop to shame. Aesthetics obviously didn't occupy a high place among the mostly Turnaway masters of Hold.

She decided to go back to her hostelry, started to rise, then sat back down again. The hair on her neck prickled. She was being watched. She took several things out of her bag and laid them on the bench as though looking for . . . her handkerchief, which she wiped her nose with as she turned toward the items lying on the bench in order to glance toward the area that had been behind her. There was a figure standing against a building at the end of the street, where the park ended. That is, she thought it was a figure of a person, though it could have been . . . anything. It was too far away to see the eyes though, for some reason, she thought they were red. Keeping her head down, she replaced the items in her bag, stood up, shook out her skirts, and turned slowly in that direction. The figure was gone.

She returned to her hostelry, had a better meal in the refectory there, and wrote a letter to Mrs. Stemfall saying she had been hired and would not be returning to the Conservator's house, though she paused a few moments before adding those last words. Staying in Hold might involve danger, but going back to Faience was out of the question. If something wanted to look at her, it could do so as well in Faience or Apocanew as here in Hold. This Fortress, with its hall keepers and bureaucratic systems, was among the safer places she could be.

She walked over to the Fortress, and in the main corridor, the one with all the dusty flags, she located the post service office, where she paid a fee to have the letter taken to Apocanew on the train; another, lesser fee to have it delivered in Apocanew to someone on the route list who worked at Faience; and still another, quite small fee to have that person deliver the letter to Mrs. Stemfall. Returning to the hostelry, she locked door and window, pulled the curtains, and settled herself to sleep, grinning unashamedly at the thought of what Rashel would do and say when she heard the news.

Just before she dozed off, however, the grin faded as she remembered what Doctor Ladislav had said. "A man, traveling with a wife, and one or more children . . ."

She was obviously expected to play the part of the wife, but where were they to get the children? She drifted into sleep with the question unanswered.

In the night, she had several dreams that half wakened her, not her usual type of dream, but something much more real and immediate. When she woke at dawn, she was the surprised possessor of a discrete section of missing memory concerning climbing down a well and traveling through caverns, and the memories were still returning, like bubbles in a mud pool, each preceded by a feeling of fullness and then a soggy *pwufl* as the bubble broke to disclose an event in all its details. Dismé lay abed until the day was well advanced, recollecting her journey underground with amazement, some embarrassment, and more than a little joy to know that somewhere Arnole still lived.

She also thought about the dobsi in her head. She could not feel it, but now she knew it was there! Should she tell the doctor? Would it upset him? Would it place him at risk? The initial impression she had of him made her believe that he and the demons might well be of like mind, but in the end, she decided not to mention it.

✦ *31*

a visit to hetman gone

Two days later, Mrs. Stemfall went into the dining room where Rashel was having her noon meal in lonely splendor. Just outside the door, she adopted a dour and disapproving face.

"Parm me, Ma'am," she muttered, with a sniff. "But there was a letter from your sister, Miss Dis. She ast me to tell you she has that job they was offering. She won't be coming back."

Rashel turned quite pale. She had received Michael's message regarding the "stuck door and extra day away" with a degree of composure, expecting Dismé to return today. Now she rose from the table and left the dining room, missing the sly smile that fled across the housekeeper's face. Upstairs, in Dismé's room, Rashel pulled out the drawers, opened the cupboards and threw wide the closet door. They were empty except for a tattered shirt and pair of men's trousers, which she regarded with momentary rage until she realized the belt around them was Dismé's own. She returned to attack Mrs. Stemfall.

"You packed her things! You sent them on to her."

Mrs. Stemfall allowed herself a measure of hauteur. "I did no such thing. I'd have had no time to do so."

"I'll get to the bottom of this. I'll question Joan and Michael. If you have . . ."

Mrs. Stemfall turned in outrage and left the room, feeling Rashel's fury crackling the air after her. Rashel raged through the house, looking for evidence, so she said, that one of the servants had helped Dismé do whatever it was Dismé was alleged to have done. Molly Uphand retaliated by providing a supper that was barely edible, but Rashel didn't notice. Carrying her rage from the house to the museum, she went on so furiously in the succeeding days that a number of museum staff took sick.

In the classroom, Lettyne bit her lips in aggravation. Tidbits of news about Dismé had been good for a few coins from her mama, and now that source of income had departed. At home, Molly Uphand smiled quietly behind a dish towel, postponing a good gossip with Joan about it until they were home. Dismé had often lent a hand and was well-liked.

Rashel's interview with Michael caused the gravest affront. He denied taking baggage from maid or cook or housekeeper to send on to Hold. He denied he had packed any such thing himself. He kept his temper very well, considering that half-a-dozen times he came within a breath of assaulting her. When a momentary lull allowed him to do so, he tendered his resignation to the Caigo Faience, thereby renewing hostilities.

"What do you mean, you're leaving?" she snarled.

"I have already secured a driver's position in Hold which is to begin in a few day's time."

"You don't have my permission to leave!"

"I'm sure the BHE will find someone for you within the next few days," Michaël replied. "I informed them earlier, and they said it would take little time to replace me."

"*You* informed them!"

"Yes Ma'am. In accordance with the rules of my contract."

"I am your employer!"

"Respectfully, no Ma'am. I work for the BHE, like the rest of the staff of Faience and this house. We all took the job on short notice, to oblige, for a minimum term that was over some time ago. Any or all of us can leave on three days' notice."

Rashel opened her mouth to shriek, but was forestalled when he held out a packet.

"Pardon me, Ma'am, but this letter was delivered a few minutes ago."

"From whom? From where?"

"A rider, Ma'am. On a black horse up from the city."

She ripped open the envelope, read the first two lines, and turned quite pale.

"Ma'am?"

She wiggled her fingers at him, brushing at him. Go, said her hand. Go away. He went, noting her discomfiture with great satisfaction.

Behind him, Rashel read the brief note again. And yet again. Nothing changed what it said. She was summoned from Faience to meet with Hetman Gohdan Gone. Damn him and damn him! She had tried to ignore him, and failed. She had tried to charm him, and failed. She had tried compliance, but mere compliance didn't satisfy him either. He was not susceptible to any form of handling, and it was all her fool mother's fault! Her foolish, stupid mother who had obligated all Rashel's future life.

She remembered screaming at her mother for involving her in such a thing. "How dared you?" Rashel had cried.

"Because it was the only thing I could think of," her mother had replied, glancing up at her daughter from the hands that twisted in her lap. "He wanted to sacrifice you. I bargained for your life by convincing him you could be of help to him . . ."

Rashel hadn't believed her. She had seen no reason why the Hetman would have wanted to kill her. He hadn't even met her!

In the face of this disbelief, Cora would have been wise to have gone away at that point, or to have sent Rashel away. She loved her daughter, however, and did not assess either the depths of Rashel's hatreds, or the shallowness of her affections. As a result, Cora died quite suddenly, just before Rashel and Ayward were married. She was quite alone at the time, and only the timely arrival of the cleaning woman allowed her to be bottled while tissue was still harvestable.

Rashel's disposal of her mother had put an end to a minor annoyance. Rashel wished a similar departure for Hetman Gone, but nothing she could do would rid her of Hetman Gohdan Gone, save die, perhaps, and she was not sure even that would serve. She knew very well what had prompted this summons. Dismé! Dismé the idiot. Dismé the "little golden bird." Dismé, whom Hetman Gone had commanded Rashel to keep close and under supervision. Dismé, who had departed without Gone's approval.

When she stormed out of the room, Michael, who had stepped only around the corner, immediately re-entered it and found the letter upon her desk. He approached it (as he thought wise to do) with his hands clasped behind his back. He read it quickly, keeping well away from it and fighting a strong urge to pick up the letter, to look at it more closely, to bring it near his eyes. Instead, with a shiver, he stepped away, glancing back to see the page disappear in a single flare of red, leaving no ash.

Though he had not heard the name of Hetman Gohdan Gone, he had been told about sorcerous documents. Such manuscripts were often designed with a dual purpose, first to convey a spell or enchantment, second to entrap the person who read or touched them, making them subservient to the sorcerer's will. It was good he had handled only the envelope.

Within the hour, Rashel ordered the carriage for a trip to Apocanew, directing Michael to the street corner where he had taken her before. She told him to return in two hours' time, and after the carriage turned a corner and disappeared, Rashel walked toward the Hetman's gate, taking no notice of the small boy who came around the corner where the carriage had turned. He followed her at a distance, obviously preoccupied with the ball he was bouncing against buildings and walkways, always leaping and scrambling to catch it before it bounded into the street.

The keeper of the iron gate was as rude as usual, and gaining the Hetman's dwelling was as onerous. The way seemed longer, the air colder in the hallways, hotter in his room.

He told her to be seated, and when she had done so, he remarked, "Quite unexpected, Dismé running off like that."

"Temporarily," murmured Rashel. "They won't keep her long. She's totally inept."

"Tsk," murmured Gone. "She was the only one left in Bastion, and you let her get away. And after you'd been so efficient with all the others. But then, Dismé was the only one you were specifically ordered to keep alive."

She looked puzzled, not understanding him.

"The others went so very neatly, too. I always admired the ease with which you disposed of her father and brother, and you barely into your teens. No one ever thought you'd done it."

For a moment, Rashel's heart stopped. This was a new tack, something never mentioned before, something she had not been sure he even knew. Still, his voice had not been angry.

She was practiced enough at these interviews not to dissimulate. She replied in a monotone, "It wasn't difficult. The man wasn't my father, and he didn't like me. Roger wasn't my brother and he slapped my face. I didn't like them."

"You didn't mind at all?"

"Roger was *his* favorite. And Roger couldn't stand being called a coward: he would walk on the bridge parapet above the river, showing off. All it took was a little push."

Hetman Gone was, for a moment, silent. When she said nothing more, he murmured, "And Val Latimer?"

"I brewed foxglove from the garden and put it into his tea. His heart was bad anyhow. It didn't take much."

"Well you did it very neatly. Your mother knew, of course."

She gasped. She had had no idea her mother knew!

"Oh, yes. That's why she brought you to me, after you killed Roger. She had to. She was under instructions to protect all three of the Latimers. You had killed one of them, which meant your life was forfeit, Rashel. Then you killed again, and for the second time she convinced me you'd be useful. I'm afraid she was wrong."

She sat, stony faced, her mind awash in confusion.

The Hetman went on. "Five of them altogether, wasn't it. Roger, your step-brother. Latimer, your step-father. Then your own mother. Then Arnole, and Ayward—oh, you didn't kill those two, I know, but you disposed of them, nonetheless. If only you'd been *told* to dispose of them, I could congratulate you. You weren't ordered to do anything to Arnole or his son, however, so why did you?"

In deep confusion, Rashel moved fretfully. "They were complicating things, attracting attention. Ayward would go on and on about Inclusionism." She swallowed deeply and attempted an appearance of candor. "It wasn't done as neatly as I planned. For some reason they both disappeared."

"True, neatness escaped you. But Arnole and Ayward are not the ones I regret. It's the three Latimers I wanted: not killed, not hurt, not maimed, only watched and kept, for we of the Fell may need one or all of them alive and unhurt. You weren't punished for killing Roger or his father, and we forgave your mother in return for her donating your life and services, and for keeping tight watch on our little bird. Then you disposed of your mother, which wasn't authorized, and the duty fell to you. Now . . . now we no longer have her. You have cost us much, Rashel, and you have given us little. What will you do about it, ah?"

"They'll send her home," Rashel blurted.

"I think it unlikely. I feel wheels spinning within wheels, circles emerging from circles, the pivoting and whirling of forces, while the danger looms still. The Latimer lineage is of unusual interest to certain powers outside Bastion, and you have let the only Latimer in Bastion get away."

"In Bastion? You mean there are others?"

"Latimers? Oh, yes. One here, one there. A dozen or so outside. Who knows how many altogether? Each new bit of information only serves to confirm their importance, as is clear from my reading of the Book of Fell." He laid a huge, horny hand upon the book beside him, a heavy book, with unevenly cut pages and patches of mold on the cover. She shuddered. The book had played a part in her dedication. At least, the thing that had emerged from its pages had played a part.

The Hetman went on. "But you weren't responsible for any of the others. Dismé was the only one of the Latimers you needed to concern yourself with."

"Why are we concerned about Latimers outside Bastion?"

"You're questioning me?" His tone was amused.

She swallowed deeply, moistening dry lips with her tongue. "I'm naturally curious, that's all. I have long thought I could serve you better if you involved me in your magic. I know you have magic. Several of my dear friends have spoken of it, to me, without mentioning your name, of course, but I knew who they meant."

"You have wanted to be involved in my magic," he said musingly. "Now that's an idea."

"And I could serve you better if I knew why Dismé is so important!"

Gohdan Gone chuckled, such a clatter as a gibbet load of bones might make, rattling in a cold wind. "You work best when you do what you were told during your dedication. You were perhaps distracted at the time? I will tell you once more. The Lost Book of Bertral says there is or will be a Guardian Council. There are a score or more members of this Council. We read this in the Book of the Great Fell, whom I serve, whom you serve. Whoever or whatever this council may be, it will be inimical to us, and the Latimers have something to do with it. We of Fell don't want a Guardian Council. Now, what will you do?"

She drew herself up. "I'll visit her in Hold! I intended to go there in any case. I am part of the commission studying The Artifact. There is a meeting there in a few day's time."

"Of course you are part of the commission," he murmured, looking her full in the face. "Another of the little benefits we have provided you." He hummed under his breath. "Have you learned yet what it is?"

"No. No one has any idea. Not at this stage."

"What do you think it is?" he demanded.

She took a deep breath. "I believe it is a crystallized process, something which was ensorceled into being but never potentiated."

He pinned her with his glance, his eyes red in the fireglow. "An interesting concept. And was there a book with it?"

"No one has seen a book. The whole cellar has been excavated, and all that's there is the thing itself."

"While you are in Hold, take care of Dismé. Somehow, you must take her back to Faience."

She licked her lips again, and murmured, "I found a recipe a few years ago, in one of the old books Caigo Faience had collected. It was an account of a potion used by black magicians in the deep past. The drug seems to kill, but the one dosed and seeming dead may rise again, subservient to the will of the person who does the raising up. It uses the liver of a certain fish, which I've obtained through trade channels."

"Does it work?"

"I'm not sure I have the incantation right, but the drug part works well enough. I've done several dogs, buried them, dug them up, brought them back."

"Pfah. Chemistry. We of Fell do not trust in that." He opened a box beside him on the table and took from it a curled pale scrap of skin, scant hair still sprouting from it. "Here on this parchment is the recipe for Tincture of Oblivion, all the ingredients spelled out. You will create this, and you will use this. If you let her escape, all our confidence in you will be gone. And once we have no further use for you . . . well, you know. What the Fell did to you before, but slightly, he will take pleasure in doing again, and this time you will die of it."

She was sweating, not only from fear and the heat of the fire, but also from the words she read on the parchment and the wrath that consumed her inwardly. Though it was a fury she dared not show, she said stubbornly, "I wish I understood all this focus on her, her father and her brother and her kin!"

He leaned back in his chair, seeming to ruminate for a

moment, chewing over the alternatives. When he spoke, it was almost a whisper. "One time, one time only, I will tell you *why*. You will never ask *why* again.

"It was revealed to me that Latimer would rise up against me. Therefore, I sought Latimer and found a lineage that began at the time of my arrival on this world with one couple and their two children. He, Latimer, was the founder of the Spared. His first woman was gone in the Happening, but the children remained, two of them, male and female, who sired or bore into successive generations. I took the Spared as my people, and I guided them to make a source of power for me. I have identified the descendants of that line, and have set a watcher over each of them against the time one of them will rise up against me. So I found Val Latimer and his children, so I set your mother, and so I have set you as watcher."

"Why don't we kill them all?"

"To do so would change a future which benefits me. Now do not ask me why ever again."

She bowed, fighting to maintain control of herself.

Gohdan Gone purred, a sound like the warning rattle of a snake. "She's perched there in Hold. Don't let her get away. And if, by chance, she eludes you, waste not a minute in following after her, for we will be following you."

She had neither resolution nor obstinacy left. For the moment she was beaten. "Yes, Master," she breathed. "I won't let her get away."

When Rashel emerged from the gate on the street, the small boy was still busy bouncing his ball off a flight of steps at the corner. He saw her emerge and went swiftly around the corner and down an alleyway, where he found Michael leaning against the carriage eating a sausage roll.

"She went into a hole down the block," said the boy. "There's a gate and a keeper."

"Ah?" murmured Michael, expectantly.

The child gave him a shrewd, completely adult wink. "Once she was in, I made myself useful. There's an apartment up above, with a window looking down on the hole, and there's an old woman living there. I helped her carry her marketing up to her rooms. She says she's seen this one and that one coming and going. She's heard one of them ask for Hetman Gone. Strangeness is . . ."

"Strangeness is what, Bab?" asked Michael, wiping the grease off his chin with his kerchief.

"Strangeness is, people go in and come out, not staying long, in and out, several over a few days, then nobody for some long time, then several again . . ."

"So?"

"But nobody ever goes in and stays. So, if there's somebody living in there, they get in there another way."

Michael felt in his pockets, discarding splits and bits until his fingers found a Holdmark. He tossed it to the boy, who caught it in one snatching fist and put it into his pocket. "You helped her carry her shopping, eh?" he said, looking up and down Bab's toddler body and babyish face.

"Well, you know," smiled Bab. "I'm stronger than I look."

✦ 32

dismé in hold

As Hetman Gone had said, Dismé was indeed perched in
Hold, though she was not singing. There was no time for
singing among the books she was to read, the dialects she
was to learn, the bare-handed fighting technique she was to
master. Since it was less troublesome to delegate this last
than to worry over it, she put the matter in Roarer's paws
and told it to learn well. Though Dismé herself was not conscious of making progress, the master seemed satisfied.

Arriving via the back stairs and the ledge outside the doctor's window—a secret way, he had told her, that could
never be disclosed to anyone else—she spent many evenings
in his quarters, reading pre-Happening books aloud to him
over dinner, or joining him in learning country songs that
were, so he said, current outside Bastion. He had prided
himself on his voice until he heard hers, which was remarkable.

"You must have sung a great deal to get a voice like that."

She shook her head. "Only to myself, when I was alone,
out in the woods. It went along with my twiddling."

"Twiddling?"

"You know, pounding on things, making a rhythm."

Though she had begun with some suspicion of his motives, as the days wore on she came to trust him. He remained unfailingly friendly and appreciative without ever

indicating he thought of her as anything but a useful person who might as well have been sexless. She was incapable of imagining that this cost him some effort.

She made one trip to Newland on the doctor's behalf, where she visited Gayla and Genna and retrieved the book of Nell Latimer. Since her quarters were subject to periodic housekeeping inspections, the doctor kept it for her among his secret things; after reading it, he was extremely thoughtful.

At the end of several spans she entered his office via the reception area, her face closed and dull, responding to Captain Trublood's greeting with a murmured "morning," and was admitted into the doctor's presence. Here she was greeted with his assessment, gratuitously offered, that she was beginning to shape up. She, who had come to his office for quite another reason, was much flustered by this.

"That was a compliment," said the doctor, sternly.

"Yes, sir. Yes, thank you, sir."

"The Fight Master says you are becoming quite skilled. He wonders how this is possible, in such a short time."

She flushed. "I . . . I really don't know, Doctor."

"He is impressed. He would like to know the secret, so he can impress it upon other students. Take it as a compliment."

"Thank you," she murmured. "But I came about something else." She handed him the letter she had just received.

"You are to receive a visit from your sister," he commented, looking at her quizzically over the top of the letter.

"My step-sister," she said, quietly. "She has never wished me happiness. I think she may be trying to kill me."

"Ah," he said, quirking his eyebrows at her, as he did from time to time when she did something momentarily puzzling. "Why?"

"I don't know. I suspect that she killed my brother and father, though I don't know her reason for that, either. I do know she uses people, uses them up, and when they've been used up, they are chaired or gone. She has never finished with someone then let them go on to something else. She goes on sucking the life out of them long after she's through with them."

"She says business brings her to Hold. Would you have any idea what that may be about?"

"Wasn't some mysterious artifact discovered here in the Fortress not long ago? Down in a cellar, I think. She is a member of some study commission for such a device."

He stared at her, unblinking. "Did she mention that?"

"To her husband. I overheard."

"Well. Since you already know about it, perhaps we can give her a surprise. She says she arrives day after tomorrow. There has been a good deal of conjecture about this artifact, and some people have drawn conclusions—unwarranted ones I think, but understandable nonetheless. Let's arrange that your meeting shall be in an unexpected manner and place, in my presence, and immediately thereafter we will depart, which will give her no time to harm you. Does that solve the problem?"

She frowned, suspecting he was up to mischief, but sure that he grasped her feelings well enough. "I suppose it solves that one. Isn't our departure rather sudden, though?"

"Not really, no. I didn't tell you everything about our making the trip. The foremost reason for going is to warn the harmless people near the borders to get out of the way before Bastion boils over and scalds the countryside. Again."

"Again," she murmured, remembering the demon's words in the cavern.

"The Regime used to do it quite regularly. Then the demons took to picking us off . . . but you don't know about demons . . ."

"I know they come into the cities," she said quietly. "I was only eight when I first saw them, going out of the city and adding to a bottle wall. I was up on the wall, in a place my mother had shown me."

"You astonish me," he said. "You remember your mother?"

"Yes. She went away when I was very young. I never knew why, though since I've grown up I've wondered if perhaps she wasn't threatened by the Regime. I came to know later that many of the things she told me were not . . . Regimic."

"I had a mother like that, as well," he said, his eyes crinkling. "And I, too, was very young and bereft when she departed, though my father seemed impervious to grief. He married again, very soon."

He mused for a moment as she stood patiently before him, then came to himself. "Is there something else?"

"Yes. I received another message, this one from Michael Pigeon, our driver at Faience. He has been working here in Hold for a short time. He wants to take me to dinner tonight."

"Aha," said the doctor, his voice tight. "Young love."

She frowned. "He's older than I, by a little bit; neither of us is really young, and love has never been mentioned, but I do . . . value Michael. I just don't know whether continuing the acquaintance is a good idea . . ."

The doctor peered at his desk for a moment, then said, "He's a driver, you said?"

"Yes, sir. He has an instinctive understanding of horses, or so I've been told. They seem to think he is another horse, or at least the ones at Faience did."

"In that case, I direct you to meet with him tonight, as he asks, and arrange for him to meet with me tomorrow."

Amazed, she agreed.

Michael had suggested a small café not far from the Fortress. She did not realize how much the separation had changed her until she saw his face.

"You look . . . marvelous," he said, his eyes wider than usual.

"It's the hair, I think. I learned a new way to do it."

"Not just that."

"The clothes, then. They make a difference in how I feel."

Michael flushed. "You never seemed to care about your clothing, but you were always beautiful."

"Michael! That's nonsense. As for clothes, Rashel always picked them, so the less I cared, the better."

He shook his head ruefully. "I came here thinking maybe I could help you, but you seem to have helped yourself."

"I fell into a job that suits me, that's all. Speaking of which, my colonel at BHE wants to meet you. Tomorrow."

"Why?" he asked, pulling from the table in sudden alarm.

"Don't get upset," she cried. "He's a very good sort of person. It's possible he needs a driver."

"Him? He can get drivers by the dozen!"

"Well, it was when I said you were a driver that he got this curious look on his face and said 'hmmm.' " She peered into his face, then said in a disappointed voice, "But then, you probably already have a job you like."

"I have a job I don't like," he said angrily. "I took a post with a Turnaway family, and I did it too quickly. The only thing good about the place is they have a Praiser cook! The Mister is a dainty lay-about, something or other in the Division of Taxation, and the wife, one he obviously married for reasons of conformity, is the worst flirt I've encountered in my thirty years. She'll get me gelded or die in the attempt."

She laughed. "Poor Michael. Come to the Fortress tomorrow. About mid-morning, Doctor Ladislav said. You may say you were summoned, if your current employer objects."

"Oh, he'll object," muttered Michael, still unable to take his eyes off Dismé.

That settled, they had their dinner. When it was over, Dismé had shared some of her secret thoughts, as Michael had, and the two knew a good deal more about one another, enough, Dismé found herself thinking, to lead to other such occasions.

When Michael returned to his quarters, he spent a few restless hours reviewing his life and questioning what he had done with it. The first twenty years had been spent on a horse farm on the Praise border, working with his father and half-brothers in the breeding of horseflesh. When he grew older he'd discovered that the same focused gentleness that worked well with horseflesh also seemed to work well with women. Though he'd had no feminine influence in his life since his mother vanished when Michael was two, Michael seemed to understand women almost as well as he understood horses.

The farms were widespread thereabout, set at the toes of the mountains, with forests full of strange creatures, earthly and unearthly, almost at the doorstep. People on the border still buried their dead without bottling any part of them, the accepted local fiction (for BHE ears) being that the old folks had just walked up into the hills and disappeared. One might go to grandpa's funeral one day (which, in local argot, was called "visiting the sick") and the next day tell BHE a long story about how grandpa disappeared, with all the other mourners chiming in, correcting details, and nodding their heads in agreement. No one felt it was lying. It was just a way of getting along.

At age twenty, Michael had gone to Apocanew in search of excitement, and he'd worked for the BHE for a while, keeping their horses, long enough to figure he didn't want to be there long. Everything was twisted in the BHE, sanctimonious reasons covering unspoken motives that were far from holy. The only thing worse than making waves was making eyes at some high-up's wife or daughter. At that level, women were a kind of coin used to obtain advancement, and if they fell in love it greatly reduced their value.

Men were also said to be chaste, except, that is, with outlanders. Rapine among outlanders was overlooked. Since outlanders weren't really people, what one did with them wasn't really sex. Some authorities even held that it was impossible for a Spared One to impregnate an outlander, since they were no doubt of different species. In the stables he'd heard a good bit about "hunting trips" outside the borders, from elderly men who'd gone on such raids when younger, for the enjoyment of the hunt.

In the stables he'd learned if a man kept his mouth shut and looked both busy and stupid, people would forget he was there. As a result, Michael learned more than he cared to about the inner workings of the BHE. At twenty-six, he'd taken leave from the BHE, planning to go back home for a while, but on the journey, he'd fallen in with some people. After a few days of their company, he'd sent word home that he'd been delayed, and he didn't actually get there until well over a year later with a story about prospecting in the highlands above Comador, where he'd found a source of gold, showing, as proof, a pocketful of little nuggets.

Then a particular someone asked him to go back to BHE, where his good credentials were still in effect, and get himself assigned to Faience. It hadn't taken a great deal of doing. He was good with horses, and he didn't mind the solitude. Of the candidates for the job, Michael had been obviously the best choice. He'd been told what to look out for, and he had looked out for it.

He hadn't been told to look out for Dismé Latimer, but it was due to her he'd stayed as long as he had. Women as a class, he liked very much just as horses, as a class, he liked very much, but a woman who made him feel protective, careful, almost brotherlike, that was new. He'd never felt for any woman what he had come to feel for Dismé, a feeling he could not name.

And now he'd told her he would meet with her boss, who Dismé had called a good man. Did she know? Was she guessing? Or worse, was she taking it on faith. Or worse yet, was he something more to her than a boss? Despite his doubts, when morning came he kept the date with Colonel Doctor Ladislav, who glanced up to wave him to a chair.

"Sit," he said.

Michael sat.

The Colonel Doctor remarked, "Understand you're a good man with horses."

"I was raised in that business, sir. Father's a horse breeder, over along the Praise border."

"Did Dismé tell you what we're going to be doing?"

"Traveling, she said. I didn't really get . . ."

"Well, she doesn't get it either." He lowered his voice. "There are only a few of us who ah . . . explore up near the border. Prospecting, really. Finding things we can use. You wouldn't mind going along?"

Michael flushed and said, stiffly, "Sir, I heard a good bit about BHE traveling when I worked for the BHE in Apocanew. The men . . . they seemed to take a good deal of pleasure in it, but . . ."

"Oh," murmured the doctor. He rose, went to the door and shut it quietly. "You're thinking of that kind of traveling. Going outside and kidnapping youngsters? Raping women before torturing them to death? Killing off this one and that one? Maybe drunken orgies thrown in, to bond the men together? Eh?"

"Yes, sir." And he gave the Colonel Doctor a straight look. "That kind of pack hunting, it doesn't sit well with me, sir."

"Nor me," murmured the older man. "You know why they allow it, don't you? It defuses aggression. The Regime wants aggression used up out there, not in here. I would prefer to train it out or breed it out of our people, but my preference doesn't govern. If a society thinks it needs weapons, it must accept killing. If it thinks it needs violent men, it must accept rapine and assault."

Michael found himself nodding. "I didn't like to think of Miss Dismé in that kind of . . . affair."

"No. You like her, do you?"

Michael kept his face carefully attentive, but only that, as he said, "I admire her, sir. Up there at Faience, she was like . . . like an owl among a clutter of hens."

The doctor blinked. He hadn't thought of Dismé in quite that light. "Her sister—step-sister. A hen?"

"No, sir. Not her. That one is a shrike. Cripple you and hang you out on the thorn tree to eat later."

"I see. Are you willing to leave your current job?"

"You'll have to requisition me, sir. This Turnaway bravo, he won't just let me go. He doesn't bear inconvenience."

"Which one is he?"

Michael said, "Gars Kensy Turnaway."

The doctor made a face. "Another by-blow from on high. I think my requisition will suffice, nonetheless. Here's how to find my quarters. Be there around noon."

"Your quarters, sir?"

"Except for this one encounter, I don't want you to be seen with me or coming and going from where I am. There's a spy planted in my office, and I don't want him getting his hands on anything real. When you get near my quarters, be sure no one is hanging about before you slip in. The door will be unlocked."

Michael blinked at that. It was a strange thing to say, unless, that is, the doctor knew more about him than he was letting on. "My duties, sir?"

"Oh. This and that. You have my word that nothing you do for me will offend your conscience." Jens wrote out a requisition slip, signed it with a fine flourish, and patted Michael on the shoulder before he opened the door. "I'm relying on your discretion, Pigeon."

"Who's that?" demanded Captain Trublood.

"Nobody much," the doctor answered, yawning. "Someone reputed to be good with horses. The vet service needs some new men." Which Captain Trublood knew, because he had been filing requisitions for the veterinarian service all span.

"Ah," said the captain, losing interest. Captain Trublood had lost interest in most facets of his job, which seemed to be either doing paperwork, running errands any ten-year-old could run, or following the doctor to see where he went. So far as Captain Trublood could tell, Jens Ladislav was just what he said he was, despite that almost heretical conversation they'd had.

The doctor returned to his office where he added Michael's putative veterinary service application to a huge pile of documents and then carried the pile out to the captain.

"Trublood, I have some things that need to be filed," said the doctor, with his usual pleasant smile. "I hate to ask you to do them . . ." his voice fell to a whisper. " . . . but quite frankly, you're the only one here I can depend upon to do it absolutely accurately. While you're doing so, look through them so you'll have a grasp of the contents."

"What are they, sir," murmured the captain, momentarily gratified.

"All manner of things. Chair specifications. Agreements we've had in the past with our . . . suppliers. Inventories. Files on my informants. Staff assignments. That sort of thing, you know? Some of it not for the eyes of people who aren't rock solid, you know." He gave the captain a half wink and a nod.

"Of course. Yes sir."

The doctor had spent part of one night collecting this pile from the stored files in the sub-basement. He had dusted them off, rearranged them, put some of the material in the wrong folders, invented several new folders to which he had added spurious documents concerning his movements and Dismé's future assignments, plus an assignment sheet of Michael Pigeon to the Regime Horse Farm in Praise. He had capped it off by making a number of mysteriously significant notations on documents of no significance at all. It should take the captain several days to go through all this, sort it out, make up his spy report for the Colonel Bishop, and then find the right places to put them all back. When the doctor left Bastion, he would leave a long list of other useless work for the captain to do.

Now, however, as a kind of capstone to this stratagem, he asked, "Oh, by the way, are congratulations in order?"

"For what, sir?"

"Oh, isn't there something about you and the bishop's daughter? Which one are you marrying? Mavia? Lorena?"

The captain turned a peculiar shade of green and swallowed with some difficulty. "No sir. I'm sure you're mistaken, sir."

"Oh. Well, sorry then. I was sure the bishop told me he'd picked you out, but perhaps he meant someone else." And with a repeat of his charming smile, the doctor retreated. He had actually heard it from his barber, who had it from Scilla's maid, who had it from Scilla, who had it from the bishop's wife, but that was of no matter.

The captain went to the toilets, where he shut himself in and put his head down. He had met both Mavia and Lorena. He regarded being married to either of them as equivalent to being married to the bishop himself, whom they much resembled, right down to the moustache. Either of the ladies outweighed the captain by a considerable margin. Mavia

had a squint, and Lorena was afflicted with continuous ca-
tarrh. He could not possibly do a husbandly and Regimic
duty by either of them. It was time, perhaps, that he develop
some kind of physical problem. Something hereditary.
Something the doctor could mention to the bishop that
would make him ineligible for the great honor the bishop
had in mind.

Michael, meantime, made his way back to the house of
Gars Kensy Turnaway, bastard son of the bishop and a Turnaway madwoman, presented his requisition, listened to the
Turnaway git whine about it, then packed his things, which
took only a few moments as he hadn't liked the place well
enough to unpack. He found a hostelry near the Fortress, the
same one Dismé occupied for a few days on arrival in Hold,
and at the appointed time was at Jens Ladislav's quarters—
walking past but not entering the last hallway until it was totally empty—where he shared a glass of wine with the
doctor while the doctor explained his plans for almost immediate departure, information not to be shared with anyone
except Dismé, said the doctor, particularly not with anyone
in the doctor's outer office.

Perhaps imprudently, Michael asked, "Why do you figure
they're watching you, sir?"

"Don't they watch us all?"

And with that, Michael had to be content. He was given a
rather large purse and sent off with a great list of things to
be bought and done and accomplished within the next day
and a half. On his way out, he encountered Dismé in the vast
main hallway and mentioned his errand. "We're leaving
morning after next, is that it?"

Dismé nodded. "Yes, because Rashel is coming to Hold,
tomorrow."

"Rashel! You're not going to meet with her!"

"The Doctor will be there. I think he has something surprising arranged."

He scowled and muttered. "I've known men like the doctor, people who will stir things up. I hope it's not he—or
you—who gets the surprise. Be careful, Dis."

The need for this was so obvious it required no answer. She left him, with a brave smile which was not entirely faked, knowing he was right; the doctor was like a boy pushing a stick between the bars at a huge, caged beast. Sometimes beasts broke the bars that held them. She would be well-advised to keep that in mind.

dezmai of the drums

And what is he up to, Colonel Doctor Jens Ladislav? What wicked thoughts percolate in his eager brain, what mischief is he turning his hands to? His prancing feet dance a razor's edge between the rigors of the Regime and his perception of the preposterous, an inborn and thus inescapable discernment which should have gotten him bottled long ago. The Regime does not allow itself to be thought ridiculous, and it is only the unaccountability of fate, thinks he, that is responsible for his impunity thus far.

So, aha, says he, there's this body that calls itself a Guardian Council, a body—so one is told—that maketh much magic, which magic the Regime has sought for a very long time, with only intermittent success—that is, if one doesn't count the kind of practices General Gowl is probably accomplished at. And so, ahum, there's this thing in the Fortress cellar that seems magical enough for whole rafts of sorcery, and also a sorcerous book that he, and himself alone, has found. And finally, aaah, there's this woman Dismé, who, providentially and damn near miraculously, has turned out to be not at all weird or tongue-tied, as described by Major Marchant, but a sensible woman who has agreed to work with him.

Now, thinks the doctor, Dismé has a sister, an inimical and dangerous kinswoman—not really kin, there's no shared blood—who nonetheless continues to assert a kinswoman's claims of courtesy and friendly-feeling with no return of same on her side. *Also*, the sister is an Inexplicable Arts functionary of the BHE, who talks a good line of jargon that the mossy-mouths in Hold have fallen for, or into, whichever! Most likely she's coaxed them into her web with sexual wiles, for Major Marchant has that look about him, and according to the doctor's spies, the major is not alone in sharing Rashel's favors. The Warden of the College of Sorcery in Apocanew, Bice Dufor, has been mentioned, as well as Chief of the Department of Inexplicable Arts, the great Ardis Flenstall himself, which would explain why Selectivism has become so popular at BHE in such a very short time.

And, chortles the Colonel Doctor, if this concatenation of persons and motives and myths isn't a wonderful opportunity for mischief, then he'll be a demon's uncle.

So down goes the Colonel Doctor by the main stairs, bowing to this one and that one, always smiling that wicked smile of his, the consequence of being born with lips that will not turn down, not so much as a smitch, not even in those times when he would trade his eyebrows for a good scowl. As for instance now, when a forbidding expression would save him a good deal of time spent in idle chit-chat and greetings when he is afire to leave the Fortress and get on with his conniving. He has shopping to do!

So, it's down the cobbled street leading from the Fortress, long enough to note if he's being followed, which, today, he is not; then off to one side a couple of times this way and that, and then a straight trot along an alley where, half hidden behind a display of masks and bonnets, is the lair of Madame Ladassa Veyair, a dealer in wigs and costumes (sold mostly to Praisers), and, by virtue of long experience, an expert in disguise. The doctor often has need of disguise in his line of work and he has made a close friend of Madame Veyair by helping Madame's people slip back and forth across the borders of Bastion. Madame and her people count themselves as rebels and could be chaired in a minute or bottled in less than that if the Regime knew what they were up to. It is in the doctor's interest to be sure the Regime never catches on.

Once inside, the Colonel Doctor, with a conspiratorial glance at the closed door of the shop, slips from beneath his cape the blocky shape of the book and moves toward the small office at the rear on jigging feet, beckoning Madame Veyair to follow. There he opens the book and points, eyes alight at her expression.

She sees a woman wearing a complicated headdress of unmistakably arcane significance, all gilt and glass, with beaded tassels that hang about the ears; a woman whose forehead is painted a brilliant blue that shades to green along her jaws; a woman whose eyebrows, eyelids, lips, and hands have been gilded; who wears a long, high-necked dress of shiny blue and a sweeping velvety cape patterned all over in blue, green, and gold.

"Who?" asks Madame, with what amazement she can summon, not a great deal. Madame has seen more of the world than would be supposed. "Who is this? Or, more likely, who is she who is to be got up to look like this?"

"The latter, a woman who works for me."

She purses her lips, running a finger along the page that describes Dezmai of the Drums. "Is she at all like this?"

"She is, I think, a mirror to this." He looks upward in innocent wonderment, eyes wide, miming his own marvel.

"And what is the so-what of that?"

Now he focuses, whispering: "Sorcery, Madame. She is, I believe, a gateway into sorcery. Perhaps merely to a rivulet running from a sourceary, or a wee spigot from the mother of all barrels, or perhaps . . ."

"I understand," she crisply interrupts this flow. "When?"

"The garb will have to be ready by tomorrow noon. We leave Hold early the following morning."

"What size is she?" she asks, busily making notes between glances at the pictured Dezmai.

"She comes to here on me," he says, placing his hand just below his chin. He is a tall man, indicating a taller than average woman. "Slender. Not a lot of . . . chest or hip. She says she climbs trees a lot." Again his eyes are dancing as he contemplates Dismé up a tree.

"With a free stride, then? And an erect posture." More notes, referring to color, to size. A quick sketch of the head-dress, done in colored inks, all within moments.

"Exactly."

She hesitates, fixes him with imperious eyes. "Jens. You've given me barely enough time. Before I stretch myself and my people, tell me you're not imperiling this woman for your own amusement."

For a moment, his dancing eyes grow wary, his prancing feet grow still. "I would never do so, Ladassa. Not this woman."

"And you do not want anyone else to know about this?"

"Oh, we will all be much, much safer if no one else knows anything about this."

"I have notes enough. My memory is acute. We will bring the costume to your quarters before noon tomorrow."

"Do not be seen, Ladassa."

"You have trustworthy helpers, Jens. So do I."

"A final trifle," he said, with a bow. "For myself I need a farmer's outfit with a full beard, and paint for a horse, and for her a cloak, one that will cover her from head to toe."

After a virtually sleepless night, Dismé spent the morning cleaning her quarters and packing for the journey, reporting for work in early afternoon by going up the back stairway and entering the doctor's apartment from the residential corridor, thus avoiding Captain Trublood's minatory eye. So far, the captain had no reason to take any real notice of her. She was plain, she was seldom around and when present was always laden with dusty papers.

The doctor was waiting for her inside, with a strange expression on his face. His hand rested on a rather large box.

"What's wrong?" she asked, thinking immediately of Rashel.

"Nothing at the moment," he said, "beyond the usual wrongness that permeates most everything under the

Regime." He guided her to a chair and seated himself across from her, regarding her with a curious combination of curiosity and daring.

"I need to discuss something with you seriously."

"Very well."

"You must not take offense."

"I will endeavor not to do so."

"Um," he said, and again, "Um. Have you ever . . . have you ever thought that you might be someone else? Some other woman?"

"What woman?" Dismé asked in astonishment. "Who?"

"I have found a picture of a woman who looks remarkably like you, but she's called Dezmai of the Drums."

"Dezmai? But that's . . ."

"I know. Very close to your own name. Even more interesting—a fact which I have found out only recently, due to diligent, even exhausting labors—is the fact that your father, Dismé, may have been great-great something grandson of Abnozar Latimer, whose drumming signalled the danger at Trekker's Halt and saved the lives of a great many people." He cocked his head, to see how she took this.

She took it with a grain of salt. "He never mentioned it," she murmured.

He shrugged. "It is interesting, nonetheless. The picture resembles you greatly."

"Who is this person supposed to be?"

"A member of the Guardian Council."

Her mouth dropped open. "You're making an outrageous joke?"

"No. I have a book picturing the members of the Guardian Council . . ."

She put out her hands, fending him off. "No one has ever had a picture of the Council! The Dicta say we have angels, so we don't need Guardians, and while I don't necessarily believe that, nobody's ever seen the so-called Council . . ."

"It isn't true that no member of the Council has been seen. There was the woman of flame who appeared to Hal P'Jardas. One the general claims to have seen but probably hasn't."

She frowned. "Oh, yes. I'd forgotten about Tamlar of the Flames. I heard about her from Arnole!"

He peered at her. "You continue to astonish me. You have seen demons. You have read pre-Happening books. Now you admit familiarity with a story that probably wouldn't be recognized by a dozen persons in the Fortress. The Archives have the original account, of course, but the book I spoke of and the Artifact in the cellars are the first bits of confirming, physical evidence."

"And where did this book come from?"

He regarded her thoughtfully. "I found it, purely by accident, but if you tell anyone I have it or where I got it, I am likely to be chaired or bottled by morning."

"Will you at least stop talking about it and show it to me!" she said irritably.

He leapt to his feet and brought it from the next room, unwrapping it with great ceremony to lay it open before her. She stared at it, unbelieving.

"It looks like me."

"Indeed. That's what I thought the moment I saw you."

"She's carrying a drum."

"As a matter of fact, I brought one for you, if you want it." He pointed to a small drum lying on the table, one he had purchased on his way back from his visit to the costumer's.

"And this resemblance was the reason you sent the letter?"

"No. I didn't know you resembled the picture, but your name had come before me three times. Once in a letter to me from a person unknown, once from the lips of an old friend of yours, a little boy you played with in the Apocanew park, and once in a discussion of Faience among certain officers. This book was only the final flick of the whip. To my mind, all that was a sufficient cause for action."

"Because of this 'Protector' bit?" she asked, running her finger along the pertinent line of text.

"That, yes. Come, sit down. Let me expatiate!"

He guided her to a chair and sat down opposite her, leaning forward intently. "I've come to believe, from experience and reading and what I've learned on the outside, that the

Regime—I suppose really, one might say any regime—is rather like a pot of porridge. If vigorously stirred every now and then, it can be a nourishing if not always tasty staple, but if left on the heat unstirred for some time it becomes increasing stodgy. If left untended, it can char into an immovable solid, like coal.

"Thereafter, it is incapable of being stirred, incapable of providing nourishment. When a regime is like that, citizens have to resort to bribery or lawbreaking to do quite necessary things like digging wells or fixing roads, thus joining corruption to congealment. Between the Dicta and the Chairs and the bottles, our Regime has been charred for at least one or two generations, not only immovable but also immoral."

She frowned at him, for he was making her decidedly uneasy.

Her expression made him blather self-consciously, "The Regime cries out to be stirred, vigorously! If there is truly a Guardian Council, then evidence of it should stir the Regime to its roots . . ." He paused, as though making room for her to object. " . . . and what would be better evidence than for one of them to show up!"

She shut her lips firmly and put on her vacant expression.

This made him even more self-conscious. He said in a wheedling tone: "If it makes you too uncomfortable . . ."

"If *I* am not to be *I*, how can *I* be uncomfortable," she said sharply. "Who am I to deprive you of your amusements, Doctor? I am yours to command, and since you take this Guardian Protector thing seriously, I presume you don't intend to endanger me."

He flushed. "No! Of course not!"

"Your whim is my command," she muttered.

He nodded, face as serious as he was able to make it be. "I suspect there's little difference between whim and inspiration at the beginning of any chain of events. It's what happens later that tells us which is which."

She rose and went to the table where the book lay, open. "What does this mean? *'This is Dezmai, in whose charge are*

*the howls of battle, the roars of great beasts, the lumbering
of herds, the mutter and clap of thunder, the tumult of waves
upon stone, the cry of trumpets, the clamor of the avalanche . . .'"*

"I have no idea," he replied. "Also, please, once we leave
this room today, don't feel impelled to quote it. Say absolutely nothing about it. Not to anyone. Don't respond to
any questions. I don't want anyone to hear your voice."

"Many people here know who I am."

"I've brought you Dezmai's costume. It will cover you
from head to toe." He opened the box and presented it with
a low bow.

"And where are we going?"

"We're going down a great many stairs to the cellar where
the device is."

"We're going to see the device?" Her face lighted up with
excitement.

"We are. The place has been fully excavated by now, and
it's well lit. When you enter the chamber, there will be a
short stair in front of you. You'll go down it, and the device
will be directly before you. All you need do is go down the
steps, walk up to the device and look at it. Really look at it.
Stare at it. As though you are . . . memorizing it."

"Why?"

"Observe the picture in the book. That's what she's
doing."

"What is this device? It looks like a frozen wave."

"It's what you see there, a shape, like a chunk of dark
glassy stone, yes, a featureless mass except for a place
halfway up one side where there is a good deal of cloudy
discoloration. Everyone thinks it's magical, of course. The
bishop is staking his career on it . . ."

"The bishop?"

"He's ambitious. If this thing turns out to be magical, it
comes under the Division of Culture, which is BHE, which
is the bishop's purview. The thing certainly looks sorcerous,
doesn't it? Though, oddly enough, the text says nothing
about it."

She nodded. "It sounds simple enough."

"Your sister will be there. You'll put in an appearance, then turn around and leave. If she follows, I'll delay her while you come back here."

Dismé reflected, trying to decide if that made a difference. If she was covered in this costume, if her face was painted, if the doctor was there, it was unlikely Rashel could do her any harm. "If you think Rashel is going to be impressed by me, or you, or the surroundings, I doubt it."

"Let's try," he said, smiling at her. "Meantime, I presume you're all packed? Good. Did I tell you, Michael's going with us when we leave here early tomorrow."

"Michael said he was going," she replied, returning his smile. "He wasn't delighted when I said I was to play the part of your wife. I think perhaps he's . . . fond of me."

The doctor turned away and busied himself at his desk while Dismé went into the adjacent room, where there was a mirror. When she had shut the door behind her, the doctor sighed deeply and murmured, "Fond of her. Well. And of course. Why wouldn't he be?"

✦ 34

the doctor does more than intended

Came a knock at the doctor's door. With a quick look to be sure the door to his bedroom was closed, he opened the door only slightly to see the unremarkable face of one of his spies.

The spy whispered, "The woman's headed down there, Doc."

"The procession's coming? As we planned?"

The spy nodded, scratching his head. "They're happy with the money, Doc, but a bit confused about the detour."

"Tell them several people along the route are celebrating promotions. They should be Praisers, as they are all the time, and keep on being Praisers down five flights of stairs. When they get to the bottom, they go away. Surely they can manage that."

"Yes, sir. I'm sure they can."

Jens shut the outer door and went to knock on the inner one. "Are you ready?"

When the door opened, his jaw dropped. Dezmai of the Drums stood before him, true to the picture in every detail except for the slightly flustered expression.

Jens shut his mouth and offered his arm. "Lady?"

Wordlessly, she took it, and they arranged themselves in readiness the doctor murmured, "When the musicians come by, walk behind me, just as though we are part of their procession."

They waited for some time before they heard music. The doctor cracked the door and peeked through, waiting until the masked and costumed musicians and dancers filled the corridor, capering and weaving while playing a joyous tune, the whole punctuated by the juggling of brightly colored flags and the occasional thwang of a three-stringed harp. As they went past, the doctor stepped out and Dismé fell in behind him, losing themselves in the noise and action.

The procession descended stairs that widened all the way to the ground floor and narrowed below that. At the bottom, a low hallway extended toward an open door, the curtains behind it hiding the interior of the room beyond. The musical troupe turned back well short of the spearmen standing guard, la-la, twiddle and thwang-banging along the walls and thus creating an aisle down which the doctor proceeded, Dismé close behind.

With a ceremonial salute, the doctor uttered the password of the day. The men flourished their spears, and stepped aside. From behind the curtain the doctor could hear Rashel's voice, solemnly explaining the research which she proposed to do upon the device or artifact or "crystallized process," punctuating her words with low, seductive laughter.

The doctor glanced back, as though to be sure the musicians had dispersed and feigned surprise at the presence of the figure behind him. He bowed and held the curtain widely aside, peering curiously within. The ladder had been replaced with a rough though solidly built stair that gave access to the central area of bare soil, now considerably lower than when he had seen it last. He stepped inside only when Dismé was at the stair.

Rashel, behind the dark slab of curving stone, was still talking enthusiastically to the intent group around her. She did not see Dismé descend the steps and approach the device from the other side. As for Dismé, she saw nothing in the cellar at all: not the people, not the circling arches, not the packed earth, not the device, but only an amorphous cloud swarming with stars, exploding with light and movement.

Two galaxies lay before her, and a distant voice told her to reach out, which she did, covering the star clusters with her hands.

Some of the functionaries from Inexplicable Arts were far enough to the side that they had seen Dismé enter. Her appearance startled them into immobility, but her approach made them move to stop her. They had taken only a step, however, when a beam of light emerged from the device first to strike Dismé's forehead and then to detonate a blast of effulgence that staggered everyone in the chamber.

The functionaries howled, Rashel screamed, the guards outside, who had seen only the light reflected from the corridor walls, shouted an alarm. For a moment the doctor saw a towering giantess, taller than the ceiling of the room, extending upward into non-existent space, her face glowing with a light that dazzled him. Within the chamber, people groped sightlessly, confusion compounded by deafness when a voice thundered:

"This is a kinswoman of Elnith of the Silences. Let no person lay hands on this woman for she is of the Guardians."

The device or artifact or crystallized process—for in this case Rashel had quite possibly been correct—at once separated into its constituent atoms, a shower of silver dust sparkling at the top and proceeding downward until nothing was left, the whole disappearing in the space of a few deep breaths. This left Dismé standing face to face with a woman she scarcely recognized, a blank-faced female who stared blindly, dumbfounded and deaf, with no idea who or what it was before her.

Dismé turned. For a moment she faced the doctor, only long enough for him to see the curled line of light that flamed upon her forehead, before she leapt up the stairs and passed swiftly before him out into the corridor. Once there, she moved to the nearest door, her action so fast that it blurred.

The doctor, who had seen as much as anyone could have seen of what had happened, gritted his teeth tightly together and swallowed several curses at himself for meddling with things that he understood so imperfectly. So, she resembled the drawing! So, wouldn't it stir things up to lend some support to the idea of a Guardian Council! Oh, yes, very bright of him to do a great deal more stirring than he'd intended!

"Colonel Doctor Jens Ladislav Praise," grated one of the blinking men from Inexplicable Arts. "Is this your doing?"

"I am as surprised as any of you," he said with complete honesty, meantime casting another glance over his shoulder to be sure that Dismé was indeed out of sight, though that in itself was a cause for worry. She had taken a door that led into the bowels of the Fortress; it was easy to lose oneself in there; and some places could be dangerous, especially for a woman alone.

As though echoing his thought, Rashel cried, "It was a woman, wasn't it. I heard a woman's voice. Where is she?"

"The voice came from the artifact," said the doctor, though he was not at all sure that was true. Certainly it had come from the vicinity of the device. Dismé had been very much in that vicinity though the voice had not sounded like hers.

"But there was someone here!"

"The person left," someone said.

There was a babble among those assembled, Rashel showed signs of emerging from shock, and though she had not recognized Dismé, the doctor decided not to wait until she had a chance to replay the event in her mind. He left them jabbering behind him and achieved his apartment by the quickest route known to him. He found Dismé already there, however, in the tiny bedroom, staring alternately into the mirror and at the Book of Bertral, open upon the bed.

"What happened in there?" he asked.

She turned on him glowing eyes and a face that seemed carved of stone. "Later."

"Dismé," he cried. "I need to know. How did you find your way back up here?"

"You need to know no more than I," she said in a voice like boulders rolling together under the sea. "And I have no idea how I got here. Something knew the way, and I followed the something." She took a deep breath and said, in a slightly calmer voice. "Perhaps matters will come clearer with a little time."

The tone of her voice was so forbidding, so different from her normal intonation, that he dared not pursue the matter. Instead—assuring himself repeatedly that he was not frightened of her, that he had no reason to be afraid of her, that he had not ever, in any way harmed her—he fetched a bottle from the bedside cupboard and poured himself a drink. When she moved away from the book, he retrieved it. The illustrated Dezmai of the Drums bore a twisted line of light upon her forehead. The line had been on the page before, but it had not glowed until now. He leafed through the book, finding that other illustrations also glowed with light. Camwar of the Cask, glowing. Tamlar of the Flames. Rankivian of the Spirits. Among others. He read the concluding lines once more:

"Let him who reads pay heed . . ."

He turned. Reading over his shoulder was Dismé—a somewhat more familiar Dismé except for the blazing sign.

"Did you know this would happen?" she asked in an angry voice more like her own, brushing the sign on her forehead with her fingers, as though to verify it was there. She stared at him imperiously, awaiting his response.

"I didn't expect anything like this to happen," he said, flushing. "I was just throwing odd rabbits into the pot."

She turned, her long sleeve dragging across the table where the small drum lay. It fell to the floor. When she picked it up, it roared like a far-off peal of thunder, and went on roaring until she set it down. She looked at it in astonishment.

She said, "Where and when did you find that book?"

He laid it down, gripped his hands together to keep them from shaking, and told her how he had found it. " . . . and it was wrapped in oiled canvas and stitched tight. There were tools there. I took a shovel and dug it up."

"Ah," she murmured. "So."

He gulped, drily. "I retained presence of mind enough to fill in and litter the hole. No one else knows it was there."

Her lips quirked in a smile. "If the Regime were aware of this, you wouldn't last long, Doctor."

He shrugged, saying wryly, "As you may have gathered, I have no great confidence in the Regime. I think some things are safer buried. I've spent days looking at this book, at your name in it. Dismé—Dezmai. Close, as you said . . ."

"Who sent you the letter you mentioned?"

He frowned again. "I don't know. I assumed it was someone who knew both you and me quite well, but it was unsigned and delivered in an unconventional way. All the mystification was intended to be intriguing, so I sent for you as soon as I knew where you were. You came, and everything . . . just seemed . . ."

"Foreordained," she said, with stone in her voice once more. "Yes, Colonel Doctor, it seems that something certainly was."

"There's something else," he said, reaching into his pocket. "When I was a child, very young, my own mother gave me this little book. See here, there's a prayer for the soul of a departed one. Can you read that?" He handed it to her.

"It calls upon Rankivian, Shadua, and Yun," she said.

"And I have called on them, from time to time. Now see here," and he turned to the gray pages that followed the blue ones in the Book of Bertral. "Here are Rankivian, Shadua, and Yun. Here, evidently, they have been from the beginning. Who knew that? How did their names come to appear in a book given to me decades ago? It is a puzzle, like the puzzle of the letter I received with your name in it."

"Your letter writer may have desired my downfall, or yours," she snarled. "Did you think of that?"

"I always think of that," he said, slightly angry himself. "Among the Spared, someone always desires another's downfall. However, if we are paralyzed by that, we never do anything."

"True." She took a deep breath. "So what do you plan now?"

He murmured, "For tonight, we hide you, Dismé. So your sister won't see you or that sign on your face."

She looked at herself in the mirror once more. "It's nice to know you can be sensible on occasion." She went into the adjoining room, where she had left her own outer clothing.

He wiped his forehead, saying, "There's a cloak in there for you. We leave tomorrow at dawn, as planned."

"We can't leave without our children. We cannot travel without them." Her voice was still remote and echoing, but it sounded amused, for all its distance.

"I meant to introduce you to them early tomorrow morning but now will be better. In fact, it may be best if you don't go back to your room until much later. I didn't count on all this much disturbance. Though I doubt it, your sister might realize who she saw down there, and decide to visit you at once."

"All my things for the trip are under the bed, so the keeper wouldn't see I had packed for a trip. You have my book."

He fetched the Latimer book from his cache, then attempted his former insouciance. "We'll get your clothing after everything calms down. Let's go call upon Bobly and Bab."

"Bobly and Bab?" She came into the room, neat and ordinary, the gleaming sign upon her brow hidden by a scarf.

"They are brother and sister, which is good, since those are the roles they play. They are in their thirties, which is also good, since they have acquired circumspection and reason."

"Children of thirty? I'm not that old myself!" Her voice was now almost itself once more. "What am I to do about this?" she gestured at her forehead. "We don't want this seen, do we?"

"You've hidden it well enough, for now."

"I'll take the Nell Latimer book. Have you read it?"

"Yes. With some understanding and more confusion." He handed it to her, and she put it in the pocket of her cloak. He led her out onto the window ledge—which he noted she walked along freely, unafraid of its height—and into the narrow maintenance hall, down that to a precipitous stair leading to other narrow corridors, one of which had several cobweb festooned doors along it. The doctor knocked twice on one of these, then twice again, then once.

The door opened and a tousled head looked out from sleepy eyes. A little light-haired person, perhaps five or six years old, dressed in an child's pink nightgown, saying, "Well, Doctor, it's a bit late for it, but how nice of you to call. Come in. Don't disturb the spiders."

They stepped inside, ducking to avoid the webs, as another little person came sleepily into the room, a male version of his sister, neither of them any larger than a small child, and each with a child's voice, face, and manner.

"Dismé, may I introduce Abobalee Finerry and her brother, Ababaidio. Otherwise known as Bobly and Bab."

"We're all packed," Bobly chirruped. "Ready to leave at the crack of dawn, if that's what you came to ask."

The doctor shook his head. "Actually, I've brought you your mama." The doctor pulled Dismé forward. "Can you give her my bed for tonight? She shouldn't be seen just now, though she'll have to pick up her things from her rooms before dawn."

Bab turned to Dismé, inquiringly. "Are you packed, Mother dear?"

Dismé blinked at the designation, smiling a little. "I packed a bundle. It's under my bed. Everything's in it including the clothes I plan to wear."

"She can't be seen," whispered Bobly to the doctor. "She's been a naughty girl?"

"No." The doctor shook his head. "She's been quite . . . ah amazing, as a matter of fact, but someone wants to harass her and I'd rather she had a good night's sleep."

"Ah, well," said Bobly, with a thoughtful look. "We'll have to think of something. Later."

"Yes," agreed the doctor, rather wearily. "Later."

Bobly looked him up and down. "You'll need to get back

into your usual haunts, won't you? We hear something weird and wonderful's happened. The place is buzzing like a hive about spectacles and marvels and all sorts of upsets! Most likely the big men will be calling meetings right and left. Wouldn't do for the Most High Colonel Doctor to be where he couldn't be found!"

"There's talk already?" the doctor exclaimed. "What weird and wonderful thing?"

"Apparitions. Angelic voices coming from the cellars, things exploding, then disappearing. Oh, my yes. Much, much talk. Music, it's said. Drummers. A whole connivance and contraption. So, you'll be wanted."

He hesitated, shifting from foot to foot, his eyes on Dismé.

She murmured, "We left connivances and contraptions in plain view in your apartment, Doctor. Items of incriminating nature that probably should be put away."

The doctor slapped his forehead with his hand, cursing at himself. The book, laid out for all and sundry to peer at. Her costume. Oh, my yes. "Later," he said, taking himself out the door. "Keep her out of sight."

"He's been up to mischief again," said Bab.

Dismé regarded the two of them, looking from face to face. "You're really twins, aren't you?"

"Yes," said Bobly. "And people of our size aren't uncommon in New Kansas, though the Regime thought we were children when they kidnapped us from our caravan. They do that, you know."

Dismé nodded. "I know. My best friend was taken that way."

"Luckily, they thought us too young for rape, so we arrived here bruised but mostly unharmed. Luckily, the doctor is the one who examines youngsters, deciding if they need whatever help he can provide, including getting them across the border and back to their families."

"How does he do that?"

"Oh, he claims children are ill with some catching disease, and he sends them to a clinic on the far edge of Praise or Comador, and then he loses the record, which isn't difficult or unusual, and the children just sort of get lost. Anyhow, he knew immediately we weren't children, and he's the one who helped us disappear before we disappointed the Regime by failing to grow up. They wouldn't have kept us, you know."

"The Regime?"

"Oh, my no. We'd have been slaughtered long since like any other freak. Any abnormal thing is demon touched, you know that. Fit only for bottling, if that. But the doctor gained us a reprieve."

"He keeps you here?"

Bobly replied, "He doesn't keep us at all. He offered to return us or let us be part of his . . . efforts. We took a liking to him. We approve of his efforts, so we decided to stay for the time being. He found us this safe lair, and we travel around among the towns, dressed as children, acting like children, then when we're in here, we're ourselves. Now, bed for you!"

Dismé looked about herself, aware of weariness for the first time, but seeing nowhere to lie down except the floor. Bab, however, bent down and pushed on a molding which ran along the bottom of the paneled wall. The molding, and the knee-high length of wooden skirting to which it was attached, slid inward a few inches, then upward and out of sight, disclosing a long, low, floor-level cubby hole. Inside, level with the floor, she saw the long side of a mattress with pillows and a blanket.

"Hocus-pocus," he said. "Grumfalokus. That's where the doctor sleeps when he's hiding from his mother."

"From his mother?" Dismé laughed, breathlessly. "I didn't think he had a mother?"

Bobly said, "The doctor's real mother was one Aretha Camish Comador, but he was orphaned young. This one is his step-mother, a sort of half-aunt married to the doctor's father. His step-mother's always on him about being nonconformist and maybe catching the Disease. You slip in there, lady, and have a bit of rest. Later we'll figure out how to get your things."

After a moment's consideration as to the best method of

getting into the bed, she lay face down on the floor next to the opening and rolled through it onto her back, which left her supine in the center of the narrow mattress. She felt of the outer wall, finding it to be built of stone, roughly mortared. The air was fresh and rather cold, so it wasn't a coffin. She wasn't really closed in.

Bab asked her curiously, "What's that on your forehead?"

Dismé felt for her scarf, which had come loose in the rolling about. "I have no idea. It came . . . today."

"Does it hurt?"

She thought about it for a moment. "It tingles. Not as bad as when your leg goes to sleep, but rather like that."

Bab bent to look into her face. "Now I'll lower the board. You latch it from your side. The latch is there by your left hand, and that way you're safe. It's counter-weighted, so you can raise it with a fingertip if you want to get out."

The board slid closed, leaving her in darkness. She fumbled for the latch and pressed it home. For a few moments, she heard muffled conversation from outside, then silence. There were blankets folded along the wall, and she pulled them over her, snuggling into the warmth. She was weary enough now to let go of the self she had been holding like a screen between Dismé and the recent happening. The person inside her was no longer herself. Something wonderful and dreadful had happened. Roarer? she suggested. Is that you?

Don't worry about it.

But I'm all strange, changed.

Not at all. I've visited here before, from time to time. You've heard my drums, roaring.

And what am I to do?

Just go on being. All will take care of itself.

Go on being what?

Why don't you start by getting some rest?

Which, after only a few more dazed and wondering moments, she did.

Above her in the Fortress, Rashel was climbing the stairs to the corridor where Dismé lived, furious at what had happened and eager to take it out on someone. She approached the keeper's cubby and demanded to be taken to Dismé's room.

"She's not there," said the keeper, one Livia Squin, second cousin to a minor Turnaway who'd provided her with the job.

"I didn't ask if she were there, I asked to be taken there," said Rashel in her most infuriating voice.

The keeper was given to irascibility at the best of times, which this was not. "Not allowed to," she said. "Not unless she asked me to, and she didn't."

"I, Madam, am here on Regime business. Dismé Deshôll is my sister."

"I don't know that, do I?"

"My identity card, Madam." Rashel handed it over.

"This doesn't tell me you're her sister." The keeper stared at her, eyes bugged out, teeth stubbornly clenched.

Rashel gave her a long, measuring look. "It's very strange. I don't know you at all, and yet I think . . . I think I detect signs of the Disease in you. Being unnecessarily obstructive is one of the symptoms. I know, because my husband had the Disease. I knew when he started getting obstructive that he must have it, and what do you know? He did! It must be that demons have gotten to you somehow. I'm meeting with the chiefs of Happiness and Enlightenment tomorrow. I think I'll mention it to them . . ."

The keeper pushed her key across the counter, saying furiously, "She's in room 415, down the hall to the end. Bring back the key when you've unlocked the door."

"Of course," said Rashel. "When I've left a note."

She stalked down the hall, hard heels falling noisily, fingers making an irritating clatter with the key. Once inside she looked about to be sure she was in the right room. Oh, yes. There were books she recognized, and a few items of clothing. They couldn't be paying her much if all she had were these few old rags that she'd had in Faience. A shelf of knick-knacks, a drawer of snacks including a half bottle of cider, tightly corked. From her pocket she took a vial half-filled with a grayish powder. A moment's search turned up a corkscrew. She opened the bottle and emptied the contents of the vial into it, meantime chanting an incantation in which the ingredients of the potion figured along with long sleeping and horrid wakening. She set the bottle on the chest, the cork slightly loosened, to make it easier to remove.

She crowed to herself, quite audibly: "She'll drink that tonight or tomorrow. I'll stay in Hold until I can find her body and claim it. She won't really be dead. Not if Hetman Gone's recipe's a good one."

She started to leave the room, then remembered her reason for being there, the note. She found a bit of paper and jotted a few words: "Sorry to have missed you, see you tomorrow, your sister, Rashel."

General Gowl had fallen into a drunken sleep on the sofa in the penthouse, following an afternoon's dalliance with a new and excitingly unwilling servant girl. He was awakened by a terrible voice calling his name. Groaning, he forced himself to sit up, then to rise and stand awkwardly in the middle of the room, hearing the summons. Where was the girl? Who had wakened him?

The girl had fled, and the waker had been, perhaps, someone from outside? He went out into the roof garden and wandered from there to the chimney. Yes, someone was calling his name inside there. He opened the secret door and went into the dogleg cleft that led past the place where the brazier stood. Arriving there, he found the place empty, but he waited, as though for an assignation, neither impatiently nor wonderingly, but blankly, as a well-fed and watered gelding might wait at a shaded hitching post, unconcerned about what would happen next. What happened next was a volume of smoke pouring from the chimney and the emergence of the general's particular angel.

"On day four of this span, the army will move," said the angel, in a voice that sizzled like molten bronze. "On day six they will be at the border of Bastion. There my Quellers will come upon them, and you will go into battle. The world is about to become yours, General Gowl."

The general accepted the idea as pleasurable, not at once, not under these dreadsome conditions, which made him want to cower like a child, like little lopsided what's-his-name, Fortrees, all those years ago. He took command of himself and repeated obediently, "Two days from now the army will move. Two days later they will be at the border of Bastion. There the Quellers will join them."

"Not join," laughed the voice. "Come upon them. Your army will not follow the Quellers . . ."

"*I* will lead them," said the general firmly.

"Indeed," said the voice as it funneled back into the chimney from which it came. "For an enemy has arisen, and battle is required. These are my orders: Each of your subordinates must select someone to travel with the army to contribute to the strength of the Quellers."

The voice and the presence were gone. The general stood for some moments assuring himself that the angel had indeed told him battle was imminent. His people would have to be told. He would call a meeting. Meantime, how strange to have thought of little Fortrees. He had not thought of him in years, decades. What was it that had brought him to mind?

Struggling with memory, he went to the penthouse and rang for his aide, who came pantingly into the room, almost forgetting the courtesies due the general in his eagerness to speak.

"The Colonel Bishop has been looking for you, sir. There's been an . . . event, down in the cellars, where the artifact was."

"Was?" cried the general.

"Oh, yessir, it's gone now. The bishop has called a meeting since we couldn't find you, sir, and he told me to let you know as soon as you were located . . ."

The aide said no more, for the general had all but knocked him down on his way to the stairs.

* * *

Colonel Doctor Jens Ladislav was awakened (or so he made it appear by much yawning and rubbing of supposedly sleepy eyes) by a functionary from BHE, who said a meeting had been called in the staff room on the third level. Col. Dr. Ladislav was wanted.

"Tell them I'll be there as soon as I can get dressed," he murmured. "I've been asleep."

The functionary bowed and left bearing the message, while the doctor washed, combed, and dressed himself. Only when he had double-checked to see that everything incriminating was put away where no one would find it even through deliberate search, did he leave his quarters to attend the meeting on level three.

There a large table was surrounded by a noisy group, with General Gregor Gowl Turnaway among the noisiest.

"There you are, Doctor," cried the general. "What do you know about all this business of somebody destroying the artifact. Somebody from outside! Now, how did they get in, I ask you."

"I guess I let the person into the cellar," said Jens, hands turned up in innocent wonder. "Someone was behind me as I came down the stairs. Naturally, being gentlemanly, I stood aside to let him or her, or . . . drat. I shall simply say she, until someone proves otherwise. Wasn't she expected?"

"Expected? What would make you think . . ."

The doctor said firmly, "The voice spoke of kinship, of Elnith of the Silences. I immediately remembered Hal P'Jardas's account of his stay here, before settlement. You know."

"P'Jardas?" growled the general. "Oh, Right! Yes. Of course. Something required by Elnith of the Silences for settling here in her land. We spoke of it not long ago."

"Well, this person was it, wasn't she?" murmured Jens, looking around for a vacant chair. "The voice said 'kinswoman.'"

"That's rather the point," growled the Colonel Bishop. "Who is she? The woman in the cellar, I mean."

"It would be difficult for anyone to say," murmured the doctor, dragging a chair up to the table. "She was painted."

"How did she get into the Fortress?" demanded Mace Marchant.

The doctor looked up at Marchant's voice, wondering why the man was here in Hold again, as though he didn't know. Rashel was here, so Marchant was here. How cozy.

"Who knows," said the doctor. "It may be someone who lives here, or works here. Or, the person was dropped on the roof by demonic forces, or hatched by a very large bird . . ."

"Enough of this nonsense," growled the general. "This is serious."

"I'm not being frivolous," Jens replied, reining himself in with some difficulty. His ebullience sometimes got the better of him, but now was definitely not the time to be noteworthy. He went on in a more moderate tone, "No amount of questioning will get an answer from people who don't know, and we don't know anything except that the event has something to do with the Guardian Council. It's being said that the device in the cellar was one of many, created to identify members of that Council."

"How do you know this?" demanded the bishop, angrily.

"I don't *know* it. I'm merely repeating what people are saying," said the doctor in an almost uninterested voice. "News that filters in from here and there. I've been making arrangements to do a bit of inquiry on the subject. Now that such creatures are actually showing up and interfering with us, it's imperative we find out something about them."

"So you'll be off exploring again, eh?" asked the Colonel Bishop in a testy tone.

"No more than usual, sir," murmured the doctor.

The Colonel Bishop subsided, glowering. "I don't like this . . . interference." He also did not like the fact that his spy, Captain Trublood, had so far been unable to find anything wrong with the doctor. According to Trublood, the doctor came to the office in the morning, went to the Hold clinic an hour later, stayed there most of the day treating various wounds and diseases. The doctor was also teaching a couple of apprentices how to set bones and sew up wounds, one of them an old man from the town, Ben, who was already far enough advanced to treat people on his own. Since Ben was an anchorite who didn't speak, Trublood had learned nothing from him.

According to Trublood, the doctor returned to his office in late afternoon, where he signed documents, gave instructions, and met with medical officers who needed help. When he left the office, Trublood sometimes followed him to his quarters and had on occasion kept watch on those quarters all night, to no point at all. It could be proved that the doctor spent a good deal of time saving the bodies of people the bishop considered only bottle-worthy, but there was no Dicta against doing that, though there certainly should be, in the interest of efficiency!

The doctor, who had read most of these thoughts on the bishop's face, made himself be still. He half closed his eyes and decided to appear sleepy. That would be most appropriate and least involving. A total lack of involvement was what he had been conveying to Trublood.

Only after a brooding silence stretched lengthily did the bishop say, "It's said that a member of this supposed council showed up in a place called Everday, where they had a device very much like the one here in Hold."

"Find out!" directed the general. "You, Jens. Find out!"

"I can try," murmured the doctor, with seeming reluctance.

Even the bishop agreed they should find out about the Council, though he felt no amount of information would ease his disappointment over the destruction of the device. The bishop was fifteen years younger than the general, and in the bishop's opinion, it was time the general was bottled and he, Lief Laron, took his place. In order for that to happen, he needed something powerful, and he had hoped the new artifact would be that thing.

It seemed to the bishop either very bad luck or extremely bad planning that after generations of experimentation with sorcery, all they had were a few eccentrics who could fly and a number of ancient devices that went off on their own and devoured investigators. Many of the Spared were coming dangerously near to Scientism in words and actions, thinking they could do things more expeditiously without magic than with it! Worship of the Rebel Angels was becoming more and more perfunctory; bottling of dissidents, once quite rare, was getting to be almost routine. Also, he was hearing more and more about magic that really worked, rumors that were growing both in number and specificity, many of them mentioning the general by name!

If, as was now apparent, the device under the fortress was not his key to unlimited, safe power, then . . . well, maybe he should find out about what the general was using. Maybe he should take some of his spies off the doctor and add them to those he had watching the general. In order to find out what the general's source was, however, he would need some time! If he could just get the general, and the army, out of Bastion for a while . . .

"It seems to me we need to shift our focus," he said firmly. "We should be talking about the army moving out of Bastion, soon. Right away."

Over Colonel Commander Achilles Rascan Turnaway looked up with his mouth open and his eyes wide. "The army isn't ready, Colonel Bishop! Believe me, we're not yet ready!"

"We certainly shouldn't delay," the bishop advised him. "Better sooner than later."

"And our treaty with the demons?" asked the doctor. "What are we to do about that, Colonel Bishop?"

The Colonel Bishop had momentarily forgotten the treaty with the demons. "Th . . . that," he sputtered. "That will have to be . . . fixed. They'll have to get out of our way. Or be subdued. We'll tell them that. They're to be subdued."

General Gregor Gowl laughed in a mocking tone. The bishop looked up to see he wore an expression of evil glee.

"You must have been reading my mind, Bishop." The general chuckled. "I was about to make just such an announcement! The fiery angel returned late this afternoon, bearing new instructions. We are indeed to make ourselves ready. Tomorrow at dawn will be threeday of this span. At dawn on fourday, the army leaves Bastion. By sixday, we will be at the border, up near Ogre's Gap, where the Rebel Angels will send us means to subdue the demons."

A silence fell, confusion on the part of some, dismay on the part of others, a rising elation so far as the bishop was concerned. When the quiet had persisted for some moments, the doctor asked:

"Did your visitor describe these means, General? Are these means devices, or weapons, or perhaps fighters?"

"Fighters," said the general, allowing his imagination full rein. "Oh, yes, Colonel Doctor Jens Ladislav Praise. Fighters before whom the whole army of demons will be like toy soldiers, set up to be knocked down. Fighters so terrible they will go in advance of our own men, for our own men would collapse in terror if they were too close."

"What fighters?" asked the commander, waiting open-mouthed for an answer.

"They are called Quellers," said the general. "And each of you in this room is to select someone to accompany the army to the border, that the Quellers may draw strength from their support." He was paraphrasing, but he thought this was what the fiery apparition had meant. He turned to his aide. "Pass out the papers, Joram."

The papers were passed. "Just write the name," said the general, in a jovial tone. "Some family member or subordinate you'd like to honor."

Around the room there was a scuffling of paper and pen. The doctor knew a euphemism when he heard one, and he inked the name of Captain Trublood on the sheet before him, folded it, and handed it in. Next to him, he saw the bishop writing the name of Gars Kensy Turnaway, his bastard son-under-the-blanket for whom Michael had worked. So, the bishop had also heard in the general's voice that same ugly glee.

Well, whoever might be named—and it would be a wonder if the doctor's name was not on someone's page—the doctor was resolved to be far, far from Bastion when the army moved in any direction at all. There was now an even more urgent reason for going: to warn the people over the borders that Bastion was erupting at once, bursting like a boil, and putrid war was coming upon them again.

In the last dark hours of summerspan five: twoday, the doctor knocked softly on Bobly's door. Only Dismé was awake, and she shushed the doctor into the room and pointed to the kettle, just put on to boil, and the teapot standing ready. "You're earlier than the roosters," she said.

"Just came by to be sure you'd be ready," he murmured. "To be sure you have your clothing and what not."

"I don't, yet. I was about to go up and get them. This late there'll be no one about. I can do it while we're waiting for the kettle to boil."

"I didn't expect to find you awake."

"Thirst," she said, shaking her head. "All that running about and being . . . whatever it was. I'll go get the clothing while the kettle boils."

"I'll go with you."

"You can't," she smiled. "The keeper wouldn't allow it."

In a moment she was gone, shutting the door quietly behind her. The doctor sat tiredly back in his chair, shortly falling into a doze, only to be startled into alertness when Bobly came rustling into the room, rubbing her eyes.

"Something," she said. "Something wrong wakened me!"

"Nothing wrong," he replied. "Dismé's gone after her clothing."

"Something wrong," she repeated, fixing him with wide eyes. "You know me, Doctor. Why else would I have wakened unless something was wrong. Very, very wrong. Someone's in danger!"

Though Mace Marchant had postponed a previous engagement in order to attend the meeting called by the general, he had no intention of missing it entirely. Several hours after the time he had been expected, he tapped at the window of a private room in a lodging house some blocks from the Fortress. After several taps, of increasing volume, the window was opened from inside by his dear friend, Rashel, who greeted him warmly. Once he was inside, she put wood on the fire and poured each of them a glass of aged cider before they settled upon the hearth rug to continue the relationship which, Marchant believed, had long been their chief amusement. Actually, the relationship had never amused Rashel, who had been unable to feel pleasure of that kind since her dedication to the Fell.

"I have news for you," he murmured. "The device under the Hold? It wasn't, maybe isn't, the only one."

She sat back, startled. "What do you mean?"

"I mean, there have been or are other devices like it. Here and there. According to Colonel Doctor Ladislav, people have come in contact with the devices, and the devices have identified them as members of the Guardian Council."

"Mere people?" she said in disbelief. "Surely the Council would be angelic, at the least?"

Hearing her annoyance, he hedged: "Well, maybe the people aren't the members. Maybe they just have appropriate bodies for the Guardians to inhabit." He pulled her close to him and began to stroke her shoulders and arms.

She shook off his hands. "Mace, this is important. What do you really know? Exactly?"

He sighed, thinking he shouldn't have told her until later. Pillow talk was more fun than inquisition. "I should mention first it's rumored some of our people actually have The Art."

"Who," she breathed, fury building. "Who has it?"

"Oh, head of Inexplicable Arts, Ardis Flenstall, for example, and Warden of the College, Bice Dufor. I don't mean it's talked about on the street, but those of us in Inexplicable Arts have heard the whispers. It seems those two, and perhaps others, have received instruction from someone. They don't mention it themselves, but their servants and students aren't totally discreet."

"How?" she breathed. "Since when? And by whom have they been instructed?"

"From what we can piece together, the source is ancient and arcane, someone or something—a warlock, a grimoire,

maybe both—that existed before the Happening. Whatever
the source, some men are really able to do it . . ."

"Move carts without horses?"

"No, no, it isn't that kind of art. It concerns itself with
summoning powers and forces to bend the will of others. As
I've heard it, the magician wouldn't try to move a cart, he'd
move himself. Be that as it may, General Gowl is one of
those to whom The Art has been given . . ."

If Mace had been able to see her eyes, he would have seen
fury. Ardis and Bice had such power? And they hadn't told
her? Shared it with her? She looked down at her hands, forc-
ing them to stop writhing in her lap, tasting gall as she
begged sweetly, "What do they say, about the . . . about
where they got The Art?"

"I can only tell you what I've heard. Bice Dufor's manser-
vant was talking in the servant's hall. He said that the warden
returned to his quarters with his clothes soaked with sweat,
remarking he'd met with someone 'heat loving as a snake.' "

"Ah," murmured Rashel.

"Flenstall got drunk one night at dinner and maundered to
his aide about this old man he knew. 'An old man who has a
grimoire called the Book of Fell . . .' " He shrugged. "I'm
putting bits and pieces together, but they do start to make a
picture."

"But you've never met this person."

He shook his head. "Never. Which is surprising. I should
have thought this source would have been interested in anyone associated with the Inexplicable Arts. Not that I want to
learn black arts. The idea is frightening."

"And what about the devices?" she asked, wiping the
anger from her face to replace it with an expression which
was merely interested.

"The doctor says he has heard from various sources—by
which he means people who live on the borders and hear
things from outside—that these devices have been found in
other places, that each one disappears after causing a change
in some person who touches it. Now that's really all I heard,
but I thought you'd be interested."

"I am," she breathed, settling against him with a languorous sigh, purposefully hiding the fury she felt toward her dear, dear friends Bice Dufor and Ardis Flenstall. "I am very, very interested."

Dismé waved at the keeper as she went by, wondering why the woman was so red in the face and even more flustered than usual. None of the keepers were what one would think of as personable, but Livia Squin seemed to be perpetually walking a fence between anger and tears. Dismé thought the woman called her name, but she chose not to stop. Better get her clothes and go.

In her room, she pulled the bundle from beneath the bed, untied it and took out the clothes she intended to wear. Time was growing short, so she would change into them now.

As she struggled with her petticoats, the keeper down the hallway shifted from buttock to buttock in indecision, wiped her nose, bit a fingernail, finally rose from her chair, went out into the corridor and started down it, only to stop at the top of the stairs when she spied a girlchild making her way up the flight toward her. The little girl was wearing a hooded cloak over her nightgown and staying tight to one wall as she hummed softly to herself. The keeper had often heard small children make that tuneless humming when they were up past bedtime and badly needing sleep. She had the lagging steps of a tired child who had climbed a long way.

The keeper fixed Bobly with slightly protruding eyes as she whined: "Child, what are you doing here? You don't belong here."

"I know," said Bobly, rubbing her eyes. "My mommy is here visiting my aunty, and I got tired, so my aunty said come up and go to her room and lie down. She gave me her key."

"She should have come with you," said the keeper, disapprovingly. "You shouldn't be wandering around alone."

"My aunty says, if a child isn't safe in the Fortress of the Regime, then where is she safe? Isn't it safe here? I can tell her you said so . . ."

A look of alarm crossed the pasty countenance, "No, no, child. No such thing. It's just, you're such a wee little one."

Bobly pursed her lips in an offended manner. "I know my numbers. I'm old enough for that. Anyhow, I like exploring."

"You're sure you know the room number?"

"It's down there," said Bobly, yawning and pointing. "I've been to my Aunty Dismé's before."

"Dismé!" cried the keeper. "Oh, my child. I'll go with you."

"You don't need to."

"Oh, yes. I do, I do. I should have gone myself, right away. I should have, after what I heard, oh, my . . ." and the keeper was off down the hallway at top speed, with Bobly trotting close behind her.

Dismé had not locked the door. When the keeper and Bobly burst in, she was sitting on the bed, a bottle of cider at her lips.

"Don't drink it," cried the keeper. "Oh, no, don't drink it."

And at that moment, the doctor's voice came from over their shoulders. "What's going on?"

"Oh, oh, you shouldn't be here," squeaked the keeper. "Or maybe you should. You're Dr. Jens, aren't you. Why, then perhaps you should be. Don't let her drink it. I think it has poison in it."

Once Dismé assured them the cider had not touched her lips, the story took some time to elicit, for it began with a great deal of information about Livia Squin herself, necessary information, Livia thought, to establish why she so resented the rude woman named Rashel Deshôll. And to establish why the keeper believed she was up to no good. And to establish why the keeper sneaked down the corridor after her to listen outside the door and hear the unmistakable sound of a cork being pulled, and the subsequent chanting which was enough to freeze one's blood.

"That one's sister left it for that one to drink, meantime making a wicked spell that I heard every word of, and talking to herself, which I also heard, and sure as certain, this wicked potion is something to send that one to sleep for a time, and wake as a mindless slave. Also, that wicked woman talked of somebody called Hetman Gone, ah?"

All in all the experience had been both mysterious and horrifying, as her tears and shaking hands now gave evidence. The doctor took the cider bottle into his hands and looked at it curiously, noting the sediment in the bottom.

"Well now, we'll take charge of this," said the doctor, patting the keeper on her bony shoulder. "It would be wisest not to say anything about it, don't you agree?"

Keeper Squin nodded frantically, still trying to stanch her tears.

"You run along. We'll see to Dismé's welfare."

"Yes," said Keeper Squin, somewhat recovering herself. "And while you're seeing to welfare, that child ought to be in bed!"

When she had gone, when they made certain she had really gone, Bobly said quietly. "We don't want to walk past her with a bundle. Even if she doesn't mention this other, she'd talk of that to anyone."

Without explanation, she pulled a chair over to the left-hand window, climbed upon the chair, opened the window and thrust the bundle out, swinging it from side to side to make it fall away from the windows that extended in a straight line below. She leaned on the sill to watch it fall to the left, a barely visible blotch upon the dark rock roots of the fortress.

"Bab can get it from there," she said. "It will take him no time at all."

She opened the front of her gown to disclose a capacious bag fastened to a belt, and into this she slipped the cider bottle, buttoning her gown up again and pulling her coat closed across it, while smiling innocently at the others.

"And what is that for?" asked the doctor in a stern voice.

Usually, the bag was used for stealing groceries from the market, or pilfering some little thing or other that Bab could sell for a few Holdmarks, enough to buy cloth or whatever else they might need. Not that the doctor didn't provide. He did, and well, too, but one couldn't sit underground all day, every day, living on largess!

"Apples," said Bobly. "When Bab and I go past the orchards. Even though they're windfalls, you'd be surprised how huffy some growers get."

"Oh, I can imagine," he replied.

"Now," she said, "let's get back down below, where the four-legged rats are cleaner than the two-legged ones up here."

They went, the doctor holding Bobly with her head on his shoulder, she humming and sucking her thumb, a ruse they had obviously used before. Dismé paused long enough to give the keeper her thanks and a small reward, which earned her far more regard than she might have supposed possible. One flight down, the doctor moved into less-traveled corridors, and they came to the lower ways quickly after that.

Once inside, when Bobly gave him the bottle, the doctor turned it in his hands, gently sloshing the contents, hearing something like an evil whisper in the movement. "It's no doubt black stuff, Bobly. I'm going past the clinic when I leave here, to pick up some supplies. I'll store it away at the clinic, behind lock and key."

"Can't you dispose of it?" she said.

"Where? Who knows what vileness is contained in it, what might leach out of it no matter where I poured it. No. I'll keep it safe until I can burn it to nothing. The demons have a furnace for doing that. They use it to dispose of ancient evils, evoked by old sorcerers, like ash-beast's toes and sigh-anigh."

"Who is this woman you're speaking of?" asked Bab, who had been wakened by their arrival.

"Rashel Deshôll," said the doctor. "Who knows someone named Hetman Gone."

"So, that's who your sister is!" exclaimed Bab, with a sharp look at Dismé. "Well, I saw her enter Gone's door not long ago, when Bobly and I were visiting Apocanew. Seeing that's where the weather lies, I think you'd better put the potion in something besides a cider bottle. Something no person in his right mind would think was food or drink."

Thinking this sensible, Bobly looked among the things

she had salvaged here and there, finding a small blue bottle etched on the outside with a skull and crossbones, though the design was almost all worn away. She transferred the stuff from the cider bottle to the blue one and broke the cider bottle to shards. Once Bab returned with the bundle of clothing, the doctor said he saw no reason they should not take the opportunity to sleep until morning.

✴ 35

wife and children

Before dawn, Bobly wakened Dismé and helped her dress, insisting that she wear the cloak the doctor had left for her.

"One never knows," chirruped Bobly. "Any little thing that can be noticed probably will be noticed. Better wear it because likely any sensible woman would wear something like it, out so early. Also, I'll braid your hair for you."

"I thought only young girls braided their hair," said Dismé.

"That's here in Hold, but out on the road you'll find it's best braided. Roads are dusty and hot water's in short supply."

When the braiding was done, Bobly folded the edge of a large head scarf into a band and bound it over Dismé's forehead, pinning the band at the back and letting the rest fall loosely over Dismé's neck and shoulders in the manner of the country women of Comador. Taking up their belongings, they went along the corridor to a door which opened easily but was backed by a tightly locked metal gate. Bab lifted out the hinge pins, and when they had gone through, he restored them, smearing mud over the bright scratches he had left. The rude stonework of the fortress wall loomed behind them, the windows reflected the waning moon.

"Softly now," murmured Bobly, turning down the wick in her lantern so the flame barely lit the cobbles. At this hour, streets were empty and smoldering cressets oozed smoke that lay pooled on walks and gutters. Only insomniac roosters called wakeful into the darkness now and again.

Bab said, "We go down this back lane through the town, just a little way, Mama and her two children. And what do we call you? In case someone overhears."

"You'd better call me Mother unless we're alone. If I need a false name at any point, you can call me by my mother's name, as it's not one I'd forget. She was called Bahibra."

"She was a Comador?"

"I'm told she was. She went away when I was a little girl."

"You and the doctor," said Bobly. "His mother did the same. Or had it done to her. And Bab and I, also."

"My friend Michael, too," she replied. "All motherless."

"Bahibra it is, then," said Bab. "We turn here," and he lifted the lantern to light the entrance to a wider street lined with tall houses, eyes shutter-lidded against the dawn.

"There," said Bab, pointing. Ahead of them, by a watering trough in a market square, a canvas-topped wagon stood behind a team of four horses who were stamping and shaking their heads as a shadowy form moved about them.

"Who's he?" asked Bobly, suspiciously.

"It looks like Michael Pigeon," said Dismé, happily.

"It is Michael Pigeon," said Bab. "He's all right. I've known him for ages. Now, give me the bundles." He gathered them together with astonishing strength for one so small and carried them down the street to Michael, returning quickly.

"The doctor will join us later," said Bab. "Come now. We've seen what the wagon looks like and we've unburdened ourselves. We turn left again here."

"Aren't we going to . . ." began Dismé, gesturing.

"No, we aren't," answered Bobly. "Come along."

They trudged down the indicated street, coming in a few moments to a slit of descending shadow through a hulking tenement, a steep lane of uneven stone that debouched almost at once at the top of a steep stair leading down to the Holdwall.

Dismé pulled down her hood as they started down the fit-fully torch-lit stairs under the eyes of two guards sitting half asleep beside the gate at the bottom. Bobly ran on ahead, taking a small sack from the basket she carried.

"What's she doing?" whispered Dismé.

"Making friends, or renewing them," muttered Bab. "She baked sweet cakes early this morning."

"Good children you have here, Ma'am," called one of the guards, happily munching as they approached.

"Oh, they are indeed, thank the angels," chirruped Dismé in a syrupy voice, lifting one hand in a casual wave while keeping eyes down and lantern low to negotiate the uneven cobbles.

"Where you off to, little'uns?" the guard called.

"Farmer down the way," cried Bab. "He's got berries for the picking. Got to get there before they're gone!"

Then they were through the gate and moving down the road, which in the space of half a mile bent itself around a hill and became invisible to the city.

"Now what was all that about?" Dismé demanded.

Bobly replied, "Our things are in the wagon, for berry pickers carry baskets, not baggage. We don't want to be seen with the wagon inside the city. We don't want to be seen with the doctor inside the city. The doctor doesn't want to be seen with us or the wagon anywhere. After the appearance of that mysterious great woman in the cellars, no woman alone should be seen leaving the city. All these matters have been considered."

"I can see that," Dismé agreed, looking eastward, where the horizon was limned with pallid light. "There's the dawn of the new day: summerspan five, threeday, and now what?"

"Now without stressing ourselves a bit we just amble along slowly until we and the wagon coincide at a time when no one is around to observe that fact," said Bab.

"And when we've coincided, we stay inside the wagon for the first day's travel," said Bobly. "Because it's nobody's business who's in that wagon. You may be sure the doctor won't be, for he went another way entirely, and what has any of that to do with a mama and her two little ones, going berry picking?"

Dismé accepted all this obfuscation as being in keeping with the rest of the languid and dream-wrapped world. Soft-fingered dawn woke to pat the cloud-pillowed mountains and smooth the mist-blanketed valleys; the first rays of sunlight tiptoed among the hills like careful house-guests, not to disturb sleeping copses. Even the birdsong was drowsy.

Dismé yawned. "That's why we left so early? So we could be out of town before others left?"

Bab said, "Exactly. We didn't sneak, lurk, or skulk, any of which would have attracted notice. But we left very, very early, which nobody noticed at all."

"The doctor says late night doings are universally suspect," commented Bobly. "But rising early is staunch and meritorious, provoking only admiration from the capable, or aloof distaste from those who are slugabeds."

They had gone some way into the sunlit morning before the horse-drawn wagon, which had left the city through another gate, caught up with them and passed them by. A little farther on they entered a narrow strip of forest, where they found the horses browsing while Michael reclined in the wagon, waiting.

Bab greeted him like an old friend.

"Where do you know one another from?" Dismé demanded.

"Oh, Bab's been very helpful to me, now and again," said Michael. "Both in Hold and in Apocanew. Finding out things."

"People pay very little attention to children," said Bab, giving Dismé a level look. "Including your sister."

Dismé's brows went up. "Rashel? How do you know her?"

"Do you know of a Hetman Gone?" asked Michael.

Startled, she said, "I never heard of him, or it, until last night. Who or what is he?"

Michael replied, "We've never laid eyes on him or it, but Rashel, it seems, serves the creature, whatever he is."

Bobly nodded. "The keeper of Dismé's corridor heard Rashel invoke the Hetman's name when she planted poison in Dismé's room."

"Poison!" cried Michael, horrified.

"Which I cannot understand," murmured Dismé. "She was eager enough to drive me mad, but she never threatened my life."

"This stuff might have left your body quite alive, but without the will to oppose her," Bobly reminded her. "So the keeper overheard, and so the doctor thought. At any rate, he took the stuff away to the clinic with him early this morning."

"Is this Hetman in Apocanew?" asked Dismé, thoughtfully.

"He is at least some of the time," Michael said, going on to tell them all about the summons that had arrived at Faience after she had gone, and about Rashel's subsequent visit to Hetman Gone.

"Ah," Dismé said. "Then there is a connection . . ." and she in turn told them of the time, years before, when Rashel had arrived home in the care of her mother, obviously injured. "It's the only time I ever saw her like that, not in control of the situation."

As the grazing horses tugged the wagon along the verges and the sun rose higher, they had time to speculate, fruitlessly but at length, before the doctor's voice came from among the trees.

"Miss Dismé. Bobly and Bab . . ." A bay horse with white leggings emerged from the woods bearing a corpulent farmer with wide suspenders, a full beard, and a squashed hat.

"Now who would have known that's our friend the doctor?" cried Bobly, clapping her hands.

"Ah, yes," said the doctor. "Farmer Hypocky Rateez, an olden name from an olden time. Call me Hypock."

"You're late," said Michael. Since hearing Dismé was in danger, he was not amused by this raillery.

The doctor made a face. "I had a devil of a time evading

the scrutiny of good Captain Trublood. When I went out the northeast gate, toward Praise, there he was behind an inadequate tree, all eyes-on-horseback, set to follow me to the ends of the earth, or a goodly way toward Praise, whichever came first. My good horse made sure to kick up considerable dust, which a helpful headwind laid upon him by the bushel. Several miles out he decided too much was enough and turned back. I couldn't change identities or horse markings until he was gone. Luckily, the horse moves more quickly than I would have managed on foot. And how is Miggle, our driver?"

Michael bowed to him, still frowning.

" . . . and you are, Ma'am?"

"I am to be called Mother, or Bahibra," said Dismé, "though I cannot truthfully answer your question."

"Not quite sure who you are, eh?"

"Not quite, though this morning I seem to be mostly myself. Enough so that I'm worrying a good bit about Rashel finding me."

"If Captain Trublood is true to Regimic form, Rashel has been or will soon be forestalled. As for your name, while Bahibra is very nice, I shall never think of you as anything but Dismé or Dezmai. Your proper costume is in the wagon, in case."

"In case of what?" she asked, taking off the scarves, which made her head ache.

"What in the name of all the angels . . ." cried Michael, catching a glimpse of her forehead.

"You didn't tell him," she said almost sulkily, clapping her hand over her brow.

"No," breathed the doctor. "Quite true. I didn't tell him, and it must be done on the way, for more recent happenings make this journey even more urgent than I thought it was!"

He hitched his horse to the rear of the wagon and got onto the driver's seat beside Michael. Dismé and her guides climbed into the wagon through the rear curtains, onto two fat and comfortable mattresses that lay atop their belongings. The airy interior was hidden from view by an arched canvas cover stout enough to provide shade and protect them from the weather. While they lay at their ease inside, the doctor proceeded to tell Michael about the general's declaration of war and also about the Council of Guardians.

"So she's one of *them*!" said Michael, awed.

"We don't even know if there is a *them*!" Dismé cried. "So far all we have is a book, and a costume, and a . . . a myth."

"It's like being an emperor," said Bab, entranced. "You have nothing to say about it. If you're born one, you're just born one, and they start feeding you the myth along with your breast milk, then as soon as you stop wetting yourself, they costume you, drop the crown on your head, and you're it!"

"I'm not at all sure I'm it," she said.

"You were it yesterday," said the doctor. "I heard it in your voice."

"Well, it's faded," she said, a bit angrily. "Or she's gone. Or something."

"Maybe just retreated a bit," offered Michael. "To let you catch your breath."

She had nothing to say about that, and her manner warned them to stop talking about it. Farmer Rateez fell silent and concentrated on the surroundings while Dismé stretched out to watch the road through a crack in the back curtain. Bobly and Bab amused themselves by singing a part song, in which, to their surprise, first Dismé joined and then Michael.

The doctor sat up straight and paid attention to the sound. Bobly and Bab carried a tune well, but they had children's voices. Dismé's voice was already known to him, but Michael . . . both their voices might have belonged to Praiser festival singers, especially here, among the trees, where Dismé let her full voice be heard. The two of them . . . together . . . were quite remarkable, which did not totally please Jens Ladislav.

Hold was at the center of Bastion, with the three counties spread about it like clover leaflets, separated one from the other by ranges of hills that approached closely from the west, northeast, and southwest. The separating hills became higher the farther one went, ascending at last into the great mountain ranges that surrounded Bastion on all sides. The wagon was traveling on the road that ran between the shires of Comador to the left and Turnaway to the right, and far ahead of them were the ever-ice peaks of the Western Wall.

By noon they were well into the rumple-lands, those uppish and downish hills that were home to small villages, farmers, and herders. Hayfields lay along the creeksides, interspersed with gardens and orchards, and an occasional village sprawled on a sunny hill, where a keg on a pole indicated the presence of a tavern, an oversize hammer betokened a smithy, and similar totems told of wheelwrights, coopers, or sawyers, even a thatcher, his trade betokened by a reed bundle cut from the swamps along the rivers. The houses were long, low shelters dug half into the sunny sides of hills, then built up of rammed earth or earth-brick or even daub and wattle, all back ditched and steep roofed, thatched heavily with long overhanging eaves that protected the walls from wet.

By afternoon, they came to a split in the road, the right leg of which wound on upward to the Westward Pass and Ogre's Gap, a way often taken by the army and still used by raiding bands. It was a way no one else used much, and the road's sapling grown appearance indicated a lack of traffic.

"Which way?" asked Michael, who was driving.

"We should get over the pass as soon as possible," said the doctor, "as there are people we have to warn. However, if we take no more than an hour, we can go look at the old Lessy Storage Yard, and there's a reason we should see it."

Accordingly, they drove to the left on an almost level road that wound generally southward along the edge of the hills. They were at the western side of a box canyon dotted with copses and centered on a burbling stream which grew more silent and deeper as they went. The canyon was not long, and they soon came to the end of it, an area of gravelly ground set about with rotted rails and faded signs that said,

"Property of the Regime. No entry." The place was almost barren except for rampant growths of briar over the fallen fence and an unhinged gate.

The doctor leapt to the ground, handed Dismé and the little ones down, and stalked toward the fallen rails, stopping almost at once to look around. South of them the forest rose abruptly among sheer precipices cleft by fringed waterfalls, froth that plummeted milkily down bulwarks of black stone. From the nearer and much lower clifftop ahead of them, a single glassy cylinder of clear water plunged silently into a rock-bound pool, only a few yards away. East of them were lower hills, hiding any view northeast toward Hold or southeast toward Newland. Mountains stood north and west, stone teeth gnawing at the sky.

"It's too quiet," said Dismé.

It was true they heard no bird, no beast, no wind sound, no water sound. The doctor prowled across the fallen fence into the yard beyond, and the others followed. The area was littered with tanks and wheels, bent axles and toothless cogs, many now fallen into piles of rust, their shapes barely recognizable. Every artifact still extant wore manacles of briar that tangled all the yard. To one side a short grass area was dotted by patches of bare earth with abrupt outlines. Something had once stood upon these bare places; something had been moved away from them. Nothing had grown back where they had stood.

The doctor knelt to examine a bare patch, then another before picking up a handful of stones and dropping a stone on each bare spot as he counted: " . . . eighteen, nineteen." He muttered. He checked to see if his count was correct, that every bare spot had a stone on it. When he returned to the others, he had deep lines of concentration between his eyes.

"What was it that sat in those spots?" asked Michael.

"My guess is they were devices like the one in the cellar of Hold. The archives say that when the fortress was built, there were a number of curved pillars on Hal P'Jardas's mound that were carted away to the Lessy Storage Yard. Archives has a map showing the yard. It's a good distance from Hold or any other habitation, which means there wouldn't likely be trash pickers out here."

"Were the pillars like the one I saw?" asked Dismé.

"The description sounded like. It all hangs together: Tamlar, the fumarole, her talk about Elnith and the pillars, all in one place."

"Where did they go, then?" asked Michael.

"I don't know," the doctor answered. "Three of those bare patches have edges so clean that whatever was there was moved recently. I've heard that one of the pillars was brought to Everday at least a generation or so past."

Dismé said, "If people were transformed by them, maybe they vanished."

"Possibly," the doctor agreed. "We know Tamlar existed before the pillars were found. We know one was still buried under the Fortress. Add those two to nineteen, get twenty-one, and there are twenty-one Guardians in the book."

"Why was the pillar left buried in the mound?" asked Bab.

Dismé said, haltingly. "Tamlar was here from the beginning, and it was she who created the Calling Stones, to summon the Guardians when the time came. Tamlar never sleeps. She needs no mortal body. She keeps time on time; she measures the age of the sun, the earth, the stars; she moves the stones to meet their chosen ones; she is Guardian of the Guardians . . ."

Around them the hush deepened, became expectant.

"How do you know that?" asked the doctor.

Dismé shivered, whispering, "Something Dezmai left behind in my head. Let's leave here, Doctor. Now."

"What do you feel?" he breathed.

"Something evil, wrong, horrid coming here, yet a bit distant in time or space or knowing, but coming, nonetheless. We don't want to be here when it arrives."

"No, we don't," he replied. "Also, today is threeday, and the army of Bastion moves tomorrow morning. On sixday, it's supposed to be declaring war on the world from the border of Bastion. They're taking this same route, so we need to keep well ahead of them."

334 • Sheri S. Tepper

"You didn't tell me it was so soon!" cried Dismé.

"New information," he said, shaking his head. "Decided late last night. It's dismaying, but it doesn't change our plans."

The sensation of menace deepened as they turned the wagon back the way they had come. When they had gone a little way, the doctor cleared his throat and asked, "They were known as the Calling Stones, by whom?"

Dismé looked vacantly into the distance. "Tamlar named them. They call in two directions; earthward to us, the embodiments; outward to . . . to something else. Something that's not in the stone, but comes through the stone into us. We give it or them a foothold in humanity. They don't live in us, but they can work through us."

Michael broke the spell by putting his arm around her gently and murmuring, "It must make you terribly curious . . ."

"Someday we may find out more about them," said the doctor, glancing at the sky. "Now we must make up for lost time."

They drove back to the fork in the road, this time turning up the slope toward the mountains, stopping at intervals to clear fallen stones or chop a few saplings. By the time dusk began to settle, they had reached a clearing beside the stream where a fire circle of blackened stones identified the place as a usual wayhalt. Michael parked the wagon on high ground before unhitching and hobbling the horses, while Dismé, Bobly, and Bab gathered firewood and the doctor laid a fire.

Dismé watched him as he took a demon stick from a small container in his pocket and struck it across the seat of his trousers. "What did you just do?" she asked in an alert, interested voice. "That's a . . ."

"That's a match," he said. "What did you think it was? Oh, oh, of course. You've never seen one . . ."

She cocked her head, regarding the flame in his fingers. "I've seen them, but not used that way. According to the sorcery teachers at Faience, you're supposed to give it a contagion first, and say a magical invocation . . ."

"And a lot of other nonsense," said Michael, grinning at

her. "I lived long enough on the border to know that matches light fires. All you have to do is get the head hot enough to explode into flame, and you do that by friction, by striking it on something. Though I hadn't seen anyone light it on his butt end, like the doctor just did."

"So I was right. It's not magical at all," Dismé said.

The doctor shook his head. "My butt end, magical? While some have admired it, even extravagantly, I would not be inclined to call it magical. Miraculous, perhaps. Or exceptionally fine . . ." The match burned his fingers, and he dropped it.

"She meant the match," said Bobly, with a glance at Dismé's flaming cheeks.

The doctor laughed. "The match isn't magic either. That's part of the nonsense the Selectivists and their predecessors have promulgated on a credulous populace."

Dismé said, "I've never thought matches were magical, I was just surprised at the way you lit it. But . . . if a child stood up, pointed at his desk and said *Hail Tamlar, let there be fire*, and the desk went up in flame, that would be magic, wouldn't it?"

"That would be magic," the doctor admitted. "Have you seen that happen?"

She held out her hand and murmured, "Hail Tamlar, let there be fire."

Fire bloomed on her palm, steady as an oak. She looked around her at the circle of staring faces. The doctor cleared his throat. Bobly made a little whimpering giggle. Dismé blew into her palm and the flame ascended into the sky, rising like a floating feather, higher and higher until it vanished.

After a long silence, the doctor murmured, "Could you do that before yesterday?"

Dismé nodded, rose, went to the wood laid in the circle of blackened stones and put her hand to it, igniting the wood. The fire was hot; the smoke smelled like smoke. It was definitely fire, not some kind of illusion. The others stared. She shrugged. She knew no more than they what it meant.

The doctor burrowed into his pack and came up with a device which he put to his eyes, looking through it at the stony wall across from the road they had traveled on.

"What is that?" Dismé asked Bobly.

"Oh, those are distance glasses the doctor found somewhere outside," whispered Bobly. "They bring far away things very close, like a magnifying glass, only more so."

The doctor pocketed his device, excused himself and went away into the woods. After a time, they saw him halfway up a rock wall opposite their camp site, one that culminated in a flat, protruding chunk of stone. Dismé, Bab, and Bobly began the preparation of a meal, and when they glanced up from their work they saw smoke rising from atop the rock, a single skein of white, pink-tipped by sunset, that rose straight in the calm of evening.

"What's he doing?" Dismé murmured, fascinated.

"Signaling someone," said Michael, who was also quite interested in this exercise. "Now I wonder who?"

The doctor returned before their supper was quite ready, breathing heavily and rather red in the face from the climb. After they had eaten, Michael spread a waterproof canvas between the wheels of the wagon, attached a canvas skirt around its edges, and moved a mattress from inside the wagon to beneath it, where it would be well sheltered in event of rain. Michael and the doctor took the under-wagon bed, Dismé, Bab, and Bobly the in-wagon one, with the little people at opposite ends on one side and Dismé on the other.

"You really hadn't lit a fire with a match before?" asked Bab from the darkness. "Even some people in Hold use them."

"Where do they get them?" Dismé asked.

"Peddlers sell them for splits, when nobody Regimic is around."

"Where do the peddlers get them?" Dismé asked.

Bab murmured sleepily. "They get them from peddlers over the edge, who get them from New Chicago."

Bobly yawned. "Using matches can get you chaired, if

anyone catches you at it. It's supposed to be magic, and fiddling with magic is forbidden, unless you have a permit. You
know that."

She did indeed know that. As well as a great many other
things she hadn't really thought about. She lay there, intending to think about some of them, but though she had
drowsed in the wagon a good part of the day, sleep came
upon her almost at once.

✦ 36

rashel rages

In the Fortress at Hold, Rashel began threeday by causing consternation among the staff of the Office of Acquisition, Department of Inexplicable Arts.

A youngish clerk said for the third or fourth time: "Madam Deshôll, we have no other information on the device. It was simply there when the men started digging."

"What about the area itself. Is there information on that?"

"P'Jardas," said an older man from the back of the office. "His accounts. Let her look at that."

Staff member know-not knew nothing, so staff member knows-a-lot, a sandy man with a short reddish beard, retrieved from the Archives a faded but remarkably dust free folder.

"There've been a lot of people looking at *that* recently," he remarked before resuming his seat. "BHE. Division of Medicine."

Rashel seethed. No one had mentioned any such file to *her*. She found a quiet corner and sat over the folder, leafing through it, scanning here and there, stopping to read all of a letter, all of another account. She caught knows-a-lot's attention with a snapped finger and said, "Where is the Lessy Storage Yard?"

Knows-a-lot rose and wandered toward the file room. "There's some old maps in the file back there."

Rashel examined the maps he furnished with increasing excitement. So, the pillar excavated under the Fortress was indeed not the only one. There were many others! And she was likely the first one to think of them! She would take the few necessary minutes to find Dismé's body, then go on to this storage yard!

Accordingly, she went up to the fourth floor and obtained a key from the keeper—not Livia Squin, who had gone to Amen City that morning to see her sick mother (mythical) with no intention of returning. As Rashel approached Dismé's door she rehearsed the panicky cries she would make when she found Dismé seemingly dead, opening the door onto an un-embodied room where she stood stupidly staring at nothing. It was just as it had been the day before. Except . . . the bottle was gone. Which meant what?

Furiously, she went back to the keeper's stall and demanded to know who had been on duty the previous night, and when that woman was said to have gone to visit her sick mother, the day person was fetched so Rashel could insist on knowing when Dismé had last been seen.

"What does she look like?" asked the woman, one Hermione Bittleby, in a voice as glacial as Rashel's own.

"Plain," said Rashel. "Braided hair. Dressed like a farmwife."

"Haven't seen her," said Bittleby. "There's no one like that on this corridor."

"Her name is on your list. The room at the end of the hall."

"I wouldn't call her plain! She works for Dr. Ladislav."

"And where will I find him?"

"Division of Health is up corridor twenty-seven a way, third floor, I think, off the main corridor."

Rashel, growing ever more enraged, stalked to the main corridor, found offshoot stairs that led to corridors twenty-two through twenty-seven, went up several flights, and went to the doctor's office, where she encountered James Trublood.

"I am Rashel Deshôll," she said haughtily. "I'm looking for my sister, Dismé Latimer?"

"Gone," said the captain, seeing her hauteur and raising her an arrogance. "The Colonel Doctor sent her to Comador to dig out some kind of statistics." He had seen the assignment sheet himself, in the pile of materials he was just now sorting out.

Rashel noted his arrogance and raised it a contemptuous. "Then you will announce me to the doctor?"

"He's gone, too," said the captain, matching her contempt with a Turnaway's disdain. "He left early this morning, gone off to the borders of Praise." The doctor's itinerary had been on top of the stuff to be filed. The most recent document in the folder was a copy of a letter telling citizen Befum that the doctor would be visiting, leaving on summerspan five, threeday.

Summerspan five, threeday was today, and Trublood had been at the Praise gate on the northeast side of the city, where indeed, the doctor had ridden out toward the Praise hills and Trublood had eaten a good deal of dust just to verify where the doctor was going! He had then gone posthaste to the Colonel Bishop, who had said yes, yes, the guards at the gate had already reported the doctor's movements. Trublood, who until that moment had thought he was the bishop's only or at least primary spy, had been offended by this intelligence, and he had added the irk to the revulsion he had stored away over the Bishop's daughters.

"Do you know when Dismé left?" Rashel asked.

The captain thought about it. When had she come into the office last? Not twoday, yesterday, when all the ruckus had taken place down in the cellars. Not the day before. And not during the span-end of span four, either. But the preceding day, he had seen her briefly, dropping off something for the doctor. "It could have been anytime within the last five days, Ma'am. She hasn't been into the office here since summerspan four, eightday." He did not like this woman's manner. She obviously did not know she was speaking to a member of the Turnaway clan.

Rashel put the captain's name on the mental lists entitled "To-be-disposed-of-when-Rashel-is-running-things," and flung herself off in a fury. The poison in the bottle hadn't reached Dismé because Dismé had already gone! And now the bottle was gone also. Making the stuff took seven days after all the ingredients were obtained, which itself had taken more than a span! Was someone walking about with it in a pocket now? By the iron-barbed prick of Fell, she could hardly ask anyone!

This was too much. Hetman Gone would expect her to follow Dismé to Newland, of course, but first she had to take a look at the Lessy Yard. She hired a guide-driver with a carriage and a pair of fast horses and reached the Lessy Yard with its tumbled fences by late afternoon, only a few hours after the doctor and his crew had left it. Rashel wandered among the trash and discards, at first looking for wavy pillars, then focusing on the places where such pillars had no doubt stood. She counted them, just as the doctor had done, noting the stone dropped on each vacant place and wondering at it.

"Wagon was here," said her driver. "Not long ago."

"Maybe the wagon took what I'm looking for," she said.

"Not likely, no, Ma'am. Most likely just a family, come to fish in the pool yonder. Wagon tracks are no deeper going than coming, so whatever they were after, it didn't weigh much."

"Why do you say a family?" she asked, suddenly alert.

"Children's feet. Woman, couple of children, couple of men. Not many tracks so they didn't stay long."

Rashel subsided. There for a moment she'd thought it might have been . . . But no. Children would explain the stones on the bare spots, too. Children did things like that, making up games. Rashel herself had never played games. She disliked rules, and she could not bear losing.

"Besides," said the driver, "if you're looking for whatever was standing there, the holes are deep in turf. The grass has grown green many a year where those things stood."

The pillars certainly had to be somewhere, and it

shouldn't be impossible to trace them, which she would do, right after she had seen to Dismé. She returned to Hold by late afternoon, which meant she had missed the train to Newland, and it was too late to start the journey in a carriage. She would hire a carriage for the morning, and spend another night at the lodging-house in Hold. It was as she was on her way there that she was rudely accosted by a stranger.

"The Hetman wants to see you, Rashel," said this person, an anonymous, ashen-skinned, dun-haired, nothing-looking man.

She drew herself up. "The Hetman? From Apocanew?"

"The Hetman, from anywhere he chooses to be," said the messenger. "Follow me."

She did so reluctantly, her stomach clenching, her jaw tight, wishing she had the courage to refuse, believing at one moment that it was a joke, a trick, and in the next that it was unacceptably real, that the Hetman was, in fact, in Hold. As, in fact, turned out to be true when her guide led her to a blind-ended street she had never seen before, between shuttered houses she found totally unfamiliar, to a grille gate she knew all too well. Inside it was an equally familiar, wizened and hairy figure who answered her knock.

"Summoned?" he sneered at her, as the guide melted away into the darkness of the streets.

"By the Hetman," she murmured, and was admitted. The corridors were not as long as in Apocanew, but the room to which she was admitted might as well have been the one in Apocanew for any difference she could detect. Gohdan Gone sat as he always did, facing the fireplace.

"The bird has flown," he said.

"Only so far as Newland," she replied. "And I will ride to Newland in the morning. She is there doing some work for Doctor Ladislav, or so his assistant says."

"Ah," said the Hetman. "Come and sit by the fire."

She went to the chair with her head down, her lips pinched together to keep them from trembling, surprised that he showed no anger. When he spoke his voice was soft, almost sweet.

"Very recently, Rashel, you asked me to involve you in my magic. Remember that?"

"I . . . I was impudent, Master. As you said at the time."

"Perhaps you were, then. Now, however, I have decided to grant your request."

She was still for a long moment, trying to guess at his motives. "To aid me in getting Dismé back to Faience?"

"Oh, yes. Your participation will help get Dismé back, to Faience or some other place."

She swallowed deeply. "I am gratified that you believe I can assist you."

He curved his mouth at her, showing the huge teeth at the corners of his lips. "I am, as you know, a follower of the Fell, and therefore the Fell grants me a measure of power to hold and use as I see fit. Still, the use of this power requires certain rites and observances."

"I understand . . ."

"I can save you the time you would have spent in journeying, to Newland, for Dismé is not there, nor anywhere in Bastion."

Rashel looked up, totally alert. Not in Bastion?

"So much was easy to determine. Where she is, we do not know. I must send . . . a personal envoy to find her."

"Master, I am your willing envoy. I'm sure I can . . ."

He interrupted her with a raised hand. "If you had followed my orders at once, perhaps you could have, but you put other tasks first. Your research under the Fortress. Your dalliance with your lovers . . ."

She searched desperately for something to divert him from this line. "I am late only because I thought you would want to know about the devices that summon the Guardian Council!"

He turned his huge head toward her, the long yellow fangs sliding outside his lower lip, momentarily exposed as he curled his long upper lip in a sneer. "Devices?"

"The one in the cellar of the Fortress. I was there, in the

cellar, and some woman came, laid her hands upon it, and it dissolved in a shower of fire. A great voice said something or other about the council, and the woman went away too quickly to be followed. We were all blinded by the fire and deafened by the voice . . ."

"This made you forget Dismé?"

"Oh, no, Master. I was not concerned about Dismé for I had already put in her room the potion you told me to make. While I was allowing time for her to drink the stuff, I inquired about the pillar. There had been many of these pillars before the Fortress was built. They were taken to the Lessy Yard . . ."

A long, thoughtful silence.

"Which is where?"

She babbled the location, concluding, "When I found Dismé had gone to Newland, I went to the Lessy Yard, first thing this morning. The pillars aren't there now, but several of them were taken away only recently. I intended to go in search of them once I had Dismé back in hand . . . but you say she is not in Bastion . . ."

He stared at her, eyes glowing from the fire. "I will send my envoy to this Lessy Yard. I will send after this woman you speak of, the one in the cellar. I will find Dismé Latimer. I will involve you in my magic, as you have suggested. And because you have brought me this information, I will reward you by assuring you will live through the experience."

Before she could speak, he rose, turning to look down upon her from a great height, while she in turn gazed up, far up, at the blazing glow of his eyes, the terror overwhelming her as she realized that the Hetman was not, as she had always assumed, a misshapen and ugly human fellow whose eyes merely reflected the red firelight. Whatever fire was about this creature burned from within.

He reached out one finger and laid it upon the skin of her breast. She screamed as she felt the blister form. He had never touched her before. His minions had manipulated an iron image of the Fell during her dedication, her "mating" as they called it, and something out of the book had occupied that image once it was coupled with her, but the Hetman had not touched her until tonight.

"To summon the envoy I need certain things," he whispered, his breath crisping her hair and brows so that the ash fell into her face. "I need the eyes of a living woman, the hands of a living woman, the womb of a living woman. The eyes will be taken first, then the hands, and finally the womb will be eaten from inside by the Fell himself."

"Dismé," she stuttered, trying not to moan at the pain of the burning. "That's why you need Dismé."

"I need the envoy to *find* Dismé," He smiled horribly. "I need your *involvement* to evoke the envoy."

A little before midnight, two guards from the Fortress found a woman lying on the street. She still breathed, so they took her to the clinic where Dr. Ladislav often worked at night, as the doctor had asked them to do in any such case. The doctor wasn't there, but Old Ben was, and he had been studying with Dr. Ladislav. He gestured that the guards should wait in an outer room, which they did, while he undressed and examined the unconscious body, taking the blood pressure, measuring the temperature. As he counted the pulse in her throat, his eyes moved from severed wrist to severed wrist, from empty eyesockets to the area between her legs, which had been mutilated. Whoever had done this had intended her to live, for they had bound the wrists, and while the injury to her lower body had no doubt been excruciatingly painful, it had somehow been done without causing enough internal bleeding to lower her blood pressure. Though her eyesockets still oozed blood, that loss was not enough to endanger her life.

What he saw was not new to him. Both he and the doctor had seen mutilations of this kind more frequently of late, mostly to women and children, occasionally to men, but never to old people. Almost always, the people were left alive. Which meant, so the doctor had told him in secretive whispers, that the continued life of the victim was an important ingredient of the ritual. "My theory," Jens had told him, "is that a black art cannot come from any natural thing, for its power is against nature. Death is natural, so black art cannot take power from death. Continued pain, however, is not natural. Nature soothes, or nature lets die; rarely does it permit continued agony. So, the ritual takes its power from pain, from death withheld, the longer and more dreadful the agony, the more power it produces. Thus, we have mutilations as the method of choice, for coping with mutilation is a continuing agony even when wounds have healed . . ."

Despite having seen it before, this was the first time Ben had seen so many parts taken from one still living victim. Ben went into the outer room and wrote a note to the guards. "Do you have any idea who she is?"

The guards, who had been half asleep, shook their heads. She hadn't been carrying anything, they said, as was quite understandable considering she had no hands to carry anything with. The younger guard offered a bit of jewelry that had been around her neck, a silver pendant set with an obsidian image, and bearing an engraving on the back. "For my dear friend on the occasion of her promotion. MM."

"It's set in a design," said one of the guards, peering over Ben's shoulder. "I know that design. It's the insignia of Inexplicable Arts, see, the I and the A woven together that way."

"Mace Marchant is head of Inexarts in Apocanew," said the other guard. "Maybe the woman's from there. Is she gonna die?"

"Not of her injuries," Ben wrote. "When she regains consciousness, perhaps she can tell us who she is. If not, you will perhaps ask the man at Inexplicable Arts?"

When the guard had read this, he shook his head. "Sorry, Ben. It'd be against orders to leave her here. We only brought her because Dr. Ladislav wants every victim brought to him, no matter how bad they are, and once he has 'em, he's got the rank to decide what to do with 'em. But he's not here, him nor his rank, and you an't no officer, Ben. Hell, you an't even in the department! Look at her. She'll never be able to work, or have children, if a woman can't work or have children . . ."

"Preferably both," said the other guard.

" . . . then she's no good to the Spared and we're s'posed to put her in the demon locker near the Praise Gate, to be bottled."

The woman inside the room may have heard this, for she began to thrash madly to and fro, emitting horrid, grating sounds. It was only then that Ben discovered she had no tongue.

"Wait a bit," he wrote. "I'll stop the pain."

He shut the door to the outer room. The doctor had shown him where all the drugs were: the red containers from Chasm by way of the demons, to fight infections: the blue containers, vials and bottles from the west, to sedate and kill pain. The individually labeled green-packaged herbs shipped from far Everday to reduce anxiety, to promote healing, to reduce fevers. He went to the shelf and looked for a certain small blue bottle. The doctor used the same colors to code his own drugs, for some of his assistants read little if at all. The small blue bottle had been here last time Ben was at the clinic.

No such bottle. Well then, the last of it had been used! Or, there might be more in the storage closet. After a search he found an old, scratched blue bottle at the back of the highest shelf, not quite the same color, size, or shape as the one he'd been looking for, but then, the woman was so bad off that any calming drug could only help her.

She would be unable to swallow, so he carefully filled a syringe attached to a tube and fed the tube into the back of her throat. When he had dosed her, she stopped thrashing and howling almost at once. Her breathing slowed. Her heart rate slowed. Ah, well, perhaps he had killed her, but the demons would have done that anyhow, after they took some of her to be bottled. He wrapped her closely in a sheet, opened the door to the hallway, and let the guards take her away. Though he felt great pity for the woman, he was not reluctant to let her go. She would either be dead before the demons came, or she would sleep through whatever they did to her. If Ben himself was on that stretcher, he would not want to go on living in that condition, even if it were possible.

He stared at the bottle a long moment, considering. If it had killed her, best it not be left around where he or any other nincompoop could make a mistake with it. The bit of silver jewelry lay on the table beside the bed. He still felt it would be a good idea to send a note to Mace Marchant. Needn't tell the man the details. Just advise him there was an accident victim, so tall, so old, such and such color hair. Maybe he could identify her by her description.

✴ 37

leaving bastion

When dawn came, the doctor told them to pack the wagon, but also to make up small packs of necessities for a long hike. When all this had been done, they drove on up the road until midmorning, then left the wagon and horses in a clearing while they went on foot to a path in the woods that very soon became steep and after that, perpendicular.

At noon, when they stopped for a much needed rest, they heard the creak of wheels and saw through a gap in the trees their own wagon, now driven by a horned demon.

Dismé stared questioningly at the doctor.

"Regime guards are instructed not to see any demons who are moving about on ordinary demonish activities," he told her. "They would definitely see me, however, and neither general nor bishop would approve of my taking a wagon into demon territory."

"How do you get away with these journeys?" asked Michael.

The doctor stopped to mop his forehead with a kerchief. "The farther from Hold one gets, the less Regimic the people are and the less the Regime knows or cares about them. Meantime, the Regime has become so smug it can't tell the difference among the revolutionary, the innovative, or the merely various. The high command knows so little about the outside that if I came back with a fully equipped chemical laboratory and told them I'd found it in a cave, they'd probably believe that, so long as I brought it back piecemeal in my saddle bags, thus proving I hadn't known it was there beforehand."

"So it's the wagon that's troublesome," murmured Dismé.

"At this pass, yes, because this pass has guards. If I hadn't really wanted to see the Lessy Yard for myself, we might have gone another way."

"How do we get the wagon back?"

"This path we're on meets the road on the other side."

The path, if so it could be called, continued to be a hard, rough scramble up a rock wall and down another, during which Dismé blessed all her tree climbing days. Bobly and Bab climbed like squirrels, while furry beasts with large heads and short tails came out of the rocks and whistled at them, ducking for cover whenever Michael pretended to throw something.

By early afternoon, they had crossed the pass out of sight of the road and descended a way down the far side of the mountain. Following the smell of smoke, they came upon horses and wagon hidden from above by rock outcroppings and leafy copses. Rabbits were roasting over a fire.

"Heya," called the doctor.

One of the demons approached them, holding out his hand. "Jens Ladislav," he said. "Who's this. New assistants?"

"Dismé," said the doctor.

"I know you," said Dismé, who had stared hard at him when she heard his voice. "You're Wolf."

The doctor looked at her in confusion, which was echoed to some extent by the demon himself.

"You never saw me," he challenged.

"I heard your voice," she said. "Yours and your female friend's. Is she with you? At least she was less insulting!"

"Insulting?" the doctor asked, his eyebrows raised.

"He called me a dead snake," she said. "A limp rag. A do-nothing, know-nothing."

"I had no idea we had friends in common," said Michael, laying his hand on Dismé's arm. "Are you sure he wasn't trying to provoke you into taking an appropriate action? That's what he did with me."

"By all the Rebel Angels and their golden footstools," said the doctor. "Is this a reunion? Someone please enlighten me?"

Dismé gave a concise account of her encounter with the demons in the cavern below Faience, to which Wolf added his own explanations: "What was really happening was . . ." while Michael offered: "We have to take into account that . . ."

"How do you know this horny one?" demanded Bab of Michael.

"Because I spent a year with him and his kin," said Michael.

"And what is it Wolf put in your head?" Bobly asked Dismé.

"The female demon called it a dobsi," Dismé replied. "A creature that transmits information to them. Everything I see or hear. Or, I should say, did transmit. I don't know what Dezmai allows to be seen."

"Thank you for the warning," said the doctor, somewhat snappishly to Wolf. "I may have said certain things I did not want transmitted!"

"But they arranged for me to meet you," Dismé cried. "I thought you were in on it; you sent the letter."

"In on what?" the doctor cried.

"Shhh," said the demon. "You'll frighten the horses. We didn't arrange it, Dismé. It was Arnole who sent the letter to the doctor. He didn't tell us he'd done so until you'd already left Faience, and since it took you precisely where you could be best helped, we simply let it be. We kept our word. We did make a plan for you, but it wasn't half as good as Arnole's."

"Arnole?" The doctor threw up his hands.

"Ayward's father," said Dismé. "My friend. Who also had a dobsi in his head." She turned back to Wolf. "And you also know Michael?"

Michael flushed and dug his toe into the ground, as the

doctor's eyebrows threatened to escape his head. "Well, well," he said. "You didn't enlighten me, Mr. Pigeon."

"I didn't think it mattered," said Michael. "So, I'm a rebel spy! A spy for them, a spy for you, rebel either way, what's the difference?"

"We'll discuss it later," said Jens, beckoning the others to join him on the blankets spread around the fire. When Wolf had seated himself, he unwound the turban, displaying a complicated bony structure attached to the horns. To Dismé's amazement, he slowly lifted the entire assembly, which separated from his head with a decided snap. He set it down beside the fire, where the horns remained for a moment upright, like a stringless lyre, then lowered slowly to a horizontal position. The bony structure between them emitted legs, and the leg part dragged the horn part off into the undergrowth. Neither the doctor nor Michael showed any surprise.

"We let them wander around sometimes," Wolf said to Dismé, scratching his head vigorously with both hands. "They like to nibble bits of foliage and mosses . . ."

"They?" she faltered.

"The Dantisfan. A race of small, psychosensitive creatures who exist in symbiotic relationships with larger, less perceptive beings, such as humans. The dobsi are the juvenile form, flat, thin, capable of inserting themselves inside the skull without at all injuring the brain. We protect the Dantisfan from predation, we feed them and give them a protected place to spawn, and they accompany us and alert us to any hostile intent in the area."

"Where did they . . ." she asked, astonished.

Wolf said, "They came with the Happening, along with the Visitor and the other Un-Earthlies. Some of them were predatory monsters, most weren't. The Dantisfan are among the most useful, at least to us. The horns are full of tissue rather like brain tissue and the outsides are studded with receptor cells, like eyes, ears, barometers, thermometers, tastebuds, smell sensors, and, most important, some organ that detects emotions in the vicinity. The middle part has the legs, and what we call the pressor organ, the one they use to tell us what they feel, or what they see and hear through their dobsi's sensors."

He took a comb from his pocket to restore his hair to order, continuing, "In addition to transmitting what the dobsi sees and hears, they'll show you what they sense as well." He cast a quick glance at the doctor, whose habitual smile seemed somewhat strained about the edges.

"No doubt it was a survival characteristic, wherever they evolved," said the doctor with a dismissive twitch of his nostrils. "It would be an advantage to be able to leave your offspring by itself and still be able to see everything that was going on around it. Do they hear only their own offspring?"

Wolf shook his head. "Their own by preference, but if any dobsi yells loud enough, all Dantisfan within range pick it up."

"And who is the Visitor?" asked Dismé.

"The big something that came with the Happening."

Dismé nodded, recognizing it as part of the story she had told her students. "The part that split off."

Wolf said, "Those of us from Chasm started calling it the Visitor because that's a relatively comfortable label. It implies the stay is temporary, that the thing will go away. We think the Visitor must be part of a race of beings who live in space, though we're guessing at that. We also postulate that they hitch rides on bits of space trash that are moving somewhere, like the huge one that came at us. Anyhow, the Visitor is getting closer by the day."

"What does it want here?" Dismé asked. "What does it do?"

"Nobody knows. It's headed inland, now, toward a wide stretch of dry prairie where there's some kind of building. We have a few Chasmites out there, to keep an eye on it."

"So demons are just . . . people?" Dismé asked.

"Quite right. People."

"Then why . . . why all this secrecy?"

Bobly said, in an amused voice, "She wants to know why you don't make friends with the Regime?"

Wolf snorted. "Why doesn't the damned Regime make

friends with us? Because we're heretics. We don't believe in sorcery. We don't believe things happen by magic. We don't pray to Rebel Angels. We don't have a Dicta that answers all questions. Also, we don't go along with all that bottle and chair nonsense, even though we make the hardware for them. Among ourselves, we tell jokes about keeping the Regime well seated and bottled up. We don't need a hundred thousand fanatical killers out here."

"But there is magic," cried Dismé. "I've seen it!"

"I'm sure you saw what looked like magic," said Wolf, in a kindly tone. "Nonetheless, I'm also sure there was a natural explanation for it."

"Heya . . ." someone called from downhill.

"Flower," said Wolf. "I'll fetch her." He got up and strolled away, pausing to stroke the Dantisfan, which had thrust itself against a rock and was busy scraping lichen with a ridge of emerald chitin that evidently served it for teeth.

The doctor murmured, "Demons are no less doctrinaire than the Spared. They refuse to believe in anything they can't measure and explain. The Regime believes implicitly in magic and thinks that Scientism is heretical, but the demons already have carts that move without horses as well as a few mechanisms that carry people through the air. They have a great many other technological things as well, and they have no patience with magical thinking."

"So I shouldn't blather like a classroom monitor about the end of the world, or how the Spared will be saved."

"Or about angels. Most particularly not angels. They see the idea of angels as a threat to their own dominance of the physical world. We're not here to debate Wolf or his people. We just need to warn them about the army, so they can spread the word to everyone who lives out here."

"Can't anyone do anything to stop the army?" Dismé asked.

The doctor shook his head. "Most of the rebels aren't fighters. They do, however, make up at least a third of Bastion's population. The night before we left, I sent messages in all directions. By the time we were at Lessy Yard, most of

Bastion knew what the army planned. When the army moves, a third of Bastion's population will leave, leaving only the Regimic types behind. The Fortress at Hold will still be full of Turnaways, but there'll be no food grown or cooks in the kitchens."

"No support for the army, in other words," said Michael. "But no active opposition, either."

The doctor shook his head. "What are they supposed to oppose? From what General Gowl said, there will be monsters joining the army, but Chasm believes all the real monsters died out centuries ago, and it doesn't believe in magical ones. Chasm will have to see them before they can plan to fight them."

Dismé said angrily, "Michael, why didn't you tell me this?"

"How could I with Rashel right there?" Michael protested.

"Arnole must have been a rebel, and he didn't tell me. How could there be so many rebels without the Regime knowing it?"

It was Wolf's partner, Flower, just arriving, who replied, "It was inevitable. Once the Regime said that one living cell is a life, real living became irrelevant, and the Regime started bottling everyone who was troublesome. Meantime, it was Regimic policy to capture young people from outside. Follow that pattern for a few generations, bottling people who believe, replacing them with outsiders who don't, and before long most of the people in Bastion pretend to be Regimic but aren't."

Wolf nodded. "Meantime, the leaders are so proud they believe pride will hold Bastion together, and as an extra incentive, they say everyone outside Bastion will be wiped out."

"Which, if true, might have made Bastion alluring," said Flower.

Wolf nodded. "We outsiders based our strategy on keeping the Spared where they are, keeping them satisfied, bleeding them out slowly while replacing their people with our people, until they wouldn't be dangerous anymore."

"It was working fine until the general had his visions," the doctor growled. "And that brings me to the reason I came this way . . ."

The warning took some time, allowing for Wolf's explosive digressions into disbelief and anger, particularly on the subject of the Guardian Council. "They've upset things already. People doing magic. People causing miracles. Bastion's bad enough without some power hungry cult gaining influence among the rabble by doing a little legerdemain."

"Is it legerdemain?" murmured Dismé.

"Of course it is," snapped Wolf.

"And do they bear a sign, on their foreheads?" she asked, innocently.

"Dismé!" warned the doctor.

Wolf said, "They are said to, which is more trickery, though I haven't seen them myself. Luminous paint, most likely."

Dismé removed her scarf and turned so the demons could see her face. Flower rose and came to her, bending to touch the sign, jerking her finger back at the sensation.

"Use soap and water if you like," Dismé suggested. "I don't mind if you remove it. I've tried."

They tried soap and scrubbing, reddening her skin in the process but making the sign glow only brighter.

"It's a substance we're not familiar with," said Wolf, at last, through his teeth. "Chasm could identify it."

"No, they'd be as baffled as I am," confessed the doctor, with a headshake at Dismé. "I'm by way of being a small scientist myself, and nothing known to me glows like that. Certainly not the way it did immediately after the device hit her."

"You saw it?"

"I did. Wolf, I respect you too much to lie to you. Something here is outside your experience and mine. You know the Tamlar story. Remember the pillars on the mound that P'Jardas spoke of? On the way here, we stopped at the storage yard where those pillars had been taken when the

Fortress was built. The pillars aren't there anymore. How many of the Council have been . . . what did you say, Dismé? Called?"

She looked into the distance and said, "Tamlar needed no call. I feel most of the others have been found." Her voice seemed to come from very far away.

"How does she make that voice?" asked Flower, in an interested voice. "It's very clever."

Dezmai turned to look at her, and Flower froze in place.

The doctor said, "It isn't a trick."

"Oh come now," said Wolf, sneeringly.

Dezmai opened her mouth hugely and roared the sound of great drums pounding. Around her the trees shivered, branches fell, leaves flew. The fire flared up and sparks went soaring away in lines of fire. Wolf, who seemed to be at the focus of the sound, was flung aside in a crumpled heap.

Dismé dropped her head and was silent.

As Wolf struggled to his feet, the doctor gulped. "Wolf, I think perhaps it would be wise if you and Flower ah . . . withheld judgement about the Council. For a time."

"I'm sorry," murmured Dismé. "She does what she likes, and she hates being ridiculed."

"We know," said Michael coming to put his arm around her shoulders, and looking piercingly at the others. "Don't we?"

Bobly and Bab assented quickly, as did Wolf and Flower more reluctantly.

"Show them Bertral's Book," whispered Bobly. "Perhaps that will help them understand."

The doctor fetched the book from his saddle bag and sat down with it in his lap, the two demons leaning over his shoulders.

"Lady Dezmai of the Drums," he read.

In whose charge are the howls of battle, the roaring of great beasts, the lumbering of herds, the mutter and clap of thunder, the tumult of waves upon stone, the cry of trumpets, the clamor of the avalanche . . .

"There must be some kind of device in the wagon to make that sound," suggested Flower. "Some kind of amplifier."

"*There is no device in the wagon*," said Dismé in a tone of fatal decision. "You have doubted once. Do not doubt again."

"I think that would be wise," said the doctor. "Please, Wolf, Flower, bear with us. I don't know what's going on any more than you do, but I do know I bought that wagon just a few days ago, and there's no device in it."

The two demons looked at one another skeptically, but they did not voice their doubts again. Instead, they crowned themselves with their Dantisfan, wound their turbans to hold the horns in place, made rather curt farewells and took themselves off, scarcely waiting until they were out of earshot before beginning to argue with one another.

"I apologize for them," said the doctor, getting up to return the book to his saddle bag.

"No need," said Dismé. "In time, they will either learn or Rankivian will take them." She rubbed her head, fretfully. "I have the strong feeling that if we don't want to encounter black arts, we need to leave this place. Dezmai, dobsi, or demons—one or all of them has set my teeth on edge. Something horrid is coming this way, and we must be far away if we are to avoid it."

They hitched up the wagon and set out again upon the road, not stopping until the dark was well upon them.

✦ *38*

anglers and border guards

Summerspan five, fourday, evening: on a grassy promontory in the Comador mountains, a pair of anglers vacationing from Newland made themselves a sketchy camp out of a couple of bedrolls and a circle of stones around a small fire. They had camped the last two nights some way north and west of Newland. They had tramped on today to intercept the Outward Road and had followed it first west into the hills and then south along the valley to the old storage yard below. From there they had clambered up a narrow and well-hidden trail to the top of the promontory, where they had spent a twilight hour fishing the pools up the stream and back again before setting up camp.

The woods were behind them and the open air before them. Their view to the north included the smoke from a village or two in the Comador rumplelands, and a little east of that, light from a village in the flatland of Turnaway, past the Outward Road. It would take a bonfire to be seen this far, so someone was memorializing a marriage, a birth, or a bottling. From above, the near end of the Lessy road was hidden by copses in the valley below, but it emerged into the open farther north, where it curved to the east around the sides of two low hills.

Behind them, their fishing stream wandered through the forest, dropping in a staircase of talkative falls and mute pools, to the edge of the precipice before them, where it slipped over a smoothed rockrim in a vitreous flow that entered the large pool, only its shimmer showing that it moved. From there on, the water was only a valley creek, running smooth a bit, then quicker and whiter over stones, becoming a crooked silver thread along the road they had come by, whiter and wider as it met other rills and brooklets until, at the road fork, it straightened north and east toward the wetlands that bordered Apocanew in Turnaway-shire: the lowest, flattest, and wettest of the shires, source of the subterranean river that drained all Bastion and kept it from becoming a lake.

The men had raked a bed of coals to one side of the fire and spitted half a dozen fat trout above it. On the fire, a kettle steamed alongside a pot of cornmush, beans, and bacon to which had been added a handful of peppers and some other common herbs, a mixture locally known as *much-a-plenty*. The fish took only a short time to cook, and the much-a-plenty had been cooked before they left home and heated several times since, so they soon filled their plates, took their jug of cider from the icy waters of the precipice pool, and sat crosslegged near the edge of the drop to enjoy their meal and the view. Darkness had fallen in the valley below them where the moon silvered the curves of the road and made of the landscape a painting in steely lights and ashen shadows, a view that brightened as the moon rose further and the fire died behind them to leave only a faint haze of smoke against the darkness of the trees.

"Look there," murmured one to the other, in a whisper.

"Where?" grunted the other, older man.

"Shhh. Look down there at that largest pile of stuff in the old yard. See it? Now look left a little. What's that moving?"

The other stared. They both did, for several moments.

"It's big," whispered the older man, suddenly convinced of the wisdom of quiet. "Really big."

"Ayup, it is that," whispered the other in response. They watched, fascinated, as the bulky shadow fell toward the ground, then heaved up and moved forward, its head moving back and forth like the head of a serpent or, though they had never seen one, that great snake-headed bear of the north, weaving . . .

"It's smelling something," whispered the younger man. "See, how it's sniffing all around the yard, and now it's sniffing the way back to the road."

Indeed, the bulky shadow had reached the road once more, and was now moving along it, away from the valley, first into the trees, then out of them onto the first visible stretch of road that curved around the hill.

"Shadua of the Shroud protect us," said the older man, getting up rather hastily and thereby dislodging his tin plate so that it went down the face of the stone like a tambourine, chingling and bashing as it went.

Far down the road the shadow froze, turned, rose to its full, ogre's height, and stared back the way it had come, head tilted to let it look upward at the promontory on which they stood.

As though by mutual consent, the two men had already frozen. Half standing, bent double, they remained as they were, every muscle tensed, their very breathing stilled, fearing even to blink. The wind blew into their faces from the valley. The faint smoke of the fire went into the trees. Both of them noticed this with heightened acuity; both silently acknowledged that the direction of the wind was extremely fortunate.

After a long, long time, an eternity to them both, the shadow on the road dropped down once more and loped away in a hideous shuffling gallop that took it beyond the curve of the hill. Even then the men did not move, for the road came into sight again, further on, and the shadow stopped again on that farther stretch to peer back in their direction once more. Only when the black blotch had reached the end of the second curve and gone on around the hill did the younger man stand erect and draw an explosive breath.

"What was it?" asked the older man.

"Don't know," replied the other. "Don't want to know."

"D'ja see the eyes?" asked the other from a dry mouth.

"Red," said the other. "Red and glowing. Like coals. Shouldn't a been able to show up so far from here, but they did!"

"Demon?" asked the older man. "Didn't believe in 'em until now, but it had to be. What else?"

The younger man shook his head. "What d'ya think? Shoudn' we pack up and get out of here? Just in case it comes back."

Without further discussion, they fell to clearing their camp, making up their packs, burying all evidence of themselves, including the ashes of the fire. They had come the easy way along the road in the valley, but without discussing it, they turned up the hill to take a steeper, wilder, and infinitely safer seeming route southeast through the Comador hill country toward home.

Part way there, one of them remembered the tin plate, which would certainly bear the scent of one or both of them. He spent the rest of the journey trying to convince himself that the thing would not come back to sniff it out.

Discipline at the guard post above Ogre's Gap had long been lax. Though considerable traffic had once passed that way, now there was so little movement on the road that the four guards, changed at the beginning of each span and assigned to watch two and two, night and day, had fallen into the habit of having one man watch the road during the day, while the rest of them slept, and having no man watch the road during the night while they all played cards and drank. Since the daytime watcher had also been up all night, he was usually asleep at his post. That is, during those times when he hadn't taken off to go fishing or hunting for his own amusement.

Thus it was an unusual state of affairs to find all four men awake and watchful late one night, a state of affairs resulting from the fact that one of them had allowed a wagon to pass that afternoon driven by two demons, a male and a female. None of the guards had ever seen a demon before, and the junior man, the one who had seen them this afternoon had been asked to repeat his description of them until he was heartily sick of it.

"Look, they din't spit fire or spout smoke; they din't turn me into a frog; they din't look like nothing weird. They looked just like people only they had horns. That's it."

"Was they real horns?" the sergeant asked, for the tenth time. "That's what I want to know. I mean, what's to stop some rebel from getting some horns off a cow and sticking them to his head and claiming to be a demon? To get out of Bastion? He could, you know he could."

"Why would anybody do that?" the junior man demanded. "When anybody could just walk up over the top of the hill 'thout any trouble at all. Anybody can walk out of Bastion anytime, you know that as well as I do."

"He'd do that to get a wagon out," said the sergeant, to the sycophantic nods of his two cronies. "That's why he'd do that. To get the wagon out and the woman out and whatever was in the wagon."

"They stopped and got out so's I could look in the wagon," asserted the youthful guardsman, very red in the face. "There was a couple mattresses with blankets, and some bags with clothes in, and some books, and some food stores, and that's all."

"Contraband," muttered the sergeant into his moustache. "They was probably carrying contraband. I should report that."

"Well, you go right ahead," said the guard, losing his temper altogether. "And I should report you wan't even here, 'cause you were off fishing, and the other two of you wan't anywhere around, 'cause you'd gone with him and the three of you was prob'ly having yourselfs a nice swim whilst I had two demons to deal with!"

This statement so far leveled the grounds of accusation that the sergeant wisely decided to let that aspect of the matter drop. "It might be the first of a bunch," he said, flatly. "Or, it might be headquarters, making a test shipment or even checking up on us. For the next few days, we'd better look sharp at whatever comes along."

All four agreed that this would be prudent. Or, as they put it, "A pain in the ass what those wine-drinking bastards in Bastion get up to."

So it was that all four of them were more or less awake when, just before dawn, the man assigned to the watchtower, the junior man, the same one who had seen the demons that afternoon, came creeping in the back door of the watch-house, leaving it open, and shook the sergeant to alertness in utter silence, with a hand over his mouth.

"What the . . ." demanded the sergeant, before he saw his man's face, which was white and stark eyed and frightened.

"Something coming up the road," that man said. "Never saw nothing like it. A beast maybe, a big one. Not nothing we can handle, Sarge. Too big, moving too fast, and I think what we ought to do is turn out the lights and get out of here."

The sergeant was braver than most, and stupider—the two qualities often going hand in hand. Already fully dressed he stalked to the door, tossed his quiver over one shoulder, took his spear in one hand and his bow in the other, opened the door with a crash, and strode out into the moonlight.

By this time the other two were reaching for their boots. The man who had reported gave his two fellows a frightened look and went out the door he had come in by, leaving it open behind him. In the wan light of predawn, the other two saw him running full tilt for the hillside and the cover of the trees.

That was about when the sergeant yelled, which brought the two to their feet. Then they heard a panicky shout, which made them turn in confusion, first toward their weapons, then away, toward the door. Then the sergeant screamed, a sound which went on interminably without any stop to draw breath, rising in pitch in a tortured shriek which neither of the men had ever heard or wished ever to hear again. They both made for the door their fellow had left by, but by that time they had delayed far, far too long.

✦ *39*

laying a false trail

When the doctor awoke on the morning of fiveday, he found Dismé seated on the ground beside the wagon, fully dressed, holding the dishpan and a considerable bouquet of herbs which she was shredding into a mush in the dishpan. As he watched, amazed, she applied that mush to her hair and body, which she had in the meantime stripped of all clothing. When green from head to toe, she dunked herself in the stream that ran down from the pass, not even noticing its iciness. When she came out of the water, she donned clean clothing and set aside the clothing she had worn.

"I'd love to know what you're doing," said the doctor, from the wagon seat.

She started and flushed. "How long have you been there?"

"I'm a physician," he said. "The human form is not a mystery to me, old or young, lean or fat, male or female."

"Well, being looked at is a novelty to me, and I wish you wouldn't," she said, somewhat angrily. "I seem to be changing the smell of myself. I got the idea in the middle of the night, Dezmai, Dantisfan, dobsi, or demon. Something's following us by smell, and we need to change the smell."

"How about the rest of us?" he asked, in an interested voice. "Should we adopt a new scent?"

"I'd recommend it," she said firmly.

"The thing in your head . . . the whatsit?"

"Dobsi."

"If the Dantisfan can receive from the dobsi and talk to the demons, then I should imagine you can perhaps listen in on the conversation? Especially when you're asleep?"

"It's possible," she admitted. "In which case the Dantisfan have been passing on to the thing in my head that something dangerous is about, which makes me even more nervous. If something evil comes, it will have grown used to the smell of the rest of you as well. Michael, you, Bobly, and Bab. And the wagon. And the horses."

"Should we use those same herbs?"

She shook her head. "No. Those herbs were for me, particularly, to disguise some particular attribute which some creatures can find by smell. Or so I am led to believe. In addition to this, we must all eat summerhay after our breakfast. And rub some on our shoes, on the wagon, on the horse's feet. If we can get them to eat some summerhay . . ."

He made a face. "Summerhay? Even cows won't eat it."

"You can make pills of it, if you like. If that would be easier."

"How much for each?"

She shrugged. "Enough to make us stink, including the horses."

He set about gathering summerhay from along the stream, making a face at the smell. So far as he knew, summerhay was used only to keep moths out of woolens, though odiferous things were usually ascribed virtues even when they had none. When he had the summerhay gathered, he put it in a pan and began drying it over the fire, then setting it aside to cool before crushing it with mortar and pestle. Finally he combined the powdered herb with some substance scooped out of a jar that bound the herb dust together.

"What's that?" asked Dismé.

"Paste. With some sugar in it." He rolled the resulting substance into pills, smaller ones for people, larger ones for horses, leaving a mass of the stuff as it was, for rubbing on the outsides of things. He had barely finished by the time Michael, Bobly, and Bab returned to the camp bearing a dozen good sized fish.

"Phew," said Bobly. "What have you been up to?"

"Dismé has had an intimation," said the doctor. "One I think we'd be wise to heed."

"It smells as though she's had something worse than an intimation," said Bab. "That's summerhay."

"The doctor has made some pills," said Dismé, her eyes vague and glassy as she gazed up the peak they had climbed the day before. "Something up there is following us. Following the trail we made over the rock. It knows our smell. It knows the wagon smell, and the smell of our horses. It is very near us now, but it does not move by day."

Michael had brought a pile of wood for the campfire. He laid it down and asked Dismé, "Do you sense that the thing is after you, personally? Or after all of us?"

Dismé nodded, dismally. "Oh, Michael, it's after me, only me, and the rest of you only because you're with me. And the reason it's after me has something to do with Dezmai, but she comes and goes so quickly, I can't grasp what she knows of it."

Michael frowned in concentration. "Well, if it's following you personally, we need to make a false trail. I'll take your clothes, the ones you've worn, and I'll take the doctor's horse—forgive me, doctor, but I've seen you on a horse, and I can make far better time—and lead the creature away from whatever route we are taking."

"It won't come after me until dark," she said firmly. "The thing travels in the dark. It's made of darkness."

"We'll still need to change our smell," said Bobly, taking a proffered pill from the doctor's hand. "And I have no doubt this will do it. Our Uncle Titus was given some once, for a bellyache, and he stank of the stuff for days!"

Michael and the doctor put their heads together while Dismé sorted her clothing, using a long stick to separate the things she didn't mind losing, and drawing the rest into a pile to be washed in the herb mixture which also had a strong smell, though one that was spicy and resinous rather than sickening.

Michael made himself a sandwich of bread and meat for

his breakfast, packed up enough food for another few meals, rolled his blankets, bundled Dismé's discarded clothes together, and tied them into a bundle at the end of a length of rope. The doctor, meantime, brought out a hand-drawn map and laid it on the tailgate of the wagon.

"Here," said the doctor, pointing at a painstakingly inked line upon the map. "This is where we are. We went west from Bastion, into the mountains to the pass, then southward, down this road. The road forks just below us, one southeast, one southwest, both of them headed toward the rim of the east–west canyon you can see there, almost a day's ride away. We'll take the southwest fork—it's better for the wagon. You take the southeast one that goes all the way to this bridge crossing the canyon. It's been there since before the Happening. Across the bridge the road runs both ways, up the canyon and down, east and west. The east way goes uphill, past some old quarries and over a pass by a waterfall and eventually ends up in Comador. It's a bad road. The west road is better. It lies between the canyon wall and the river, and it works its way down to a river ford in a wide valley. If you cross the river there, the road climbs north to rejoin this road, and the Seeress we're going to see will be just a few miles west. I figure, two days."

Michael nodded. "I'll drag the clothing across the bridge, throw it over, then dose me and the horse with summerhay and follow the west fork to the ford, cross the river and rejoin you at the Seeress."

"We won't throw them," said Dismé in a worried voice, putting her hand on his arm. "We'll dangle the clothes down the side of the canyon on the rope, to leave a scent trail down the stone, then drop them at the bottom. And we'll rub the rope with summerhay as soon as we've done, or it will still smell of my clothing."

"We?" he cried.

"I'm going with you, Michael. If the herbs don't work, I don't want the thing going after Bobly or Bab or the doctor. Let it come after me if it will."

Michael shook his head firmly. "You're not coming."

"Dezmai says I am," she said with equal firmness. "Dezmai says I am because Tamlar says so, and neither of them are anyone I can argue with."

Michael turned to the doctor for help, but he only shrugged helplessly. "I can't argue with members of the Guardian Council or Rebel Angels or whatever they are, Michael. If any force can outwit whatever's after us, it's more likely to be them than it is us!"

A few moments later, with Dismé's cast-off clothing at the end of a rope, his face set in frozen disapproval, Michael mounted the doctor's horse and pulled Dismé up behind him. He rode off in a mood of considerable confusion, for he had been hugged by women, many a time, but he had never really been touched by Dismé until now. Her arms were tight around him, her body was pressed against his back. He found the experience unsettling and chose to deal with it by picturing her as Dezmai, huge and powerful, not at all girlish, not at all someone to be . . . lusted after. This vision, once well summoned, was slightly terrifying and worked almost too well for comfort.

The doctor looked after them, shaking his head. "I wish she wasn't going off alone like that."

"She isn't alone. Besides, Michael's fond of her," Bobly offered tentatively. "She's fond of him, too."

"The question is, can he be fond of Dezmai? Or she of him?"

"I don't know," Bobly whispered. "I haven't any idea. Don't plague me with questions like that."

Bab summoned them to breakfast. They took their pills, gave some to the horses, then smeared summerhay on everything in sight, including the wagon and everything in it. When they left shortly thereafter, they moved in a traveling stink. At noon, they did not want to eat. When thirsty, they could barely stand the taste of water.

Meantime, on the road to the bridge, Michael broke his silence to ask, "Where did you learn this use of summerhay?"

"I dreamed it," Dismé said into his ear, her lips brushing his neck with each stride of the horse. "Perhaps Dezmai of the Drums leaves messages for me while I am asleep. I get them at times when I know she is away, otherwise occupied."

"Away from you?" he asked, trying to keep the question merely interested and impersonal.

Dismé shook her head. "Michael, I don't know. I can only guess. I've always been curious about birds and small creatures. Sometimes I've wished I could inhabit one, to learn how it thinks and what moves it and whether it hopes or not. This being treats me like a . . . a house she is visiting. She comes in and looks around, very curious, turning things over, opening the cupboards, but remaining aware the house cannot be my house if she fills it with herself. So, most of the time, Dezmai goes elsewhere, perhaps leaving some tiny part of her alert within me, to warn her if something goes awry. She is close enough to intervene if I am in danger, but she does nothing to stop my fear, and I am deathly afraid of that thing the dobsi senses."

"You think it is stronger than Dezmai?" he asked in dismay.

She tried to come up with an answer, saying finally, "I think she feels it may be someday if it isn't yet."

In the wagon which was now some distance to the west of them, Bobly broke a long silence to ask, "Where are we going?"

"To see a woman named Allipto Gomator," said the doctor. "She's a seeress. A good one."

"And where does she live?"

"In a cavern, some distance along this road. It was she who told me years ago where a large cache of medical books and equipment was, a discovery that secured me a place in the Regime. This time I had planned to ask her about the Guardian Council."

"Why not ask Dezmai?" Bobly asked.

"I would do so happily. Do you think she'd answer me?"

"It's no sure thing," said the little woman. "She seems to come and go, doesn't she."

They came to the top of a rise where the world opened out, the road falling before them, then rising again, though not again to the height they had just surmounted. Beyond the hills lay a vast stretch of prairie with cloud shadows moving upon it, including one such shadow that moved against the wind.

Bab pointed southward. "What's out there?"

The doctor stared at the horizon, his face set. "South across this prairie, in the hills, is an enormous canyon, miles deep, and in that canyon Chasm has its buried city. The demons keep its exact location a secret so the Mohmidi, among others, won't find them . . ."

"The Mohmidi?"

"The shadow you see is their tribe, a prairie people who are fierce and violent to other tribes and scarcely less so to the people within their own. They travel in wagons, following the pasture with the seasons. They leave girl children to starve on the prairie, or to be eaten by wolves, and when they need wives to bear their sons, they raid other people to obtain them. Another people, the Laispos, send out bands to follow the Mohmidi and rescue the girls who are left behind. They live in secure towns at the far, southern edge of the prairie, and in that tribe, the women are warriors, sworn to enmity against the Mohmidi, and they suffer no man to ride with them."

"And this seeress is where?"

He pointed to a notch in the skyline, where the road lay like an ashen thread between black mountains. "There, at that lower pass, in a cavern. She says she lives behind it, in a stone house built for her by those who have come with questions."

"And you have questions."

"Yes," he replied. "I do indeed have questions."

Well east of the place where the doctor had long since driven off the road and made camp, Michael still rode along the twisting way, dragging Dismé's tattered clothing behind. All during the day he had kept a mental picture of the map in mind while urging the horse to the fastest pace that would not tire the big gelding utterly. Luckily the way had been fairly level, with only a few long climbs, and the stretch ahead actually seemed to be downhill so far as the bridge, where they had to arrive before darkness if they were to avoid becoming the victims of whatever it was that followed them. Hurrying was almost always a mistake, Michael thought, as it led to falls and broken bones and other misfortunes, so he had contented himself with an easy trot or an easy lope that ate the miles slowly but surely, Dismé's arms around him, her cheek against his back, so silent he thought she might be sleeping.

They had stopped once at a stream to water the horse and themselves, Michael watching carefully in all directions as Dismé knelt at the bank. They had stopped again to stretch their legs and go briefly behind a tree. Other than that, he had kept a steady pace and as the sun dropped toward evening he was gratified to see the bridge just ahead of them, a thin gray line supported by a wide arch below, the whole appearing almost magical in its lightness.

The wall of the canyon at the near end of the bridge seemed steeper, so it was there they lowered the now ragged clothing at the end of the rope so that it dragged along the canyon wall before they pulled in the rope and dropped the clothing on the scree slope at the bottom. Michael had summerhay in hand to anoint the rope, plus pills for both of them and for the horse, who was too tired to make a fuss about it. When all that had been taken care of, he lifted Dismé to the saddle and led the horse across the bridge, only to stop in amazement. At the far end of the bridge, across the road that ran along the canyon, towered a stone.

He had heard such stones described enough times on this journey that there could be no doubt what it was. Black, wavy, with golden lights, taller than he, an armspan wide, thick at the bottom so that it sat securely upon its base. Dismé's reverie was broken by the stop, and she looked up as well.

"Another one," she said.

Looking around to be sure they were alone, Michael went to the stone to lay his hands upon it. It hummed at him, but there was no burst of light. He laid his ear against it, heard resonant harmonies, then pulled away to examine the darkening sky. Some distance back from the road and high above them, a huge section of the canyon rim had broken off and fallen to make a wide, arched slope of scree that extended from the road almost to the top of the mesa, where it met a short collar of rimrock, vermillion in the setting sun. On either side of the fall, other cliffs stood entire, the road squeezed into a narrow ribbon between their crimson walls and the foaming river.

The slope before them had grown up in dark firs, more thickly in the higher reaches. Leading the horse around the stone, Michael began the ascent, tugging the reluctant beast after him. Within a hundred meters or so, they were in the cover of the trees, sparse grasses around their feet. When the horse was picketed with a long rope, he began to graze, reasonably content even though still saddled, for Michael wanted no delay if they had to leave suddenly. Building a fire was out of the question, so he shared out their cold food, picked a fallen tree as backrest, and cushioned a place beside it with pine boughs covered with one of their blankets. There, with the other blanket warming their knees, they ate their evening meal, almost too weary to chew it.

When they had packed everything away, they lay back on the blanket, covered with the other. Michael drew Dismé against him, her head pillowed on his arm, and she turned toward him with a little sigh, her arm across his chest.

"Dearest Dismé," he whispered. "Dearest one."

"Aaah," she bubbled at him, a tiny snore.

With a half smile of almost amusement, he lay still, letting her sleep. The sun had set far down the canyon. From where they lay, he could barely see the bridge, and as it grew darker it vanished into the general gloom. He dozed a little, then woke, then dozed again. At the third or fourth waking Michael saw a light eastward, slowly moving down toward the bridge on the near side of the river. He put his hand over Dismé's lips and shook her. When she wakened, he whispered to her, and she joined him in feeling their way down the ridge toward the forest edge, where they lay prone to watch the light coming closer. As it neared, they made out the form of an old man, not bent but weary, carrying a lantern and obviously hurrying as fast as possible. When the figure reached the end of the bridge, he stopped, so close that Michael could make out the astonished circle of his mouth, the widened eyes reflecting the lantern light.

Dismé started. "Why . . . that's . . . I think it is . . ."

"Shhh," Michael cautioned, drawing her tight against his side. Below them, the old man set his lantern down and approached the stone to lay his hands upon it, as Michael had done. A blast of light engulfed stone, man, and the surrounding area, and in the second before becoming blinded, both of the watchers saw something huge, dark, and hideous standing half erect at the far end of the bridge.

Dazzled, they put their hands before their eyes, removing them a moment later to blink at the scene below, where the stone was shedding its substance in a fountain of fire that lit the approach of the monster. The old man, alerted by sound or intuition, turned his back to the fiery stone and held his staff before him, facing the horror that approached.

"Are you Bertral?" the monster roared, a coughing roar that seemed to come from the pits of the earth. "You have no Book, Bertral. Without the Book, what are you?"

Michael saw the staff tremble. Behind him the horse whickered in fear and Dezmai spoke firmly into Michael's ear. "Get him the book from the saddlebag, boy. Take it to him."

Though he was unaware of any decision to obey this command, he scrambled to his feet and ran to the horse, who immediately became as uncooperative as possible, tiptoeing one way and another and throwing his head about. "Speak to the damned horse," growled Michael in his throat, only to hear the same voice say, to the horse, "Be still." Which it was, immediately.

With the book in hand, Michael started down the slope, all too aware of the diminishing light of the sparkling stone, the looming darkness crossing the bridge, the glowing red eyes an impossible height above that bridge, a monster ogre-ish in size, far greater than any man.

"Go," said the voice in his mind. "Hurry!"

He slid down the hill, half falling, getting up and running, only to trip and fall several feet, knocking the breath from his lungs. Something went past him in the night with a great roar and the smell of hot metal, flinging itself against the enormous bulk of the monster in a tumult of shouting, crashing, and drums. Deafened by this assault, from which even the monster recoiled, Michael gave up trying to remain upright and simply slid to the bottom of the slope, fell at the old man's feet, rolling onto his back to offer the book.

Eyes peered down at him from beneath a twisted line of light. Old hands gripped the book. The ancient straightened, and stood up, and up, and up until his height was as a great tree and his voice an avalanche that spoke. "I have the Book! I am Bertral, servant of the Guardians. By Tamlar, Ialond, and Aarond, by Rankivian, Shadua, and Yun, I command you, go hence."

Where the monster had been was only a core of retreating and shapeless darkness and a small form standing utterly still. As the stone sparkled away into nothingness, a voice cried:

This is Bertral of the Book, in whose charge are all histories, accountings, and settings down of happenings that these shall be rightly told, weighed neither to one side nor the other. His is the accomplishment of justice when he shall stand before the assembly of the mighty to answer for the honor of his people.

Michael blinked. The old man was merely an old man, though the light upon his forehead shone as brightly as before. The oldster reached down and offered a hand, which Michael took and pulled himself onto his feet. From part way across the bridge, Dismé turned and came toward them, though how she had reached that place, Michael had no idea.

"Michael Pigeon," Michael introduced himself. "That's my friend Dismé."

"Arnole Gazane," said the old man. "Any friend of Dismé's is a friend of mine."

"Arnole!" cried her glad voice from behind him. "Oh, Arnole. It is you." She came toward them, eyes beaming beneath her scarf, her face shining with joy.

Arnole had left his wagon some distance up the eastern road where it had lost a wheel on a protruding stone, so he said when they had finished hugging and exclaiming and brewing tea. "I couldn't raise it, couldn't unload the wagon. No help for it. I had to go look for help."

"We'll go back with you," said Michael. "What's in the wagon?"

"Three more of those stones," said Arnole. "I remembered reading about the Lessy Yard, so I went there. Don't know why I hadn't gone before. Most of the stones were long gone. Three were gone more recently. I asked questions. Farmer said some strangely clad folk took the last three away in a wagon within the last year, and they said they were going to the marble quarry. Well, there was only one marble quarry I know of, one in the high mountains almost due west of Apocanew. So I got me a good wagon and a team, with a couple of strong fellows to help, and we came there to the quarry. There they were! Two standing amid some cut marble, right out in plain view, the third one between them, wrapped in sacking. Took some doing with felled trees and ropes and tackle, but we got them in the wagon. At that point, my helpers got on their horses and went back home, and I came this way because it's downhill and I'm going to see a lady who lives along that road. I have this niggling hunch about her."

"The Seeress?" asked Michael.

"You know Allipto?"

"The doctor does. He's headed there, too," said Dismé.

He grasped her by the shoulders and shook her gently. "So you left that house at last, girl. Oh, by all the powers and spirits, by the separators and celebrators, you left that house."

"Rashel didn't want to let her go," commented Michael.

"Oh, I know that. I don't know why, exactly, though I've a feeling . . . I've always thought Dismé was more than she seemed . . ." He reached for her and patted her shoulder.

Michael laughed, without real humor. "You were right about that. She's already more than she seems. She's Dezmai of the Drums. The stone under the Fortress was meant for her. Dismé, I mean."

Arnole's mouth was open, and it was a long moment before he shut it. "Dezmai?"

She took off the scarf and let him see her forehead.

Arnole shook his head. "It was you who hit that ogre where he stood?"

Dismé murmured, "It was Dezmai, not me. Not exactly. She uses my body as I might use a knife, to fight with. She uses me to speak through. She uses my mind to receive messages from all of them, or whatever ones of them are talking. Whichever ones those are, they say the monster is only a small manifestation. An envoy of the real evil, so to speak."

Arnole nodded. "Things are coming to a head."

"How do you know?" asked Michael.

"Twenty-one Guardians. Different classes of them. Tamlar was first, I guess we know that. I found *her*, that was no problem. I didn't have the book, so she read me the roll. One to call, two to answer, three to protect, four to rock the cradle, five to spur intelligence. I'm one of the five. Camwar's one of the five. He was called ages ago. The six aren't needed yet, not for what we're supposed to do, whatever that is, but one name among them is that of Befun the Lonely, and I know him! Protector of animals. I went to see him, and sure enough, he had the sign! He says those of us who are involved need to get to the new place, west of here."

Dismé cried, "Why are we supposed to go there?"

"Tamlar says if we don't get there first, the monster wins the first round. It's a kind of race, or contest, or battle.

Befum says the monster—the thing behind the monster—is the reason. It's a synthesized monster, partly made of a creature that came with the Happening, and partly out of old gods buried here on earth, and it's the worst parts of all of them. It lies under Bastion, the place it both nourishes and feeds upon." He sighed deeply. "No point talking about it now. There's too many things still unknown."

He stared at the sky. "Best we get a move on, young ones. Wherever we want to get, we'd best get there before tomorrow night. That thing won't give up. He'll be on our trail again, bigger next time."

"I don't know if we can raise a heavy wagon," said Michael, tiredly.

"Don't worry about it," said Dezmai in a muted roar. "Bertral and I will see to it."

Michael fetched his horse and the three of them plodded up the northern road where, if all went well, they would be able to mend Arnole's wagon.

✦ 40

at ogre's gap

Summerspan five: Sixday. Sweltering, swearing, only half ready for movement, much less battle, the vanguard of the army of the Spared approached the guard station at the border of Bastion by dawn of sixday, as demanded. The outriders came back to report an empty post and evidence of some butchery in the road. The general spurred his horse; the bishop followed.

"Demons," said the general, staring at the mess of blood and bone squashed on the road. "You see what they get up to?"

"I see blood and a good many chewed bones, but I don't see the promised warriors," said the colonel bishop.

"Do you doubt the word of the angel?" huffed the general.

The bishop shook his head. "Not at all. Since all the men are here, perhaps I can do the blessing now." He was impatient to return to Bastion, to light a fire under his coup d'etat.

"You'll bless them when the Quellers are here," said the general in a voice that permitted no argument. "We'll bivouac here and the men can rest while we await the supply wagons."

"As I was about to suggest," grated Colonel Commander Achilles Rascan Turnaway. "The men can use some sleep."

The bishop dismounted with an audible moan. The gen-

eral bellowed at his aides, demanding breakfast, bed, water
to wash himself. The ranks came plodding over the pass and
down toward a wide meadow, an area called Ogre's Gap on
maps, to memorialize a battle with monsters some centuries
before. This fact occurred to the general as he took a paper
from his pocket.

"Here," he said when his aide approached with a basin of
water. "Give this to the runners. Bring these men here."

"What's that?" asked Rascan.

"The ones we named to give strength to the Quellers. I
named a man of yours, fellow named Fremis. I recalled your
telling me he was the best fighter you had."

"You named Fremis? He's head of the Honor Legion,
General. He needs to be with his men, not undergoing some
formality."

"If we're going to strengthen the warriors who'll assist us,
we have to do it with our best people. Dr. Ladislav knows
that. He named that favorite of yours, Bishop. Trublood."

"Trublood? I hope this strengthening business won't damage him, General. I want him for one of my daughters."

The three separated in mutual annoyance, the bishop and
commander going in one direction, the general in another.
"Last person in the world who should be distracted right
now is Fremis," mumbled Rascan. "What does Gowl think
he's doing?"

"I think he's depending more upon the *Quellers* he's been
promised than the army he has here," said the bishop.

The two diverged toward their separate campsites, the
commander toward rest, as any soldier did whenever he
could, and the bishop to fret about getting back to Hold and
usurping power. Around them, the men slumped, too weary
to grumble, which would have been their usual response to
a camp without food. Soon there was only the snargle and
whump of snores, the murmur of voices as officers went
about identifying the nominees. Within the hour, the
"strengtheners," around a hundred of them, were assembled
outside the general's tent, where most of them went to sleep
on the grass.

✦ 41

a seeress sees

At Omega site, very early in the morning, Nell was hunched over her breakfast, marshalling further arguments for leaving the redoubt, when the alarm sounded in the cavern above.

"That's for you," said Jackson.

"I hear it," she said irritatedly. She was sick of the redoubt, sick of playing games, sick of Janet's obstructionism for obstructionism's sake. Neither she nor Jackson seemed to realize the purpose of their lives had changed. Nell had just decided that today would be her last day in Omega, regardless of what the others said, when the alarm rang, postponing her announcement of that fact. Of course! Day after day of useless nothing, and then someone had to come looking for prognostications just at a crucial moment! As she climbed the stairs, she heard Jackson's voice, counting coffins again.

"Counting them won't change anything," she snapped at him over her shoulder. "Twelve wake-able, counting us. Eighty-two maybe alive but not wake-able. A hundred six dead."

Jackson ignored her, saying to Janet, "Raymond and Nell are the youngest. What? Thirty-six elapsed years?"

Raymond said, "Thirty-six is right. And I was thirty-two when we started."

Janet said, "Nell was thirty. She's sixty-two. The rest of us are closer to seventy . . ."

From above them, at the mirror in the anteroom to the cave, Nell could still hear them discussing her age as she confronted her own image. She always expected to see a young woman in her mirror, and seeing her real self next to that mental image always shocked her. She laughed, abruptly. What difference did it make? Youth, attractiveness, being a good mother, a professional success, all those important things now meaningless. Family gone, except for remote descendants who knew nothing of Nell Latimer. Her only associates those incessant talkers down below, intent on arguing their last years away. Alan was among the wakeable. If she could do nothing else, she'd wake him! At the very least, he could break the tie vote!

The alarm sounded again as she straightened the golden wimple and moved through the lock to seat herself at the table. The supplicant stooped as he came through the outer doorway.

"Admit him," she said to the computer as she reached for the cards, the bones. Few of them would trust a simple statement of fact unless it was dressed up in some kind of cryptic make-believe. A scatter of bones. Cards laid in an arcane pattern.

"Allipto Gomator," said the man, more matter of fact than awed, which was unusual.

"I am Allipto Gomator," she said in the throaty voice she had once strained to produce. Now her facade of wisdom was buttressed by wrinkles and the rasp of years was in her throat.

The supplicant surprised her by chuckling. "Of course you are, Madam. We have spoken before. I know your many times great-granddaughter, Dismé Latimer. Don't you know me?"

She had not thought she knew him until he stepped farther into the cavern. He looked ten years or more younger than when she had seen him last, which had been quite recently. He had given her information then, and he had gone seeking more! "Arnole . . . Gazane," she said, wonderingly. "You were going in search of certain . . . miraculous devices!"

His face cracked wide in a gleeful smile. "Yes, Seeress. And I have so far found four of them." He stooped in a half bow. "One of which was evidently meant for me."

When he bent forward, she saw the sign on his forehead and put her hand to her throat. "You? Your face . . ."

"Awe-inspiring, isn't it?" he chuckled. "Don't know what use it is, though."

"When . . . how . . . ?"

"A story too long in the telling for now, Seeress."

"Was the device meant for you . . . only, or was it meant for anyone who found it?" she asked, rising from her chair to come closer to the glass bubble that separated them.

"Oh, meant for me particularly, I think. I fetched three of the stones from a quarry up the mountain, and it's certain two of them weren't meant for me, for I handled them repeatedly while getting them loaded. The other one is wrapped in sacking, for some reason, and I haven't unwrapped it. They are strange things, marvelous things. Come out and see for yourself!"

"I? I don't . . ." She fumbled for words.

"Your many times great-granddaughter is outside. Don't you want to come out and meet her? It's less than ten steps to the wagon from your outer door."

The protocols, under which Nell had lived for centuries, were very clear on the point. The only correct thing to do at this juncture was to have Arnole wait while she went downstairs and got the rest of the awake team to agree she could put on an emergence suit and go outside. That, however, would merely extend the argument she had been having with them for days. Janet and Jackson would say no, she and Raymond would say yes.

She was tired of it. The rules were outdated. She rose from the table in Allipto Gomator's green robes and golden wimple, opened the lock with a manual override, and went out of the cavern into the clean, pine-smelling air, feeling the wind on her face for the first time in almost forty waking years. For a moment her eyes closed and she simply leaned on the wind, letting it fill her with delight.

"Ma'am," said Arnole, taking her by the arm.

He led her to the wagon where two stones stood next to the sacking-wrapped bundle. She thought they were slabs of obsidian, perhaps, big pieces, standing taller than she, curved, glassy, with a good many lights in them. Wide and thick at the bottom, the slabs tapered to a knife's blade thinness at the curled upper edge. Rainbow obsidian it had been called. Indians had used it in jewelry.

A young couple stood beside the wagon. She didn't know the man, but the young woman . . . yes, she had a recent ping-picture of this young woman, though the picture did not show the swooping line of light upon her brow.

"Dismé?" she asked. "I'm Nell Latimer."

The girl's eyes opened wide. She drew a quick breath and fumbled in the pocket of her cloak, drawing out a bundle that she unwrapped to disclose a book.

"This is yours," she said, awed. "You wrote this."

Nell stared at the book, then at the girl. "My journal. Now how on earth did you get that?"

"My father said that a wiseman named Alan or Ailan—not one of the Spared, someone else—gave it to one of my father's ancestors when we first came to Bastion. My father's people were Comador, and we are not far from Comador here. Perhaps it was given here, at this place. You are my ancestress."

"You've read it?"

"Oh, yes. It took me such a long time. Things are spelled very differently now."

"Did you understand it?" Nell asked, intrigued by the contrast between the sweet naivete of the girl's voice and the ageless gravity of her eyes.

Dismé's voice roughened. "I understand what it is like to live with someone who conspires at one's destruction, as your husband did you. My step-sister has conspired at mine."

"Come," Arnole interrupted impatiently. "You can talk family later, but for now, Allipto . . . Nell . . . step up."

Michael helped her into the wagon, and she took one step

to the nearest of the stones, running her hands over it curiously. It was glassily smooth, with a kind of humming vibration . . .

The world stopped. She was somewhere else, learning things she had no names for. She was being instructed. Nell was in abeyance. The mind she shared was full of those treasures she had always sought, the workings of the universe, the reasons and intentions of the galaxies. Time passed forever.

And then, the lights went out, she blinked, and came back to herself standing in the bed of a wagon beside a dusty track, high on a mountain, while before her the chunk of whatever-it-was glittered its way into darkness like a bouquet of sparklers on a long-ago Fourth of July.

A similar stone confronted her across the dwindling fountain of sparks, its glossy surface reflecting her face. Though some of the lines had disappeared from her face, she was still recognizable, even with the twisted line of light she wore upon her forehead, a duplicate of the ones worn by Arnole and Dismé.

"Elnith? Elnith?" Arnole was crowing, as he did a stiff-legged war dance around the wagon. "I knew it had to be you. Who else could have slept here all those years . . ."

Nell sought for the word, the denial, perhaps? The comment? The affirmation? Nothing came. She knew . . . everything. She had no words for what she knew. The pause became an anticipatory silence. There were no words she could use for the reality and truth and understanding she had been given.

"Elnith is of the Silences," Arnole murmured to no one in particular, as he and Michael helped her down from the wagon. He took her arm to escort her back toward the cavern, saying, "We need you, and we will wait for you out here. However long it takes."

Nell paused, turned, beckoned to Dismé. When the younger woman approached, Nell took her by the hand. At the touch, Dismé felt a wind blow through her mind, a quick riffle of memory, fleeting images, a catalog of happenings.

Then Elnith's hand drew her down into the cavern where the two of them confronted three people sitting at a table, so deep in argument they didn't even look up at their approach.

Elnith struck the table they sat around, startling them into annoyance that turned at once to amazement. Jackson lurched to his feet, knocking over his chair. Janet turned very white, while Raymond sat unmoving, his mouth open. Standing silent before them, Nell placed her hand on Dismé's lips, which opened to say commandingly, "All those in the coffins are to be taken outside, where Rankivian, Shadua, and Yun may reach them."

"What the hell, Nell?" demanded Raymond.

"Hush," Dezmai said in her own voice, and he was still.

"Good Lord," murmured Janet. "Look at their faces!"

Elnith stilled Janet with a glance, then turned to go up the sloping floor toward the coffins. In that moment, Dezmai departed, leaving Dismé behind in her own self to face the gaping incomprehension of the trio before her.

"I know who Nell Latimer is," Dismé said. "I don't know any of you, but I'll tell you what has happened. My friend, Arnole Gazane, brought three devices in his wagon. The devices identify members of the Council of Guardians. Nell was identified by one of the devices and she is now . . . a host for Elnith of the Silences, as I am a host for Dezmai of the Drums. Arnole has been identified as Bertral of the Book . . ."

"What is this nonsense?" snarled Janet. "This playacting, this . . ." She sputtered into silence, turning to the other two for support, but their eyes were fixed on Dismé.

"Go up and talk to Arnole," she said. "He knows more than I do, and it won't do any good to expect Nell to talk while Elnith has hold of her. Our . . . visitors know more than we do. When they speak, they speak from knowledge. When you've spoken with Arnole, I think you'll decide to do what Elnith asks."

"Who are you?" Raymond demanded.

"My name is Dismé Latimer. Nell Latimer is an ancestress of mine. Dezmai is my inhabitant."

"I don't believe this," muttered Janet.

"Believe or don't believe," said Dezmai, in sudden thunder. "We do not care for your disbelief." She went to join Elnith.

Janet stared after her from an ashen, angry face. "This is gibberish," she said. "This is . . . ridiculous."

"Look at her," whispered Raymond, pointing in Nell's direction. "Really look at her. This is frightening, awe-inspiring, marvelous, maybe, but not ridiculous." He got up and started for the stairs, Jackson following, though reluctantly. When they had disappeared above, Janet stood looking alternately upward and at Elnith, indecisive as ever. Finally, with a grimace of frustration, she went after the two men.

Elnith was left below amid the ranked coffins of Nell's people. Inside Elnith was Nell, enclosed in a space of hazy distances. Without warning, a third entity entered the space and spoke. When she left, Elnith went with her, and Nell bent forward, gasping, as though she had bled out, her life power exhausted. Dismé held onto her sympathetically, knowing how it felt at first when the visitors departed.

"Is she gone?" Dismé asked.

Nell nodded. "While she was in there, I wanted to know who Rankivian and Shadua and Yun are, and SHE told me we used black arts to let ourselves sleep all these years. SHE says it was done for a good reason, but the technique is black because of the danger to the souls of the sleepers."

"The ones who won't wake up?"

"Even some of those who do wake up, maybe. They get lost. They turn inward. Rankivian is the one who can reclaim them. He's coming here to reclaim them. SHE says so."

"Elnith says?" Dismé asked, like a cricket chirping from beneath a hearth stone, shrill and incredulous. "She speaks?"

"No. Not Elnith. SHE! The one who came with the Happening. SHE who has come down from the dark north-lands . . ."

She looked about to collapse. Dismé held her arm.

"I have to sit down," Nell gasped. She did so, putting her

head down on her knees, hands linked behind her neck, crouched into the smallest possible volume, as though wishing to retreat into nothingness.

"It gets easier," said Dismé, putting her arms around Nell to warm her. "After a while, you can let them come in and go out without feeling like that."

Nell whispered "How long have you . . ."

"Several days now, four or five. The first few times are the worst, really."

"SHE said you can speak to people, at a distance. You need to tell them the monster takes its strength from pain. Tell them to kill those in pain, not to let them go on hurting . . ."

Dismé regarded her thoughtfully. "You're sure? I'll have to go up, outside . . ."

"First we have to wake the sleepers. You can help me."

Dismé watched Nell do the first two, then went down the aisles of coffins, doing the same, setting each of them on emergency waking cycle, both the living and the dead. Finished, they went up and out, and Dismé went to find a quiet, high place for her dobsi to speak from.

Raymond was talking with Arnole and Michael, all three of whom turned as Nell approached, saying, "I'll need your help, yours and anyone else we can get. The coffins will open soon, and we have to bring the people out into the sunlight. It must be done before the horror, the beast arrives."

"The thing is coming here?" cried Michael. "How did you know about it?"

"SHE knows it," Nell replied. "Yes, it is coming here. We need to be gone before then."

"Is there a lift that goes down into the cavern?" asked Arnole, suddenly practical.

Raymond replied. "It will hold six or eight people at a time, once they're out of the coffins."

"You want the dead out here?" Jackson asked.

"The Council wants the dead out here," said Nell. "The Council of Guardians. This place is awash in trapped souls."

"Would someone please tell us what's going on?" demanded Raymond, querulously. "How did this Council of Guardians get into the act?"

"Later," said Nell, heading back toward the cavern, Arnole following her.

Raymond found Dismé wandering thoughtfully, so he asked her the same question, at which she took a deep breath and told him what she knew of the Council of Guardians and the book of Bertral, summoning Michael to fetch the book from the saddle bag. Soon the three sleepers were looking through it—Raymond with belief, Jackson wavering, and Janet remaining convinced the Council was pure superstition. The three argued among themselves, finally taking their argument back into the redoubt, from which the elevator rose and fell throughout the afternoon. By late afternoon, all the sleepers had been carried into the light where lines of still bodies lay upon the stone.

The doctor had been delayed by copses and collapses on a road he accused of being uncooperative. The obstacles had eaten time, preventing the doctor and the little people from arriving until evening. It was still light, though barely, when the doctor halted the team and stared down into the rocky pit where the seeress had her lair. Laid out on an area of flat, gray stone were a great many bodies, with people moving among them. From far down the road, lanterns were approaching.

"That's the seeress," said the doctor, amazed. "She's outside!"

"Seeress?" said Bobly, doubtfully. "Doctor, that's Elnith's costume from the book."

"I'll look her up," said Bobly from the back of the wagon.

"The book's in the saddlebag," said the doctor, inattentively.

"Then Michael has it," said Bobly, in disappointment. "I wanted to know what she's Guardian of."

"I can quote it from memory," said the doctor.

This is Elnith of the Silences, in whose charge are the secrets of the heart, the longings of the soul, the quiet places of the world, the silence of great canyons, the soundless depths of the sea, the still and burning deserts, the hush of forests . . .

Hers the disciplines of the anchorite, the keeper of hidden things; hers the joyous fulfillment when high on daylit peaks she shall answer for the discretion of her people. No hand of man may touch her scatheless, beware her simplicity.

"Who are the others?" Bobly asked. "And who's that old man on the high rock, looking at the sky?"

"I don't think I've seen the oldster before. That's my horse, so Michael and Dismé must be here, but whose is that other wagon?"

By the time the tired team had plodded down the several switchbacks to arrive at the cavern, the people there had gathered to face them, as if they feared what or who might be arriving. Seeing this, the doctor stopped at a good distance, jumped down and helped Bobly alight.

"It's Doctor Ladislav," called Dismé.

Above them, the figure on the high rock was slowly descending. From among the lines of bodies, the seeress came. She walked directly to the newcomers and took the doctor by the hand.

"Allipto Gomator?" he asked, wonderingly, for she was unlike the woman he had last seen here.

"I am Nell Latimer," she said. "Allipto Gomator was a part I played as a way of getting information from the outside world. I am also, so it seems, Elnith of the Silences."

Dismé came forward to greet them. "My old friend Arnole is coming, doctor. He's Bertral of the Book. He really is! The Book belongs to him and I don't think he'll give it back."

Nell was moving inexorably toward the wagon, tugging the doctor along beside her. "Come. I was told to show you this." When they arrived, she pointed imperiously at the stones.

"Aha," cried the doctor. "Another one! Or is it two? Who found them? Where were they?"

"Get up in the wagon," she said. "Get a good look at it."

The doctor climbed into the wagon and confronted the stone, examining it with curious eyes. There were lights within it, as there had been with the one he had seen before. He wondered if this one also hummed, and leaned his ear against it, listening. Those watching saw his body grow rigid, his face empty, his hands fall limply to his sides as he leaned against the stone, his face pressed tightly to it as it exploded into light.

"Aah," murmured Dismé.

"It could only be Galenor the Healer," said Arnole at her side. "These things happen at appropriate times, in appropriate places. Who else could it be, with all those bodies laid out?"

"Most of those are beyond Galenor's help," Dezmai said. "They can only be helped by Rankivian, Shadua, or Yun."

"If you're expecting other people, they may be coming up the road," said Bobly, from beside her knee. "We saw lanterns moving this way from up above."

Even when the stone had sparkled away to nothing, the doctor did not move from the place he had slumped. His contact with the stone had created no frantic energy as in Dismé's case. Instead it had plunged the doctor into profound concentration which allowed him no motion or speech, though he showed no sign of distress. After a time, Michael laid him flat in the wagon bed and covered him with a blanket. Then at Bobly's suggestion, he drove the wagon down the road and into a grassy cleft where the horses could be hobbled and left to graze. The doctor's wagon was brought to the same area, where Bobly, Bab, and Dismé laid a fire and began preparing a meal.

They were busy chopping onions when the people from down the road arrived, three of them, far taller than most people, very slender, with long, bony faces, each one clad in a tight bodysuit covered by a loose, metallic, sleeveless ankle-length garment that fell straight from the shoulders, one in white, one in gray, one in black. They stopped at the wagons first, their extreme height allowing them to lean half over the wagon bed to examine the doctor.

"Who is this, Dezmai?" asked the one in gray, glancing at Dismé. "He bears our sign."

"He is Doctor Jens Ladislav," said Dismé. "I think he's unconscious. Perhaps he is Galenor."

"Yes, this is Galenor the Healer, in whose charge is the battle against the ignorance and ills of mankind. His is the accomplishment of intelligence when he shall stand before the living and the dead to answer for the wisdom of his people."

The gray-clad one stood tall. "Forgive me. I am Rankivian who was Jon Todman of Secours. This is Shadua, once Ellin Loubait from Murgia, and Yun, who was Karm Lostig, from the Sierra Isles."

"Elnith has been expecting you," Dismé said. "She has a great many of her people around on the other side of the rock."

"Dead or alive?" asked Shadua, bending from her great height to look intently into Dismé's eyes.

"Dead ones. Live ones. Some who could be either."

The three went around the rock and across the stone to the place Nell stood, among the bodies. They laid their hands on her shoulders. She stiffened, seeming in the instant to grow larger and taller, and for a moment all four stood very still, as people do who are consulting one another on matters of critical importance. They moved down the line of bodies, Rankivian first, the others following.

At this body or that one, Rankivian stopped and touched the face or head, and at his touch a green flame sprang up and ran flickering across the supine forms.

The others had gathered at the edge of the great rock to watch what went on. "Ninety-one," murmured Arnole, who had been counting the ones Rankivian touched. He turned at a sound behind him to find that the doctor had joined them.

Jens stared at the figures moving among the sleeping and the dead, murmuring:

" 'Rankivian the Gray, of the Spirits, in whose charge are the souls of those imprisoned or held by black arts, and the souls of those who cling or delay, for his is the pattern of creation into which all patterns must go . . .' "

When Rankivian had finished and moved to one side, the white-clad Guardian moved among the bodies, touching some of those Rankivian had touched as well as some of those he had ignored. From those touched, a small smoke arose, white as snow, and the bodies fell at once into dust. Body after body went into smoke.

"One hundred twenty," said Arnole.

Again the doctor spoke:

" 'Shadua of the Shroud, in whose keeping is the realm of death to which she may go and from which she may come as she pleases, for its keys are in her hands.' "

When Rankivian and Shadua had finished, Yun went among the bodies that were left, his black garments disclosing and revealing as he knelt to touch every person who was left upon the stone.

" 'Yun of the Shadow, by whose hand all those locked from life may be restored or safely kept until the keys may be found.' "

Where Yun walked, people began to stir, to sit up and move, to stare around themselves, as though in a dream.

"Seventy-six," said the doctor. "Seventy-six of them were alive."

"What was all that?" exclaimed Michael.

The doctor replied in a voice almost his own, "That monster, the one that followed us, is part of something larger, some kind of devil that's responsible for the Terrors. The Terrors have weakened their life force, sucked them into a halfway state between life and death. Rankivian released them from that stasis: some went one way, some the other. Shadua touched only the dead ones, unknitting them, raveling them, letting their patterns depart.

"When Shadua had finished, the remaining ones were alive, though some were lost in dream and refused to come out of it. Yun woke all of them. From the apparent youth of some of them, they may have waked seldom or never in the cavern."

Michael said, "There are more alive than Elnith thought!"

The doctor nodded. "Some of them carry wounds of the spirit, however, and I should see to those."

The doctor did not move, however, and Dismé turned to find him staring at her, into her face, at the sign on her brow. He touched his own forehead, then smiled his familiar smile, took her hand and touched her sign with his lips before moving off. She stared after him, puzzled. He was talking quietly with Nell, who shortly moved away from him to climb the high ridge where Arnole had spent part of the day.

People began to gather at the campfire, for the evening was growing chill. Around them was much coming and going, as wakened sleepers went below to find clothing and blankets, as those already dressed came back up into the world, as food stores were sent up from below for the hungry.

"Has anyone told Elnith about the thing that was following us?" Bobly asked no one in particular. "Seems like she should know, and those new three who just came."

"Elnith knows," said Dismé. "The others may not."

The three were approaching them now, with Raymond trailing behind. Bab and Arnole rolled several lengths of log near the fire, for sitting on.

Bobly demanded, "Someone tell them about the thing."

Arnole stirred the fire with a stick as he told the story of the three stones, his broken wagon, and his own awakening at the crossroads, concluding, ". . . Michael gave me Bertral's Book, and Dezmai chased off the monster. Not forever, though, according to her."

The doctor had returned to sit beside Dismé, taking her hand very gently in his own.

Shadua asked, "Does anyone know what all this is about?"

Rankivian said, "I feel that some great task awaits, but I know . . . nothing."

"Nor I," said Dismé. "Yun?"

"The same," said he. "Something momentous needing doing, but no idea what. Perhaps the doctor has a better idea of it."

The doctor nodded, saying very softly, so that they had to lean forward to hear him, "It has something to do with people who should be dead but are not. I thought at first it was just those of the cavern, the sleepers, because the freezing kept them alive, or parts of them alive year after year, century after century. Rankivian released them, however, and Shadua unknit them, but I still feel the pressure of regret . . ."

"The bottle walls," cried Dismé.

The doctor's face lighted with sudden comprehension, and he cast a quick glance over his shoulder and put his finger to his lips. "Quietly, Dismé. We may be watched. Or, we may be searched for in order to be watched. Let's speak softly."

"What are bottle walls?" asked Shadua.

The doctor stared at the fire for a long moment, as though he were having some internal discussion of the matter. Then he raised his head and said clearly, "According to the Dicta of Bastion, any cell from a person is equivalent to the person. This doctrine originated some decades before the Happening and was at first applied only to fertilized egg cells. Later, still before the Happening, it became possible to use complete cells to make clones. There were great religious and political arguments about it, all of which came to an end with the Happening.

"However, during and after the Happening, those who had held the belief concerning egg cells decided that the doctrine logically had to include any living cell at all. If a single cell of a person was kept alive, that person was said to be alive. One would have thought that the survivors had more urgent things to think about, particularly inasmuch as the technology necessary for cloning was no longer available. The Spared, however, made the doctrine part of their Dicta.

"At first they froze bits of the dead or dying in glaciers, in ice walls. Then, taking advantage of their beliefs, the demons showed them how to build bottle walls with nutrient pumps and traded them the technology in return for a non-aggression treaty. For centuries, every person in Bastion has been bottled either after he dies or immediately before he is disposed of, unless, that is, he disappears, leaving no living cells behind.

"This allows the Regime to bottle anyone they please and dispose of the actual person. The Dicta say that the person is present in the bottle, and when the world ends, the Rebel Angels will re-embody the person from the cell."

"But the ouphs come," cried Dezmai. "Weeping for their lives that are gone and their rest that has been taken from them!" Her voice was like wind, surging through their senses in a great gust, then gone.

The doctor said, "Dismé! Quietly."

"It wasn't me," she whispered. "I can't control *her.*"

After a moment's silence, Rankivian asked, "What are ouphs?"

After waiting, to be sure Dezmai wasn't coming back, Dismé said, "The unquiet spirits of those in the wall. They come singly or in a mass, like fog or a bank of mist. They slide along the walls where their patterns are kept. I have heard them grieving endlessly for life that is not lived, for a return that is withheld. They can neither live nor rest."

Rankivian nodded. "Yes, they would grieve. Their patterns are being imprisoned rather than released into the great pattern. All life is in the great pattern. Each microbe has its tiny spiral, each sparrow its arc of flight, no matter whether the life is self-aware or not. The pattern is generated by the universe along the time front, emerging ever richer and more ramified. For the aware, to feel oneself part of the pattern is heaven. For the unaware, it is the totality of being. For the unaware, to be withheld from the great pattern is sadness; for the aware, it is hell."

"The ouphs play at being people," said Dismé, softly, looking over her shoulder, as the doctor had.

Shadua whispered, "Can that happen?"

Arnole spoke, also quietly. "As a young man, when I was a menial who cleaned the offices in the fortress at Bastion, I lived in cheap lodging behind the Fortress. I often saw ouphs there, frequenting abandoned neighborhoods where they slid along vacant sidewalks arm-in-arm. There was a dilapidated theater where the ouphs queued up or sat within, as though witnessing performances. They held tea parties in abandoned houses where they sat in ramshackle chairs beside broken tables to pour invisible tea . . ."

"Why?" Dismé asked. "What were they doing?"

"I don't know. No one saw them but myself. I learned not to speak of them, for doing so drew too much attention to me. I couldn't risk being thought a madman, for crazies are bottled as soon as symptoms present themselves. Instead of reporting them, I followed them and watched them. Their forays always ended in one of two ways. Suddenly, the event would be over and they would slide off in different directions, like leaves scudding on a pond. Or, sometimes, they would be drawn into a kind of vortex, as though sucked up by some unimaginable force."

"I've seen that," cried Dismé. "They scream as they go, thin voices like the blades of knives, as though something were eating them!"

"Ah," said Shadua. "I see! They repeat little plays they were accustomed to. They go here and there. They play at eating or drinking. Their patterns remember that much, and those with similar patterns gather together because it feels companionable."

"Is the memory in the cells?" demanded the doctor in an astonished tone.

"Is the wine in the empty bottle?" asked Yun. "No, but the bottle still smells of the wine. And if Dezmai and Bertral both saw them, then perhaps all of us who were destined to be Guardians could have seen them, if we had looked . . ."

He fell silent, for Nell had run into their midst, her eyes wild. "Dismé," she cried. "Come with me, now. You were right, doctor. Something dreadful, dreadful . . ." And seizing Dismé by the hand, she drew her away toward the height.

"What happened?" whispered Yun.

The doctor answered, also in a whisper. "I told Nell about the mutilated people we've been finding in Hold. I told her what I had inferred from the evidence, that pain is what empowers whoever is behind all this butchery. With that to look for, Elnith must have heard something, or sensed something, however she does it. It's a power only she has. Now Nell's going back up on the hill because she can . . . receive the information better from up there . . ."

"Why did she take Dismé?" demanded Michael, who had been listening to all their discussion from among the shadows.

"Dismé has a dobsi," said Arnole. "It is likely Elnith needs her to send a message."

Inside the shieldwall of Hold, near the road that runs northeast to Praise, a room was set aside for demon business, a place where the dead and nearly dead were put to await their bottling. There, on sixday morning, the triage demon came to a particular body which she listed among the recently dead, those who could still have flesh taken for bottling. As she wrote, however, something about the choice troubled her, and she paused, staring at the lax form for some time.

"This one isn't dead," she said.

"It isn't breathing," muttered one of her colleagues.

"Well, it really is breathing, though you can barely detect it. Plus, there's healing going on. See the cut on the face. See there, at the edges. That's new flesh."

The other made a face. "I wouldn't want to be alive, like that. Chasm knows what was done to it."

"You're right. Chasm might know. I think we'll send the body there."

"You're out of your mind. Chasm will have a fit!"

"No they won't. They particularly want to see victims like this. They collect them. There've been many of these cases lately, and Chasm wants to know why. Maybe this person knows."

"Her tongue is gone, she can't speak. Her hands are gone, she can't write."

"Chasm has machines that can read Dantisfan emissions as though they were print. Call for pick up, pack it up, and get it on the road."

Shrugging, the other complied. When they left the room

to go out into the air, bottles clinking as they headed for the bottle wall and the forest, the person's body was among some other living persons, hidden beneath straw mats in the wagon. As they approached the bottle wall, none of the demons noticed the fog of ouphs that descended upon them, nor did they feel the presence of a subservient entity who was searching the vicinity for what remained of a sacrifice.

✴ 42

the ogre's army

At the pass where the army of Bastion was camped, the supply wagons arrived toward midafternoon. They were met with considerable eagerness by the men, though any eagerness the officers might have felt was diluted by their suspicion that either the general's visitation had been fictional or his interpretation of that visitation had been faulty. The bishop's belligerence was coming off the simmer into a full boil when the general came from his tent and summoned them with a gesture.

"They'll come tonight," he said crisply, when the bishop, the commander, and a group of others had arrived. "I should have remembered: the angel of fire always comes in the dark. We marched all night, so of course we couldn't have gone to battle immediately. We should be ready to march at sundown. The Quellers will arrive then. They fight in the dark."

With the pronouncement, he returned to his tent, leaving the others to look at one another with slightly raised eyebrows but without comment. If any part of their current situation made sense, then what the general had just said also made sense. Several of them huddled together to discuss the matter only to be interrupted by an outrider who pulled his horse to a stop nearby, dismounted and came running toward the commander.

"What?" barked Rascan.

"There's a peak up there to the north, sir. Goes up well above timberline and gives a good view of the country in all directions. There's people leaving Bastion, or at least leaving from the direction of Bastion, though they might have been forest dwellers up in the hills who saw our march and decided to get out of the area."

"How many?" demanded the bishop.

"Hard to say, sir. We only see them when they cross open ground, and there's not a lot of open ground up this way. I shouldn't think enough to worry about. As I say, probably just farmers from up there, decided to get out of the way of any battle that might take place."

"Then why didn't they go into Bastion instead of away from it?" demanded the bishop.

Wisely, the outrider offered no interpretation.

Rascan said, "Keep your eyes open. Let us know if anything changes."

The outrider went back to his horse and left the area at a trot, passing a sizeable number of demons and rebels who had been alerted by Jens Ladislav and had been hidden in the forest before the army arrived. Some were mountain people, unencumbered by baggage and able to move very quickly. The demons among them could hear and speak at a distance, and all of them were assigned to follow the army, to overhear its plans, and to carry that information forward while the rebels spread out to inform any farm or hamlet close enough to be in danger.

Elsewhere, on other roads leading toward other passes, wagons, flocks, and herds were leaving Bastion by hundreds and thousands. Within several days there wouldn't be a farmer or his produce, a stockman or his animals, a craftsman or his tools left in the country. Those leaving, in fact, included about ninety-eight percent of the useful inhabitants and one hundred percent of those who could actually do magic.

On Ogre's Gap, the warriors of Bastion had been fed, which made them feel less weary and ill-treated, and when the sun fell toward evening, they began to assemble their gear and repack it for the march. A number of the general's own guardsmen had been told to move quietly through the camp to form a line around the so-called strengtheners, though it was a line half-hidden in shadow. At Ogre's Gap the dark would come early, for the great peaks that thrust themselves into the western sky intercepted the lowering sun to cast deep shadow across the nearer mountains, plunging the meadow into dusk while the lowlands of Comador and Turnaway still basked in light.

As shadow came, so came an ominous quiet among the men. Even the officers took to looking over their shoulder, as though something dangerous might be descending upon them from the open air, or from among the trees on the darkling slopes of the mountains. With the dark came a cold wind from the forest, one that sent sparks fleeing from the campfires and silenced the men who'd been warming themselves. Officers came from their lantern-lit tents into the night, fastening their armor and testing the edges of their swords with their eyes fixed on the ceaseless movement of the wind-stirred trees. The first sound of something approaching came from among those trees, over the ridge, the loud cracking snap of large branches.

The sound dropped into absolute silence, for every man on the meadow was holding his breath. Next came the rattle smash of broken wood, a whuffling and snorting such as a huge pig might make as it came through the trees, which again cracked and crashed, broken trees falling outward into the Gap as something monstrous emerged from cover, elephantine and black, its arms reaching to the ground, its knees half-bent, crouching forward to sniff the soil, then rising to full height, arms raised, only to fall once more onto its knuckles as its head turned from side to side, nostrils wide, sniffing.

The wind blew from behind it, and the stench of it came in waves that made the waiting soldiers gasp with dizziness, as though being suffocated. The creature bellowed, and though no words could be discerned in that great rush of sound, each person present understood the howl to have meant, "Where are my strengtheners?"

The hundred or so men who had been nominated, including Captain Trublood, turned to flee, but the general had foreseen this possibility when he set his spearmen behind them. They were chivvied forward at spearpoint, pressed back toward the place the monster waited. Nearest the beast was Fremis, the great warrior, who spun toward the monster and, as it grabbed for him, jabbed his spear upward with all his strength into the huge, hairy belly. The howled response to this attack felled the army like wheat before a scythe and those few who looked up saw Fremis dangling by one leg from the creature's fist, saw the giant jaws gape, saw Fremis's head bitten off and heard the crunch of the skull like a piñon shell between huge, black teeth.

The monster threw its head back and held the man above its open mouth, the enormous hand squeezing the body as blood gushed from the severed neck into that cavernous maw. The giant gulped and swallowed. The desiccated body was thrown aside. It was done before the fallen men had even struggled to their feet, and Fremis's fate fell on ten others of the strengtheners too swiftly for any reaction except that of some few men who had chosen to sleep at the very edges of the forest and who now lost themselves in its shadows and crept away.

Energized by these draughts, the monster reared itself almost upright, yammering into a chorus of echoes:

"Go west from here, down the mountain, go west. We go to kill the Council of Guardians!"

The bishop whispered to the general, next to him, "We're fighting against the Guardians? I thought that was another name for the Rebel Angels?"

The monster seemed to have preternaturally acute hearing, for it screamed, "I am Rebel Angel! I am one who saved you! My kind, we saved you, you follow us now!"

And with that, it fell to its knuckles and selected another victim. The next man decapitated, instead of being drained into the monster's mouth was swung at the end of a huge and hairy arm like a whirling censer, filling the air with red rain. So with the next dozen slaughtered, until all who stood in Ogre's Gap were soaked with blood. As the men were reddened they began to grow, taller and wider and more horrid with each moment, teeth lengthening into fangs, armor becoming living bone and shell, skulls becoming scaled casques that gleamed with an ashen pallor. The beast bawled again. All still capable of hearing anything, heard the words, "Behold the Quellers!"

The crimsoned drummers began to beat, the sanguined trumpeters to blast, the general—scarlet from plumed helm to boot-toe—rode a horned and carmine dappled beast that no longer resembled a horse. The commander rode, teeth showing in a ferocious grin. The bishop rode, forgetting all about his coup. The officers rode. The men marched. The ogre bawled again, and this time the message was, "Westward. Move westward!"

The army began to move. From the woods, the rebels watched, aghast. They were not believers in magic. They could not have imagined the enormity that went against all nature, the warlock's horrid horde. Fortunately for them, the army had no eyes for them, nor did the monster who had called the army into being, for that creature was busy with the remaining strengtheners, assuring that no one of them should be left unmutilated though well over half the original number would be left alive.

When the army had gone so far down the mountain that the drums could no longer be heard; when the monster had ravaged the last of the strengtheners and had shambled off in the same direction, only then the demons crept from the forest to move among the bodies. One of them stood silent at the edge of the clearing, sections of his horns becoming transparent as the Dantisfan upon his head transmitted what he saw to others of his kind west and south and east of him.

Far from where he stood, two days journey at least, a dobsi spoke, and to the demon's mind, his Dantisfan interpreted. "Person, maybe human, label Dezmai cries loudly: *They must not be left alive. From their pain the monster takes its life. None living may be left alive! From their pain the monster takes his power!"*

The demon spoke to other demons, and they to a troop of rebels who had just emerged through the wood. Neither demons nor rebels were armed, but there were arms enough upon the field. Swords sharpened for battle served to behead those who had been left alive. Captain Trublood was among them, and his last thought was that he need no longer worry about the bishop's daughter. Axes meant for war were keen enough to chop the trees needed for a great pyre. The smoke of that burning rose throughout the night and into the following day. When it was done, all that was left on the high field was ashes, armor, and charred bone.

As the pyre burned at Ogre's Gap, the rebels sent riders to warn the people that the horror lived on blood and pain, that the only way to conquer it was to deprive it of blood and pain. "Do not fight," the riders cried. "Do not defend. Give up bravery or honor, for they are meaningless. Only run, hide, deprive the horde of the agony that keeps it alive."

Elnith said the Guardians had to go west, at once, and quickly. At the cavern of the seeress, while some people slept and others tried to convince themselves they should stay in Omega Site, those with the sign readied themselves for the long march that Elnith told them they must begin at dawn. Bertral, with his eyes shut, sat on the wagon tongue with his book, calling the role of the Guardians and Elnith moved restlessly about him, searching silently for the beings he named. Intent upon this distant communication, she did not see the shadow that detached itself from the cavern entrance and came to the side of the road.

"Nell," he said.

Elnith stopped. She did not know the man before her, but Nell did, and Nell had come awake at the sound of his voice. Elnith retreated, not far, waiting to see what was happening to her link with this present day.

"Alan?" Nell asked. "Oh, God, Alan."

He stepped forward and hugged her, the two of them clinging together in the darkness.

"They said you didn't talk."

"Elnith doesn't," she replied. "But she's an intermittent inhabitant."

"It's not you, then, who's changed. It's someone else."

"Oh, it's not me, Alan. No. But it isn't anyone . . . foreign, either. I mean, she fits into me like a hand into a glove. It's not uncomfortable. I could resent being a glove, of course, but the things I catch sight of when the hand inside me moves! The things she knows! We used to argue all the time, at the observatory, Neils and me, and now . . . if he were here . . . I could tell him where to find how it works, how it all works."

"She picked someone in her field, then." He smiled tenderly at her, smoothing her hair back from her face, searching the sign on her forehead as though to memorize it.

"Maybe that's it. I know her language, at least a little."

"Her language is silence?"

"It's just . . . words are so imprecise. They have different meanings to different people. She . . . she speaks in certainties. Directly, mind to mind."

"Do all of them do that?"

She shook her head. "No. I don't think so. Dismé doesn't mention it . . . Dismé. Did you know she has my book?"

He smiled. "I passed it along to a Latimer descendent a few centuries back. By that time, the written language was beginning to deviate quite a bit, and I thought if I waited any longer, no one would be able to read it. The last bit, the bit you taped, I transcribed that into the book as well, so it was your complete account of the Happening. There's a copy in your stasis locker, just in case you want to review."

"I don't need to review. I remember it far too well. The Darkness, when even the pings couldn't see. The endless numbers of the dead. The monsters. I thought that was over, and here it is again!"

"When you make this journey, may I go with you? Will Elnith mind if I go with you?"

Nell was silent, as though waiting for a signal or a comment, but none came. "It may not be possible. In any case, you have no reason for going except me."

"Isn't that enough?"

"Not in this battle, Alan. I don't know what's happening, but I know it's more important than we are as people."

He inspected her face, looking at each part of it as though searching for something.

"I've grown old," she said.

"I've been looking at you in your coffin every time I've waked. You don't look any different to me. Does she have a personality, this . . . inhabitant of yours?"

Nell considered this, the emptiness of her face showing her thoughts. "No," she whispered. "She doesn't. She has no . . . agenda at all. No . . . hope, fear, anything. Just this pure intelligence, loaded with curiosity, picking up every detail of everything she comes upon. Almost without self-awareness . . ."

He hugged her again, whispering, "Frightening, I should think. Despite her, I'm here, if Nell needs me."

She held him for a moment almost frantically. Seeing the world through Elnith's eyes was like peering from a dizzying precipice at a foreign landscape where perspective and content coalesced into an alien and unrecognizable whole. She said, "There's something vertiginous about it, though Dismé says it will get easier." Tears flooded her eyes and Elnith came.

"Hush," Elnith said without words. "I will not harm you. You are the hand with which I hold this world. I will care for you well. I will not take you from yourself or from your love forever. Do not be afraid."

Nell came back to herself staring into Alan's face, and he into her eyes, dazzled at what he had momentarily surprised there. When he left her, Arnole spoke from the wagon, startling her.

"Old friend, ah?"

"Very old, Arnole. Not a lover, ever, but closer to me than any lover could have been."

"I envy you that friendship. I worry that we . . . we Guardians may not have friends, though perhaps . . . among ourselves."

She cried, "What do we have, Arnole? What are we for?"

He shook his head, saying, "See if you can call Elnith back. It is urgent that we find all members of the Council, but of the twenty-one, we still have found only nine."

✦ 43

various pursuits

Summerspan five, sevenday: Some people left Omega Site before dawn, others decided not to leave at all.

"I don't believe any of this nonsense," Janet told Dismé, Nell, and Arnole as they put the last few items into the wagons. "Jackson doesn't either. We're going to sit tight along with some of the others."

"Will you accept some advice?" asked Nell, looking across Janet's shoulder at Jackson, who was shifting uncomfortably.

Janet shrugged, her lip curling. "You'll give it, anyway."

Nell spoke directly to Jackson. "There's an army headed this way. If they can't see, hear, or smell you, they may pass you by. If they do see you or hear you or smell you, they'll dig you out, like a rabbit out of a burrow. When we've gone, clean up every scrap of anything left out here that smells of people, spray it with . . . I don't know, something natural and anonymous, hide every indication of people and shut the place up tight."

Janet pursed her lips. "Except for Allipto's booth."

Nell turned on her. "Any opening will get you killed."

Janet jeered, "The booth is tamperproof."

"It was never tested," said Nell, as she turned toward the wagon, speaking over his shoulder. "There are monsters with the army, much like those that came during the

Happening. The booth wasn't built until after they were gone."

Unconvinced and angry, Janet watched them go, two wagons heavily loaded with people from the redoubt, trailed by a long line of walkers. Rankivian, Shadua, and Yun had gone during the night, stalking with great heron strides. Janet had been glad to see them go, for those with signs on their foreheads troubled her. Though she was certain it was a trick, she couldn't figure it out. The best she could do was stay away from them, and she had prevailed upon Jackson to stay with her, to care for the few newly wakened ones who had chosen to stay, most of whom had never wakened in the redoubt and now only whined about it.

"Monsters!" Janet said, with a sneer.

"There were monsters," Jackson reminded her. "You know there were, Janet."

"I know that they all died centuries ago!"

He tried to persuade her. "You believe that, because we've seen nothing of them since the darkness ended. Some of them might still be here, able to harm us."

"If they were here now, the pings would have seen them."

"Not necessarily," he said, looking with some regret at the wagons moving down the hill. "Nell gave us good advice."

"Nell! 'Elnith of the Silences,' for Lord's sake. And she called herself a scientist!"

Jackson's eyebrows went up and he said stiffly, "Nell never called herself anything. She was a scientist. We all were."

"Perhaps, but she always had something peculiar about her."

He gritted his teeth. "Such as?"

"Raymond told us the gametes had all spoiled. It seemed a strange thing to have happened, so I actually opened up the compartment and examined the vials. No question they were spoiled, every vial except Nell Latimer's and the ones in the animal file. There was no residue in those vials. Her embryos hadn't spoiled. They'd been taken."

"After they spoiled, she could have cleaned them out herself, any time in the centuries we've been sleeping."

"Why would she have done that?"

"Sentiment, possibly. Fastidiousness."

"Then why not say so?" She turned away in irritation.

"She probably considered it a private matter."

Janet turned to give him a look of frank derision and went back toward the redoubt, while Jackson cast another uneasy glance at the empty road, wondering if his decision to stay behind with Janet might not have been a very stupid one.

Two days later, the monster army arrived in the vicinity of the redoubt, quite early in the morning. The demons and rebels had forerun the army, cutting directly across country to warn every living person in the way, so the army had found only vacancy. The few crofts visible from the road had been abandoned, their livestock driven away into the woods. From a high pass at dawn after the first night's march, the only living persons visible were the Mohmidi on the plains below, headed away southward at some speed and at a great distance.

The ensorcelment in which the army had left Ogre's Gap had lost much of its force by the end of the second night's march. Though the huge and horrible monster shambled along at the army's rear throughout the night, at sunrise it departed, letting the exhausted men and leaders collapse into sleep. By late afternoon, when the men began to waken, the sorcerous urgency that had moved man and horse away from Ogre's Gap was entirely gone. The army woke to find themselves no longer devilish Quellers but only hungry men who had lain all day in blood-stiffened and reeking garments beneath great clouds of stinging flies.

Their first action was to scramble down the canyon wall to the river, where they bathed and washed their clothing. As soon as the officers' tents were set up, water was warmed and brought to them for the same purposes.

"I'm finding it hard to think strategically," said the commander to the bishop, when he had cleaned away the blood and dressed himself in clean garments. "I feel foggy, as though my head was stuffed with wool."

The bishop held his own head with both hands. "Can you remember what happened?"

"The . . . thing, you mean?" Even to himself the commander's voice sounded hollow, echoing, as though he were in a cave.

The bishop mumbled, "There was a monster? I mean, really a monster?"

"Oh, yes. It strengthened itself very quickly, as I recall. Blood seems to be the key to the whole matter."

The bishop gulped, lowered his head still further, then asked, "Did we stop to eat on the way? Have we eaten at all since then?"

The commander looked momentarily confused. "I don't recall."

They subsided into silence. Eventually, the bishop asked, "Is the monster still with us?"

"At the moment, probably not," said the commander. "It seems to show up a little after dark. It was with us last night, I know that. It took a dozen or so of the men as strengtheners."

Another silence was interrupted by the arrival of a young officer. "The general asks for the bishop," he said. "And for you, Commander." He hesitated for a moment, then turned to the bishop, crying, "Sir . . . don't, don't let him take us any farther. That thing, sir. It's eating . . . it's eating us. There'll be none of us left if we go on with it."

By the time the bishop rose to his feet, Colonel Rascan had already run the young man through with his sword. "Rebellion and disobedience. They must be dealt with relentlessly!" he cried with fiery emphasis, totally unlike his usual grave demeanor.

The bishop surprised himself by being outraged, though he kept his voice level. "Isn't the monster eating enough of us? Do we need to kill each other?"

"A rebel is not one of us!" Rascan turned furious eyes on his companion, the bloody sword still in his hand. "The creature is on our side. Working for us. Nothing must interfere!"

The bishop, eyes on the quivering blade, said nothing more. He followed the commander out of the tent and across the few paces of stony ground to the place the general awaited them.

"Something's wrong," said the general, conversationally. "Something's gone quite wrong. The wounded men up there at the Gap should have lived for a long time yet!"

The bishop murmured, "I don't understand, sir."

The general looked surprised. "I thought you'd know. Well. It's this kind of magic. I've used this kind. You have to do it so the pain goes on. The spell takes power from the pain to make us Quellers, but we aren't Quellers anymore. We've reverted! Something's gone wrong back at the Gap."

The bishop paled. "I thought, that is . . . we believed it was an angel, one of the Rebel Angels who strengthened us. That's what it said! Was that wrong?"

"No, no, I'm sure that's right, I'm only saying the angel used *magic* to do it. That shouldn't surprise us, should it? The whole thing seemed very familiar, and then I realized when I woke today why that was. One has to oppose nature in each step, you see. The killing or maiming of a healthy innocent old enough to be aware, that's necessary; and the drinking of blood or eating of flesh of one's own kind; that's necessary, and the infliction of lasting pain; that's necessary, too. To make it work, you see?"

"To make what work?" the bishop whispered.

"Gone's magic. Hetman Gone. Never mind. You don't know him. He showed me how to do it, that's all." The general stepped away from them and peered down the river valley to the gap that gave a view of the plains. "What are we doing here?"

"We came to conquer the world outside Bastion," said the commander, firmly. "But we have received new orders to kill the Council of Guardians!"

"Before we kill them, we must have battles. What about the people outside Bastion? The farmers? The settlers? What about the canyon roads, where the caravans come through?"

"We saw no farmers or settlers, sir. We're a great distance from the canyon routes. To reach them, we'd have to go down to the plains, then a good way eastward."

"We need someone to fight!"

The commander marshalled his thoughts. "The first town on this road is Trayford. Or, we could pursue the nomads, though I seem to recall seeing them far across the plain from us, and going farther . . ."

"Trayford," mused the general. "I remember Trayford. It's only a village. I want a battle, Commander. A big, big battle. We need a larger target than Trayford . . ."

"Henceforth?" offered the bishop, with a sudden spurt of hope. "We could leave this road when it reaches the plain and go cross country. That's the direction the . . . thing told us to go anyhow." Which would have the added advantage of taking them through largely unpopulated country where some of them could sneak away. Also, the fewer people, the less likely the Spared could be slaughtered during the exhausted sleep they fell into after these forced marches.

"Got to get us Quellers back, right?" said the general. "I'll need a few young women."

"There are no young women with us," said the commander. "Nor have we seen any."

"They're here," said the general, his head bobbing up and down as he agreed with himself. "Got to be here. Somewhere. We'll just look for them, that's all. Or Ogre will. When he gets here."

Squatting solidly at a crossroads, the Inn at Trayford was a sprawling building built upon and added to over the centuries. The several stable and barn wings surrounded enclosed yards for carriages, oxen, horses, and other livestock being driven from one part of the country to the other. The windows were of a style called "salvage," which meant ancient bottles with the bottoms cut off, threaded in nested stacks onto long sticks that were abutted in vertical rows in wooden frames. While the undulant surface gave no view during the day, it allowed a greenish-amber glow to guide travelers at night.

It was this light the travelers spied late in the evening of summerspan five, eightday, after two days travel that had felt like forever. None of the sleepers had been in condition to walk the distance, as the doctor had said to begin with, so the trip had been a succession of halts to dress blisters, to bandage sprains, to let some folk ride awhile, to convince others they could walk, to dole out painkillers from the redoubt, to fill water jars at every stream and take comfort breaks at inconvenient locations. Still, as they approached the town, all who had started on the way were present, though many were at the end of their strength.

"We can't take them the rest of the way," Dismé murmured to the doctor, when they had achieved the stableyard. "I even worry about Nell and Arnole."

"I've talked to Arnole," said Jens. "He says he'll trade the heavy wagon for a lighter one to carry the last stone; he'll take four horses instead of two, so he can trade teams. He and Elnith will ride in the wagon, along with the little folk. You, Michael, and I will get two riding horses each and change them often."

"And how do we pay for all this?"

"Jens Ladislav the doctor has been traveling for some time, and he has built up a credit account in many little towns. The hostler will be glad to get some of his stock out of danger, and our tired beasts can be set free to graze in the canyons."

"And the people we've brought from the redoubt?"

"They'll have to take cover with the people of Trayford. The villagers have had to take refuge before; the nearest canyons have caves big enough for all of them."

"There's nothing we can do to protect this town?"

"What power do you have, Dismé?"

"I don't know."

"Well, neither do I. I don't know what power Elnith has, or Bertral. You and he fought off the monster, back at the bridge, so we Guardians have some potent force, but we don't know how to use it. As I read Bertral's book, the three most powerful in terms of sheer force are Tamlar, Ialond, and Aarond. Tamlar is at the fortress, along with Camwar, but no one knows where Ialond and Aarond are."

"What has Camwar been doing there?"

"Building a barrel, Elnith says."

Dismé spluttered, then began to laugh helplessly. "Doctor Jens. If only you had foreseen all this when our journey began!"

"Like a bit of flotsam foresees a flood? All I had in mind was a neighborly warning! This whole . . . ogre, Goodland, guardian bit is so far from my understanding that I wouldn't have believed it if you'd told me."

"Galenor doesn't explain things?"

"He does not. I feel this cold, precise intelligence standing just behind my right shoulder, evaluating everything I sense. As for offering help, the only thing he's done is lay hands on a few of those ex-sleepers who had given up on living. They were immediately healed, but since I had nothing to do with it, I didn't find the experience particularly edifying."

She nodded wearily. "I'm incapable of being edified until I've had something to eat."

They went in together. Those who had come from the redoubt had already filled the long, rambling room, their talk echoing from the smoke-darkened beams of the ceiling and adding to the chatter of a lesser number of local folk. Dismé looked for a demon, thinking she might transmit or receive some news thereby, and immediately saw one crouched at one side of the fireplace.

She went to sit beside him. "We have just come from the guard post at Bastion's border."

He gave her a haunted look. "Then we came from the same place by different routes, woman."

"We didn't see you on the road."

"No. And likely you didn't see what happened to the army of Bastion two nights ago, at Ogre's Gap."

"Ogre's Gap," said the doctor, coming up beside them. "That's an old name for the meadow just below the guard post. What happened there?"

"The Ogre arrived," said the demon, his shoulders hunched, as he stared into the fire. "If I describe it, I make it sound like something that could exist when, in fact, it is a being out of nightmare. Imagine a thing part bear, part snake, part ape, part prehistoric creature from the old books. It bit the heads off a number of soldiers and squeezed their bodies dry to drink the blood. Then it bit off a few more heads and sprayed the blood over the men, turning them into a horde of devils. Even the horses were changed. When the army marched away, the Ogre maimed the ones who were left behind. We received a Dantisfan message from someone named Dismé, so our people came out of the forest and killed the maimed soldiers. We are not killers. We do not relish it, though we knew it had to be done. I have had the grues since then."

"You did them a service," said Galenor in an icy voice. "Do not grieve over them."

The demon laughed. "I am grieving over me, sir. Over ideals I had that are lost." He shuddered as he went on: "The army and the Ogre move only at night. We demons are posted at relay points along their line of march. Every crofter or farmer capable of hearing has been warned." He fell silent as he picked up his mug with shaking hands.

Galenor said, "You're having trouble believing this."

The demon shivered violently, almost a convulsion. "We don't believe in magic . . ."

"Don't be misled by your eyes," said Galenor. His voice was very deep and resonant. "If an inexplicable good thing happens, you do not call it magic. You call it good luck, or perhaps a miracle, wrought by some power you know nothing of. So, if a bad thing happens, it, too, can be a miracle, also wrought by power."

"Magic!" cried the demon. "Miracle! What difference between the two?"

"There is no difference at all," said Galenor. "Except

that people allow themselves to believe an event if it's called a miracle while disdaining the same event if it's called magic. Or vice versa. Life arises naturally; where life is, death is, joy is, pain is. Where joy and pain are, ecstasy and horror are, all part of the pattern. They *occur* as night and day occur on a whirling planet. They are not individually willed into being and shot at persons like arrows. Mankind accepts good fortune as his due, but when bad occurs, he thinks it was aimed at him, done to him, a hex, a curse, a punishment by his deity for some transgression, as though his god were a petty storekeeper, counting up the day's receipts . . ."

Galenor pressed the man's shoulder, once, twice. The demon relaxed and took a deep breath, color coming into his face. Dismé looked up to catch only a glimpse of the other being behind the doctor's eyes before he turned away and left her.

Dismé did not follow him. She was too weary to encounter Galenor or anyone else. Instead she sat down at a nearby table where an old woman was finishing a cup of tea, her empty plate before her. She took one look at Dismé's ashen face and imperiously summoned the server to order a draught of spirit, which she pressed into Dismé's hands.

"I'm not sure I can keep this down," Dismé murmured.

"You will," said the woman, pressing the cup toward her lips with a wrinkled hand. "This first, then you must eat." And she turned to the server again to order a meal before welcoming the doctor who had returned to sit beside Dismé.

"My name is Skulda," the old woman said, smiling at him.

"Did you arrive today?" Dismé managed to ask.

She nodded, taking a sip of cider. "It seems I got out of Bastion just in time."

"Especially since Bastion does not approve of people getting out," said the doctor.

"I wasn't a long time resident. They won't miss me."

Dismé accepted the broth, bread, cheese, and fruit put before her by the innkeeper's daughter. Though she didn't feel hungry, hunger would return, and the old woman was right, she had to eat.

"Where are you from?" she asked, as she picked up the spoon.

Skulda sat back comfortably. "Oh, I've spent time along the New West Coast, in Mungria and New Salt Lake and Henceforth and Secours. I've lived on the Old West Coast, the Sierra Islands. I spent time in Everday and in Bastion. I've journeyed eastward to New Kansas and New Chicago, and there was even a brief time among those touch-me-nots down in Chasm, lah-me. The subterfuge and playacting it took to become part of *that* close little group!"

The doctor tented his brows, accepting his own bowl of steaming broth with thanks. "You've traveled enough for several."

"Oh, not only traveled." She chuckled. "I've been several. I've been Aretha and Bahibra and Clotho. I've been Hathor and Moira, almost the whole alphabet full from Atropos to Ziaga. And, the children I've had, lah-me! Nineteen at last count. I even stuck around to raise some of them. I may have great-grandchildren by now."

"Don't you know?" Dismé sputtered around a mouthful of broth. It smelled of onions and herbs, and it was full of lamb and barley. "If you have great-grandchildren, I mean?"

The woman frowned, a little sadly. "That wasn't the task, dear child. I was to vanish from all their lives before any longstanding claims of affection could be made. Not that they weren't good children. Oh, they were good enough. That's what the whole point of having them was."

The doctor put down his fork and took a sip of wine, looking at her thoughtfully. "But you've not had a child for some time."

"I suppose that's true," she said, nodding. "The youngest would be getting on toward thirty by now. And Befum . . . he'd be eightyish I suppose. Ah, but I was young when I began. And there were all those syrups and tinctures to keep me young. You introduced yourself as a doctor, lad. You'd make a fortune if you could duplicate such tinctures to keep teeth solid and skin smooth and all the insides of you ticking as though you were a teenager still, even old as I was. How old d'you think I am?"

"I'd say, eightyish," the doctor opined.

"Aha. See there. You missed it by a league, mile, or kilometer, whichever's to your taste. I'm a hundred twenty-one. My first child was born at forty, my last at ninety-three."

The doctor turned to Dismé, winking his amusement.

"No more children," mused the old woman. "God says enough is enough. All the miraculous pharmacopeia can be dispensed with. Good thing, too, for I'm tired of it all."

Arnole, who had been sitting nearby, came to slip onto the bench beside Dismé. "Tired of what, grandma?"

"Being savior of the human race! The constant pregnancies, labor, deliveries, all that suckling, then the trial of making quite sure my current husband or lover could cope without me, or finding foster parents who could."

"When you moved on," Arnole said.

"Surely. When I moved on. Many babies to bear, and only a finite number of years to do it in! Oh, my boy, I always made quite, quite sure the child would be well cared for before moving on, very well cared for. But it's over, and now's time to lay down the fatal beauty, the erotic body, the seductive charm." She winked at the doctor. "All those accoutrements of fascination and captivation that let me do my job with the least possible confusion. No more being bewitching."

Michael had joined Arnole on the bench, and now all four of them confronted the old woman with total fascination, which did not at all dismay her. She smiled at them as she continued:

"I knew it was time to retire last time I was in Henceforth when I saw a poster in the little shipping office. Come to Urdarsland, it said. Natural beauty, leisure, intelligent companions, charm and relaxation. A retirement community for the connoisseur. Ah, good people, if there's anything nineteen children can make of a person, it's a connoisseur of leisure and relaxation. So, I've hired a carriage to take me to Henceforth. When I get there, I'll buy a one-way ticket to Urdarsland where it's full of warm springs and moss grows on the great trees . . ."

"Gardens too?" breathed Dismé.

"Oh, yes, my child. The booklet made it look like Eden."

Dismé chewed the mouthful she'd forgotten about, and the doctor asked, "You want to leave this world behind?"

"It's getting too crowded with memories. In Bastion I took a short walk to buy myself a pair of shoes, not more than a hundred fifty paces from my hostel, and I saw two of my former husbands on the street. They couldn't recognize me, of course. I don't look at all as I did when I was ninety, claiming to be thirty-six, convincing them I was bearing their children."

"They weren't your husbands' children?" asked Michael, in a strangled voice.

"Oh, no, my boy. No. They were the children of other men, long gone, children perfect for the purpose, God said."

"And you were doing this at God's behest?" asked Arnole.

"Ah, yes, my boy. I was born to duty. Aging is my retirement benefit. There in Bastion, picture this, I was peering nearsightedly over my spectacles at this man I'd been sheet leaping with some thirty or forty odd years ago, thinking I should be reveling in erotic memory when I was actually grateful for being old. Let's see. The baby I had with that one had been . . . James? Jasper?"

"Jens," said the doctor, tonelessly.

"Could have been. Something with a J, at any rate. A bit of a whirlwind, that wee bratty, though maybe the child only seemed more energetic than normal. He was among the last half dozen, and when I had them, I was already looking forward to the retirement God promised me."

"Was your life that . . . distasteful?" whispered Dismé.

"Oh, child, not in any way distasteful. I always found many secret pleasures to make up for quotidian tribulations, don't you know? I hated leaving a few of the men, and hated even more leaving some of the children. Baby Cammy, ah, he was such a dear. And my last one, dear, dear Dizzy-Dimples! I stayed longer with that little love. But I had to go . . ."

A driver came into the room, whip curled at his belt and leather gauntlets folded in his hand. "Skulda?" he asked the room at large, looking about. "A carriage for Henceforth?"

The old woman rose, took her cloak from the back of the chair and put it on. As she left, she turned to them. "So nice to have seen you again. Dismé. Jens. Arnole. Michael." Three more steps and she was at the door. "Say hello to Abobalee and Ababaidio for me. So nice to know you all turned out well."

"I heard my name mentioned," said Bobly, climbing onto the bench beside the doctor. "Who was that. Somebody's grandma?"

"Somebody's mother," said Dismé, staring at the doctor, at Arnole, then, with covert unease, at Michael.

"Come," said Galenor, urgently. "Dezmai. Bertral. We must speak with Nell Latimer."

The bishop and commander had been kept at the general's side during what was left of the day. The general, moving restlessly around his tent, had rehearsed a certain rite he would do when the ogre arrived, and the bishop had listened with growing revulsion as the details became increasingly clear. As the day waned, the bishop had asked, almost hopefully, "General, perhaps the creature isn't coming back."

The general slapped the bishop on his back and gave him a jovial grin, displaying teeth which seemed larger than the bishop remembered his having. "Oh, he's still with us. Not as strong as he was, but he will be, when I do the rite. I remember it. Oh, yes, I remember it. Ah . . . see, there, the sun's going down. Now he'll come . . ."

They waited, and within the hour, he did come, monstrous and terrible, to drink the blood of half a dozen men. When the general howled at him to find women for the rite, he rose to sniff horribly the surrounding air, to lurch toward the cliffs at the roadside, and there to set his claws into a cleft in the stone, where the doorway of the seeress had been left un-sealed by a woman more interested in being right than being careful. The airlock designed to keep out heat, dust, and radiation had not been designed to restrain an ogre who could smell young women inside—fairly young in elapsed years, at any rate—who were soon dragged out and brought to the general.

The general did the rite from memory, cutting off this, chomping that, drinking this other thing, calling upon the Great Fell for power, while the other officers looked on, or looked away, or looked, as the bishop did, at his feet, wondering why the Rebel Angels had brought him to this place. Wondering what the Rebel Angels really were. Wondering if they ever had been angels or if he and his people were not now servants of some horrible antithesis.

Other people were found in the redoubt. They were "fixed," as the general said, then left there to keep the magic strong, including the oldest woman among them who kept screaming, "Jackson, where are you, Jackson. Help, Jackson . . ." There was no one to help, and the general said it was important that there should be no one to help. This time, when the army marched, the pain of the victims buried deep in the redoubt should suffer for many days before they died. Now they were well hidden, well provided with water and warmth to extend their lives, but with the rock wall collapsed over them, they were unreachable by anyone at all.

Before dawn on nineday, the exodus from Trayford took place with Dezmai, Bertral, and Galenor raging at the populace to get them moving. Nell, in the absence of Elnith to keep her mute, had spent the few hours with her old friend, Alan, before seeing him depart with the others.

"I wonder if we will see one another again," he said. "This is a stranger future than any I ever thought of."

"I know. It's like a nightmare, one of those vivid dreams that are terrible and enticing, all at once. The kind you are relieved to wake from, but don't want to forget . . ."

"Don't forget me, Nell."

"Alan, my dear. We've been together, in a way, for almost a thousand years. I shan't forget you. I figure we still have fifteen, twenty years to spend together, and if Elnith will allow it, I'll be back here, looking for you. Keep well until then."

The town was empty by the time Arnole and the others were ready to set out. As they mounted their horses, Nell went into one of the trances that were becoming familiar and emerged to say:

"Elnith says Bastion's army was at the redoubt. The redoubt is fallen. Janet left the door unsealed because she didn't believe in monsters. She's inside, with others, maimed like those at Ogre's Gap. They have water, they have warmth, they're not mobile, they can't reach anything to ease the pain . . ."

She turned away, retching, unable to continue for the moment as she thought of kindly Jackson and the foolish few who had stayed. "Elnith says to get someone to go to the redoubt and put those people out of their pain. There are no demons nearby. Even if they come, the mountain has been tumbled down over where the entrance was. The army is near the foot of the mountain and turning westward. They march swiftly. We are nearer the goal, but not by much. If we are to get there first, we must go."

Dismé climbed into the wagon, stood tall, covered her eyes with her hands and concentrated on broadcasting horror through the dobsi in her head. She could almost feel the stranger in her skull screaming, a sharp pain, like a stab wound. When she had kept it up for some minutes, she slowly relaxed. "That's the best I can do, Nell."

Nell drew her cloak around her, sighing. "Tamlar awaits us where we're going, but Ialond and Aarond are not there. We have only one stone left, the wrapped one . . ." She fell silent as Elnith came upon her once more, for a moment, then departed.

Dismé asked, "If the stone in the wagon is for either Ialond or Aarond, where's the last stone?"

"We haven't time even to wonder," cried Nell. "There's no time, no time at all."

*   *   *

Bice Dufor, Warden of the College of Sorcery, received a note from the Hetman, asking him to drop in as soon as possible. All Bice's instincts were to go in the opposite direction, quickly and with no intention of return, and his mind occupied itself visualizing this retreat while his body stood before his mirror, fingers busy buttoning his jacket, mouth telling his servant to bring the carriage to the gate. He tried, momentarily, to escape from whatever his body was doing, but it was useless. No matter how he screamed inside his head, his feet carried him out the door and down the walk, where he encountered Mace Marchant.

"I have an errand, Mace," he said in a cheery, totally false voice. "Come with me, and I'll treat you to dinner, afterward." He caught hold of Mace's arm in a grip of iron and held it tightly until they were seated in the carriage.

"Where are we going?" asked Mace, eyes fixed on the man beside him who had already sweat through his jacket, whose eyes were full of panic, yet whose voice was jolly as a Praiser after a service of adoration.

"See a man," the warden said. "Only for a moment."

Mace had come to the warden's place with a message, and since the warden was saying nothing, Mace shared with him the account of Rashel's death as he had learned of it from the anchorite at the medical clinic.

"Rashel?" said the warden, in a strangely disembodied tone. "Rashel Deshôll?"

"Arms gone," said Mace. "Eyes gone. Mutilated, Warden. Mutilated. Have you heard of any such thing?"

"Ah," said the warden, with a panicky sideways glance. "How would I have heard of any such thing. What are you suggesting?"

"I wasn't suggesting anything. I can't explain it, that's all. She was doing . . . doing good work. She was . . . very intent upon her . . . usefulness to the Regime. She was . . . I can't understand it, that's all."

"Well, no more do I. Here's where my man lives. This won't take long." He dragged Mace out of the carriage with him.

The gate was opened immediately, subterranean hallways were negotiated at what amounted to a dead run, and never for a moment did the warden release the hold he had upon Mace's sleeve.

Inside the overheated room, the Hetman waited in a fever of impatience. Dufor was not a pawn he had expected to sacrifice so soon, but there was no alternative. The army must move relentlessly to dig out and kill the Council of Guardians and destroy the being from the north. The Hetman had arranged for the army to be strong, led by one monster and transformed into thousands of others, but this intent was being inexplicably weakened. He had to add power, much of it, and since he had foolishly discarded Rashel, believing her usefulness was over, the warden would have to do.

The warden, however, did not come unencumbered. He brought with him a strangely silent Mace Marchant, a man who started at a sound, who seemed inclined to fade into the furniture, who did not, in fact, look as though he had wanted to come.

Dufor was babbling, "While Marchant may be mistaken, Hetman—and I apologize sincerely for taking up your time with nonsense if he is mistaken—he received information today that Rashel Deshôll, near death, was taken to the bottling room near the Praise Gate in Hold. I thought you might want to know."

Hetman Gone smiled, a sight from which Mace Marchant hastily averted his eyes, at the same time opening his lips slightly so he could breathe through his mouth.

The person called Gone rumbled, "How thoughtful of you to bring me this word, Warden, though in fact I am not interested in the woman and deeply regret the inconvenience you have caused Major Marchant. Major, thank you for attending the warden. I look forward to meeting you at another time, but just now, the warden and I have some urgent and private business to discuss."

Marchant bowed and tried to back away, but the Warden's hand was still locked upon his arm.

"Let the major go," said Gone, in a voice like a knife, keen as a scalpel, cutting through all obstructions, all contrary ideas or intentions.

The warden's hand fell away, and the major got out of the place into the torch-lit courtyard, only to wait there an interminable time until one of the dwarfish servants came into the area.

"Still here?" crowed the creature, prancing about and giggling, as though drunk.

Mace gestured at the gate.

"Oho, it wants out! Not the only one, no, no, no." It giggled frantically. "Many people want out. What's my name?"

What had Bice called him? "Thissel. Please let me out."

"Thissel, Thissel, that's my name." He pranced around the courtyard, circling, giggling.

Mace shuddered. What was the creature doing? He turned his eyes from the enormous erection protruding from the creature's clothing. Surely . . . surely that was some kind of physiological abnormality! Surely, this one should have been bottled long ago.

"Knows my name. Says please. So, we let him out . . ."

Mace stood close to the gate, pretending not to notice how the creature looked at him while it unlocked the gate, then moved quickly, slipping from the creature's sudden embrace and into the tunnel where he ran up the many stairs and seemingly endless corridors until he reached the fenced area abutting the street. The grille was locked. The vertical bars were too narrow and slick to climb. He waited again, quietly, refusing to scream though the scream welled at the base of his throat, refusing to panic though panic nattered at him, refusing to admit fear though he was frozen with it, waited seemingly forever before the one called Gnang came to open the grille. This time he asked at once.

"Gnang, please open the gate for me."

And this one, too, giggled and muttered and tried to touch him intimately as he fled.

Once outside, Mace stumbled away, his heart pounding dangerously, only now fully aware that he was terrified to the point of paralysis. He stopped for a moment, leaning against the wall as he panted. Near his feet, where the walkway met the cobbles of the street, a barred culvert led, so Marchant had always supposed, into the storm sewers of the town. Such openings were found at intervals on all the streets at the center of Hold.

As he panted, hand pressed to his chest, a sound came from the culvert, a voice, gasping words. No, he told himself, he was imagining it. After hearing what had happened to Rashel, after the warden's dragging him off that way, and that . . . man and his servitors. By all the Rebel Angels, it would be odd if he didn't imagine awful things.

He plodded slowly on, taking deep breaths, gradually calming himself. As he approached the next culvert, the sound came again, a labored gasp, panting, words, gargled. He stood over the opening, trying to decipher the sounds. Again the panting, grunted monosyllables that sounded like, pleez, pleez, pleez. Mace looked around to find himself completely alone on the street. He knelt down and listened.

Gohdan Gone's voice. "You have been a good servant. You have done well, building that collection of sorcery at the college. All those spells in your office, all those slabs of human skin, all that critical mass of sorcerous intent, there in the college, a place from which I can draw the power in my necromancy."

"The college?" squeaked the other voice. "The college?"

"Colleges. Churches. Schools. All of them, fertile ground. Full of people jockeying for position, easily corrupted. You have been useful, and I regret the necessity of using you now. I had intended to reward you better than this, at least temporarily. But still, you know what must be done in the attainment of power . . ."

Then came a horrid gargling, an agonized though muffled scream, and Mace began to run, as fast as he had ever run, for though he wanted to believe he was imagining things, he knew the scream had been the warden's.

*   *   *

Four of the travelers sat beside a well in the prairie lands west of Trayford while Michael shifted saddles on the horses. Arnole was speaking. "I first heard of Nell Latimer's children when Dismé said that she had a book written by Nell Latimer. Dismé said Nell had written that she saw the being fall to earth and heard it say, 'Come to me quickly, with all your children.' "

"Yes, I did hear that," said Nell.

The doctor mused, "The book also spoke of donated ova. Of your embryos stored in the redoubt, were there as many as nineteen?"

"I suppose, yes. But all the embryos were destroyed at some point. Not only mine. The gametes of animals, too."

"Some were no doubt destroyed," said Arnole. "Perhaps on the same occasion when yours were taken from the redoubt and implanted in a woman calling herself Skulda who bore nineteen infants, leaving them in the care of men who thought they were the fathers of the children. Plus you, Nell, plus Tamlar makes twenty-one."

Nell shook her head. "I know nothing about it. One person could, I suppose, be the biological mother of all nineteen human Guardians, but why? And who arranged all that?"

Dismé asked, "And what did the being mean, 'Come to me quickly with all your children?' "

Arnole spoke harshly. "It meant that Nell and we who are her children had better get to this place we're going before that monster does. I wish I knew where Ialond and Aarond are."

They mounted and rode on, Dismé and the doctor side by side. "I've just realized," she said in a stifled voice. "We are brother and sister."

"Yes," he said with a wry twist to his mouth. "I guessed that some time ago. I have been working on brotherly feelings ever since."

At the railway station in Hold, Mace found a great many people wanting to travel to Apocanew on a train that had no engineer, no stokers, no conductors. An angry official from the Office of Maintenance dragooned a crew from the street and went along to keep the volunteers at it. Finally, the train set off on what was to be a nerve-wracking journey that ended prematurely when the boiler blew up some distance northeast of the city, killing both the dragooned crew and the official.

Mace abandoned his luggage and walked the rest of the way. He wouldn't need luggage. He was not going back to Hold, where the monster was. He had never . . . never used a black art. Despite all the rumors going around, he had never, never inquired into that side of things, never hinted that he wanted to know. Nonetheless, he had read old books, as they all did, those who searched for The Art. He had read of a certain ancient people in middle America who had a religion based on torture and blood. He had read of tribes in North America who routinely tortured and ate their captives, including children. What had happened to the warden was no new thing, but an ancient evil practiced by many primitive men publicly, and by a few civilized men privately. Disappearance. Torture. Hideous death, too long delayed.

He could only guess what was happening, but he could extrapolate a little from what he knew and had heard. He greatly desired to use that little for the general . . . good. Something to upset the balance, perhaps. Frustrate the dark powers, perhaps. The monster had done that terrible thing to Rashel, and Mace had cared deeply about Rashel. He would have married her, if she had consented. There had been something about her, a kind of hidden vulnerability, that had moved him. Perhaps he could do something to the monster who had killed her, perhaps only a mosquito bite, but whatever he could do, he would do.

Within the hour, he was at the College of Sorcery, bustling in with every appearance of officialdom, calling for the warden's aide, who happened to be the only one in the building.

"The warden has sent me down from Hold to pick up some papers for him, private papers. Something he needs for his business in Hold. He's told me where to look for them, and which ones he needs, if you'll be kind enough to let me into his office. I had a note from him, but the train blew up outside town, can you imagine? I lost my cloak and everything in the pockets!"

The aide had heard of the train disaster and was not prepared to contradict the head of the Apocanew sub-office of Inexplicable Arts. He opened the door and offered his assistance, but was shooed away by Mace, who then locked the door and began a careful search of the warden's room. If what he had overheard there in the street was true, then the warden would have a cache of sorcerous stuff in this room. Among such a cache, he might even find something to aid Rashel . . .

Mace would have found nothing had he not stumbled over an irregularity in the floor near the back wall of the office, where a strip of flooring came up when he put the tip of his knife under the edge. The cache he had expected to find was there, a quantity of spells written on pieces of skin with hair still attached to them. Not pigskin. The hair wasn't pig hair. It was human skin, and the bones with them were human bones. From the hair pattern on one or two, he could suppose the belly hair of a mature man or woman. From the texture of others, he presumed young children. His eyes skimmed one or two of the spells, and he sat down quickly, eyes closed, trying not to be sick all over the warden's possessions.

One of the skins was a love spell, so named, though it actually subordinated the will of the ensorceled to the will of the sorcerer, which did not describe what Mace had thought of as love. The spell called for bits of the . . . victim's hair. Rashel had several times taken bits of Mace's hair, as keepsakes, she had said. The words of the ensorcelment were words she had said to him—so he had thought—in the heat of passion.

He wiped angry tears from his cheeks. Well, well, then why was he trying to avenge her? He owed her nothing! Except, said a small voice he heard from time to time, you owe yourself something, surely?

The warden had recently said some rather odd things during lectures at the college, odd enough that they had been remembered and mentioned, here and there. The warden had said that the very words of a spell, and the stuff on which those words were written, could have a power of their own that was separate from the putative purpose of the spell. Like the boxes the demons used to power the Chairs: those boxes could be taken out of the Chairs and power other things, and they, too, were dangerous if one tried to open them. So, if the power was a separate thing from the spell, then that power could be used for other things that the magician didn't even know about. There could be fatal spells that ate the magician who used them while increasing the power of someone else.

Which was no doubt what had happened to the warden. Mace could almost feel the gathered menace that attended these parchments. It seemed to him that the room was full of hazy ghosts, watching him, tiny vortexes where their heads should be.

Shaking his head to clear it, he sat for some time in thought, then replaced the parchments where he had found them, though not before laying a trail of candle wax into the recess beneath the floor. There were explosive powders in the cabinet, used for magical effects, and he poured some of these into the recess also, and from there in a trail leading under the warden's desk, where he placed a candle stub in a pile of the same stuff. He poured the lantern oil about and under the desk, then gathered together a folder or two, lit the stub of candle with a striker (it would not take it long to burn down) pulled the shutters closed across the only window, and let himself out, locking the door behind him.

"Did you find what the warden needed, sir?" The aide, being officiously concerned.

"I think so," said Mace, consciously summoning up the reality of himself as he had been yesterday—a little pompous, a little sarcastic, a little too sure of his own importance. He adopted a slightly admonitory tone, "He said he wanted the lecture he'd given to the graduates last spring. I presume this is it."

The aide took the folder and looked into it. "Yes, sir."

"And also his notes on the Inclusionist Selectivist controversy. Which is what this seems to be."

"Again, yes sir, it is."

"I don't know why he couldn't simply have sent a note asking you to bring them to Hold. I'm sure if you were too busy, someone could have done it." Mace strained to sound a trifle haughty.

The aide shook his head. "As a matter of fact, sir, I'd have been hard put to it to find anyone. All our ordinary workers seem to have disappeared! Just quit. None of them showed up for work since before last span-end. There were only two workers here this morning, besides me, and they've both gone!"

"The professors? The students?"

"It's vacation time. We don't expect them back for summer term until summerspan six. I don't know if they'll show up or not. There were no farmers at the market this morning, either. And the butcher's shop was closed. The barber, too."

"What's happening?" Mace was honestly curious.

"I don't know. No one knows. It's just, all the ordinary folk seem to have gone somewhere."

"Nonsense," said Mace, striving to remain in character. "Where would they have to go?" Except where he, himself, intended to go, as rapidly as possible. Away.

The aide shrugged and followed him to the door, so intent upon sharing his worry that he didn't ask for the warden's key.

From the corner Mace watched the college entrance. Very shortly the aide came out carrying the cash box and locking the door behind him. Mace retreated to a tavern he sometimes frequented, only a block away. Aside from the couple who owned it, it was occupied only by a few aimless people crouched over beer pots. Mace ordered a meal and was halfway finished with it when people began yelling *Fire*. Not to seem uninterested, he went out to the street with the

tavern couple and the other drinkers still capable of movement, where they all gaped at the fire and waited for the firemen. A horrid purple smoke rose from the fire, with a stench
that drove the crowd inside, where they peered out through
the windows. No firemen appeared. By the time everyone
realized that no firemen were coming, the fire had completely gutted the College of Sorcery and the adjacent buildings were burning from foundation to roof.

In Mace's opinion, the least traveled way out of Apocanew was the road that ran past Faience and on into the
mountains to a little used and unguarded pass. From there,
he would go to the nearest village and seek work as . . . a
teacher. He was literate, his only real skill, and he intended
to leave Bastion forever.

In Chasm was a cold place of blue-white light and glittering
machines where voices came from the walls. Rashel was
standing when she woke. She opened her eyes with a sharp
click, click, to peer down at her shining self. Inside this polished skin were polished parts, metal and silicon and ceram-
ics of various kinds, all of them impervious and almost
eternal. Only the crinkled gray matter well protected in the
center of her was fleshy. She was unaware of this, and also
uninterested.

"Me," she said with her speaker, raising her metal hands,
clack, clack, in a gesture of defiance. "Me. Rashel. Nemesis
of Gone and all his beings." The hands were three-fingered,
two hooks with one sharp blade opposed, good for cutting
things off.

"That's right, Rashel," said the voice from the wall where
someone twisted a tiny wheel that sent a signal to one of
Rashel's new parts, a tiny reservoir, which flowed, briefly,
producing an intensity of pleasure she had never felt in her
life before, a total ecstacy.

"Good Rashel," said the voice. "Good Nemesis of Gone."

"Go?" she asked, eager to go, eager to kill, maim, destroy,
feel ecstacy again. "Go now?"

"No," said the voice. "Not now. Soon. Soon Rashel can go

and earn many hours of happy. So many hours of happy. Later."

"So many," she murmured, clack, clack, folding back the hooks, the blades, the lower arms, the upper arms, into their resting position. "So many," closing her eyes, click click.

Elsewhere in the hard, blue place one person asked another, "Who's this Gone it always mentions?"

"No idea," said the other. "It really doesn't matter."

the visitor

Arnole, Nell, Bobly, and Bab were in the light wagon pulled by four horses; Dismé, Jens, and Michael were on fresh mounts with spares on lead ropes. By the end of the day, the group remained well ahead of the army, or so Dismé told them, having received word from demon, dobsi, or Dezmai. When it grew dark, they stopped, unhitched, hobbled the horses, and settled themselves to a cold supper, knowing they could not risk a fire. On the flat and seemingly endless plain, they could not hide a blaze. Instead, they drank tepid water from the water barrel and tried not to think about hot tea.

Despite exhaustion, Dismé could not relax. The dobsi in her head was picking up urgent emanations from many sources, and she could not shut off the sensations that fled through her mind too quickly to consider or even, in many cases, to recognize. She murmured fretfully to Arnole. "I'm not sure it's actually telling me what I think it is! Arnole, you have a dobsi too, and you have more experience with it than I do! Why aren't you doing the listening?"

Arnole rolled his head about, trying to get rid of the neck stiffness that resulted from a day spent sitting in an unsprung wagon. "A few years ago, a friendly demon in Chasm had its Dantisfan whistle my young one out of my head. They grow slowly, but they have to come out before the host starts having headaches."

"You're from Chasm, aren't you?" said Dismé. "That's how you knew so much."

He nodded, smiling. "From near there."

She went on, "I don't think the thing in Bastion reads people's thoughts. I think it tracks them by their . . . brain waves, like a dog tracks a smell. I was tracked like that, once when I was just a child and again in Hold, the first time I went there. Rashel said something once about 'Watching all the damned Latimers,' and I wondered if that's what the thing was doing, watching all the Latimers."

Arnole mused, "None of the other Guardians we've found were named Latimer. Latimer wasn't Nell's birth name, and it was probably pure coincidence that Skulda chose Val Latimer to father you. Whoever was watching picked the wrong person."

The doctor said, "Whatever, not whoever. Gohdan Gone isn't human. Perhaps he came with the Happening."

Nell, who had been very quiet for most of the day, stood up with startled suddenness and said, "We must travel tonight!"

Michael shook his head. "It's dangerous. There's no moon until late. We could cripple the horses."

"We have to go tonight, no later than moonrise," she said. "Elnith just showed me. The army travels at night. We have to get farther ahead of it before we can really rest."

"Bab and I'll watch," said Bobly. "We can sleep in the wagon later, so we'll wake you at moonrise."

They agreed to this, rolled themselves in their blankets, and fell into restless sleep. Bobly and Bab had already made a comfortable nest of blankets in the wagon where they sat back to back, swiveling their eyes over the flatland around them.

North were mountains, invisible in the dark. South and east of them were the prairies, all the way to New Chicago, and beyond that, the ocean. It was a smaller world they looked out upon than the one Nell had known. At the Happening, ocean bottoms had been raised, spilling the seas over the lower land. The Arctic and Antarctic ice had melted, driving the waters still higher. Under the weight of water, the continental plates had riven and thrust up new ranges of mountains to tower under the slow wheel of the stars.

Bobly and Bab poked one another occasionally to be sure they were awake, the intervals becoming less, the need more urgent, both of them becoming inexplicably anxious as their eyes swiveled from side to side.

Bobly put her hand on Bab's arm. "What's that there?" she asked, pointing to the east, in the direction they had come. "In the sky, see, a kind of shadow?"

It could be seen when it crossed the stars, a thin shadow, moving north to south then north again.

"Get doctor's distance glasses," directed Bobly, her eyes fixed on the flying shadow. "Let's try to see it closer."

"If it isn't too dark to see anything," murmured Bab as he searched. "Here they are, in his bag. I'll look."

He put the glasses to his eyes and fiddled with them, drawing in a horrified breath. "A flying thing. Like a huge dragonfly. Bigger than anything. Its eyes shine. They give enough light to see it's got fangs and talons. It's searching, down here, below. Oh, by all the Guardians, Bobly. It'll see us."

"Wake the others," she said. "And do it quietly."

Deep in the redoubt, far at the end of a winding access tunnel that ran through solid rock toward the reactor room, a storage compartment hatch slowly opened. After a time Jackson's ashen face peeked out, remaining hidden for some time before protruding itself farther into the aisle, eventually to be followed by his body, crouching, then slinking slowly down the tunnel to the sealed door that opened on the storage area. It was locked from his side, and it squeaked slightly as he unlocked and opened it. At the sound, Jackson shrank visibly, as though trying to dissolve into shadows. Nothing. No sound. No movement. Eventually, he gained the courage to open the door far enough to get through it, leaving it open behind him as he went down the corridor he had traveled . . . when? The day before?

He had heard the monsters not long after dark. With the upper door and the panel next to it sealed—he had sealed them himself—the entrance became invisible. Though it looked like the stone around it, it was stronger than stone, and it did not admit sound from the outside. He should not have been able to hear anything smaller than an earthquake from outside. When he woke to the sound of howls and falling stone, he knew at once that the door was unsealed and that Janet, as part of her quixotic rejection of Nell's advice, had done it.

The knowledge moved him into frantic, unhesitating action. He made no effort to save the others. He simply fled, down through the labs, past the food storage, and through a small access door to the maintenance tunnels, which he sealed behind him. The tunnel was so low that one had to stoop to walk through it, and at its far end, he had crawled into a storage compartment and curled himself into a tight ball. If he had gone to Trayford, with the others, he would not have been here at all. If it hadn't been for Janet, he would have gone to Trayford. If he had been in Trayford, he wouldn't have been here to save the people in the redoubt, so he would pretend he had gone.

It became a litany, over and over, one recited alternately with another: "I closed the upper door. I remember closing it. I sprayed stuff around on the rock. I wouldn't have done that and leave the door open. So I didn't leave it open. I closed it. That damned fool Janet opened it. She's determined to prove Nell wrong. She was going to prove it by opening the door."

She'd had plenty of time to do it while he'd been clearing space for the people who were staying behind, more of them than the redoubt had been designed to house. The thought of double-checking the door had crossed his mind, but the recently awakened needed help, so Jackson hadn't thought, and Janet hadn't believed, not until the moment the monsters came in.

Now, after a full day in hiding, he expected to find the place empty. Bodies maybe, but otherwise empty. There had been terrible sounds as he fled, but once the maintenance tunnel door was locked behind him and he was deep into the innards of the place, he couldn't hear anything. Now, as he approached the living quarters, he heard sounds again, sounds that told him he was wrong about finding only bodies, sounds that led him to them, each of them in turn: moans, screams, a terrible grating noise some of them made in their throats, the horrible look in their eyes. "Kill me," the tongues said. The eyes said, "Oh, for the love of God, kill me."

He would not. He could not. He did not believe in killing. He had never believed in killing. Instead he wept, crouched, put his head between his knees and howled, made useless by fear, pity, horror, and an empathetic ghastliness of pain.

On the prairie, the doctor peered through his glasses.

"What is it?" breathed Nell.

"A monster," he answered, in an expressionless voice. "A flying one. Evidently Gowl—or the other thing, whatever it is—isn't content with the speed of his approach and he's decided to catch us out here in the open. The moon is rising! Is there anywhere we can hide?"

Dismé searched inside herself. Dezmai was away, as, indeed, all of their inhabitants seemed to be. No Bertral, no Elnith, no Galenor.

"Can you panic your dobsi?" Arnole suggested. "If you work up a good fit of fear, it'll pick up on what's bothering you and broadcast it. There may be a demon close enough to hear you."

Dismé put the glasses to her eyes and had little trouble in working up a fit of horrors. The thing had huge, multi-lens eyes. It did indeed have fangs dripping from complicated jaws, and many legs with long, cutting talons.

Nell asked for the glasses and examined the creature for herself. "It's one of the ancient ones. I've seen that kind before, during the long darkness. The fangs are venomous. One touch and the victim is past help."

"Add to that," said Dismé, "that compound eyes like that are extremely useful in detecting motion."

The doctor took the glasses from Nell, leapt upon the wagon seat and began to search the area around him. "I'm looking for shadows," he said. "Any kind of swale or wash we can drive into. Hitch the horse, Michael. If we move it will have to be quickly."

Michael did so, as Bobly and Bab ran to help him, and very shortly, the doctor pointed a little way to the north. "There's a shadow that way, some kind of low place."

The others had already put their belongings in the wagon, and as Arnole took the reins, the others mounted their horses and went northward, slowly, both to reduce the chance of injury and to keep the noise and movement to a minimum. Bobly had the glasses again, and she lay supine in the rocking wagon, trying to keep the flying monster in sight.

When they arrived at the shadow, the doctor was already there, regarding it with dismay. It was indeed a wash, but one little wider than the wagon and quite short, a mere cut in an otherwise rounded, smoothly eroded bank separating the level prairie from a wide, dry riverbed.

Without a moment's hesitation, Michael jumped onto the wagon seat, drove the wagon into the riverbed, then lined the wagon up with the wash and made the horses back up, which they did unwillingly, tossing their heads to show their displeasure. When the wagon was as far back as it would go, both it and the horses were below the level of the surrounding land. "Get the canvas cover off," said Michael. "There are tent stakes in the wagon. Peg the cover to the sides of the wash. Throw some grass on it."

He was dropping the wagon tongue, talking to the horses, twisting their ears gently in his hands, murmuring sweet nothings, getting them to lie down in the traces, backs together, feet to either side.

"No time to take off the harness," he said to no one in particular. "And besides, we may need to leave in a hurry."

"What about the riding horses?" asked the doctor.

"Bring the saddles in here, hobble the horses, and let them

graze. There are other horses here on the prairie, wild ones or escaped ones. That thing won't know the difference, and in this deep grass, it won't be able to see the hobbles."

Everyone scattered, tossing saddles into the wash, pegging the cover from bank to bank, cutting handfuls of grass to toss atop it. The gravelly soil of the wide river bottom was grown up in tufty grasses where the riding horses settled to graze. The others were in or under the wagon while Michael lay prone among the wagon team, murmuring to them, keeping them down. Dismé knelt in the wagon bed, only her head thrust over the lip of the wash, watching the sky through the glasses. The monster quartered the sky, north and south, then came farther west to do it again, over and over.

"It's coming closer," she murmured, panic threatening to take her by the throat. "It's coming much closer."

"Oh, by all the . . ." said Nell suddenly. "What are we thinking of! That thing is a predator, and it's huge. What does it normally eat? What will it do when it sees the horses?"

"Damn," said Michael, feelingly. "I assumed it was hunting us . . ."

"It is hunting us," said the doctor, "but that doesn't mean it isn't hungry enough to eat horse. If it comes down on the horses, it won't need to hunt us any further. We'll be right in front of it, like dessert."

The army had turned westward at the bottom of the mountain road. It had not gone on to Trayford, for when the ogre arrived at dusk, it did not arrive alone. With it was a thing, a monstrous ropiness, a heaving slime, an amorphous stink which could, when necessary, compress itself into a loathsome cloud that half rolled, half crawled alongside the marching monsters of General Gowl. Worse than any other aspect of the thing was its voice, a slimy insinuation which slipped like a slug through the ear into the skull and ate holes in the mind. Upon arrival, the loathsomeness ate ten or a dozen soldiers and called up several monsters, including one that could fly. Then it sniffed the ground and pointed southward, toward the village. The flying thing went there while the army itself turned westward, toward some unmentioned goal that none of the men including the general knew anything about. This evening there had been no rain of blood, and the men were more or less themselves, so the bishop took the opportunity to ride up beside the general and ask a few whispered questions.

"General Gowl, do you know where we're going?"

"Um," said the general, nodding. "The thing that came down from the north is out this way, somewhere. We're going to kill it. My friend, Hetman Gone, doesn't want the thing to come closer. Also the Council of Guardians. We're going to kill the Council, too. And on the way, we're going to find Latimers and kill them because they have something to do with the thing from the north."

"What are Latimers?"

"Latimers, Latimers, you know. First Leader of the Spared, he was a Latimer. He had two children."

"And why are we looking for them?"

"Because he . . . my friend, Hetman Gone, he looked into the future, to see he would fall to the family of Latimer. So, he's kept an eye on all the Latimers, but one got away. And now he's got that flying thing looking for Latimers."

The bishop thought deeply. Why was the name familiar? Oh, yes. "Rashel Deshôll's sister," he said. "She was mentioned during one of our meetings. Up at Faience."

"I don't recall. Possibly."

That wasn't the only place he had seen the name. Where else? Written. He could visualize the paper, a long, long list of names. Of course, Trublood. Trublood's report on people who visited the doctor, either in the office or at the clinic. Dismé Latimer had visited the doctor . . . actually worked for him, and had been sent to . . .

"The thing's looking in the wrong place," he said firmly. "Dismé Latimer went to Newland."

"No," said the general. "My friend, Hetman Gone, doesn't look in the wrong place, ever. He can smell her out. He can put a hook in her mind; he can find her if anyone even thinks of her name. We are behind her, but we'll catch up. The flying thing will find her and bring her back to my friend, Hetman Gone."

In the redoubt, Jackson's spate of uncontrollable weeping gave way to dry and hopeless heaves. He stood up, his eyes fleeting over the control panels beside him, the lights, the dials, the power circuit for the coffins, for the infirmary. The infirmary. He stopped, vacant-headed, only gradually realizing his own stupidity. There were opiates in the infirmary. He almost tore the door from its hinges, getting through it. Within moments he had scooped the loaded hypodermics out of their stasis bin and piled them onto a lab apron, which he gathered up like a sack.

He instructed himself to take them as he came to them. Otherwise he'd be going back and forth, back and forth. First this nearest man, then the woman next to him. Okay, then the next two men lying under the table. Then the women . . . Janet it was, the hell with her, let her wait, go on to the next woman. Three more men. Why wasn't he seeing any of the younger women? There had been several younger women, but they didn't seem to be here. Now this . . . God, where was he going to stick the needle. There wasn't any place on this one left to stick the needle. Now this one, now . . . now . . . now . . .

He went back to Janet when he had done everyone else.

"You left me for last," she howled from a raw throat. "Until last."

"You killed all these people, you bitch," he said angrily. "You didn't like Nell Latimer, so to prove her wrong, you killed all these people. You killed yourself!"

She tried to scream at him, but she couldn't. In moments even her rasping moans began to die.

"It's coming closer," said Dismé in a level voice. "It's turned directly westward, toward us. I think it's seen the horses."

"Keep still," murmured the doctor. "Keep very still. Maybe it won't notice us."

"If the riding horses scream, these will react," said Michael in an emotionless voice. "I won't be able to keep them quiet. Can you find Dezmai somewhere? She helped with the horse when we met Arnole."

Dismé didn't answer. She had no way to search for Dezmai, or summon her, or evoke her. All the volition had been on the other side of the relationship. Above her, only a little to the east, the great creature whipped the air with its wings. She could hear the buzz, huge and deep.

"Like an engine running," said Nell.

"Engine?" asked Dismé.

"For a cart that moves without horses," said Arnole. "Or a machine that flies. As in Chasm."

"It's coming directly here," said Dismé. "It sees the horses. Everyone be as quiet as you can."

The deep sound grew closer until it was directly overhead. Out on the prairie, the horses looked up in sudden panic and tried to run. The hobbles panicked them further and they began bucking and screaming, throwing their heads wildly. The pitch of the hum grew higher. Something screeched from directly above them. The horses went mad with fear as the thing dropped directly above them and pivoted on its own axis . . .

Where it stopped. Its eyes were fixed at the wash, at the thrashing horses under the blankets, at Michael who had just erupted from among them to prevent himself being struck with a flailing hoof . . .

The thing darted forward, one taloned leg extended, and Michael was swept into the air, dangling from one leg, his mouth open, his hands reaching for the large knife he always carried at his belt.

"Michael," Dismé screamed, thrusting her way up, out of hiding.

The thing heard her, turned, dropped toward her, another leg extended. She tried to get down, but someone was behind her, she couldn't move . . .

Dismé was knocked far to one side, rolling over and over. Beside her something crashed into the ground. Michael yelled, then stopped as he fell beside her.

Silence except for the screaming horses, the muted curses of people trying to struggle to their feet in a tangled mess of wagon cover, blankets, and harness. The riding horses indulged themselves in a few more crow hops, then gathered together to talk it over with much neighing, tossing of heads, and attempts to run. One or two of them gave it up and started to graze.

From behind Dismé, Arnole asked, "What happened?"

Dismé was trying to catch her breath. She whispered, "The thing landed. Michael's here. I think he's hurt . . ."

The doctor said, "Michael?"

"Over by Dismé," said Bobly. "The thing isn't moving."

"Let me out," said the doctor.

He climbed out of the wagon and surveyed the surroundings. The moon was well above the horizon. The monster had skidded about fifty feet down the river bank, where it lay silent, and as still as though dead. Michael lay nearby, with Dismé on her knees beside him, cradling his head.

"It's not moving," she called to Jens. "Michael needs you!"

Jens went to the fallen man, Nell close behind him. Dismé, catching a glimpse of her eyes, realized that Elnith had at last arrived.

"About time," she muttered, drawing Michael more closely into her embrace.

The doctor was beside her. "Did you see what happened?" he asked.

"It just dropped," cried Dismé. "It hit me with a wing. Is he all right?"

"Nothing broken," said the cold voice of Galenor, as the doctor ran his hands down arms and legs, around the skull. Then, in Jens's own voice, "I don't think he's badly hurt. Michael. Hey, Michael."

Michael moaned.

"What stopped it?" asked Arnole, joining the rest of them with Bobly and Bab trailing behind.

"Something happened," said Nell, her eyes staring toward the east. "There, in the redoubt. Elnith felt someone . . .

someone is in there, not injured. The army didn't get him when it got all the others. Whoever it is has stopped the pain. Killed them, maybe. Or drugged them. It has to be, because that's the power that moved the flying thing, maybe even the power that summoned it in the first place. When the pain stopped, it stopped."

"We can't count on that happening again," said Dismé, rising shakily to her feet. "There's the moon. Let's put as much room as possible between ourselves and whatever is coming after us."

"If you don't mind," said Michael, sitting up with a pained grunt and holding his head with both hands. "I prefer a little preventive effort. I thought I was . . . fly-food. If this thing is still here, that means it isn't any kind of magical construction, right? It's a real thing, though it's probably powered by your warlock. It's not working now, which doesn't mean it won't work later. Somebody bring the axe from the wagon. This thing can't fly again if it doesn't have any wings. And it can't use talons if we lop 'em off."

In the redoubt, Jackson could find no way to get out. The way up through the seeress's booth was full of rock. Rock had fallen in front of the elevator in a high pile. He passed it a dozen times as he stalked to and fro, muttering to himself, fragments of old, half-forgotten prayers, nursery rhymes from childhood, the words to songs that had been popular before the Happening. It took him a long time before he really looked at the rockfall before the elevator. It was a large pile of rock, true, but the individual rocks weren't large. Not that much stone, really, if he could just get up the impetus to move it. He considered this for some time, moving a step or two toward the pile, then away from it. If he cleared it, he'd have to go up there. He didn't want to go up there. *They* might still be up there . . .

He couldn't move. Maybe it was just as well if he didn't move. Just let things go, for now. There was probably plenty of painkiller in the infirmary. Probably.

• Sheri S. Tepper

After a long time of blankness and inaction, he went into the infirmary and counted the doses of opiates, those in storage, those in the machines. Then he counted the wounded and divided the one into the other, doing it several times because he disliked the result. Two days supply, at best. Because Nell had taken a lot of it with her, for the people who had to walk to Trayford. Given a week, he could synthesize more, but when two days passed, he'd be back where he started. Still he didn't move. He couldn't move that stone and go up into the world. He'd have to do something else.

The pings. The pings were still there. Still functional. In Chasm there were survivors from old times. In old times, there would have been a rescue mission. Perhaps the survivors of Chasm remembered when men had cared about men and risked their own lives to save others. At least, they knew about those times. He sat down at the ping console, dizzy from lack of sleep, lack of food, terror, empathetic agony, rounding up pings, bringing pings home, sending pings out, one after another, to the little trading posts, to demon haunts, to the location Raymond had thought Chasm itself would probably be found. Hundreds of pings. Not all functioning, of course. Hard to tell how many there were in full working order.

Then another dose of opiates for everyone, so he could sleep for a while. Sleep, which he did, longer and sounder than he would have thought possible, only to wake at last to the rumble of machinery . . .

He half fell over himself getting to the elevator, and it was already on the way down. The doors opened and the ones inside cleared the stone themselves, coming out to find him there, crouched against the wall, fearing what he might have summoned.

"Jackson," said one of them: glittering, featureless, uninflected, robotic. "Where are the injured people you pinged us about?"

He pointed, they moved. More of them arrived. There was confusion. Jackson was ignored, mostly, though they finally seized him up and dragged him into the elevator, and once above ground, into a vehicle that was going to Chasm. Someone inside it spoke to Chasm on a radio. It was a cargo vehicle that had been fitted up to take wounded, for the survivors were on stretchers suspended on either side, three stretchers long, three stretchers high. Eighteen plus Jackson. Two white-clad technicians sat toward the front of the cargo space, separated from the drivers by a transparent shield.

"Can you help them?" Jackson asked, indicating the drugged bodies.

"Yes," said a technician, indifferently.

"Prostheses, I suppose," Jackson said, reaching for the word, not one he'd used recently. Not for . . . some hundreds of years.

"You might say that," said the other man. "They'll be fully mobile."

"Pity we couldn't have saved the severed limbs," Jackson murmured, almost to himself, thinking about it for the first time. "Back in the twenty-first, we used to be able to reattach them."

"Not needed," said the first man. "Hiram, there. The one who's driving. He lost most of his body."

Jackson looked at the shiny, robotic figure maneuvering the vehicle down the mountain road. "Most of his body?"

"That's one way to say it," said the other man. "Another way would be to say he lost everything but his head. All of yours still have their heads, so it's no problem."

Near the chopped off wings of the gigantic fly, they rehitched the wagon and resaddled the horses. Michael insisted on leading them on foot, just to be sure there were no pits or ditches that could wreck either horses or wagon. The prairie went on and on, dotted with scrubby bushes here and there, the only trees found in the occasional swales where rain gathered.

When Michael was tired, Arnole took his place, moving with an easy stride, obviously a man accustomed to covering long distances. Near dawn, the doctor took his turn, with much the same air of easy competence. They came to a long rise, a ridge extending north and south as far as they could see. Over the top was a trough, and beyond that another rise, and another trough, over and over and over again.

When the sun rose, they saw a growth of small bushes and cattails in one of the troughs. They dug a seepage hole from which the horses could drink and the water barrel could be refilled. While Dismé plodded up the rise on the far side, the others added a few dry branches to the store under the wagon, picked up along the way.

Michael said, "Now that we have light we'll be able to make better time, though we should let the horses rest before starting again."

"Starting for where?" cried Dismé, from the top of the rise, where she stood, staring to the west. "I think we're there."

The others went to join her. There were several more and lower ridges, and beyond them only a flat and featureless plain with, at the far side of it, a wall. It stretched the entire distance between low hills to north and south, and it had a huge, open gate at its center. Through the glasses, they could see two figures, white as snow, standing inside the gate.

"Like the sentries in the maze at Caigo Faience," said Dismé.

"Let's see," said the doctor, firmly. "It can't be more than an hour away."

They rode for an hour, but the wall was no nearer. Another hour, and the wall seemed some taller, but was still a great distance. The doctor cursed; Arnole sat up straight on the wagon seat; Bobly and Bab fixed their eyes on the goal ahead, and they went on. When the sun was straight up in the sky, they had crossed the last ridge and could see that the wall was not a low wall but very high indeed.

They let the horses rest, then began again. When evening arrived, they pulled up between the open gates. On either side the walls loomed like precipices. The two gigantic figures that stood inside were white-robed angels lifting their great stone hands to the sky and between them, in the space between the walls, was a wide, level-floored canyon, the wall tops so high above that a mere slit of sky showed between them. It took some time even to drive past the thickness of the walls, and when they came to the end of them, they were confronted with another such wall, perhaps a hundred yards away, stretching endlessly to either side, with other statues set in huge recesses, the flat land between the walls carpeted with grass. Dismé laughed.

"This is funny?" whispered Michael.

"This is the maze of Caigo Faience," she said. "More or less. Though, seeing the size of it, I suppose one would have to say more. Either way will get us there, but decisions can come later. Night draws on, the army will move in it, but if we work our way inside a little, they won't find us."

"Dezmai says that?"

"No. I say that. I'm speaking from experience."

They turned to the right and rode to the nearest opening in the wall. Dismé spent some time consulting the huge figure beside this gate, then remounted and gestured them forward.

"They'll be able to follow our tracks," complained Bobly.

"No tracks," said Dismé. "We have a following wind. The maze at Caigo Faience had a following wind too."

They turned to look behind them, seeing the little whirlwind that came after them, stirring the dust, straightening the grasses, erasing their passing.

"This one," Dismé said, when they came to the second gate. "Inside and to the left."

"Listen," said the doctor.

They stopped. From a great distance came the sound of howling, like an enormous beast.

Arnole said, "The ogre. Will it be able to scent us?"

Dismé shook her head. "Actually, it's nowhere near here. The maze tunnels sound from outside. If it should come inside, the following wind will carry our scent past each turning and on to another gate."

"How do you know that?" asked Nell.

"I just know," she replied.

By the time they had made two more turns, it was getting too dark to see their way.

"Here," said Dismé, indicating the nearest statue, set in a half-domed recess the size of an apse in some mighty, pre-Happening cathedral. "Let's park the wagon here and get behind and under the statue. We'll be out of the weather, if any. The horses can graze in the open. The grass is low, but plentiful."

"And Gowl's creature can't find us here?"

"I think not," said Dismé. "We were told to come here. Something here is awaiting our arrival. Seeing the place, I don't think Gowl or the thing that runs him can do anything at all to prevent our meeting it."

They went behind the giant statue and made camp between its heels and under the hem of its long robe, a cave into which they settled with sighs of exhaustion.

"Fire?" asked Arnole.

Dismé shrugged. "If we put it well under the statue, I doubt it can be seen. I, for one, would relish something hot."

The others felt the same, and the fire was lit, the smoke rising up inside the stone robes of the mighty figure and seeping upward through invisible channels to emerge far above them. They brought their blankets from the wagon and huddled near the blaze. From far, far away they heard a great cacophony of roaring, yelling, and screaming. Dismé turned, listening to the dobsi.

"That's Gowl," she murmured. "One of the demon spies is lying hidden in one of the army's supply wagons, and he's sending information my dobsi can pick up. The ogre's there, along with some new horror. Whatever the new thing is, it's eating soldiers. That's what the yelling is about. Gowl's given up trying to find victims, so he's letting it eat his army."

"He's still far away," said Nell, in a voice of chilly certainty. "They haven't even seen this place yet."

"Given the size of these walls, how long will it take us to get . . . where? To the center?" Bab asked, shaking his head.

"It's not far," said Dismé. "Not if you know the way."

"And you do?"

"The statues point the way. You just have to read them. The Great Maze at Faience was the same."

When the fire burned down, they curled into their blankets and slept. They were in an east-west aisle, which let the morning light in to wake them. They heated water for tea and to wash sleep from their faces. During the night, a copse of trees had grown up in front of the statue, surrounding the horses. There were no horse droppings on the ground.

"It's meant as a latrine," said the doctor. "Whoever lives here doesn't want us fouling up the place."

When they left, shortly thereafter, they looked back to see the trees disappearing into the earth, leaving only the grassy expanse that had been there before, utterly unmarred.

Dismé guided them throughout the morning. The walls grew shorter as they went, admitting the slanting rays of the sun. By noon, she said they were only a turn from the center of the maze, so they kept on, coming at last into a square enclosure. The floor was paved in marble set in eye-bending patterns. It was centered upon a staircase leading down. There was also a black figure upon a plinth. Dismé went to it at once, for it was much like the figure in the maze at Caigo Faience. This one pointed inexorably downward.

"Let's have lunch," she said. "We have to go down. The horses and wagon will have to stay here."

"There's nothing for them to eat here," Michael objected.

"We can leave them in the grassy aisle," Dismé said. "Water them well before we go."

"What about the stone?" asked Arnole, again.

Dismé shook her head. "We can't take it with us, Arnole. We leave it here. Either someone will come along and find it, or we'll find someone and bring them here."

"I brought three stones," he said stubbornly. "Evidently so much was intended. I don't want to leave one of them here for any part of that army to capture while we are elsewhere. Let's at least get it out of the wagon and hide it."

"We can try," said Michael. "The statues in these lanes

aren't as huge as the one we slept under last night, but there's still room behind them to hide the stone."

Dismé waited for objections but heard none. She shrugged. "Drive the wagon to the nearest niche, and we'll see if we can move it, then."

They did so, retracing their way, though not far. The statue in the nearest recess was leaning on a sword looking rather pensive, which meant, Dismé said, that the goal had been achieved. When they explored behind it, they found a sufficient space.

"It's heavy," said Arnole. "But all of us should be able to lift it."

They got into the wagon bed to do so. The wrapped stone was neither as wide nor as tall as the others they had seen. They were able to lift it and move it toward the rear of the wagon, where both Dismé and the doctor lost their grip at once, and the thing slid from their hands, landing right side up, with the sacking torn from one side of it.

"Why was this one wrapped up?" Bab asked. "None of the others were."

"Probably to make it easier to handle," said the doctor, examining his abraded hands with annoyance as he climbed down from the wagon. "It's the same as the others, except for that."

Bobly and Bab lifted the torn edge away from the stone and looked at it. "It got dirty," said Bab, as he and his sister reached out to dust off the splinters from the wagon bed.

The aisle erupted in two great fountains of fire, and giants stood at either side of the stone, growing taller with each spark. One great fur-clad figure carried an anvil on her shoulder. The other wore a leather apron and carried a hammer in his hand. The anvil was set down, the hammer fell upon it, the sound fled away, in one direction only, and in that direction, far from the place they stood, something happened. All of them perceived that a consequence had occurred. Their presence had been announced. Something had wakened to greet them.

When they blinked, the giants were gone. Only Bobly and

Bab stood where the stone had been, their faces blank with wonder.

Arnole heaved a deep breath. "Ialond and Aarond. I told you we shouldn't leave it here."

"Yes, Arnole," said Dismé. "And you were right, as always."

"My," said Bobly. "Oh, gracious, goodness me."

"One does hope so," said the doctor, thoughtfully. "Goodness being the operative word."

"I'm still the same size," said Bab, looking down at himself. "You'd think I could have kept a little of it."

Nell laid her hand on his shoulder. "Though I've known you only a little time, I think you've always been sizeable. It just doesn't show all the time."

The group returned to the center, each of them casting wondering glances at the little people until Bobly said, "Don't look at me like that. I don't feel any different. Except I know a lot of things I didn't know before, but even that is . . ."

"Remote," suggested Dismé. "It comes and goes."

"And is often unhelpful," said the doctor.

The little people nodded. Arnole cleared his throat and said, "We have somewhere to go, don't we?"

"How far?" asked the doctor.

Dismé shook her head. "From here on it's uncharted country. I know what's under the maze at Faience, but I don't know what underlies this one. We'll have to go down there and see."

Leaving the wagon and horses behind, they went down into darkness, lit only by the two wagon lanterns they had carried with them. Here and there, patches of fungus gleamed with phosphorescence that led them sometimes in narrow ways, sometimes in caverns that reverberated distantly like the footsteps of passing armies. Hours seemed to pass before Dismé stopped.

"Are we lost?" breathed Arnole.

"No," she said in a perplexed voice. "Just confused."

They had come to a hub from which tunnels radiated to

all sides. In addition, there was a hole before them into which a stair descended and another in the ceiling through which another stair rose. Dismé concentrated on the half dozen statues that were within sight. The way to the left was signalled, as well as the way to the right. The other ways were frowned upon with tight lips and closed eyes.

"Two ways," she murmured.

"Which?" asked Arnole.

"Either," said Dismé. "As you used to tell me, Arnole, there are more ways than one to reach the truth. We will go right."

They went to the right, past abysses and through more caverns, past tunnels that seemed to lead upward toward faint light, in every case forbidden by the tutelary images that stood at their entrances, coming at last to a circular tunnel that turned and turned leftward, always leftward, always downward, like a corkscrew descending, with no way out until they came to a flat dead end.

"Well, that was interesting," said Michael. "Now what?"

"Shhh," said Dismé, raising the lantern and making a circuit of the space they were in. At one side a figure was carved into the dark stone of the wall, a figure with its arms flung up, eyes wide open, mouth either singing or laughing. At its feet lay a fragment of color, and Dismé knelt to pick it up. She showed it to them: the wing feather of a mountain bluebird.

"Here," she said. "I gave one of these to the image in the maze at Faience. This is the place."

"There's no way," said Michael, taking the lantern and shining it on the sides of the statue. Nell ran her hands across it, as did Dismé.

"Put the lantern closer," said Dismé, looking into the stone. "There are lights in this stone. Like the other stones . . ."

They looked at one another, then at Michael, who shook his head. "I don't think so." Then, directly to Dismé. "I don't want to be . . ."

"Nor did any of us," said Dismé in a sorrowful voice. Oh, she had not wanted Michael to be her brother. "If it isn't meant for you . . ." She shut her eyes, not wanting to see.

He took a deep breath and laid his hands upon it. The stone did not emit light, but Michael did. He shone like a faceted gem, brilliance darting away from him to light the space in which they stood. He looked at Dismé's sorrowing face and smiled, then he laughed, and laughed again, every gust of laughter thinning the stone before him, light shining through, then brighter and more until brilliance gleamed through the pane of thin ice that stood between them and what lay beyond.

"I am Jiralk," said Michael. "Jiralk the Joyous," and he struck the remaining ice into shards.

The scent of a garden flowed around them.

"Sandalwood and roses," Nell murmured, as though entranced. "A coral-pink smell . . ."

They stepped through into a garden beneath a sky of shifting color, as though they looked upward through an opal sea. The land was cupped; the horizon hung above them. Exotic trees surrounded them, strange flowers and stretches of green led their eyes to a vision of upturned oceans and far mountains that bowed toward them. Behind them was the door they had come through, an upright plane of darkness, and upon a pedestal before them sat a being, multi-armed, multi-winged, shape-shifting, light-reflecting, dark as space is dark, glistening with galaxies.

"You were in the maze at Caigo Faience," Dismé murmured.

A moment's silence, then the distant reply.

"I have been near each of you to give you birthing gifts. To Dismé I gave a garden; to Arnole, old manuscripts; to Camwar, a craftsman's skill; to Jens Ladislav, medical books; to Michael, the grace and joy of horses. And to Abobalee and Ababidio, years of learning to be small without letting it matter, to be large without letting it show."

Nell heaved an aching sigh. "You called me, and I'm here. These are the ones we believe are my children."

The voice came nearer. "I sought you out as suitable for my purpose, Nell Latimer, an ironic choice, knowing who your husband was, but a pleasant break from the usual melo-drama of mid-level planets. These *are* your children, even those older than you are now, and there are still others whom you have not met."

Dismé started to cry, "Why Michael . . ." but instead bit her cheek to keep from whining at the unfairness of learning to care for someone she was not allowed to love! She breathed deeply and demanded, "Who are you? Why are you here?"

The voice said quietly, "Nell knows. She smelled the prayer as I did, the lush purple waves of it, inviting me . . ."

"But that was because of the Happening!" cried Nell.

"I was on my way long before that, Nell Latimer. Hu-mans are unique in holding their gods so cheap they peck at them like pigeons, constantly intruding upon them with prayer! Prayer from all sides of every conflict, prayer be-fore each contest, during every issue. Private prayer, pub-lic prayer, shepherded prayer baa-ed from congregation, sports prayer before games, prayer parroted and prayer spontaneous, endless instructions to god, endless . . . plockutta.

" 'Intercede for me and solve my problems; give me; grant us; hear the words I'm saying; suspend the laws of na-ture in this instance; cure her; save him; don't let them; lis-ten to me; do this! ' " The Visitor sighed. "Beneath it, one hears devils' laughter."

Nell looked up, saying sharply, "Devils?"

"The voice was slightly louder, slightly warmer, as though it had come from a distance and was now beside them. "Each race creates its own devils. You had so many that they specialized. Devils of racial hatred, devils of greed and violence. Devils who killed their own people in orgies of blood. Devils who bombed clinics, devils who bombed school buses, devils who bombed other devils. I got to know every one of them by name. As soon as I arrived, I sent my monsters out to kill them all. They had tarnished my reputa-tion, and though I have lavished much care on mankind, vengeance is mine."

The being shifted, only slightly, as though to take a more comfortable position as the doctor asked, "What are you?"

"This place is a godland, you may call me god. Small g, for I am not proud. We are a race evolving in this Creation to serve the Maker of it. We act as temporary deities during the childhood of individual peoples and planets. I was the midwife who brought forth this world, who stirred the primordial ooze, and noted the life that crawled up from the sea. Our race is not unlike yours, but I am very old, and you are still very young.

"We come and go. I came to teach your people language. I raised up oracles, whispered to soothsayers, wove bright visions for sorcerers, and spoke marvels to your alchemists. I came again to raise up prophets in the Real One's name: Bruno, Galileo, Newton, Fermi . . ."

The doctor interrupted, "The Real One? Who?"

"The Being whom I worship. The Ultimate who stands apart from time. The Deity some men think they are addressing when they pray with words. The Real One doesn't even perceive words. If IT did, imagine what IT would have to listen to! The Real One sees only the pattern of *what is*, where it begins and where it comes to rest. The only prayer IT perceives is action."

"I don't understand that," said Nell, stubbornly.

"An example from your old world, Nell. A child being shot and everyone weeping. What does the Real One see? IT sees the maker and making of a device that kills, the device itself, the selling of the device that kills, the buying of the device that kills, the placement of it near the child, the occurrence, the death. Only actions enter the pattern the Real One sees. *What is. What was done.* IT perceives neither intentions nor remorse."

Nell said angrily, "What do you mean, what is?"

The small god seemed to shift impatiently on its pedestal, "*What is, is!* Reality. Nature. The laws of a Universe that contains all things. Expansion and contraction, matter and anti-matter, light and dark, joy and sorrow, ecstacy and horror, supernovas and black holes, euphoria and pain, governing and politics, life and death. All the goads and all the stumbling blocks that force intelligence to grow by conquering."

"Conquering what?" asked Arnole, his hand on Nell's arm.

"Anything. Stink, or disease, or hatred. Pain, bugs, or brambles. The shortness of life or the frailty of age."

"Why not just leave those things out?" Dismé protested.

"It's been tried. If you give a being only *feelgood-joy-life,* nothing happens. Dinosaurs lived here for hundreds of millions of years in *feelgood-joy-life,* and at the end of it they had conquered nothing. Sixty-five million years ago, I judged they'd had long enough, so I brought an asteroid to start things over, just as I have done this time."

A long silence. Then Arnole said, "*You* did that?"

"It's part of what we're for. That asteroid yielded several intelligent races. Three of them, including yours, are still living here. Now if any one of the three gets to the point of honoring the Real One, I can pack up my gear and go home."

"But we got to that point," cried Nell. "Many of us worshipped . . . truth! And still you came!"

The voice was remote once more. "There weren't that many of you, Nell. Even when you went to the moon, you didn't go in search of truth. Oh, you *said* it was to learn about the universe, but you really went because you were playing a dominance game with another country. Once the other side no longer played the game, you only pretended to go on while actually you started the long slide back into magic and miracles."

Nell said angrily, "Miracles are religion!"

"It doesn't matter what name you call it," said the small god. "Magic or miracle, sorcery or religion, it's all the same."

"We didn't slide into magic," Nell argued. "I mean, yes, some did, my own husband did, but the rest of us . . ."

"Aside from earning their livings, what did your people do, mostly? Games. Sports. Casinos. Loud machines that went fast. Shopping. Lawsuits blaming others for whatever went wrong. What did they believe in? Conspiracy theories. Racial superiority. Heroes with superpowers. Faith healers. God-loves-you religions. State-supported lotteries. All that enormous energy expended to conquer nothing at all, stadia full of people watching no conquering going on. For every scientist or person in government who really tried to conquer, there were a thousand people buying lottery tickets, drinking beer, watching football, and growing old."

Nell objected, "We would have outgrown that . . ."

The voice grew more conversational. "I think not. Once a race has technology, life is so much easier that conquering loses its urgency. I blame myself for leaving when I did. I could have delayed the acquisition of technology until you had killed your devils. Technology concurrent with devil worship never works out well."

"Devil worship?" said Arnole, in a skeptical voice.

"Intelligent races always worship something. It's a kind of yearning that intellect has, to see and worship the eventual goal. It may not always go after the truth, but it always wants a story. People start out with magic, and turn that into religion, and then, if they don't go on to worship the Real One, they settle for a temporary godlet like me, or for any one of a thousand convenient devils. You can tell which by the actions. Those who worship the Real One are problem-solvers. They experiment and pay attention to the result in order to see what's good, what's bad. They work to give every person and creature the good stuff, variety, food, space, cleanliness; and they do it because sane, healthy creatures exposed to complex environments conquer better! They work to eliminate the bad stuff like pollution, extinctions, overpopulation, weapons, because sick starving creatures in impoverished and threatened environments don't conquer at all. Did your race do that? It did not, so you weren't worshipping the Real One, and you certainly weren't worshipping me because I hadn't returned yet.

"Your leaders worshipped the greed devil when they sold their votes and influence to spread bad stuff; they worshipped the power devil when they valued votes over the health of the planet; they made a pretence of mercy and justice by advocating human rights while they sucked up to dominance devils whose law was torture and whose rule was the enslavement of women."

They felt the being's sorrow, as it said:

"There was no cure for it. You were too many, too set in your ways, so . . . it was time to start over. Which is what I've been doing this millennium. There is no more oil for dominance devils to use as a weapon. I've put it out of reach. I've reduced the human occupied land area by two thirds, cutting your space but giving more room to the other intelligent races. One aquatic, one arboreal, as it happens. Almost all humans live on this one continent, now, and they are still in the magic-cum-religion stage that requires a certain level of godhood. Bastion worships the Rebel Angels. Chasm worships itself, so far as I can make out. New Chicago and New Kansas have dictators who are becoming icons. Each of the Sierra Isles has its own tutelary deity, as does Everday. One of your first tasks will be to schedule godhood contests between me and the local deity in each place."

"That's absurd," said Arnole.

"Not at all. There's a human tradition of god competitions. Moses's god against Pharaoh's gods, for example. I included descriptions of god competitions in several holy books from two to six millennia ago. At any rate, I will win, and I will become deity of all the humans, temporarily one hopes.

"Before we get to that, however, there's a devil on his way here who wants all of us dead, particularly me. Gohdan Gone, who was once called Baal, was driven out of the middle east millennia ago. Part of him went to Central America, where the Aztecs called him Huitzilopochtli, and part went to the Iroquois in North America, to be fattened in both places by torture and cannibalism, until they were conquered by other men with subtler devils. Gone is still an unsubtle pain drinker, but he's had a long time to ramify, and you'll need to get rid of him quickly, before he changes into something worse . . ."

"We don't know how to do that!" cried Dismé.

"That's why we're bringing him here," the small god said patiently. "So you can learn how. His arrival here is not an accident, it was planned to give you the practice!

"Once he's dead, you'll need to clean out Bastion. You'll need Tamlar and Hussara to help you do that. Possibly Volian and Wogalkish as well. Be sure you get down to the bottom of the caverns where the devil had its roots. When Bastion is clean, I'd recommend that you settle there. It's centrally located, it will hold a good number of our recruits, and since all of you but Tamlar are basically human, you'll need a humanish place to live and study and enjoy your lives."

"Not much of that left to enjoy," said Arnole, wearily.

The small god laughed. "You all have a very long lifetime left, if you don't get killed. Even those of you who are eightyish have at least that long to live again. My contract with you is a fair one. I give you very long life and good assistants. You give me your best effort to start this world over. If I don't succeed this time, my superiors will replace me, and I don't want to fail."

"As everybody's god, what will you do?" the doctor demanded.

"You mean immediately?" asked the small god. "I will raise up prophets to make conflicting pronouncements that will inevitably be garbled in transcription, resulting in mutually exclusive definitions of orthodoxy from which the open-minded will flee in dismay. As they flee, I expect you to identify them and move them to Bastion."

"Recruits?" asked the doctor, raising his eyebrows.

"Exactly. Also, I will be capricious. I'll reward and punish arbitrarily. I'll peek through bedroom windows and admonish what I see there, sometimes one thing, sometimes the opposite. I will have purposes men know nothing of, and when men begin to catch on to them, I will change them. This will convince some of your people that I am unreliable."

"We bring those people to Bastion also?" Michael grinned.

"Precisely. Occasionally, I will do a conspicuous miracle to save one dying child while a thousand children starve elsewhere. This will convince sensible people I am perverse, and they will curse my name. Be sure to recruit those who do, they'll be invaluable. Only by repudiating both devils and small gods will they ever know the Real One.

"I will be a sham, but not a snob. I will let every man, woman, or child, no matter how greedy or wicked, claim to have a personal relationship with me. In other words, I will be as arbitrary, inconsistent, ignorant, pushy, and common as humans are, and what more have they ever wanted in a god?"

"The truth!" cried the doctor and Arnole, simultaneously.

All of them smiled, unable to stop smiling as they felt the being before them laughing. "Oh, tush, they never wanted anything of the kind. Creation has the truth written all over it—the age of the universe, the history of the world—but nine-tenths of mankind either don't know it or think it's a sham, because it isn't what their book or their prophet says, and it isn't cozy or manipulable enough."

"My people wanted truth," said Nell, stiffly. "My friends."

"They were a minority. Not many years before the Happening, one of your country's largest religious bodies officially declared that their book was holier than their God, thus simultaneously and corporately breaking several commandments of their own religion, particularly the first one. Of course they liked the book better! It was full of magic and contradictions that they could quote to reinforce their bigoted and hateful opinions, as I well know, for I chose many parts of it from among the scrolls and epistles that were lying around in caves here and there. They're correct that a god picked out the material; they just have the wrong god doing it.

"The sooner we can separate salvageable skeptics from self-righteous absolutists, the sooner we can move along. Game shows where people betray one another to one group, brain busting challenges to the other. You'll fight the devils and I'll provide distractions, and within a few generations, we'll have them all sorted out."

"And we're to be killers?" asked Arnole, sadly.

The voice became gentle. "Only of ignorance, Bertral. You will divide the sheep from the goats and you will encourage the one and shepherd the other. You always had a leaning that way. Each of you will find the fight that suits yourself and your being. You will triumph, suffer, weep, rejoice, possibly die . . . If you die, another will rise up in your name, if you don't die, you'll live an extremely long life. You are *my* angels, for whom an almost heaven waits in Udarsland, with Skulda and Caigo Faience. Your work will be long, however, long and hard before you may rest in it."

The being turned on her plinth and stretched many wings, the face appearing darkly, as through veils, each of them seeing a different image. Multiple arms beckoned and a man came toward them out of the gardens, a simple, brownish man dressed in a simple, brownish robe. He wore a leather apron, carried a drawknife and bowsaw and bore a great axe on his back.

"This is your son and brother, Camwar," she said. "Camwar has spent some years preparing for you. Also awaiting you is Tamlar, the only one of you without human parents, a being of another star, sister of those beings who are guiding each of you. I asked for their help, for this is my last chance with Earth."

The space began to move around them as the being on her plinth receded. The splintered world hurtled toward them as though they were in a kaleidoscope, images whirling to join, spinning outward to disintegrate, vortices of jagged light, horizons of endless time, pinwheels of splendor that rushed at them and receded through which they heard the small god cry, "You will not see me soon again. It is not fitting that gods, however small, consort casually with their servants. I leave you as Guardians for all that live on this world."

When the dazzlement stopped, they were standing outside the gates of the great maze, their wagon and horses beside them.

Michael cried, "Where's Dismé?"

They looked about, and then, suddenly Dismé was there, among them, staring dazedly outward, where their sister Guardian burned in the evening air.

"Greetings," Tamlar said, with a fiery grin.

On the other side stood Camwar, beckoning them to follow him, and as they turned, the walls disappeared without a sound. Far to the east, over one of the long north-south ridges came the first rank of the monster host, bloody banners waving.

✦ 45

not in conclusion

As he followed Camwar up the slope, Arnole had time for analysis.

"It is interesting," he said to himself, "that this small god implied devils were made of ignorance, for I have always believed this to be true. Ignorance perpetuates itself just as knowledge does. Men write false documents, they preach false doctrine, and those evil beliefs survive to inspire wickedness in later generations. They are like the spells woven by wizards, lying in wait for the credulous to find them and use them. Conversely, some men write and teach the truth, only to be declared heretic by the wicked. In such cases, evil has the advantage, for it will do anything to suppress truth, but the good man limits what he will do to suppress falsehood.

"One might almost make a rule of it: 'Whoever declares another heretic is himself a devil. Whoever places a relic or artifact above justice, kindness, mercy, or truth is himself a devil and the thing elevated is a work of evil magic.'

"Magic, yes! How interesting that the small god should describe magic as a normal stage of development. I have seen that, too, though most magic is only pretence or hope under another name. What I do not understand about magic today is where the power comes from? Gohdan Gone does have power! He raises actual monsters who actually kill. Is power given him by those who follow him? Do followers supply the evil their devils use?

"I am relieved to know there are many ways to wage this battle. I would be lost on the battlefield if that field were only for slaughter. But if that field were also for teaching, and preaching, and evangelizing . . ."

Dismé, behind him, was thinking. "She kept me back for a moment to tell me. I'm the only one she told. I can tell Michael or keep it to myself. How strange. One would think she would have told all of us, but she didn't. There's no time to sort it out now. No time to do anything now except . . .

"There they are, coming over the ridge! That horde coming at me is what Arnole meant long ago when he told me Rashel was going somewhere I didn't want to go. She is Regimic to her eyeballs, and I'll wager she's inside this battle somehow! We, on the other hand, have been given permission to look for truth! Which Jens and Michael and Arnole have always done, and I suppose Nell, as well. We are to find truth and keep ourselves out of the devil's hands and sort out the people . . .

"If we pick only those who flee from falsity, does that include all the good ones? The woman who ran the sweet-shop in Hold, she was a good woman, but she worshipped Gowl. She called him 'My general,' and she had his picture on her wall. If I had to sort her out, where would I put her? Should I try to make her more like us or leave her as she is? Can virtual innocence live at the borders of evil? Live off it, without becoming it? On the other hand, not all who worship the truth will have the kind of minds who can find it. Should they be prevented from supporting those who can? Even those who conquer ignorance will need grocers and tailors and men to build their houses . . ."

"Surely it would not really stop ignorance to let ignorance keep a separated half of us? Though, come to think of it, Arnole told me when creatures evolve, the change starts with only a few of them, maybe only one. The change spreads from that small start, and all the others of that one's kind stay as they were while the evolved progeny move on.

Is this to be like that? Will our progeny live on, while everyone else stays behind and does what? Die away?

"There are imperfections in this task. Still, if I must choose, I choose to believe in the side I am standing with. If only the Real One is perfect, then small gods no doubt have imperfections, as we do. I was not like those in Bastion. Arnole wasn't, nor the doctor, nor Michael, and it wasn't simply because we had one mother among us. We may well find others of our persuasion, elsewhere in the world, who worship the Real One, who always have.

"For this moment, I choose to believe and I choose, oh, I choose not to think of Michael just now. What she said to me! And I haven't even time to think about it . . ."

Michael was thinking, "She's beautiful. I've always thought she was beautiful, but she's become more so, somehow. There she goes, look at her, striding along as though it were a summer day in the garden at Faience, not facing horrid enemies on the plains of this strange little world of ours. As soon as we have conquered this mob of miscreants, which we can do merely by laughing them to death, if it comes to that, I'm going to tell her . . . What? Oh, what are you going to tell her, Michael? Jiralk? Tell her she's my sister, but I love her as more than a sister? Does her being my sister really matter . . ."

And Nell thought, "This is a strange dream I am having. When I wake, I usually dream about Jerry and the children and the Happening. Where did this detailed strangeness come from? It hangs together so well, one would almost think it was scripted just for me. Well, suppose I were actually here, in this predicament, what would I do? I would certainly depend upon Elnith to do the necessary quashing. It's obvious one old woman—even one with a few well meaning assistants—isn't going to get far without supernatural help, though the being seemed to say our inhabitants aren't really supernatural . . ."

And the doctor thought, "I knew it. I've known it all along. He's in love with her. And maybe she with him. Which is only right and proper, I suppose, given their ages and proximity. Why didn't I have the sense to stay out of it, not that anyone's going to be able to stay out of it, and why must I go on feeling! Our angelic sides are long on ability but short on emotion, while the small god seems to wallow in feelings almost as much as we do. All I've done is drag Dismé into the middle of it. If that army wins, chances are everyone in the world will be in the middle of it, we'll all be devils-food and I suppose that godlet will chuckle over it . . .

"No. She will not. I heard what she meant when she said this was her last chance to make this world work. Dividing the population sounds like desperation, but perhaps, with our help, there's some better way we can make it work . . ."

He stopped, just short of the crest of the hill and tugged his glasses from their pouch. "What are we up against? Gowl on a white horse. At least the horse was white, when they started, as Gowl was himself. Look at the mess you've made of yourself, General. Spattered and befouled that way. Why did I keep you alive, Gowl. Time after time, you infected or dissipated yourself to the edge of death and I brought you back. Should I ride to you now and ask you to listen to reason, dripping with blood as you are, and with that monster leading you. I think not. No, Gowl. I don't know the end of this, but it is sure you will find an end in it very soon, one way or another."

Bobly and Bab thought, "Oh, botheration and obfuscation, we hope to heaven Ialond and Aarond are as big and powerful as they seemed to be, for we're going to need every hammer blow, every anvil strike. Heavens to Betsy, isn't this an excitement!"

And Camwar thought, "Now, at last, at the top of this rise, no more work, no more waiting, at last . . ."

And Tamlar thought, "Burn, burn, burn, burn, burn . . ."

They topped the rise and found themselves on the edge of an eastern facing butte, the rock and clay beneath them falling sheer to the level prairie, several stories down. In front of them, level with the ground and extending all the way to the prairie below, was a ship, or so the doctor thought at first. But then, he had seen pictures of ships and they weren't shaped like that. So very up and down. So very round. With great metal rings around to hold the . . . well, they were shaped like barrel staves . . .

"A barrel," said Dismé, flatly.

"It will be a drum," said Camwar quietly, though with considerable pride. "As soon as we have a skin to stretch across it. Up here," and he started across a gangplank that led from the butte to the upper edge of the huge construction. The barrel was not as tall as the fortress walls of Godland, but it was very tall for a drum, enough that Nell and Arnole were dizzied by the height. Dismé sauntered after Camwar, and the others after her, except for Tamlar who remained on the butte, her eyes fixed on the horde that was still pouring toward them over a far rise, its vanguard momentarily hidden in the trough between the ridges.

Those on the drum regarded the great width and thickness of the staves with awe, for each of them must have been cut from a single, very old and large tree. The great hoops that bound the barrel were riveted with bronze. The top edge was finished with a circular wooden rim wide enough to walk or work upon. Hooked to this rim were thick leather laces that dropped down the outside to run through blocks fixed halfway down the barrel, then came back up to thread through others just beneath the rim, before dropping to the ground, where each lace went through a great eye bolt.

"To tighten the drumhead," Camwar said, following her eyes. "When we have skinned it from its owner."

"Why a drum?" asked Dismé.

"I am told that Dezmai knows," said Camwar, smiling at her with unaccountable fondness. "Dezmai knows very well."

Dismé regarded the great open vat with wonder. It could hold a small village, complete with bell tower. What sound this thing would make when it could be drummed upon!

"What animal carries a skin large enough to . . ." the doctor started to ask, stopping as his eyes were caught by the horrid leader of the approaching horde, cresting a nearer ridge. The ogre. More colossal than ever.

"There," pointed Camwar. "It was built to fit the hide of that beast."

"How can we kill it?" the doctor whispered.

"You could starve it," called Tamlar from behind them. "If it gets no blood, it will die. Make it pursue and pursue, but don't let it catch you."

"We can't outrun it," said Dismé. "Michael's the swiftest of us, and even he . . ."

"The race is not to the swift," laughed Michael. "Haven't you heard that? We have horses. And demons."

"Demons?" Nell turned toward him. "What about demons?"

He shook Dismé by the shoulders. "Dismé, you have a dobsi. By this time, the demons know everything about our last day, or hour, or however long it's been. They've been watching us. Ask for help, Dismé! Everyone, look at Dismé and ask for help!"

She saw all their faces, the open mouths, heard the screamed, uttered, muttered command. Help. And how could the demons help?

"They'd better hurry," she said. "That army is getting a lot closer."

Michael was already across the gangway and running down the sloping side of the butte toward the horses. Within moments he had mounted the swiftest of the riding horses and was off toward the horde. Even from this distance, they could hear shouted commands and the ogre's roar.

Nell grimaced in anger, her arms rising, every atom of her being focused on that distant horde as Elnith took her. Her hands came up. Her lips formed one silent word. A wave went from Elnith's hands outward, visible in the air as it went, past Michael, past the ridges of earth between them and the horde, and across the horde itself.

Silence. No more roars, no more commands, no more trumpet sounds. The horde kept coming, but it began to fray at the edges as its parts turned questioningly to those behind. Some stopped moving, shaking their heads. Others turned back only to be knocked down by those behind, who then stumbled and fell to make an obstacle for others in their turn. By the time the ogre's head appeared over the nearest ridge, Michael was halfway there.

Elnith stood tall upon the butte, robed in green and gold, eyes fixed on Michael, hands outstretched to hold fast the silence that wrapped the world. Michael and the horse had become something other than Michael and the horse. They too, were larger than life, brighter than life. They glowed and sparkled. The horse's golden hooves gamboled upon the grasses. Michael become Jiralk stood in his stirrups and laughed in the face of the monster. The ogre gaped wide to utter a soundless roar as it plunged down the slope toward the horse, which spun on its hind legs and came galloping back the way it had come. Eyes fixed on the retreating horse and rider, the ogre pounded after it.

"No time to starve it," cried Bobly. "No time!"

She took the same route Michael had taken, Bab in close pursuit, short legs padding down the slope, growing longer, and longer yet as they neared the bottom of the butte and circled it to the rock strewn slope at the bottom of the great drum. Aarond's hair touched the rim of the drum, but Ialond was taller by a head. Aarond jerked a boulder loose from the butte face and heaved it atop another farther out on the flat. Ialond towered above it with his hammer over his shoulder, body twisted for a mighty swing. His body uncoiled, his hammer struck the stone, and it shot toward the ogre like a ball from a cannon. While it was still in the air, Aarond had set another stone ready.

The first stone struck the ogre on the shoulder. The arm on that side went limp, but in deadly silence the beast came on. The second stone struck it on the chest. Ribs shattered and jabbed through bloody flesh, sawing at it as the ogre moved, as it did, without even slowing. Michael was almost back to the other horses; the ogre was very near. Those on the butte top held their breaths. The third stone struck the beast full in the face, felling it. Aarond and Ialond ran toward the body, which was trying to rise, the earth shaking to their footfalls, Ialond with his hammer ready, glancing over his shoulder to see Camwar thundering behind him, almost as tall, his axe over his shoulder.

It took only one swing of that great axe to behead the creature. From the butte, Dismé watched unmoved as Camwar hewed the monster's thick hide from neck to groin and lopped the short legs and long arms, but she turned away when the skinning of the long, wide torso began, trying to reason her way past her revulsion at the thought of drumming upon that hide. She could not fathom what the drum was for. For herself, obviously! Was she not Dezmai of the Drums? But what good would drumming do? She stared at the great barrel Camwar had built. Each stave a whole tree. Felled. Cut. Shaped. Again and again. Then the monster staves fitted around that huge bottom, itself made from gigantic planks, pegged and glued together. The labor of years, and for what? Did Camwar himself know?

She looked up into the silence. The ogre's death had gone unnoticed by the army, for all that horde was entangled with itself, spilling into the trough of land between ridges, unable to hear commands or curses, screams or simple talk. Elnith kept her hands outstretched, her eyes fixed, as the men of Bastion screamed silently for help and struck out at their brethren in frustration.

Skinning the monster took some time, though there were three huge flensing knives busy at the process. When the hide was off, Ialond and Aarond set the ogre's head upright in a pit and laid the bloody hide over it, hair side down, tugging it to and fro as Camwar scraped it free of fat and flesh with the drawknife he carried. Though the three were still giants as they returned, even they staggered under the weight of the reeking bundle, half-carried, half-dragged to be draped over the huge drum. They pierced the edges of the hide with their knives and attached the laces. Even when the laces had been drawn tight by the three of them, the hide sagged wetly, stinking like a sewer.

Camwar summoned Tamlar with a gesture. She stepped to the edge of the butte and leapt upon the drum, fire blooming at her feet as she moved, flame darting from her hands as she gestured, here, there, charring bits of flesh, drying the hide, shrinking it, tighter and tighter. As she danced, the hide hummed and the laces stretched while the drum moaned as though it were a living thing. Camwar watched the great staves anxiously as they creaked under the pressure.

Michael, who had been watching from the foot of the hill, rode up to the place Jens and Dismé were standing, dismounted, put a hand on either side of Dismé's face and kissed her—a joyful rather than erotic greeting—then put his arm around her shoulder and looked across the low rise where the host struggled against itself.

At that moment, Elnith dropped her hands and Nell turned to them saying in a troubled voice, "The thing is with them."

Sound returned. They heard shouting from the army and a hideous roar from the same direction.

"That's it roaring," said Nell. "The devil from Bastion. The thing you called Gohdan Gone. It's got them organized again. It can speak directly to their minds, without speech."

In a moment they saw it, a netted filthiness, like a roiling skein of rotted sinew, coming over the nearest ridge, one only a few hundred yards away. Toothed tentacles lashed out from it, a slime trail followed it, a terrible shrieking and slobbering came with its movement.

"Look," said Arnole, gripping Dismé's arm. "Look at the cloud around it. Ouphs."

She had already noticed the vortex that whirled above the monster, already heard the thin screaming as the ouph cloud was drawn into it, feeding the monster with its pain. At last, she realized what the drum was for.

"Tell Elnith to put silence around the rest of you," she said to Arnole. "Tell her, quickly." And with that she leapt upon the rim of the drum, gesturing to Tamlar to leave it. The drum had been made for this, this one thing, this thing only. She should have known at once. She felt Dezmai pour into her, looked down at her elaborate robes, her long full sleeves, felt the tassels of the headdress tinkling by her ears. She looked back at Tamlar, who gave her a fiery grin from the lip of the butte. There had been sufficient time, just. The drum head was taut. Tamlar could do no more.

Arnole went to Elnith, grabbing Michael by the arm as he went. He gestured to Bobly and Bab to join them while Michael dragged Camwar and the doctor into the tight circle. Elnith gave Dezmai a long look and put her arms around the others as they bent their heads and covered their ears. Dezmai, towering above the drum, extended one foot and stamped with it.

The peal was greater than thunder. It resounded, again and again. It sped across the approaching host, across the plain, across the mountains beyond the plain as Dezmai counted the miles between. Before the sound died, she brought her foot down again, and again the thunder roared. Now she stepped back and knelt on the butte, leaning forward to drum with her hands:

BOOM! aTum/ BOOM! aTum/ BOOM! aTuma/ BOOM! Tum. And again. And again. Her eyes were fixed on the approaching thing that was Gohdan Gone, a vast ropeyness like graveyard roots that feed upon the dead, a stringy filthiness, dripping as it came, and above it the vortex of tortured ghosts whose everlasting sorrow kept it strong. The army fell before the sound, but Gohdan Gone was less susceptible.

He is not supernatural, Dismé assured herself, as Dezmai raised her hands again. Not supernatural, merely unnatural in this world, at this time.

BOOM! aTum/ BOOM! aTum/ BOOM! aTuma/ BOOM! Tum.

From far, far away in the east there came a piercing cry, a lance of sound, growing as it came toward her and arrowed past:

Thank . . . Blessing . . . Good child . . . all . . . all . . . all . . . rest . . . rest . . . now. Behind that first sound, a volley of others, whishing like arrows as they fled by.

And again, BOOM! aTum!

Last . . . last . . . go now . . . last . . .

Above the approaching filthiness, a clearing. The cloud of ouphs was thinning, fading . . .

BOOM! aTum!
Wait oh wait . . . coming now . . . all all all

The ouph cloud was fading, thinning, was no longer. The thing rolled toward them still, but smaller. And nearer yet, but smaller yet. And almost to the place they stood as it reared itself into a towering being still, with red, glowing eyes and a body made of ten thousand writhing serpents.

As though in response to this advance, a glittering bug came low across the grasses from the south. Unlike the monster fly, this one made the sound of an engine, a fluttering, whipping noise. It was followed by others that dipped into the grasses all around the loathsomeness and disgorged dozens of silvery metallic figures before rising to return the way they had come. Among the metal figures were two quite ordinary persons, except that they wore horns.

"Wolf," said the doctor, his distance glasses to his eyes. "He's coming this way. I don't know who the other one is. He's headed toward the army."

As the loathsomeness continued to advance, several of the small silver creatures surrounded it, and one of them attacked it at once, leaping in to cut and slash with its three-fingered hands, then retreat, then leap forward again, over and over, too quickly for the monster to react.

The thing that was Gohdan Gone turned, fixing its red eyes upon its attacker. "What are you?" he howled. "Where have you come from?"

"Me," cried the attacker, as it leaped and tore. "Nemesis of Gone. Me, killer of Gone. Me. Come for vengeance."

The monster howled, thrashed at her, threw his great weight atop her and buried her as the watchers gasped. In a moment they saw flickers of reflected light as those cutting hands emerged, the nemesis slicing its way up through the very body of the horror, chortling with each snick of its knife hand, "Me, Nemesis of Gone, gone, gone."

Wolf arrived at the bottom of the butte, where they had gathered to greet him.

"What are they?" cried the doctor, pointing out the silver

478 • Sheri S. Tepper

creatures, attacking Gohdan Gone, to others of them running toward the army.

"People you sent from Bastion to Chasm," said the demon. "All the maimed ones you've been sending. We're doing the same thing with the ruined people brought from the redoubt up there on the mountain."

"Inside those machines?"

"More than machines, Jens. Part flesh, part metal. New bodies to replace the ones that had been sacrificed. Most of them have a score to settle with Bastion. We believe they will manage by themselves, though if they need more help . . ."

"They may not need help," said Dismé, regarding the figures with strangely mixed emotions, half-relief, half-horror. "If that one kills the Hetman, perhaps the army will fall apart rather easily. Who is that?" She pointed at the silver figure that was still slicing its way through the already fragmented monster.

"That's the last body we received from Bastion," said Wolf. "When she was wakened in Chasm, she had no will of her own at all, but she was eager to be commanded."

"Who is she?" asked the doctor.

"We have no idea. The men who picked her up didn't know. As soon as we had her brain installed, even before the speech module was in, we told her to write answers. We asked who she was, and all she wrote was 'Nemesis of Gone.' We assumed she'd been maimed by whoever or whatever Gone was. Later we found out she'd been dumped on the street, picked up there and taken to the clinic in Hold—at your standing orders, doctor. You weren't there, but one of your students was, and since the clinic was out of whatever you usually use, he gave her a dose of something different as pain medication. Some kind of potion."

"Potion?" asked Bobly, eyes wide.

"Potion!" said the doctor, trying to remember where he had put the bottle he had taken from the fortress.

"Potion," replied Wolf. "Chasm found traces of very

strange stuff in her body, what was left of it, but they have no idea what it is."

"How did you find out all this?" cried the doctor.

"Backtracking. Chasm asked the demons that sent her. The demons found out which guards brought her to the disposal room. The guards told us about your student at the clinic, Old Ben. He's a mute, though I suppose you know that. He wrote saying he used the stuff by mistake, that it was entirely gone."

"There hasn't been time to do all that," cried Jens. "It's only been, what? Seven or eight days since we left Hold?"

Wolf said, "You were in that fortress place for four days. It's summerspan six, fourday, fourteen days since you left Hold."

"Four days in there?"

Dismé said, "Time is probably quite different in there and out here." She was staring toward the silver figures on the hillside, slashing and tearing at the enemy, seemingly impervious to sword or spear or arrow. On the far side of the ridge, they could make out many officers and men of the Regime who had turned their backs on the field and were fleeing the way they had come.

Dismé strode down the hill and forward to the place the silver figure still chopped at the remnants of Gohdan Gone. Only shreds lay upon the prairie, a puddled filthiness. When the silver thing saw Dismé, it crowed like a cock and came swiftly toward her, knife hands clicking, but Dismé roared at it, and it turned to run after the other silver warriors who were moving up the nearest rise. Dismé turned and trudged back up the slope to the drumhead where she struck the drum once more, just to be sure. The sound fled; only the echo sped in return. The ouphs were gone.

"What did Dezmai do with the drum?" asked Michael, from behind her.

"She broke the bottle walls," Dismé said. "All of them, I think. If any are left, in Bastion or elsewhere in the world where Gowl's missionaries have been making conversions, we will need to break those, too. Camwar's drum was made for that thing alone. Now we have only Gowl to deal with."

They spun around, their momentary relief ebbing as the army, diminished but still numerous, came over the last rise with the general at its head. They were confronted by the line of silver warriors. The demon who had come with Wolf was waiting to one side, and without a moment's hesitation, he went at a dead run directly into the army, past groping hands and gaped jaws to reach up and pull the general from his horse.

Atop that distant ridge, the general howled at his captor. "We have a treaty! Don't kill me. I can give you information. Don't . . ."

"Think, Gowl!" said the demon. "Don't you remember me?"

"Remember you? Why should I remember you?"

"You should remember the friends you betrayed, Gowl. Don't you remember little Sandbur Fortrees?"

Gowl did not. Gowl gazed into the eyes before him, searching, searching, coming at last to one, far back memory of a white horse carrying a man all in white and five boys hidden in the straw bales . . .

He had time to remember it fully while the demon holding him grew huge and tall, like a tree three thousand years in the growing. The general was carried high above the fray as Fortrees grew, mighty as a tower. The general could not fathom what was happening to him. Sandbur had been the orphan boy. Sandbur had been the little follower, the nothing. Sandbur? Come to this? What was this?

"I am Tchandbur for the Trees," the giant demon whispered. "One of the Guardians, Gowl. I was begot to be what I am. I was named to be what I am, chosen first and named first, and you were moved to call me by that name from the beginning, Gowl. You were a tool in god's hands. I was put under your tutelage to learn what you had to teach me, which was to be wary of men's friendship and their words. Are you going to apologize to me, Gowl?"

"Apologize?" Gowl howled. "For what? We went on an outing. You were caught, I wasn't. Why should I apologize . . ."

"Oh, Gowl. So old to be so much a boastful child still. What shall I do with you, Gowl?"

"Oh, Fortrees, Fortrees, just put me down, put me down . . ."

"Gladly," said the Guardian, doing so from a very great height, then placing his foot firmly on what he had dropped. He turned and trudged away to the south while the other Guardians watched, amazed.

"Who?" asked Bobly.

"Tchandbur," said Bertral disapprovingly, as he looked up from his book. "Not summoned here, not needed here, merely divagating on private business."

"Is that in the book?" whispered Dismé.

"It seems everything is in the book," said Bertral. "And it changes, day by day."

The squashing of the general signalled a widespread and disorderly retreat by the army, though the silver shapes still pursued.

"Thus endeth our war against Bastion?" whispered the doctor.

Dismé shook her head, saying sadly, "Thus endeth one battle. Only one. Think what the small god said, Brother Jens. There are many devils."

Gowl's horse and those of his slain officers were running free on the prairie. There was no sign of their riders.

The doctor murmured, "I'll wager Bishop Lief Laron took himself back to Bastion some time ago."

"Bastion is hell," said Dismé. "Why would he go there?"

"Because he belongs there," said the doctor. "For a little time."

The silver warriors were halfway up the second ridge to the east.

Dismé turned to Wolf. "Can you call them back?"

"Do you want them called back?" Wolf asked, curiously. "It seems to me they're doing a good job."

"There has been enough slaughter," she replied. "Many of those men are as much victims as murderers. Call them back, now." She searched the surrounding land with her eyes. Somewhere here were the ones who were needed. Certainly they would always be at the site of any battle. Eventually she found them, three tiny figures dwarfed by the flayed and dismembered body of the ogre.

"Tell your creatures to go there," Dismé said, pointing at the ogre's corpse. "Tell them to go there quietly, and just stand there, don't kill anyone else."

Wolf took a small silver box from his belt, flipped it open, and keyed in a command. The far-off figures, all but one, slowed, turned, and trudged back in the direction they had come. Wolf cursed, keyed in a specific number, then the command again, and this time the lonely silver figure stopped, turned, and came toward them with lagging feet.

He said, "The others are fighting at command, but that one loves to kill."

"Have them go farther right," said Dismé, tonelessly, as the silver fighters neared. "Where those three people are, next to the ogre's body."

"Who?" said the doctor, turning. "Oh. Of course."

They watched silently as the silver figures came to the ogre's corpse and arranged themselves silently in ranks. The three Guardians there went among them, touching them. Even at the great distance, Dismé saw the green fire, and then the thin, white smoke.

"Who are they? What are they doing?" asked Wolf.

"Rankivian. Shadua. Yun," said Dismé. "They are releasing your captives."

"They aren't captives," complained Wolf. "And you can't release them. There isn't enough left of them to exist outside the shells . . ."

"She knows," said the doctor, expressionlessly. "Believe me, she knows."

All three of the distant figures were gathered around one of the silver warriors, the last one to arrive. Dismé felt a tickling summons in her mind. She went off down the hill, both Michael and the doctor hurrying to catch up to her. The ogre's body was not far away. As the wind shifted, they caught a momentary whiff, which made their eyes smart and their throats catch.

Shadua, looking up, saw their reaction and went at once to lay her hand upon the mountain of oozing flesh. It exploded into leaping black flames that melted the body like wax, and in moments only a pile of ash remained beneath the charred bones on a darkly stained patch of soil, the ashes already blowing away among the grasses.

"You called me?" asked Dismé, wearily.

"This one," said Rankivian. "All the others chose to die, but not this one. This one chooses nothing."

"Can you find out who it is?" asked the doctor.

"It says only one name, over and over. Your name: Dismé, Dismé. It hates you. It wants to kill you. But it has no volition. It can do only what it is told. If told to hate and kill, it does it with enjoyment. If told to do anything else, it will obey."

"Then order her to tell us her name."

They turned their attention back to the silver form, intent upon it. Shadua said imperatively, "Tell us your name."

Mechanically, the being answered. "Nemesis of Gone . . ."

Dismé said, "What was your name before you were Nemesis?"

"Rashel was my name."

Dismé stared at the shining carapace, her own image reflected in it, a distorted personage that grimaced like a clown. What a vengeance! Rashel had hated and feared Gohdan Gone. He had done to her as he did to all his servants. And then . . .

She asked, "What was the potion Old Ben gave this woman, Jens?"

"I don't know what was in it," he said, "but you know it was meant for you. The power in it came from Gone, not from the stuff itself. I took it to the clinic and put it away where I thought it would be safe . . . I knew it was evil, but I had no idea what it would do . . ." He fell silent, realizing Dismé was no longer listening.

"A potion meant for me. One made by Rashel, at the command of Gohdan Gone. Because I was a Latimer. As, it turns out, we all are, all of us. Guardians." She looked over the doctor's shoulder at Wolf, who was approaching, but still at some distance.

"Rashel," she said quickly to the silver form. "Who is Gohdan Gone? Is he dead?"

"A servant of the Fell," said the metallic voice. "The Fell is not dead. The Fell is not here to die."

They felt a chill, as though a harsh wind had blown across them. Dismé asked, "What is the Fell?"

"The Fell is in the book, greater than . . . greater than . . . greater than any being here."

Dismé checked Wolf's progress again and said quickly, "Rashel, I order you to choose to die."

For a long moment nothing happened. The three fingered hands clicked and clicked, the knife edge extending as though in longing. The optics in the silver face glowed.

"It's either that or imprisonment forever. I order you, choose to die," said Dismé again, eyes fixed on Wolf who was very near.

"I choose to die," said Rashel.

Shadua put her hand upon the silver figure and a fine white smoke came from a grilled opening near the neck. Dismé turned and started back toward the others, Michael and the doctor still at her side. They passed Wolf, who went by them purposefully on his way to his silver army.

"He'll be angry when he finds they are dead," said the doctor.

"Very," agreed Michael. "So will all of Chasm, even if they get their hardware back."

As they passed the amorphous scattering that had been Gohdan Gone, Dismé lingered beside it. The stuff of it was leaking slowly into the sand. A thin whining came from it. She stooped to hear it better and made out the words. "Fell is not dead; sing while you can."

She knew in her heart she could defeat Gone, had defeated Gone, but evidently Gone had been only part of the evil. The Fell still lived. Somewhere. After a moment, she rejoined the others at the bottom of the butte where they were saddling the horses and hitching the wagon. Nell, Arnole, and the little people slowly gathered around them.

"Are we finished here?" Michael asked.

Nell nodded. "Except for your friend there. He looks upset."

Wolf was storming back toward them, his anger palpable.

"What in hell have you done?" he shouted as he approached.

"I told you," said Dismé, when he was near enough to hear her speak quietly. "We released your captives. What you had out there in those silver shells is the same thing Bastion had in the bottles. It doesn't matter if they fight for us or against us, what's kept there is pain, and Gohdan Gone can feed off it just as he could the ouphs."

"Ouphs?" said Wolf.

"The spirits of those who had their patterns kept alive in bottles. Not full-fledged ghosts, just meager spirits, but taken all together, they felt enough pain to feed that monster."

"You're talking magic again," snarled Wolf. "Those warriors had no pain. We gave them pleasure, great pleasure."

She shook her head. "If you could not detect the evil, you weren't looking for it. They hated and they were in captivity. Hate is pain, captivity is pain, even when the hater is euphorized into accepting it. If you could not detect the ouphs, you were not looking for them. Just because you can't see it, doesn't mean it isn't there. As for magic, yes, I may be talking magic from time to time, but then, I am the temporary servant of only a small and temporary god."

"We saw your small god," sneered Wolf. "The way we at Chasm figure it, you had a collective hallucination. You only thought you saw and heard it, but your dobsi picked up on what you thought you sensed."

Dezmai turned on him, took him by the shoulder and grinned fiercely at him. "I call upon my sister, Volian, Guardian of the Air," she cried, keeping her eyes fixed on Wolf's face so the dobsi would catch it all and send the image to every demon within reach. "May he fly until the sun sets. I call upon my brothers, Hussara of Earth and

Wogalkish of the Waters. May dust devils annoy him and rain pour upon him, and may he hear the ridicule of Jiralk the Joyous throughout his suspension."

She picked up a stone and threw it high into the air, so that it fell sharply on the drumhead, creating a resonance that carried Wolf aloft and spun him face down, slowly, staring at them from widely opened eyes as the sound went on, and on, and on, and laughter rang in his ears. Lightning split a cloud that began to move in their direction. Small dust devils began to collect.

"Magic," whispered the doctor.

Nell said tiredly, "Arnole told me once that sufficient power would look like magic to a person who didn't have it. If we are to believe the little god, the power is hers, not ours, or perhaps it is the natural power of Tamlar's kinfolk. Do I need to say I don't feel like a Guardian of anything at the moment? My children seem to have taken to it better than I."

"Let's head back to Trayford," said Arnole. "They may need our help in dealing with the remnants of the army. Whether they do or not, we need some time to ourselves."

He helped Nell onto the wagon seat. Camwar, Bobly, and Bab climbed into the wagon bed behind them. Michael lifted Dismé onto her horse, then mounted his own as the doctor had already done.

"Tamlar," called Nell. "Will you come with us?"

"I will come when you need me," she replied. "But now I will help Shadua dispose of all this carnage."

"Burn it well," called Dezmai. "Be sure none is left for either Chasm or the Fell to use."

Camwar turned to take a last look at his great drum. "I know it's too large to move," he confessed. "But, I will miss working on it." Then he smiled at Dismé. "You will need others, however. Smaller ones that will not take so long. I brought you a sample," and he took from the wagon bed a set of three small drums, set into a curved frame that fit over the pommel of the saddle.

They rode eastward, up the rises and into the troughs, toward the distant mountains. As they crested one of the ridges, they saw the flying machines from Chasm returning to the field. They stopped long enough to look through the glasses at the pilots of these machines gathered by the great drum, peering into the air above it where Wolf still revolved, around and around.

Later, as the sun was setting, they heard one brief drum roll from behind them.

"He fell. He bounced," said Dismé, with a small, self-satisfied smile. "Dead snake."

Jiralk, Michael, erupted into laughter which sped away like the wind along their back trail. "You didn't kill him, did you," he cried.

"Of course not. I was just returning the insult he gave me."

"And what now?" Michael asked her

Dismé reached out her hands to Michael and the doctor. "Bastion, I think. We know the devil there. We know what he eats. Maybe we can smoke him out. Maybe we can find out more about . . . the other thing."

"You think we'll have access to our . . . counterparts to do that?" the doctor asked.

"I said we," Dismé said, smiling ruefully to herself. "I didn't necessarily mean them, though I admit they're useful. Then, after Bastion, maybe other places for the same reason. And after that, to meet our brethren, those who live in the forest and the sea . . ."

Nell remarked from the wagon, "I knew there was a reason to come out of the redoubt. Also, if we're stopping in Trayford, I'd like to find Alan. I promised him I would. And poor Jackson. I suppose he's in Chasm. Perhaps I can visit him there."

There was silence for a time, except for the creaking of the wagon, until Bobly asked Arnole:

"How many Guardians are there in the book, Arnole?"

"Twenty-one. We know some of them only by name, Ushel, for instance, and Geshlin."

"And how many stones were there?"

"Twenty, one for each Guardian but Tamlar."

"But Bab and I only used up one," she said. "So if you count us as two . . ."

"As you certainly should," said Bab.

". . . there should be twenty-two Guardians."

"Odd," Arnole said thoughtfully. "You're right, of course. I wonder who that could be?"

No one had an answer. Camwar drew a long-necked stringed instrument from his baggage in the wagon and began to make a gentle music in time with the horses' hooves. Dismé touched the drums and then stroked them, bim, bom, and boom: tinky tunk, tiddle, tunk tunk. Jiralk began to sing, Dezmai joined him, and for a time, they rejoiced, while unseen far behind them the fortress of the small god emerged once more, silently from the grasses.

nell latimer's journal

Alan and I are living in a large apartment in the Fortress of
Bastion. It used to belong to General Gowl, and it has access
to the roof garden the general built to reward his wife for giving him a son. Gowl's wife, son, and unmarried daughters are
now living on a farm somewhere in Praise, learning to raise
sheep. Dismé wanted them moved completely out of Bastion,
but the doctor preferred to have them where he could keep an
eye on them until we start separating the sheep from the goats.

We returned to Bastion by way of Trayford. The town had
escaped any serious depredations by the army, which had
pretty well scattered to the points of the compass, along with
most of their leaders, including the bishop. Alan was there
waiting for me, along with Hussara, Volian, and Wogalkish.
I've forgotten the names they had before, though they told
me, and when the huge, hairy bulk of Hussara hugged me to
his chest and called me Mother, I was . . . a little put out. I
cannot yet think of them as my children. Hussara is a very
big man, wide-shouldered, with great muscled arms and
legs. Wogalkish is built like a swimmer, very lean and fit and
androgynic, and Volian is a graceful woman with white hair
and light blue eyes, slender but tremendously strong. We
stayed in Trayford just long enough to tell several demons
what was intended and ask them to spread the word to the
people of Bastion and the surrounding area.

From Trayford, we went north by wagon. Dismé and I traveled in the same small wagon, spending most of the time in talk. Of them all, I think she will be closest to me for she feels like a daughter whereas the others feel like . . . creatures out of myth, too strange to humanize. Oh, except for Arnole. And Michael. And the doctor, sometimes. I told Dismé a lot about the world before the Happening, and after we had established a friendly relationship, Dismé told me what the small god had told her at the end of our audience. The god said none of the Guardians had any deleterious genes, and therefore any cultural taboo against brother--sister sexual alliances had no meaning. The small god had taken my embryos, yes, but she had made sure they carried nothing hurtful.

I spoke supportively to Dismé about this, telling her that *what is* is no doubt more important than what people think. She replied, rather pettishly, I thought, that Arnole had told her that years ago. Nonetheless, believing that Dismé might be too shy to mention this to Michael—she seems to be totally inexperienced in such matters—I told the doctor and I presume he spoke to Michael about it, for on several occasions, I've seen Michael talking quietly to Dismé, and no one could mistake the message in his eyes. Or hers.

The trip over the mountains was uneventful, except that on the third day, we began to encounter refugees streaming out of Bastion. Most of them were on foot because the horsemen had taken their stock out of Bastion earlier, about the time Dismé and the others came out. Throughout the fourth and fifth days, the exodus continued, but by dawn of the sixth day we crossed the pass on virtually empty roads. At that point, Bertral, Galenor, Hussara, and Wogalkish went into conference, that silent sharing of views the inhabitants do when they take us over.

We camped at the pass, for we arrived there late in the day, not far from the great black scar on the meadow of Ogre's Gap, where the pyre had burned the bodies of the dead. There was a scatter of bones, pulled from the ashes by small beasts. When we woke in the morning, Tamlar had arrived amid a good bit of smoke, and the bones were gone. I imagine her fires burn a good deal hotter than any the demons could set. Besides Tamlar, there was a wan and wistful-looking man sitting on a log, waiting like a patient hound, and Tamlar said he had come to tell us something.

Since several of us were in conference, Bobly and Bab had gone down to the stream for water, Michael and Dismé were "picking wild strawberries" (an unseasonable excuse, at best), and I was less threatening than Tamlar, I summoned him over with a gesture and offered him morning tea, which he accepted.

"My name is Mace Marchant," he said. "I used to be head of the Apocanew office of Inexplicable Arts."

"What does 'used to be' mean?" I asked him, in as gentle a voice as I could manage.

"It means I don't want to be connected to it anymore, not to any of it. It's because I loved this woman. Rashel . . ."

My ears pricked up at that, for during our long drive, Dismé had told me everything she could remember about Rashel, including her end.

". . . but she wasn't in love with me. I think she put a spell on me, or someone did, so I would love her. And because I knew her, the Warden of the College of Sorcery dragged me along to meet this . . . this sorcerer. Gohdan Gone? Do you know that name?"

I told him we knew the name and we knew where, in Apocanew, he had resided.

"Apocanew? Really? The warden took me to a place in Hold. He, Gone, told me I could go, but he kept the warden there, and Gone killed the warden. I heard some of it, through the grates in the streets. It was . . ." He had to set his cup down, for he was shaking. Galenor glanced at me from his position with the group, and I beckoned. He came to stand behind the wretched man, laying a firm hand on his shoulder.

"Is that what you wanted to tell us?" I asked.

The shaking stopped, and he said, "No. Not all. When I was there, before they told me to go, I saw a book. I noticed it because it moved, as though it had something alive inside it. On the cover it said, 'The Book of Fell.' And when I heard the Guardians had come, when I heard that Bastion would be cleansed of all that, well, I thought you should know about the book . . ." He picked up the cup and sipped at it. "Such books . . . grimoires, are like collections of evil spells, aren't they? Sources of dark power, and this one looked very, very old."

As he set his cup down, he glanced up at the person behind him, and rose, crying, "Jens Ladislav?"

"Galenor the Guardian," came the reply, in such tones of awful power that the poor man was quite stricken, a state made even worse when Dismé came out of the trees.

"That's Rashel's sister," he whispered. "They killed Rashel."

I gave Galenor a forbidding look and told Marchant that indeed, Rashel was dead. I saw no reason to upset him with the details when he would need his wits about him in telling Arnole and the others what he had seen. They gathered around and began to question him, at which point Elnith joined the group, and we soon had his life's story among us. When we had drained him quite dry of useful information (including the location in Hold of Gone's place and Mace's destruction of the warden's documents, which quite frankly surprised me, for he didn't look capable of stepping on a stinkbug), we fed him and suggested he join a nearby demon encampment in case we needed him for anything further.

Bertral said firmly, "He's right about the book of Fell. There is now a reference to it in my Book. The only way we'll know we've destroyed it is to see it done."

"Let Aarond and Ialond go as children," Tamlar suggested. "Gohdan Gone slaughtered many children. Let them say to the servants of this necromancer that they have been summoned. I will follow them into the lair, and together we will find the book."

Hussara nodded. "That may gain you entrance, but let Volian and Wogalkish walk with me to the street where this entry is, to wait there for the book to emerge or for Aarond's call. It may be a more difficult task than you imagine."

"All of us," said Tamlar, her voice crackling. "If it is to be a difficult task, then we will all be needed."

Elnith decided to go with the small ones, and if Elnith went, I had to go along. The journey was made more quickly than I could have imagined, quite as though we giants were striding in the magical seven-league boots I had read of in fairy tales as a child. Giants did not knock upon the gate, however. It was just Bobly and Bab and Nell who knocked upon the gate, in our own unthreatening guises. The street was empty, but the gate was just as Mace Marchant had described it, as was the dwarfish, hairy person who came to greet us. I felt a spasm of pure revulsion when I saw it, an instinctive loathing. The creature tittered and pranced, but after a bit of this it decided to admit us, though he said his Master was away.

Below, at the end of long corridors, we found another gate, guarded by another such, who said Master wasn't home, to which we replied as before. We had been summoned. We would await the Master. This creature led us to another door which a third monster opened, letting us into the room Merchant had told us of. Despite the smoldering fire that burned, the room was in virtual darkness. It smelled . . . oh, how can I describe that smell. To me it was wet ashes, hot metal, rot, decay, blood, sewers, a stench the color of bruises. The chair stood beside the fire, heavy legs, arms, back, but the seat was only an empty frame over a precipitous hole that went endlessly down into darkness.

The three of us just stood there, trying to breathe, hideously aware that the pit before us was not empty. Each of us knew it was occupied. Gohdan Gone had departed, but the power that had moved him was still here. Elnith had taken over once we entered, but she didn't insulate me from her fear, which I felt for the first time. She was suddenly, terribly afraid, taking a long moment to gain mastery of herself and reach out toward the book. It was on the table next to the chair, and I saw my own hand go out to grip it. It was like touching the base of a great cliff, immovable as mountains. My hand fumbled with it, unable even to open the cover.

Outside the door, the creatures who had let us in were peeking at us, tittering. In the vast hole beneath us, something turned its attention toward us. Elnith felt it. So did Bobly and Bab, for Ialond and Aarond were suddenly there, laying their hands upon the book, struggling with it, unable to open it any more than Elnith had done. Elnith called, and from elsewhere Hussara and Volian and Wogalkish answered.

We felt the cavern begin to shake. The floor shuddered beneath our feet, things fell from the shelves; we three moved against the outer walls just before the roof of the cavern came down, narrowly missing us. Light flooded in. It was noon, and the sunlight streamed downward into the abyss beneath the chair. We heard something from below uttering words we did not know, had never heard, strange words that went to our hearts and chilled them. Hussara leaned above us, with Volian, whose wind came down in a great vortex and scooped everything in that room away, upward, burning as it went, for Tamlar was there to burn it as it came. A sharper gust pulled out those small, tittering creatures who had served their master, and they too were burned as they swept up into the sunshine. With the earth riven wide, as it was, there was enough light in the place to see the book was not a separate thing. It was part of the stone beneath it, part of the bedrock beneath that, rooted into the substance of the planet.

I felt Elnith summoning. We all stood as we were, without moving, hearing that movement from below, listening to it climb from the pit that held it. Then, suddenly, Dezmai and Jiralk came sliding down the sides of the pit that Hussara had made, she with her drums that Camwar had made for her, and he with Camwar's instrument. They stood tight against the wall, not to throw any shade into the pit, and Dezmai drummed, Jiralk strummed, and the two of them began to sing. Their voices twined like snakes mating, turning and twisting and lacing themselves together, pure purpose untroubled by thought or need, and we saw the cover of the book rise, only a tiny bit.

Oh, from that book came such sounds and smells and tastes. The clangor of bars and gates, the rattle of chains. The shriek of imprisoned and tortured beings. The taste of blood on our lips. Dezmai drummed, Jiralk played, they sang, the cover opened, and the first page of the book rose up as Volian leaned above it and ripped it from its binding with her breath. It came loose with a sound of ripped metal, fluttering upward like a living thing, only to fold itself into a deadly arrow shape and plunge toward Volian's breast.

Tamlar caught it with one fiery hand and melted it with her breath, and the next, and the one after that.

The book was thick. It held hundreds of pages, every page a history of some bestial cruelty mankind had committed against his own kind or other kinds. The first few were only sticks and stones used by one kind of proto man against another. Then came spears and slings, used to more purpose. Then horsemen, with bows and swords of bronze. I saw pyramids of skulls left in the lands conquered by marauding hordes; I saw living children thrown screaming into the flames of Moloch; I saw impalements without number, and crucifixions and burials alive; I saw blood poured upon high altars until the pyramids ran red to their bottoms. I saw wars of religion against religion and people against people. Every page was one such; every one had to be raised separately, separately ripped away, separately melted into a tiny blob of metal that writhed on the broken stone like mercury, crawling toward the dark. None escaped. Bobly and Bab caught them all, scooping them into a pitcher they had found among the wreckage.

The farther we went into the book, the more recent the pages became. I saw despots releasing poison gas upon their people and others; I saw torture raised to an art form in the dungeons of police states; I saw hordes starved by their rulers; I saw the ovens, the gibbets, the laboratories, the suicide bombers, the blowers-up of busses, the terrorists, the nihilists, and I heard the lip-smacking of that being in the pit that fed on it, all of it, including the souls of those who had committed the acts.

And near the end of the book I saw the Spared Ones repeating every evil man had ever invented. One by one the pages opened with cries and shrieks and howls and an outpouring of terrible spirits that stank of hatred. One by one they were silenced and the page was ripped away. One by one the pages rose on the wind like fallen leaves and were burned to the accompaniment of a far off sound, as of chains broken or walls fallen, or great cages rent wide.

We did not know what or where the captives were that held that book in place, but when the last page was burned, there was only silence in that place and the scritching feet of a small, skittering black thing that tried to escape from between the book covers and flee. I brushed it to the floor; Ialond hit it with his hammer; and Tamlar burned the place where it was squashed. She also took the pitcher of crawling evil that Bobly and Bab had collected.

"I will put it in the earthfires," she said. "Where it may stay forever, or as near as makes no difference."

Then we left the place, quickly, for Hussara, Volian, Wogalkish, and Tamlar told us they intended to clean all the valleys of Bastion from their center at Hold to the Walls of the Mountains, collapsing every cavern upon itself and flooding it until it was clean, and opening every cave at either end so Volian and Tamlar could blow through it and burn every musty corner clean and bare.

Then dust rose in monstrous clouds that shut out the sun. Flames ran across the valleys. They found Gone's habitation in Apocanew, and others like it elsewhere, but there was no other book. Span after span, the world shook and fires burned mightily, smoke and dust filling the air, until at last the wind came to blow it away and the rain poured down to settle it and put out the fires. When they were finished, the three valleys lay stricken before us, like vast open pit mines from the days before the Happening, all destroyed except for the fortress at the center of Hold, for it stood upon Tamlar's mound where the Guardians took up residence.

Only then, my other children arrived. The doctor soon found a new friend in Geshlin, the Gardener. She is very lovely and she knows a great deal about the use of herbs in medicine. She arrived almost immediately after the cleansing of Bastion along with Tchandbur of the Trees (whom we had seen briefly at the Battle of the Plain), and with Ushel, the dweller of the Wilderness, whose charge is the creation and maintenance of variety, botanical and zoological and, for all I know, viral and bacterial as well. With Tchandbur's arrival, trees sprang up as though by . . . well, as though by the power of the small god. We would go to sleep seeing a barren one night and awaken to find it a forest the next morning. We have flowers and fruits everywhere.

Befun, the Guardian of Animals, dropped by with Pierees and Falasti, beautiful women both, with voices like singing birds and falling water, Pierees to fill the trees with birds and Falasti to fill the streams with fishes. With the arrival of Rankivian, Shadua, and Yun, all twenty-one of us were together for the first time, and we celebrated the occasion with a feast. Shortly thereafter, Bastion was entered by a group of anchorites who, it seems, have been followers of Elnith for several generations. Ben, a student of the doctor's, brought them to meet her, bringing a petition to build an abbey of the Silences on a forested hill in Praise. The anchorites take vows of silence, and even their meetings are silent. When Elnith attends their gatherings, I usually sleep through them.

With the rooting out of the devil Fell, and the restoring of Bastion to a natural and beautiful place to live, we were ready to start separating sheep and goats, which, with the not-quite-willing cooperation of the demons, seems to be going well. Whenever the demons try to tell us that there is no small god (much less any Real One) Dezmai and Michael sing them into stupefication and I, Elnith, silence them for hours at a time. They go on working with us, nonetheless, because they are intent upon finding out how we do this. We continually find them searching places we have been for signs of the device we have supposedly used, though they as consistently refuse to believe our explanations. To the Chasmites, truth is determined by how well it fits their expectations, and doesn't that sound familiar?

After Alan rounded up the survivors from the redoubt, the Chasmites sent a group to meet with the fifty of us sleepers who are left. The Chasmites are indeed, direct descendants of pre-Happening survivor scientists who managed to keep track of the years since it happened. Strangely enough, they have kept themselves separate from the rest of humanity for almost the same reasons the small god gave us for separating the race. Their initial reasoning was that if science had been pushed, hard, in the century prior to the Happening, mankind would have had some way to avoid the catastrophe. I mentioned that the small god said she brought the asteroid because of what man had become, and they retorted that man might not have become that if we had been relentless in our education of our young people and had not perpetuated ignorance under the guise of cultural sensitivity and the politically correct.

I warned the people from Chasm to be careful in their research and behavior, for any cruelty to people or animals might be met with violence from the Guardians. When I speak about the Guardians to the Chasmites, however, they tend to turn off and swing their eyes over my shoulder to focus on infinity. They have the same reaction to mention of the small god or the Real One. They have consistently refused to have a god contest, and I fear they will have to encounter the godlet rather forcibly before they believe there is anything there at all.

Arnole has set up a school at the fortress for the children of the recruits who are coming in. He calls it the university of the Real One, and it teaches only things that are known to be true, which means it is largely devoted to mathematics and sciences. Dismé and Michael have threatened to set up another school nearby which will teach only things known to be helpful, such as medicine, music, and horsemanship. Needless to say, no Regimic materials have remained except what is in the Archives of the Fortress.

Camwar and Jens, Bobly and Bab, have arranged to join a caravan to New Kansas at the end of the year in order to carry the message of the small god and arrange for the first god contest. As yet, we have heard nothing of the small god's threatened prophets, and Dismé and I have wondered if, indeed, her peroration on herself as deity was not hyperbole designed to rub our fur the wrong way. The impression I got was that the small god is not above amusing herself at our expense a great deal of the time.

In speaking to Alan and the doctor, I have suggested we take a leaf from the Real One's book and focus on *what is,* which includes a few people on the moon and a growing population on Mars. Surprisingly, the small god has said nothing at all about them, quite possibly because both places have small gods of their own (or they are worshipping The Real One, which is not unimaginable). *What is* may also include one aquatic and one arboreal intelligent race. We all guess cetaceans and gray parrots, and Falasti and Pierees have gone away to see if we are right.

One year has passed since I last woke in the redoubt. Michael and Dismé are expecting a child in mid-fall. I feel like a grandmother. Alan says he feels like a grandfather, too, and though he is uncertain which of my children may also be his, he pretends to find in Michael a likeness to his grandfather. I don't think it matters, personally. Dismé sought me out to tell me the room set aside for a nursery was evidently invaded during the night, for a stone stands in the corner of it. This is, she believes, the twentieth stone, and she is driving Bertral mad wanting to see the book every hour on the hour to see who is about to be born.

It is almost dinner time, and Alan and I have planned a special meal for our anniversary, just us and the children, any who happen to be nearby. This last account has filled the last page in my journal. Perhaps I will find another one and write more, as time passes. Then again, I may leave the story as it is.

Signed: Nell Latimer Block.
Summerspan ten, nineday,
Year one of the Small God. Chasm date: 3052.

Don't Miss Any of the
ACORNA ADVENTURES

"Entertaining fare indeed."
Booklist

ACORNA
by Anne McCaffrey and Margaret Ball
0-06-105789-4/$7.50 US/$9.99 Can

ACORNA'S QUEST
by Anne McCaffrey and Margaret Ball
0-06-105790-8/$6.50 US/$8.99 Can

ACORNA'S PEOPLE
by Anne McCaffrey and Elizabeth Ann Scarborough
0-06-105983-8/$6.99 US/$9.99 Can

ACORNA'S WORLD
by Anne McCaffrey and Elizabeth Ann Scarborough
0-06-105984-6/$6.99 US/$9.99 Can

ACORNA'S SEARCH
by Anne McCaffrey and Elizabeth Ann Scarborough
0-380-81846-9/$7.50 US/$9.99 Can

And in hardcover
ACORNA'S REBELS
by Anne McCaffrey and Elizabeth Ann Scarborough
0-380-97899-7/$24.95 US/$38.95 Can